The Legend Of Jackson Murphy

RENÉE MILLER

For the men I've loved and the few I could have lived without.

CHAPTER 1

At one time Jack loved his wife. He couldn't pinpoint the exact moment he stopped, but it wasn't as though he suddenly woke up hating the way Jenny drooled on her pillow or how she ruined his favorite songs with her shrill nasal whine. Like rust on an old car, the love he felt for her slowly eroded to an intense loathing that ate away at the framework of their life together.

The past year had been the worst. Jack could no longer stand anything she said or did. Once upon a time, he would have tried, but love couldn't be forced—despite what those bible-thumping freaks up the street claimed.

He knew he should have left. Most men would rather die than live with a bitch like Jenny, but after serving a fifteen-year sentence in the institution of marriage, leaving wasn't so simple; not with three kids and a successful business.

The kids weren't an issue. He didn't see them much anyway, and he knew that courts these days made sure parents shared the children. Jack loathed the idea of paying her money for a job she'd nagged to have.

That was the bottom line for Jackson Murphy. Money. More importantly: *his* money. He'd worked his ass off while she shopped, had babies, and joined the Parent-Teacher Association. He lunched with assholes, built up a reputation, and a healthy bank account by working eighteen-hour days while she watched the Late Show from the comfort of the king size bed *he* bought. If he left, she'd take it all and then some. Jack couldn't stand the thought.

Call him greedy, he didn't care. He worked for what they had while she did nothing.

Seated in his custom-made kitchen, with its built-in stainless steel fridge and stove—and the many other high-priced appliances that Jenny never used—Jack pondered how to escape without getting fleeced in the process.

Jenny sat at the oak table she pestered him to buy tapping a manicured nail on its scratched surface. He counted the nicks that she and the kids had left in the once-beautiful piece of furniture.

She set her empty cup down on the table.

Jack tore his gaze from her lacquered nails to the paper she'd ripped apart to find the gossip column, leaving the rest in a crumpled heap. He picked up the wrinkled pages, and tried to press them flat enough to read. She could have at least put the fucking thing back together.

The cup Jenny had set on the table for him was empty. He swallowed a curse. She used to fill his cup every morning. Jack didn't think he asked a lot from her. Just serve the damn coffee. He often wondered if she despised him as much as he despised her. Jenny seemed to enjoy doing things to annoy him. Was she trying to shove him out the door?

Jack pushed his chair across the floor, and grabbed the empty cup before standing. He made a big production of setting it on the counter and hefting the pot. He managed to fill half the cup with the little bit of coffee she left before returning to the table.

If she did hate him, how long before she'd had enough? Probably not long. Jenny wasn't made of the same stuff he was. He knew Jenny well enough to be pretty certain she'd already been to a lawyer and waited for the ink to dry on her demands. And there he sat, just waiting for it like a moron.

"Are you going to be late tonight?"

Her question caught him by surprise. He blinked, pausing

in the task of not reading his wrinkled paper. The light from the window over the sink created a halo above her head, bringing out the blond highlights she spent hundreds of dollars of his money to put in. Jack would never understand why anyone would want stripes on their head.

She raised an eyebrow.

He considered her question. Why did she want to know? She usually didn't care. Was she hoping he'd be gone? "I'm not sure," he lied. "Why? Do you have plans?"

Jack bit the inside of his cheek. Jenny could look a person straight in the eye and lie through her teeth. The only evidence lay in the slight blush that dotted each cheek, so faint that most people missed it. Not Jack. His wife was about to lie.

Lowering her gaze—eyes he'd once compared to dark chocolate—Jenny picked at the chipped enamel of her cup. "No, I was thinking of taking the kids out for dinner if you're going to be late. They don't get to go out much." She stared at the paper as though it might contain the secret to life. "If you'll be home, you can come with us."

"Where are you going?" He sipped his coffee and grimaced. For crying out loud, the bitch couldn't make shit properly.

"Just to Frankie's."

Jack choked as he swallowed the bitter liquid. It burned his throat and seared up into his sinuses as he swallowed the scalding sludge. Just to Frankie's? She had to be kidding. "Jen, you aren't taking the kids to Frankie's. Christ, just a salad at that shithole costs more than my shoes."

She closed her hand around the paper, balling her precious gossip section into a fist. "It's my money too. If I want to go to Italy to buy pizza, I will. Don't tell me what I can and can't do. If you're coming I'll make the reservation for five."

"You do know that pizza didn't originate in Italy. It's actually—"

"Jack!"

Jenny glared, coffee cup midway to her lying mouth. She didn't really want him to go with them. He knew it and the last thing Jack wanted to do was to share dinner with Jenny at that snobby overpriced spaghetti house, but he couldn't resist calling her bluff.

"Fine. You're right. We can go. I'm sure I'll be done around six or seven."

"You better show up then. They get pissed when you don't keep a reservation."

"If four out of five show, I'm sure they won't care."

"They will care and I might not get another reservation on short notice."

"We're just finishing up the Sampson job. That's all I've got on the table for today. If anything comes up I'll get Ray to take care of it."

Biting her lip, Jenny narrowed her eyes.

Ray could handle things for an hour or so; he'd financially committed nearly as much as Jack. While he didn't like having anyone look after the business but himself, Jack would do it to get under Jenny's skin.

Ray had little knowledge of the construction business, materials, or bids; all he really did was handle the books. Though Ray was one of the best when it came to numbers, Jack made Jay-Ray one of the busiest construction companies in Hanover Springs. It wasn't a big area, but being the best in any area was better than nothing. If anyone had earned half of Jack's money, it was Ray, though he wouldn't get it. Still, it never hurt to make him earn his share now and then. Besides, getting on Jenny's last nerve was one of the only joys left in his life.

Jack stood and checked his watch. "I should go if I'm going to finish in time for dinner. See you around six."

He left before Jenny could haggle over the time. She couldn't get a reservation at Frankie's on such short notice. They were booked solid for months. Jack knew this because he wooed a client or two there. She must have made one in advance. He figured she was pissed because now she'd have to expand a reservation for two to accommodate all of them. Her faint blush told a story she wasn't revealing, but what kind of story? As he pulled out of the drive, Jack considered the possibilities. She could be running around under his nose. Nah,

Jenny wouldn't cheat, it wasn't in her to lie and deceive on that level. Or was it?

CHAPTER 2

As he drove the familiar route to his office, doubt seeped back into Jack's brain. He stopped at a red light and explored the possible ways Jenny might fuck him. Was she having an affair? If she was, how long had he been oblivious to it? A horn sounded and he almost jumped through the roof of his car. *Oops. Green light.*

One arm out the window, Jack offered the jackass behind him an eyeful of his middle finger and slowly rolled through the intersection. The horn sounded again.

Impatient prick.

Less certain of his wife's virtue than he'd been when he left the house, Jack turned off the main road, slowing the car as he entered Delaney Drive. Halfway down the quiet residential street, he pulled into the circular drive of the apartment complex that housed the offices of Jay-Ray Builders, Inc.

Jack's thoughts jumped all over the place. Small half-forgotten details: blushing, nervous glances, and the occasional odd behavior, combined to draw a disturbing picture. As he stepped out of the car, his foot slipped. Jack flailed both arms to keep his footing. "Son of a bitch," he muttered, and scraped his shoes on the pavement, the distinct smell of shit assaulting his nose.

When he got a hold of that rat-bastard Chihuahua and his fat whore owner, he vowed to shove the yappy fucker right down her throat. That damned dog couldn't be worth near as much as his shoes.

"Seriously, the miserable animal shits pebbles, how hard is it to scrape them up?" Jack muttered mostly to himself, knowing she probably couldn't bend over far enough to reach it.

Cursing and wiping his sole repeatedly, he walked to the building and up the steps. It had been Ray's idea to rent an apartment rather than office space. An apartment was cheaper.

According to city bylaws, running a business out of an apartment wasn't technically legal, so they hadn't listed it as the business address. They used a mailbox. So far, no one had said anything.

As he pushed through the door, Jack's gaze fell on his wedding band and the fat lady's Chihuahua slipped from his mind. He could run it by Ray, but Ray always sided with Jenny. Jenny could be sleeping with Ray for all he knew. Entering the elevator the thought made him laugh out loud.

Jenny with Ray? Absurd. Definitely trading down in Jenny's case. Jack may not be George Clooney, but he knew he was a damn sight better than Ray. Jack rated himself an almost-Brad Pitt-level of attractive. Ray, at barely five and a half feet tall, thick glasses and thinning hair—with a personality to match his good looks—didn't come close. He repeated himself every time he spoke and his allergies kept him inside all day during the spring and fall. Jenny would choose better company than Ray. Besides, who would choose Woody Allen over an almost-Brad Pitt?

The elevator stopped on the fifth floor. Jack stepped out shaking his head. If she'd found someone else, it might give him leverage in a divorce. If she wanted to be free to be with her new lover, she might let him have what he wanted.

Not likely, Jack.

He strode down the hall toward his office located near the

end, across from an old guy who Jack swore couldn't leave his apartment unless he'd shit his pants. The shit-man's door opened, hinges creaking over the shuffling of slippered feet. Jack rushed forward. The "C" hung crooked on his door. He straightened it before opening.

In the apartment, Ray sat at his desk. He'd already dimmed the lights and closed the pale yellow drapes so the sunlight streaming through the patio doors behind him couldn't reflect on his computer screen. That gave Ray migraines.

Ray's office was in the living room and faced the door. Jack's was in the master bedroom. Both had great views of Carrey Park and featured small balconies. Ray preferred to host clients either at the job site or over dinner. Jack thought it was a bit eccentric, but who was he to judge? He liked two-hundred dollar shoes.

Dirty cups lined the edge of Ray's desk and the dust on the coffee table was thick enough to write in. The older gal who came by to clean had been out sick the last couple of weeks. Menopause or a stroke, Jack really didn't care. Ray dealt with that shit.

The apartment worked better for Jack than an office. He stayed many nights until he felt like returning home. Ray used to burn the midnight oil with him. Lately though, he left at least twice a week before Jack arrived back from the job sites.

Jack paused. Was it always Mondays and Fridays? No, he remembered that sometimes Ray left early on Thursday... the same day Jenny usually went to the gym. The question was whether Jenny worked up a sweat on the treadmill or on top of old Ray. He shrugged the thought away. She wouldn't. *Ray* wouldn't; he couldn't stand dishonesty. An affair with his best friend's wife would drive him over the edge.

Jack smiled and cleared his throat, still amused that he'd ever considered Ray and Jenny fucking around. Ray was too smart to ruin a good thing by sleeping with Jenny. Jack wasn't really sure he'd ever slept with anyone. The possibility of someone's germs contaminating his body probably horrified Ray.

"You're early. Early for you," Ray muttered without looking away from his computer.

"You're earlier."

"You wanted the bid ready for the mall over on Elm. I just got the materials cost figured out. In about an hour, I'll have an idea of labor and the final figures."

"That's great. Let me know and I'll call John when we're ready to tender. He'll put it in with the rest. You got my list of the other ones?"

"The other bids? I don't want to know how you got those. It's not legal you know. No not legal. Nope." Shuffling his papers, Ray shook his head and sniffed. The faint light from the draped window highlighted Ray's rapidly receding hairline and the unfortunate attempt at a comb over.

"You think the other guys are bidding blind? Fuck, you're naïve. You still let your mama wipe your ass too? It's just business; no one is getting hurt."

"If you say so."

He was far too honest. Jack teased him about it all the time. Ray rarely mentioned Jack's dishonesty because he also avoided confrontation.

"Listen." Ray said without meeting Jack's gaze. "I need to be out of here by six at the latest. If you need anything, let me know or you won't get it until tomorrow. I need to leave by six." He turned to the computer, his face red as a tomato.

A little bell pealed at the back of Jack's mind. *Mondays, Fridays, and sometimes Thursdays... if Jenny could get Jasmine to watch Allie.* "Funny, I have to leave around the same time. We should have driven in together."

Ray grimaced. He drove like an old woman, and called Jack's driving "maniacal" and "dangerous." Jack felt he drove offensively, and he got where he needed to go in a timely fashion. No accidents; yet.

"You don't leave before nine, ever. What's the hurry tonight?" Ray asked. "Why would you hurry home? Are you going home?"

The bell rang louder. "Jenny wants some family time. I figure I better go with her so she doesn't waste twenty bucks on a burger that Jasmine won't eat, and another ten on a glass of water. What are you up to tonight? Hot date?"

It might have been Jack's imagination, but Ray seemed to search for an answer. "I just wanted an early night. No plans really. Not like dinner or anything. Come on, who would have dinner with me? Just wanted an early night."

Maybe Jenny did prefer Woody Allen.

Ray moved papers around, still not meeting his gaze. No, thought Jack. This was Mr. Honesty. The man could not tell a lie. He'd been hardwired to tell the truth and nothing but. Ray couldn't stab anyone in the back like that. Could he? Maybe he knew who Jenny was fucking and didn't want to be the one to open the can of worms. As Jack watched his partner pretend to be absorbed in the Elm Street bid, the bell's clangor now deafening, a plan formed in his brain. If Ray was up to something, Jack would catch him before the night was over.

"Hey, if you aren't doing anything you should come with us. You'd save me from getting nagged all night. Jenny loves talking to you and you haven't seen the kids in months."

Ray's hands froze. "I don't want to intrude...."

"Intrude? Shit, I'm insulted. You're family." Jack found Ray's acting skills pathetic; either he was nailing Jenny or knew who was. "I'll call Jenny and tell her to make it for six. I'm sure they can pull an extra chair over."

Before Ray could object, Jack turned toward his office and clenched his fists before the open door. Fuck, how many times did he have to tell Ray that his door did not open until he arrived? Ray just couldn't stand leaving anything in that little box on his desk. He crossed the room to the balcony doors to open the blinds and allow some light in. His eyes burned after the gloom of Ray's office and blinked to adjust to the bright May sunshine.

Turning from the windows Jack sighed as his gaze fell on the stack of papers Ray had left on his desk. Signatures mostly, but still he hated beginning his morning with a mountain of paperwork. He pulled out his chair, sank down into the plush leather, and reached for the phone. How would Jenny react? How awkward would it be if there was something going on between her and Ray? Jack didn't particularly care. He just had to know if they were fucking him over. Watching the two of them together would at least put his mind at ease. If not, he couldn't let them get away with it. No one lied to Jackson Murphy.

He punched the speed dial and tapped his fingers on the desk. Jenny picked up after only ten rings. With a phone in every room, Jack would never understand why it always took her so long to answer. Did she screen calls and decide whether she wanted to talk to him? *Bitch*. She knew he hated when people didn't answer their phone.

"What took you so long? Why are you out of breath?" he asked.

"Um... I was outside in the garden and I forgot to bring the phone. Is that a crime now? Am I not allowed to sit in the garden?"

"Maybe you could pull a weed or something while you're out there and we wouldn't need a landscaper. Seems like a waste of time for you to just sit there staring. Wait, you're allergic to bees aren't you? Sitting among the flowers is like taking your life in your own hands. That's what you told me when you wanted me to pay someone to take care of your damn flowers."

"I know, Jack; it's terrible how everyone else in the world wastes valuable work hours. We can't all be as driven as you are."

Sarcasm. Jenny was great at it. Once upon a time, he found it amusing. At this point, it made him want to blacken her eyes. Maybe even snap her neck.

"I'm working like a dog so you can do things like stare at the flowers I paid someone else to plant. Don't get bitchy because I'm providing you with the life you've wanted so desperately. If I don't work like a dog, you can't sit and smell the roses."

"Whatever. Why are you calling? Can't make dinner? I'm so

surprised." Scorn dripped from her voice.

"Actually, dinner is still on. Call the restaurant and add Ray into the reservation.'

"Ray?" her voice rose just a fraction.

The bells quieted, leaving behind a hollow echo soon re-placed by soothing cold fingers that spread through Jack's brain. "Yeah, Ray. He's kind of lonely and I thought it would be nice to include him. He doesn't have many friends, you know. We used to have him over all the time. Now I only see him at work."

"That's your fault not mine. You're never here. How would it look if he came here while you were gone? I don't want that kind of stuff going around the neighborhood."

I bet you don't, you lying little slut. "So you'll do it?"

"Sure. The kids will be excited to see him."

Just the kids? Something didn't add up. It might not be Ray, but it was *someone*. Jack secretly hoped it would turn out to be anyone else. Someone with more money, better looks, anything that meant she didn't want to leave him because of Ray. Jack wanted her gone, but a man had his pride. When your wife screwed around, it damaged even the biggest ego. To know she hadn't even traded up did more than hurt that ego; it slaugh-tered it.

Jack knew Jenny couldn't do much better than him. If not for her selfishness, they might have made a go of things and he might have managed to like her again. Not enough to give up on his own philandering, because men weren't programmed for monogamy, but enough to spare her feelings by hiding it. Jack didn't see it as a double standard. Just reality. Men had needs, and wives couldn't fill all of them.

Disgusted with Jenny and himself, Jack hung up the phone without saying goodbye. She'd start to ramble anyway. He hated that. Don't talk unless you have something to say. If you're only interested in hearing your own voice, you'd best talk to yourself. Jack Murphy was a busy man.

After checking his planner, Jack made a few calls and real-ized he could finish by lunch. Instead of going home, he booked a meeting with his lawyer, Harvey Daniels. Maybe he'd put some feelers out about his situation with Jenny. Harvey might be able to give him some advice on how to keep what he'd earned. Aside from killing her, Jack didn't know what he'd do to keep it all. She would not get a cent from him. What belonged to Jack, belonged to Jack. Period.

CHAPTER 3

Though Jack found Harvey amusing, the man had a big mouth. The upside was lunches were always interesting. As he picked at his undercooked pasta, Jack realized Harvey was so drunk he probably wouldn't remember their discussion anyway. His old friend waved to the waiter and held up his sixth empty gin and tonic.

It was now or never. "Do you handle divorce?"

"Why? You want a divorce, Jackie?"

"No, a guy I know asked for advice. I mentioned we were having lunch. He knows you're my lawyer and he needs someone he can trust. Poor bastard could lose everything he's worked for over a simple mistake."

"What did he do?" Harvey furrowed his brow, but serious wasn't an expression he was capable of with big eyes staring out of an ugly face.

His greasy mass of curly black hair sprung from his oversized, square shaped head as though trying to escape. Sometimes if he got *really* drunk, like now, his nose made a whistling sound when he breathed.

When Harvey was a kid, he took a hockey stick to the face. The result was a broken nose and a glass eye. Unfortunately, all his mom could afford at the time was a *used* replacement. Over the years, he could have bought himself a new one at least a dozen times. But old Harvey said he liked his used eye, despite its morbid beginnings. The effect, however, was like looking at a Siberian Husky—Harvey's blue glass eye staring blankly at the seat next to Jack, while his brown one drunkenly ogled the waitress as she walked by.

"Are you awake, Jackie? What did the guy do that was so wrong?"

"He married the bitch."

Harvey frowned for a second before erupting in hysterical laughter, his good eye watering as he leaned back in his chair.

Jack didn't understand what Harvey found so amusing. He was serious. Still, he joined him with a half-hearted chuckle. Harvey's big white teeth reminded him of an old mule Jenny and he rented on their honeymoon in Mexico. It used to bare its chompers for treats from the tourists. He wished the man would stop laughing. Jack glanced at the other tables and sank into his chair as people turned to stare.

"Isn't that always the problem? So he divorces her, big deal." Harvey shrugged.

"No Harv, he doesn't want to lose his money. He earned it. She's never worked a day in her life."

"Did he earn the money before or while he was married to her?"

"Most of it was after they got married, but she never did anything except spend it. Why should she get half?"

"Okay, here's the thing. Your *friend* needs to understand the law. As long as they're married, she is entitled to one-half of every single dollar he brings in. All of it whether she earned it or not. Just as he would be entitled to half of what she made if the roles were reversed. The court doesn't care who did what, marital property and all that shit."

"It's not right though. She's a leech. Why should he pay her anything?"

"That's why I don't do divorces anymore. Too messy. I can send your friend along to a good guy, but you better tell him it doesn't matter how good your lawyer is; the only way he won't pay is if she's dead. Then she'll be paying him won't she?" He laughed at his joke.

Jack smiled. He couldn't kill Jenny, not with his own hands, but someone else might. It was something to think about. Could he do it? Jack didn't ponder the question for long.

Yes, he could.

"So how's your old lady?" Harvey asked.

"Still kicking," Jack muttered.

Harvey laughed again.

If Harvey could stay sober, he'd be a great guy to pal around with. Too bad he only managed sobriety a few hours each day.

Jack arrived at Frankie's at six on the nose. Jenny hadn't graced the other diners with her presence yet and Ray was still puttering away at the office when Jack left. He'd have the advantage of watching them come in.

Glancing around the restaurant Jack curled his lip. *Fucking snobby pretentious place.* The tables were covered in white cloth edged in lace, with a single rose in a crystal vase adorning each one. They looked randomly scattered but Jack knew there was nothing random about the layout. The waiters ran around in tight black pants and faggoty shirts with goofy sleeves. Soft classical shit played in the background and sconces lit the room with a dim glow for a fake classy feel. In his opinion, classy meant so dark you couldn't look a person in the eye or notice the dirt on the floor or the crap they tried to pass off as food. Otherwise, why wouldn't they use enough light so you could see the damn place?

The maître d' led him to a quiet corner at the back of the restaurant. Jack took the far seat, his back to the wall. It would piss Jenny off that he took the only seat that could afford her a view of the room.

Take that, bitch.

Jack was sipping at his third beer when Ray arrived, impossible to miss as he tripped through the door.

The maître d' led him to Jack's table. Ray blinked furiously as he approached.

Something had upset him enough to get into the blinks. Jack offered a friendly smile as Ray sat next to him. "Well, imagine that. For once, I'm not the one who's late."

"Are you sure she said six?" Ray glanced around, as though Jenny might be seated at another table.

"Expecting someone?" Jack asked.

"Uh, Jenny. Jenny's not here. Shouldn't she be here by now?"

"She's always late. You know how she likes to piss me off. Won't show up until she's good and ready."

"You're drinking," Ray pointed to the bottle in Jack's hand. "She won't like that. She doesn't like when you drink. You get nasty and she doesn't like it."

"I'll do what I want. Jenny is not my mother and she's thirty minutes late. If I want to get pissed fucking drunk while I wait for her ass to show up, I will. Living with her, I should be drunk every minute of the day."

"I wish you wouldn't say things like that. She's not so bad, and she's your wife. Why do you say mean things like that? She's the mother of your children. She deserves some respect for that. Don't you think she deserves some respect?" He eyed Jack with contempt, his thin lips pressing together until they disappeared.

What the fuck? Why did Ray care how he treated Jenny? What the hell did he know about it anyway? The alarm tripped again in his mind. Time to up the ante. "Listen, you don't have to live with her. You haven't had to put up with her bullshit every single day and you haven't been married to her for more than a decade. I'm wondering if you might be wishing you were me, though. Is that it, Ray? Do you fantasize about Jenny? She's a good fuck and all when she puts out the effort, but that wears off fast. Trust me."

"I hate when you talk like that. Can't stand it when you do

that. God, she's the mother of your children. She carried your children. Isn't that enough?"

"Enough for what?"

"Never mind, she's at the door. She's here now."

Jenny walked toward them, the kids trailing miserably behind her. Jack would never understand why she made them dress up. Shit, Jasmine looked more like twenty than thirteen. Paul tugged at his tie as though it strangled the life out of him. Fourteen-year-old boys did not wear suits. Jack told her every time she forced him into one that she'd turn him into a damn sissy.

The only one who managed to get away with minimal primping was Allie; but then, she never did what her mother wanted her to and Jenny refused to argue with her. If Jack fought for any of his kids, it would be Allie. The seven-year-old was more of a man than most men Jack knew. She said what she thought and did as she pleased, no excuses and no apologies. The kid didn't care about what other people thought she should do. Jack encouraged her to be an individual instead of a sheep. She was daddy's little girl.

Wearing a purple Barbie T-shirt and blue camouflage pants, Allie proudly walked up to the table, her plastic princess shoes—complete with neon pink feathers—clicking on the tiled floor. Nothing on her tiny body matched, and Jack suspected she knew it. Knowing Allie, she'd dressed like a freak show just to get her mother's attention. She got so little of anything from her.

"Daddy!" Allie cried, running ahead of her scowling mother.

Yes, he might just keep Allie with him. If not for the money, Jenny would happily let her go.

"Hey, Allie-cat, I see you dressed up for dinner like everyone else."

"I wanted to go to the Chicken Pen but Mom said that place is for welfare bums and losers."

Frowning at Jenny as she approached the table Jack said nothing.

Jenny raised an eyebrow and gave him a tight smile. "Daddy can take you to the slums when he's not working, honey. It takes him back to his roots."

She patted Allie's head and took the window seat.

"We can't all start out in a doublewide like you, honey," he fired back.

Paul snickered. Under his mother's scowl, he reddened and stuffed his face in a menu. No backbone in that boy. Maybe Jack should have spent more time at home. He might have prevented Jenny from ruining them all.

"Ray, I'm so happy you could make it." Jenny smiled. She leaned down to kiss him, on the mouth, before taking her seat. "When Jack said you were joining us I almost didn't believe him. Where have you been hiding?"

"Work mostly. I hide at work." Ray smiled back.

Christ, thought Jack, the stupid ass was lit up like a fucking Christmas tree. His stomach clenched at the sweetness in their voices. What a pair of phonies.

"I don't hide, but I'm working a lot. Lots of work to do. Jack is always onto something bigger and better. Something greater every time with Jack."

"Can we order, Daddy?" Allie interrupted. "Mom wouldn't let us have a snack after school and I am starving."

"Sure we can order." Jack ruffled her blond head eliciting a sigh from Jenny. "What do you want?"

"Do Italians make fries?"

They ordered and Jenny continued to speak only to Ray, leaving Jack to talk to the kids. Jasmine, of course had nothing to say, she seldom did. She played with the phone Jenny insisted Jack buy her for Christmas, texting some equally empty-headed friend about boys, clothes or whatever it was empty-headed teenage girls texted each other about. Paul asked if Jack could make it to watch his team in the play-offs this year. He played football—quarterback Jack thought—and this year they'd made it to the big game. Jack promised to try.

Allie chattered about her friends, her enemies, and worse than her enemies, her teacher. Miss Canton was old and miserable. Jack met her at the one and only PTA meeting Jenny forced him to attend last September. She no longer asked him to go. Was it his fault the damn teacher provoked him? Some people need to be told to fuck off now and then. In Jack's opinion, the woman hated life. Jack couldn't understand why she'd think teaching would be her ideal career choice. Although he shared Allie's opinion of the woman, he didn't want to spend any time discussing her. He wanted to hear what Jenny and Ray were talking about, but Allie's babble made it impossible.

When dinner arrived, all was silent.

"Thank you for eating at Frankie's," the waiter, who Jack imagined dressed as a waitress in his off time, said in a singsong voice as he set a black tray on the table in front of him.

Jack's dinner threatened to come back up when he saw the monstrous bill, and still he had no clear idea of what Jenny was hiding. He shoved his chair back.

Jenny and Ray whispered across the table.

If not for the tablecloth, would he catch what their hidden hands were doing? What if he dropped his fork and bent to retrieve it? Maybe the kids knew something. Only Allie met his gaze, a smirk playing on her lips.

Fuck.

Stalking to the cash register hidden in the darkest corner of the restaurant, *God forbid anyone pay their bullshit bill openly,* Jack wondered if the rest of the restaurant saw what he couldn't prove. He slapped the little tray with the check and his credit card on the counter.

Although he didn't want to, he glanced back at the table. Just in time to see Ray brush Jenny's cheek with the back of his hand.

Motherfucker.

CHAPTER 4

After settling the kids in their rooms, Jenny went to bed. Good old Jenny always did excel at avoiding her problems. She knew he suspected something and tried the ignoring routine hoping he would forget. Jack wouldn't let the lying bitch off that easily. He showered and joined her in their room after looking for boxers in his nearly empty drawer. Laundry, it's a wife's job in Jack's world. Jenny, apparently, didn't get the memo.

He stepped into shorts that he hadn't worn since the eighties; the elastic had stretched and the blue cotton faded to a dull grey. *Fuck*. He'd have to get a maid. Or a new wife.

Jenny lay on her side, her back to him while she feigned sleep.

He wasn't buying it. "No Late Show tonight?"

She heaved a loud sigh and rolled over, a pained expression on her face. "I'm too tired to watch TV. If you're going to, can you watch it somewhere else? I can't sleep with the noise."

"I'm not watching anything. I wanted to talk."

"About what?"

"Us."

She opened her eyes and stared as he pulled back the covers. "Jack, can't it wait until morning?" she groaned when he climbed into bed and turned the lamp back on. "Really, I'm too tired for this right now."

"That's too bad Jenny, because I really want to discuss this and get it resolved."

"Get what resolved? Are we having a fight?"

"We sure aren't getting along. I just need to clear a few things up, start fresh."

"Say whatever it is you need to say so I can go to sleep." She sat up with another loud sigh, and then arranged the covers with exaggerated care.

Jack waited for her to finish with her annoying little performance.

"Well?" she asked.

He was overwhelmed by the urge to knock the sarcasm right out of her. Well let's see how cocky she was when he finished. "Do you want out?"

"Out of what?"

"Don't play dumb with me. You know what I'm asking."

"Why would I want out? You've given me everything I want. You're a perfect husband and father. You tell me so every fucking day, so how could I possibly want out?"

"I tell you because you don't seem to appreciate what I do for you guys. It's always about what I don't do and what I should do. A little gratitude goes a long way, you know?"

"Gratitude? Seriously? I should be thankful that you leave me alone with three kids every day? I should be happy that you never come home at a decent time like other husbands, so I have to make shit up so the kids don't think you hate them?"

"You don't tell them anything good about me. Allie told me the other day that you said I never come home because they irritate me. You told her I never wanted any of them. Maybe I should give her the number of the doctor who was going to suck her out of your fucking belly. He'd be able to straighten out who wanted her and who didn't."

"We only planned on two children. Remember? We should be saving for a trip around the world right now, or something else that didn't involve soccer and dance class. But no, instead

I'm raising another child. The other two are nearly out of the house and Allie will be here for years yet. When do I get a life?"

"That's my fault? I don't think so Jen. This one is all you. You didn't take your pills; you didn't like the extra weight they made you gain. What did you think would happen?"

"You should have used protection. I think you wanted to tie me down to you."

Jack glared, unable to believe her words. What a piece of work. Did she actually believe he wanted to keep her? He'd happily let her go as long as she just left. He was not about to pay her off. "Anytime you want to go, just say the word and I'll pack your shit."

"And the kids? Who has to take the kids?" She raised an eyebrow, arms crossed over her chest.

"Don't you want them?"

"Because I'm their mother? Why can't you take them?"

"This is exactly why I can't stand you. You're the most selfish bitch I've ever met. How can you not want your children?"

"I've been raising them on my own for fourteen years. It's someone else's turn now."

"You won't get a dime, you know. Leave if you want, but I'm not giving you a cent of my money."

Her face reddened and she scrambled to sit straighter. She tried to speak, but no words came out. Then her eyes narrowed and she made the snorting sound that betrayed her temper hung by a thread. "I am entitled to half, and I will have it. You won't get rid of me that easily, you miserable fuck. I have earned every last cent for being married to an asshole like you."

"Really? So because you spread your legs whenever I begged and managed to have a few kids, I should pay you? I wasn't aware you were a whore, but it seems appropriate."

The slap echoed in the room.

Jack barely flinched, smiling as she gathered up the blankets and stumbled out of bed.

"We're through Jack, and you will pay for *everything*," her voice trembled. "But let's be clear on one thing; I will not take the kids, but I will take everything else from you. Just watch me, asshole."

Jenny stormed out. Jack leaned back on the bed. She wouldn't get one red cent. He earned it, not her. If he had to give half of his money, half of his half of his business, and half of the house, he would have to start over again, and he'd worked too hard to allow some greedy little whore to have it all.

He needed a plan. Divorce wasn't an option. That much she'd confirmed. She wouldn't leave quietly and he wasn't about to sit like an idiot while she cleaned him out. So, what was left?

He also had a little problem named Ray. *Fuck*. Jack had more than a *little problem*. If Jenny was sleeping with that pathetic shit, the two might team up and Ray knew almost to a cent what Jack had stashed away. Ray could really fuck him. But would he? Was he in love with her? The image of Ray brushing Jenny's cheek flashed through Jack's mind. He closed his eyes. Yeah, the idiot was definitely in love.

Maybe he could convince Ray that Jenny was using him. Yeah and maybe he'd meet the fucking Queen at Wal-Mart.

Jack's thoughts went back to his lunch with Harvey. The law stated Jenny was entitled to half. Even if she got a quarter or a tenth, it was still too much in Jack's mind. She'd done nothing for fifteen years and even if it killed him, she'd get nothing in return.

But if she wasn't around to steal his money... He rubbed his chin. Yes, Jenny would be worth much more to him dead. That's all there was to it. It seemed like a rather drastic conclusion earlier, but really, there was no other option. He couldn't divorce her. She just said she'd take everything. And Jenny would. She'd hang around until she sucked him dry. Jack had given her reason enough to run screaming from him for years. Lord, how he'd tried.

Jack hated to think he could be capable of murder, but desperate times called for desperate measures. Then a thought hit him like a runaway train: What if Jenny realized the potential windfall *his* death would bring?

Morning brought sunshine and silence. The kids left for school before Jack even made it to the shower. He came down the stairs, thinking tomorrow he'd be going commando if she didn't do the laundry. He'd be damned if he'd ask her for anything.

Jenny moved in silence about the kitchen. She'd made just enough coffee for herself.

Bitch.

The entertainment section of the paper was spread out in front of her but the rest of the paper wasn't in its usual crumpled heap. He looked to the door and bit his lip.

Jack made his own coffee and retrieved the rest of *his* crumpled paper from the blue bin next to the door. As he stood, he looked out the window. The neighbor across the street stared, craning her flabby neck to see into his house. *Nosy cunt.* He would not be drawn in. Not now. He joined Jenny in the kitchen.

Sitting in front of her at the small table, Jack made as much fuss as possible while straightening the business section and slurping his properly made coffee.

From the way her nostrils flared while she read her section of the paper, he could tell she was doing her best to ignore him. She was no match for him, though, and finally looked up, her lips pressed into a thin line. Jenny hated slurpers.

"What?"

"Do you have to do that? Really, it's annoying."

"Well, every time you breathe I'm annoyed, so we're even." Jack smiled and returned to his paper. He wasn't really reading. Who could concentrate with tension hanging in the room like thick acrid smoke? Even if he could ignore that, the metaphorical knife that dug into his throat would not be ignored.

When sniffling sounded from Jenny's side of the table, he

gave up the pretense and looked up.

"Where did we go wrong?" she bawled, wiping her dripping nose with her sleeve.

Crying usually worked with him, so he wasn't surprised that she'd resort to that. Still, it irked him that she would assume he gave a damn about her feelings.

"Why don't you love me anymore? she asked."

"Why don't you love me? It's not like you give a shit about this marriage, you're just angry that I'm not giving you what you want. Stop the theatrics. I'm not bothered in the least by your tears."

Jenny continued to sniffle as Jack attempted to return to his paper.

"I don't want your money. I just want things to be the way they were."

"I think it's a little late for that, Jen. The last straw was when you decided to spread your legs for your boyfriend."

"I don't have a boyfriend."

Lying bitch.

"How could you think such a thing?" she pressed on. "I want to work this out, I'd never betray you."

"Really? Forgive me for not believing you but you're a shitty liar. There's nothing left to work out anyway. I'm done."

"Even if I was having an affair—which I'm not—what about you? You've been sleeping with that slut for God knows how long. You never miss a chance to rub it in my face. I just—damn it, Jack. Just let's try to make this marriage good again."

Jack eyed her tearful face. She sure looked sincere but he wasn't born yesterday. Those looks between her and Ray set his defenses up. She had something up her sleeve, but what? Poisoning his food? Cutting his brake lines? It might be wise to play along and see what she'd do.

"All right, what do you want from me?"

"We should take a second honeymoon, just you and me. We could go on a cruise or something."

Aha! She'd push him off the boat and leave him to drown.

Well, not if he pushed her first. "All right, you make the plans but I'm not promising anything. Get rid of the boyfriend while you're at it."

"There is no one else, Jack."

"Whatever." He sipped his coffee.

"This can't work if you won't try."

"I'll try," he lied. "Make the plans and I'll be there. I gotta get to work."

"Come on Jack. Can't you just be home one day each week?"

God, he hated whiners. "I don't work Sundays. What more do you want?" He stood, leaving his cup and the paper on the table.

"Are you *home* on Sundays?"

"Can we talk about this later? I really do need to go into work. I'll come home early if that makes you happy."

Or shuts you up.

"When should I book the trip? Can you take two weeks off?"

"Two weeks? No, I can take a week, but not two."

Her eyes welled up with tears again.

Although he didn't care about her, her fake grief gave him a good excuse to give in. He couldn't stand criers. Crying showed weakness and weakness was contagious. "Give a guy a break. I'll go, but I can't spare two weeks. It's my business and if I'm not there I could lose out on jobs. Ray can't bid, he'd put us in the poor house for sure."

"You don't give Ray enough credit. He'd do fine."

I bet....

"A week. End of discussion."

Jack left as she sputtered her arguments. All that talk about second honeymoons and making it work made him nauseous. Next thing he knew, she'd want to have sex.

He wouldn't be on any cruise, but it made a good excuse. How could a man kill his wife while planning a second honeymoon? Only people in love went on second honeymoons and people in love didn't kill each other.

RENÉE MILLER

CHAPTER 5

Jenny planned the cruise for July. A little over two months should give him enough time to make sure she'd be unfit to travel in anything other than a wooden box. He needed a plan that ensured the cops didn't point the finger his way, but Jay-Ray's problems barely left him time to sleep, let alone plot someone else's demise. Some bastard with a new setup had popped out of nowhere and was cheating him out of jobs. Every time Jack submitted a bid, the asshole bid lower. They had lost four bids in two weeks. The fact that they also won three was unimportant. He should have had seven jobs on the table or five at the very least. A couple of them were major projects that Jay-Ray couldn't complete in time.

Ray didn't help, he just bitched and moaned about the things they might be doing wrong. Jack needed solutions, not nagging.

Seated opposite his partner, Jack stared, counting backward to control his temper. When Ray was angry, he puckered his lips as if he'd just sucked a lemon or something. Jack wanted to reach over and smack the damn pucker from his face.

"We can't go lower. Can't go lower on the bids," Ray fumed. "We're going to miss this year's target. You want to retire in ten years? That won't happen if we don't top the projected turnover, and with the right profit margins. We can afford to lose these jobs. They aren't very good anyway." His hands shook as he pointed at the figures. "We're just exchanging money. There isn't enough margin. Just extra work is all these are, just extra work."

"That extra work gives us more clients later on. If I take on little jobs, then they'll remember us later for bigger ones. Clients stay loyal to a good contractor. If we had these jobs, then cutting our price wouldn't matter. It evens out in the end."

"No it doesn't. It does not. You never listen to me. I've explained this before. You never listen—"

Jack tossed the folder containing the newest bids on Ray's desk and stood. "Okay, we'll see what happens. I gotta get some shit done." He stalked down the hall and into his office to the echo of Ray sputtering behind his back.

Fuck him.

Jack slammed the door, sank into his chair, and rubbed his temples. Pussies like Ray gave him migraines. He didn't have time for someone that was too afraid to grab the world by the balls. Ray wouldn't even grab *himself* by the balls.

Seething, Jack leaned forward, opened the top drawer of his desk, and rummaged for an aspirin through paperclips, pens, and other shit he never used. He focused on his newest threat and how to get rid of it. One lone aspirin hid beneath a dusty calculator. Jack popped it in his mouth, scowling at the bitter taste.

Thorne and Sons was a new venture, but growing fast. Thorne must have had money to begin with. Jack knew firsthand how tough it was to come into this business with nothing. Most new contractors couldn't afford to bid on the types of jobs that Thorne sought. According to one of Jack's contacts, the so-called family business was comprised of a single man—who had no sons. Lucky bastard wasn't even married. Brilliant. Using a name that implied a family-owned company appealed to clients. It inspired trust. Jack wanted to kick himself for not doing the same.

"Fuck," he groaned.

He didn't have time to worry about this. After stabbing a button on his computer, he waited for the old beast to boot up. He knew he should focus on getting Jenny before she got him, but instead he had to waste time trying to get information on this new pain in his ass.

Jack forced himself to pause and steer away from panicking. Panic just made things worse. Which was the lesser of the two evils? If Jenny wasn't taken care of before the cruise, he'd lose everything or she might just kill him first. Neither outcome made Jack feel all warm and fuzzy inside.

On the other hand, if Michael Thorne wasn't dealt with soon, Jay-Ray would continue losing jobs; and money. The important question, he mused as the pain slowly ebbed from behind his eyes, was how much would he lose to that prick while dealing with Jenny. Well, he could lose a lot.

I can get it back later, but only if I'm still alive.

The computer chimed its greeting as the answer became clear in Jack's mind. First, he'd get rid of Jenny, and then he'd figure out what to do about Michael Thorne.

So there they sat; two miserable people in a happy little kitchen.

Jack didn't know how to go about finding a killer. He knew of some guys and had heard rumors, but how did one ask something like that? "Hey, you don't know me but I heard you kill people for the right price."

Nah, that wouldn't work. He knew he'd probably just get himself killed instead.

Although he hated the idea of getting his hands dirty, Jack figured it might be best to do the job himself. If he hired someone, he would be giving him the opportunity to turn around and bleed him dry. Jackson Murphy would never knowingly give anyone the tools to blackmail him.

He'd be patient and wait for the right opportunity if he had all the time in the world, but the cruise was a deadline of sorts. Pretending to read the paper, he considered messing with her car, poisoning her food, or setting up a suicide. He wondered if she had any idea of the images running through his mind and risked a glance across the table. She chewed her nails and thumbed through a fashion magazine. Not a fucking clue. It might work, but it would require the kind of planning he wasn't capable of. With science being what it was, he'd have to consider how much the cops could work out from one simple mistake.

Poisoning her food could take a long time. Too long. He'd need a drug that wouldn't be traceable in her system once she croaked. Jack had watched enough shows to know that shit took a long time to work and you could never count on those forensics bastards not finding it. He needed Jenny dead as soon as possible. He couldn't wait for her to slowly waste away.

Why wasn't she attempting to be nice to him? If she wanted him on this cruise so bad, why not suck up a little to seal the deal? Yeah... something smelled wrong.

She looked up, as though feeling his gaze on her as he stared over his paper. "What?" she asked.

"Nothing. Just thinking,"

"Stop it, you're creeping me out."

Jack hid a grin behind the sports page as his mind revisited the idea of tampering with her car. Cutting the brake lines was too cliché. He mulled the idea over, shifting his gaze as Jenny stood to get more coffee. She smoked, usually only in her car because he enjoyed forcing her to hide it. Perhaps he could do something with the gas line. The thought of blowing Jenny up had a nice ring to it.

Jenny stared from the counter.

He grinned. "What?"

"Are you okay?"

"Fine. Why?"

"You're acting... odd."

"Sorry, it's just nice to have a peaceful morning with my

wife. I like not fighting."

Oh, yeah. He was brilliant.

Jenny's face reddened. She sipped her coffee before joining him at the table. "See? I told you we could make things work. But stop staring, you're making me nervous."

"Sorry."

Jack went back to his paper.

Jenny flipped the page of her magazine, shaking her head.

Really, if they could get along like this for longer than a minute, he'd have reconsidered the whole thing. Sadly, they couldn't. His acting skills were the only barrier to another fight.

Late the night before, listening to her soft snore across the bed while he pondered possible murder scenarios, it crossed Jack's mind that he should see a therapist. His thoughts couldn't be healthy. But crazy or not, he didn't want anyone to talk him out of the plan. Jenny had to die.

His brain ached from the cruise's ticking clock as he struggled to solve his dilemma. Christ, he'd never make a serial killer, too many things to think about. Too many possibilities. Staring at his empty coffee cup, his headache subsided.

I'm thinking too small.

Every report on the news about the ones that got caught, involved tampering with cars or some stupid, amateur shit like that. Jack could do better. He *had* to do better. Like something that had never done before.

Then, as Jenny delicately dug a booger from her nose, sniffing most unattractively, the solution hit him.

The answer to all of Jack's problems lay in a tiny little insect that inspired fear in the hearts of grown men and women. A bug that could cause a man to squeal and flail around like a little girl.

Bees.

CHAPTER 6

The problem with bees, Jack found out a couple of days later, is that you can't just pick them up at your local pet store. You had to find them. Unlike hornets' nests, beehives didn't just hang around. Bees liked to make their homes inside things, not on them.

Thanks to his gardener, Jack's yard didn't have a single hive. He found out quickly that the efficient asshole even removed the ones from the neighbors' houses on both sides. Jack nearly gave himself an aneurism trying to figure out how he'd ensure Jenny encountered a bee. Then he remembered the vacationing family near his house. The Anderson's yard had lots of fruit trees.

Once he figured out where to get them, and before sneaking down the street to pick them up, he had to come up with a way to transport the little bastards without getting swarmed.

Jack solved his problem with only a few stings. He spotted a swarm near the Anderson's garage. The family stayed at their cottage for the spring and summer months, so the bees were mostly undisturbed but quite active, and partial to Mrs. Anderson's blooming fruit trees.

That night, he waited until ten for Jenny to leave for her gym class. She claimed she didn't like working out in front of crowds. Fucking liar. She went that late because she knew he couldn't leave the kids alone at that time to follow her. Jack didn't care. When her car disappeared up the street, he went about enlisting his killers.

He crept into each bedroom to make sure the kids slept soundly before heading outside. Walking through the tree line that ran across the back of the street, Jack made it to the Anderson's unseen. He slipped around the front, thankful for the cover of darkness as he waited for Mr. Norton to walk his dog inside the house next door. The dog glanced over. Jack shook his head.

Damn yappy fucker, if he—

Jack let out his breath as Mr. Norton dragged the dog up the front steps. The bees buzzed above Jack's head; he wondered if bugs ever slept. He'd hoped they might, but apparently, he'd been wrong. The hive—did bees live in hives or combs? He couldn't recall exactly what he'd read about them. Didn't matter. Whatever a bee's home was called, he'd found it tucked into a gap between the roof and the wall of the Anderson's shed. He could easily reach up and grab a handful of bees out if he were retarded enough to do so. Instead, Jack readied the garbage bag he'd tucked into his pocket and searched around for a stick. Damn, he should have brought his own. He fumbled along the edge of the driveway, keeping an eye out for nosy neighbors, until his fingers came upon something hard: a handle, smooth wood, and then cold steel. A shovel. Perfect.

With the handle, Jack poked at the gap, clumsily prying out a section of the hive. It broke free, and fell into the bag. A few bees buzzed angrily around him. He held the bag up to tempt them to join their precious honeycomb, while trying to shield his face as the little bastards swarmed his hands and head. Jack swatted them away. He cursed when a piercing pain shot down his neck.

Fuckers.

With a clap, he crushed the bee and flung it away. The bag hummed. How many had flown in?

Only takes one.

He sealed the bag, returned to the tree line and ran to his house.

The bees grew frenzied inside the bag. Jack dreaded opening the damn thing. He'd intended to hang a hive somewhere hidden, so the gardener wouldn't fuck up his hard work, but close enough that Jenny would encounter them. He didn't have a hive though.

Should've read up on bees a little more maybe.

As he listened to the hum of the angry insects, he revised his plan. He didn't have to hang anything. The bees would still be attracted to a honeycomb on the ground. Wouldn't they? Sure, the queen wasn't likely to be in there, but they'd be attracted to its sweet smell. Did bees have noses? Jack shook his head. It didn't matter. He only needed one bee to hang around, and it'd be easier to conceal a small portion of beehive in a bush, or under something like the front step.

Jack rushed through his yard, to the shed next to the pool. Jenny liked to dip her feet in the water as she read a book and drank whatever it was she drank while lolling about wasting his money and plotting the perfect way to kill him. Between the pool and the shed was a row of hydrangeas. On the far side of the pool were her rose bushes and a lemon tree that produced absolutely nothing. The rose bushes would be the perfect location but they weren't close enough to Jenny's favorite spot.

Holding the bag closed while he readied himself to run, Jack upended the bag over the hydrangeas. He counted to three and released the top. The bushes rustled as the honeycomb slipped down and out of view. A soft thud followed. Now he just had to empty the syringe in her bee kit, and it'd be bye-bye Jenny in no time.

Jack went out the back door, squinting at the bright morning sun. Walking past the pool, he moved casually toward the driveway to check on his bees. One or two buzzed along the side of the shed. Jack knelt next to the hydrangeas—to tie a shoelace he'd left loose—pleased to see about a half dozen more hovering around the fragrant blooms.

"Fucking brilliant."

He grinned, admiring his handiwork.

Standing, he brushed off his pants and walked to his car. Now he could focus on Mr. Thorne while he waited for Jenny to spring his trap.

Jack waved at the nosy bitch across the street before sinking into the leather seat of his car. His gaze wandered to the backyard. He shouldn't look, but his trap was magnetic. He smiled. If only he could witness his little killers doing their job, but he didn't have that kind of time. Jenny wasn't his only problem. Jack forced the bees from his mind and turned his thoughts to more pressing issues.

How to get rid of Michael Thorne? Murder wasn't logical. Killing your wife was different than offing some Joe off the street. Jack wasn't a criminal mastermind, after all. Brilliant as enlisting the bees to do the job had been, after a couple of freak-type accidents, someone might catch on. Coincidence only works so many times.

Even hiring someone to rough Thorne up a bit was unappealing. With the luck he'd had lately, he couldn't risk a hit. So, his options were limited. He could undercut every bid Thorne put in or maybe mess with his jobsites. Jack tapped the steering wheel, his gaze once more drawn to his backyard. A bee flew around Jenny's apple tree, the one that never produced apples. What about putting a bug in the ear of a union boss? He'd heard Thorne employed nonunion laborers. Nah. That stuff took a long time, and it would cost too much money in bribes by the time he managed to put the little prick under.

As he pulled from the driveway and accelerated away from his nosy neighbor, who still stared from her front lawn, Jack wondered if he should meet this Mr. Thorne and determine how much competition he really represented. He might be a dumb ass who got lucky a few times. Anyone can win a few bids, but could they build an empire? Not usually.

He turned onto Delaney, his thoughts drifting. He hadn't seen his girlfriend Whitney in weeks. She'd called the office several times but Jack put her off, telling her Jenny had put the heat on him. God, he missed her though. Whitney knew how to treat a man. She never pushed for anything, but accepted her position in Jack's life.

He often wished he'd met Whitney before tying the knot. Of course, she'd have been in grade school at the time. Jenny hired Whitney when she decided to go back to school to finish what she figured the kids had stolen from her. One of Jenny's friends from the gym had recommended Whitney, said she'd left home but she was a good kid. Jack had asked about her parents once, but Whitney refused to talk about them. Maybe they both died in a horrible crash. Jack didn't really care. No parents meant no bullshit.

What it was Jenny earned from her brief time in school, Jack never determined for sure. She sure as hell didn't get a job from the education. All he knew was that it cost him a couple grand and she didn't finish. But he considered it money well spent in the end. Whitney made a great babysitter. Allie adored her. And so did Jack.

On Whitney's eighteenth birthday, he and Jenny took her out to dinner. Whitney slipped Jack a note when he'd dropped her off at her apartment that night. That note contained a single sentence that changed Jack's life; *I'm legal if you're interested. W.*

Jenny must have smelled a rat because she fired Whitney a week later. Whitney started college the following month and Jack looked after her. He set her up in her own apartment off campus. She returned the favor.

Of course, Jack being a smart man paid everything in cash. He'd never leave a trail for Jenny to use to her benefit; or any evidence for Whitney to use when he got tired of her.

Jack flipped his phone and pressed the menu button. He scrolled to the "work contacts" and punched in his code. He wasn't dumb enough to leave Whitney's number easy to find. Jenny would have too much fun with that. He punched the key for Whitney's number and waited. His pants tightened just thinking about her.

When Whitney answered, Jack couldn't help grinning. He slowed at a crosswalk, nodding at an old woman who hobbled her way inch by inch across the road. Even that couldn't piss him off at the moment. "Hey there, *señorita*. Are you lonesome for your cowboy?"

Whitney didn't miss a beat. "Oh, *señor*, I'm so lonesome I've had to let the burro in the house to keep me warm. I feared the *bandido*s might have caught you and left your beaten and bloody body on the roadside. Then I'd be alone forever. I worry so about those bad men."

"I took care of the bandits, love. Now I can come home and love you all night long."

Whitney liked playing Spanish maiden and rodeo cowboy, one of her favorite games. Jack's too... especially the way she rode bareback.

"What about the *señora*? She will be looking for you, no?"

"Don't worry about her, little lady. I can come tomorrow if the burro has moved along by then."

"I think the burro is longing for the wide open space. Besides, he bites, and he kicks in his sleep. Sometimes he passes a wind that makes my eyes water like a fountain. He will be gone before you arrive."

Jack laughed. "I'll see you tomorrow then."

"Don't forget your spurs, cowboy."

He set the phone on the seat; one more reason to end Jenny's miserable life. He had a lot of making up to do for leaving Whitney alone so long, and Jack looked forward to every minute.

CHAPTER 7

Daylight faded into a purple-grey haze as Jack parked his car in front of Whitney's building. He stepped onto the pavement and reached down to shift the bulge in his jeans to a more comfortable position. God, he was pathetic. Shuffling up the steps to her apartment, Jack counted himself lucky that her building had exterior entrances. The idea of passing anyone in a narrow hallway with Little Jack at attention did not appeal to him at all.

He fished in his pocket as he neared her door, but Whitney flung it open before he'd managed to pull the key out.

"Jack! I can't believe you're finally here. I thought maybe you'd forget again and I would have to hunt you down and haul you back."

"That sounds like fun." He kissed her hard. She tasted like tacos.

She giggled.

"Maybe I should leave."

Whitney grabbed the front of his shirt and dragged him into the apartment, to the sound of buttons hitting the steps as she kicked the door closed behind them. "I don't think so, Cowboy. You're here and I'm not letting you go for at least a few hours. Can you stay the night?"

"I wish I could, but Jenny is on this big kick about making our marriage work. If I'm not home by midnight it will be another all-night tirade."

"Why can't you just pay her off and be done with this bullshit?" Whitney pouted, collapsing on the pink sofa.

When he'd handed her a wad of bills and told her to decorate the place, Whitney had gone pink crazy. The apartment resembled the inside of a Pepto-Bismol bottle. "Whit—"

"How long are you going to kiss her ass, Jack? She's a bitch."

Sitting next to her, Jack nuzzled his face in her hair. She smelled like strawberries and pot, not a bad combination. "I'm working on a way out." He kissed her neck. "I just need some time. It's not like you're waiting around for me. I know you've got your own deal here."

"I don't see anyone else. You know I'm not like that. It's been only you. You are all I need." She turned to face him and reached for his crotch.

Jack groaned as she squeezed. Then he lay back, pulling her with him.

"Obviously you aren't getting it anywhere else either. Are you? Did you fuck her as part of your "making it work" deal? Tell me you didn't." She trailed kisses down his neck, and worked at the button of his jeans.

As if he'd tell her if he'd fucked Jenny. "I wouldn't touch that bitch with a ten foot pole. Nailing her would be like screwing an old cow when I've been here with you."

"Good, I don't want seconds. Now, tell me what you want, Cowboy."

Whitney pulled his pants down his legs, nipping the exposed flesh as she drifted lower, past his thighs, to his knees and back up. They did this every time but she liked to hear the words.

Jack usually humored her. He didn't feel so indulgent this time. "I don't know what I want. Why don't you surprise me?"

"If you don't know, how can I decide? So many possibilities... are you sure there's nothing you need? I guess I could just climb on so you can be done with it and go home to your wife," she said, her voice turning cold.

Jack rolled his eyes. Whitney was still a child in so many ways. She looked like a woman and moved like one, but she could be as spoiled and unpredictable as a twelve-year-old.

"Don't be that way. You know I like to spend all of my time with you." Jack pulled her back over his chest.

She purred deep in her throat and ground her hips.

"I want you to take that damn blouse off first, and then I want to taste your skin. How's that?"

After pulling the blouse over her head, she leaned back. Jack's mouth watered. Whitney had magnificent breasts. Even before the kids, Jenny's tits never looked that good. Jenny's had been small and pert. Whitney's were round and heavy.

"Are you sure you want to taste? Maybe you want me to do something for you first. Then we can play with these later." She pinched her hardened nipples and lowered her head to lick herself. "Mmmm, that is good though, maybe I won't need you after all."

"I doubt you need anyone. But I need you."

She smiled and slid down his body until her face hovered above his thighs.

"That's a good girl, now show me what that pretty little mouth can do."

"What do you want? You want me to kiss it?" Whitney raised a wide blue gaze. "Is that all you need? Or do you want me to lick it?" She flicked her tongue across the top of his dick.

Jack's legs turned to jelly. If someone burst in with a grenade and threatened to blow them up, he couldn't have moved. He knew he'd have to say it or she'd torment him like this until he rolled her over and just fucked her. Jack had been dreaming about her mouth on his cock since he talked to her the day before, and he wouldn't leave without feeling it. "I want it in your mouth and I want you to suck it. Then I want you to keep it in there until I come."

"And after?"

"After what?"

"What do I do after you come?"

"Swallow, or let it dribble down your chin like you always do."

"That's so boring. I have something better in mind. Can we try?"

"Are you going to suck it?"

"A little. You'll like my idea, I've been doing some reading, and my plan is way better than anything you've done yet."

What could they have possibly missed? Whitney had a chest full of toys and creams and they'd used all of them. At some point, they'd tried every position known to man or beast. She let him do almost anything he pleased with her. What could she have that was new? A friend?

Oh, please be a friend.

"Let me get ready," she whispered and moved to stand next to the couch where she peeled off her skirt and panties.

Jack's mouth went dry. He cleared his throat, his gaze riveted between her legs. She'd shaved everything... every damn thing. When he finally met her eyes, she winked.

"No, that's not the surprise, but I'm glad you noticed."

How could you not notice that? Jack wasn't sure he'd last longer than a minute if she kept these surprises coming. It would be embarrassing. He prided himself on making sure his partner got off before him. Lots of guys claimed to do that, but Jack *really* did it.

"I can't imagine what you're up to. I think I should leave you alone more often if this is what you do when you're bored and lonely."

She chuckled and walked into the bedroom, her ass swaying and jiggling as she moved away from him. Jenny never walked around naked. She liked the lights off and changed in the bathroom. Whitney loved her body and played with it regularly. Jack had arrived many times to find her in the shower, already pleasuring herself and quite happy to let him watch. Most times, she preferred he didn't "interfere."

"Are you coming in here?" Whitney called from the bedroom.

She didn't have to ask twice. Jack jumped off the couch and ran to the bedroom.

"Lay down, Cowboy. I'll teach you a new game."

"I like games," Jack said as he lay on the bed.

Whitney joined him, setting a vibrator and a bottle of lotion next to his head.

"I wish you wouldn't put that so close to me. I don't like them."

"You're just jealous. Don't worry, it doesn't compare to the real thing. I'll need it later and you'll be glad once you see what it does." She took his cock into her mouth and set to work her magic, as promised.

Jack wound his hands in her hair and pushed her face, leaving her no choice but to take in all of him. Whitney liked that. Jenny did not.

"God, I love your mouth," Jack groaned as she trailed her teeth along the shaft and then back down again sending shivers down his spine and fire into his balls. "Faster, I'm almost there."

She stopped.

Jack wanted to push head her back down, but she must have had a different plan.

When she picked up the lotion and rubbed it on his cock Jack was intrigued. When it started tingling and then went numb, Jack was confused. He hated the stuff. It made it impossible for him to get off and she knew it. "Whitney, you know I don't like that shit. I don't have all night."

She smiled but said nothing. Squeezing more lotion on her hand Whitney reached behind her.

Jack blinked. Was she rubbing it on her ass? Oh God, she was. His heart raced. Shit, he was too old for this, but what a way to go. Was she about to let him do what he thought she was going to let him do? No one had ever consented without payment, and Jack didn't recall ever asking after Joanie Simpson told her friends he'd tried to do it to her in eighth grade. One horrible year of homo jokes was enough to forget the idea. But now...

"Are you serious?"

She capped the bottle and knelt on the bed. "Why don't you come up here and see?"

Jack jumped up and moved to the end of the bed. She pointed her ass at him. He positioned himself but hesitated. "Are you sure? It might hurt." Jack didn't want to hurt her, even if she did ask for it. She enjoyed it rough, but if he left more than a bruise or two on her, she'd pout for days, even if it was her idea.

"It won't hurt. It will feel amazing. The key is lubrication and relaxation. Now do it."

There she goes again. Talking to him like he'd never fucked a prostitute before. Jack eased his way in, not ready to believe she would really let him do it. If she stopped him now, he'd cry. He expected her to do so any minute, but she didn't, pushing her ass against him instead. His breath caught in his chest as her muscles clenched tight around him.

Whitney's soft moan followed the unmistakable hum of the vibrator. She quivered as she pressed it against herself, and Jack followed suit when she shifted it to his balls.

"Sweet Jesus..." Was that his voice?

"See, Jack? When I'm done, I'll just help you along with my friend here and everyone is happy." She moved the vibrator back to herself and pressed hard, as if trying to expel him. All resistance gone, she backed up and let him all the way in.

"Nguh," Jack grunted. *Nguh?* He didn't care how he sounded anymore. This was just too fucking good to be true.

"That's what I'm talking about. Now push, Cowboy. You can move around a bit."

He snapped out of his shocked stupor and moved in and out. The sight of her bent like that would have been enough to end it without her lotion. She cried out and pushed the dildo deeper where it hummed against him. Jack nearly fainted, his heart racing painfully in his chest.

This woman had to be an angel.

She climaxed.

Jack moved faster, slowing only when Whitney laid the vibrator against his balls again. Yes, he could learn to like that little piece of technology.

"Come on, Jack. Harder," she urged. "Faster and harder. Don't you pay me good money to do this? Make me earn it."

He loved it when she talked like that.

She knew it and urged him on. When Jack lost control, she squeezed her ass rhythmically around him. He yelled out something about her mother. Jack didn't even know if he made sense, but she seemed to like it. His legs gave way. He collapsed over her, spent, and more satisfied than he'd ever recalled being in his life. Even that hooker his dad hired for his eighteenth birthday had nothing on Whitney.

"Did you like that baby?" she murmured.

"You are fucking amazing. That was unlike anything I've ever done before. What the hell were you reading?"

"One of the reports we had to do for class."

"You're joking, right?" He rolled off her.

She raised her face, running her tongue over his lip and nipping gently. "No, in psych we're reading about deviant sexual addictions and practices. You know, like bestiality, pedophilia, and stuff like that. In many cultures, anal sex is illegal because it goes against nature. I was so turned on when I read about how it's practically an art in some places. I just had to try it."

"And the shaving? I asked you to do that ages ago. Why now?"

"Well, many girls do it nowadays, and according to this one report, men like to feel like they are with young girls. Morally it's wrong, and most would never want to have sex with a child, but studies prove that when a woman shaves her crotch and behaves like a schoolgirl, some men report a better sexual experience than if she was dressed like a woman, acted like a woman, and had a full covering of hair like a woman. It's really interesting. Utter bullshit, but inspiring."

"I think it's just the novelty, or they're sick perverts. I hardly think I'd want to fuck a kid. That's nasty. Besides, like you said, lots of women shave it now. It's not like it's unusual."

"You didn't want to fuck me the day you met me?"

"You were sixteen going on thirty, baby. That's a different situation." Uncomfortable with the conversation Jack leaned in and kissed her neck. "And you were a woman in every way."

"I guess. But the deviant part is interesting. I think they call it deviant if it feels too good. Some people think using toys is deviant too, and group sex, and bondage."

"Group sex? I don't have that much time tonight."

"Silly boy, I wouldn't share you with anyone. But maybe some night, I'll let you watch me with one of my friends."

He stared at her. Was she serious? "I can't join?"

"No, you'd hide somewhere and watch, like a peeping tom. You could jerk off or something, I haven't really planned it all out."

"Have I told you how amazing you are?" He kissed her again and rolled off the bed. "You got any food? I skipped dinner to get here early."

"There's some Chinese from last night in the fridge. I need to get cleaned up, but you go ahead."

Jack went to check the fridge but his phone chirped as he emerged from the bedroom. He detoured by the couch to retrieve his pants. Pulling his phone from the pocket, he checked the number. It didn't look familiar. Maybe a problem with a job?

"Jack here."

"Jackson Murphy?" a male voice. He sounded serious.

"That's right, and you are?"

"I'm Detective Logan, with the Hanover Springs police department. Are you alone sir?"

"No, I'm at a friend's house right now. We're having dinner."

"Have you been home today, Mr. Murphy?"

"Not since I left for work this morning."

"Have you spoken to your wife today?"

Excitement bubbled in Jack's chest. His hand shook so hard that had trouble holding the phone. "Yes, we had breakfast like we always do." Something had happened to Jenny. Dizzy with glee. Jack sat on the arm of the couch.

"I'd like you to come home. Are you close?"

"I can be there in twenty minutes. Are my kids okay?" Time to play the concerned father... and husband. "Is my wife okay?"

The detective hesitated. "There has been an accident, Mr. Murphy."

Jack covered his mouth to stifle a giggle.

"Your kids are fine, but you really should come home."

"I'll be there as soon as I can."

Whitney stared, eyes wide with concern. "What's going on? Are the kids okay? You asked about them. Who was that?"

"I've gotta go. That was the police. They're at my house; I think something happened to Jenny. They said the kids were fine. I really have to go."

"Is she dead?"

The tone of her voice, the barely contained glee that bubbled just beneath the surface, made Jack pause. Damn, she looked as happy about this as he was. "I don't know. I'll call you."

"Okay, I'll wait up for your call. Don't forget."

"I won't." Jack pulled on his pants and then kissed her cheek.

Her face flushed and her body trembled under his touch. "Are you okay?" she asked.

"Yes, it's just that I always wanted something to happen to her. I kind of feel bad now that something could have. You know?"

Her big blue eyes watered.

Jack ruffled her blond hair as he would Allie's.

She looked close to tears.

He smiled and squeezed her hand.

"If she is dead," she whispered, "it was nothing you did. It was probably some freak accident. I don't think she is, though. They would have said something."

He left her standing there with her quivering chin and watery eyes, feeling a little guilty that he couldn't tell her what he knew, but he was too smart to give anyone, even Whitney, anything that could be used if things went bad.

As he unlocked the door of his car Jack looked up to the heavens and whispered a prayer to the god he'd barely believed in up until the police's phone call.

CHAPTER 8

Jack tried to calm down on the drive home. Working on his story made it easy to get serious. He worked late, as he did often. Jenny wasn't expecting him for dinner because he'd told her he'd be late. He was shocked and angry about the bees. The landscaping company was paid to make sure there were no hives around the house because she had an allergy. Her kit? She kept one in the shed. Not in time? What a shame. A tragedy.

Jack turned off Elm Street, every town had one, and onto Holden, his street. Emergency lights flashed, illuminating the cul-de-sac. As he drew near his house, Jack's gaze fell on a navy blue Ford Taurus at the end of his driveway.

Mildly annoyed to see Ray's car, Jack cursed before it dawned on him that Jenny registered Ray as an alternate contact at the school; he usually located Jack when no one else could. Either they didn't try his cell first, or Ray was already there.

If things went bad he could always turn it on Ray. After all, Jack had an alibi; and he'd use it, even if it meant broadcasting his unfaithfulness to the world. What did he care now? If Jenny really was dead, she couldn't leave him or take his money.

Could she?

"Oh God Mr. Murphy, I'm so sorry."

Jack glanced to his left.

His neighbor, Mrs. Norton, ambled toward him. The woman never gave him the time of day. One dead wife and suddenly he's worth speaking to?

"Sorry for what? What's going on?" Jack smiled when her hand fluttered to her mouth.

How do you feel now bitch? You've let the cat out of the bag with your big unthinking mouth.

"Oh... I thought you knew. I mean... the police called you, didn't they?" She chewed on her little finger, her face flushed.

"They just said to come home."

"Mr. Murphy?" A uniformed officer walked from the house. The man looked to be about Jack's age, early forties, but his hair had more grey and he was definitely wider in the middle. Jack worked hard to stay as fit as he'd been twenty years before. "I think you should come with me, sir."

Mrs. Norton scurried away and Jack followed the officer into the house.

At the door, the officer let him walk in ahead. Jack headed toward the sniffling and murmurs from his living room. Ray sat with the kids, head buried in his hands. Jasmine patted his shaking shoulders. Why was his daughter comforting Ray when her mother just died?

"Daddy!" Allie cried. She jumped off the couch and ran into his arms. "Oh Daddy, it's just so bad. Ray says Mommy isn't coming back. Is that true? Is she dead?"

"I don't—" Jack pretended to be lost for words.

The officer laid one hand on his shoulder. "I'm Detective Logan, we spoke on the phone." He cleared his throat and motioned for Jack to sit down on the loveseat.

Jack waited for the good news.

"Apparently your wife was in the garden today, at the south end by the pool in our estimation."

"Yes, she likes to sit on the bench and look at the flowers. Sometimes she puts her feet in the water…." Jack let his voice fade as though too overwhelmed to continue.

"Well, she seems to have slipped and fallen into the water. She would have been fine except for two other unfortunate accidents. There was a gash on her head. Nasty looking, it was. Must have hit her head on the side of the pool. She also had bee stings on her face and hands. If she went into anaphylactic shock, due to her allergy before falling... well, you know. We figure she didn't drown but.... The autopsy will tell us more, but it's likely she wasn't breathing before she hit the water."

"The bees aren't possible, sir."

Logan raised an eyebrow.

Jack offered a smile, hoping he looked pathetic enough. "We pay our landscaper to get rid of any hives around here and Jenny always has a kit with her out there. Always."

"Yes, but your neighbors aren't so diligent, right?"

Jack hung his head.

"We found her kit on the ground. It was empty. Looks like she tried to give herself an injection... but we won't know until the coroner has a look at her body." Logan coughed. "Sorry, I meant—sorry. So anyway, we found a couple of dead bees too. I suspect that your wife came out with a fruit drink; the glass is still on the patio. It must have attracted the bees, which I'm told would have become quite agitated if she'd panicked or swatted at them. I'm terribly sorry, Mr. Murphy."

Jack looked at his hands to hide the excitement he was sure lit up his eyes. He couldn't have planned it any better. Hit her fucking head? Brilliant. Jenny always kept the kit in the shed near the pool, just in case. He'd gotten rid of that one, but completely forgot about the one she kept in the house. If she'd brought the spare kit out with her, his plan wouldn't have worked. She'd have had a full shot, probably wouldn't have panicked or fallen, and Jack would have still been trying to get rid of her.

"What do I do?" he asked in a small voice. "The kids, her funeral, there's just so much to do now."

"I'll help you, Jack," Ray whispered from the couch opposite him. "I'll help wherever you need me. I feel your pain as if she were my wife. As if she were my very own wife."

The cop frowned and so did Jack. Had Ray lost his fucking marbles? *As if she were his wife?*

"Thanks, Ray. When did you get here?"

"Oh, well Jenny called me this morning, said you'd be out. She said you would be gone and she wanted me to help her to plan your trip. Your cruise you know. She wanted everything to go right." He paused to draw a shaky breath.

Planning my cruise? More like planning how to how to get rid of me, you worthless fucknut.

Ray shrugged. "I said I'd come after work. I had stuff to finish up, as you know, and I said I'd be here as soon as I could get done."

"Who found her?" *Please let it be Ray.*

"I did," Jasmine whispered. She paced behind the couch wringing her hands. "I was the first one home from school. I called the ambulance, but I knew she was dead. Allie came home later with Paul."

"Her school called mine because Mom didn't come to get her," Paul added. "I just thought she got distracted again, so I took Allie to my practice and then we came home."

Jack looked at his children. Jasmine was visibly shaken, but then she would have seen her mother floating in the pool. Who wouldn't be upset about that? The other two looked sad enough, but not really devastated. Was it a bad thing that they weren't torn up about the death of their mother? Maybe they were just in shock.

Jack leveled his gaze at the cop. "What are we supposed to do now? Do I need to make a statement or anything?"

"No, it won't be necessary. We've done our investigation. I spoke to your daughter and I'm satisfied. This was a terrible accident and I'm very sorry for your loss. All of you."

Nodding, Jack murmured the appropriate words while the kids looked away.

The police gathered up their things. They'd taken Jenny's body away before he arrived so he didn't get to see it. The kids looked almost guilty. That wasn't possible, though. How could they have been responsible? Sure, they had reason to hate Jenny. She'd been a piss poor mother to them... maybe they got home before it all happened. Maybe one of them helped their mother into the pool or just watched as she died. Maybe they.... Nah, they weren't as smart as their dad.

Jack put the kids to bed and made sure they were reasonably okay before he returned to the living room. The girls cried, as girls do, but Paul was quiet. After forcing some tears to his eyes, he'd told them that rest would help put things into perspective. It sounded wise and fatherly to Jack's ears. He probably should've been more worried about them, but kids lost parents every day. That was life.

Ray still sat on the couch. How would he get rid of him? Ray acted as if it was his loss—which it probably was—and it pissed Jack off. He still couldn't believe what Ray said in front of the cops. Could he be more of a moron? How did Jack ever think he'd make a good business partner? The man was a fucking idiot.

"I'll stay if you want." Ray stared at his hands clasped loosely in his lap. "I can stay with the kids. Is there anyone you want me to call?"

"Jenny's parents died five years ago. I don't think she has any other relatives." Jack didn't think she had any friends either. Of course, he never cared enough to ask her. "I need to call that nanny service though, and soon. With Jenny gone, there's no one to look after the kids and I'm gone a lot."

"That can be done later. After the funeral and after you've had some time. You need some time. Why aren't you upset? You should be more upset when your wife dies."

"I think the best thing I can do is work. I'm not going to mope around the house grieving for someone who hated me."

Ray's face reddened.

Jack nearly laughed. Boy, he really did care about her. "Listen, I'm sorry she's dead. It's going to be a hard adjustment for my kids, but I'm realistic. We would have divorced before the year ended and I would have been on my own anyway. I'd like to get on with my life and forget this happened."

"I see. I'm sorry I asked. Sorry I asked anything," Ray grumbled.

"Don't be sorry; I know you cared about her. I did love her... sort of. I used to... you don't forget those feelings. But I need to deal with things my own way. If you want to do something, I would really appreciate it if you could stay with the kids tonight. I have to go out, clear my head and stuff."

"If you think that's best. The kids might want you, but if you think it's best."

"They won't need me, they love you more." Jack held up his hand when Ray opened his mouth to argue. "I know I've been a failure as a father and maybe I needed this to wake me up. I'm going out to drive around and sort out my thoughts, maybe stop at the office. You can reach me on my cell, okay?"

"The police said you need to call the insurance company. You have to handle the life insurance before too long."

"I'll deal with it in the morning. All that stuff is at the office anyway, I'll figure it out. Tell the kids I'll be home soon if they wake up."

"Okay, I will. I'll tell them." He looked down again.

Jack had to get back to Whitney. With Ray there, he couldn't call her and he really wanted to announce the good news.

"Thanks Ray. You are the best friend a guy could have."

"Yeah sure, the best," he grumbled. "I am that for sure."

Jack let himself in Whitney's apartment using his key.

She greeted him wrapped in a pink silk robe, her hair piled on her head. Puffy eyes and flushed cheeks betrayed that she'd been asleep. "So? Is everything okay?"

Jack walk past her into the living room and waited for her to close the door before replying. "It's better than okay baby."

He reached for her hands.

"Is she—?"

"Yes she is. The bitch is finally gone."

"I don't understand. She actually left?"

"No she didn't leave. She's dead. An unfortunate accident happened, and she's gone forever. It didn't cost me a dime. Glass half full, right?"

"You're okay?" She frowned.

"Okay?" Jack picked Whitney up and twirled around the room before setting her down and planting a kiss on her mouth. "I'm better than I've been in at least ten years Whit. Now I can live again."

"With me?"

"Of course with you."

"When do I move in?"

When did she what?

His smile froze.

Whitney ran around gathering clothes and makeup.

He couldn't stop smiling although he really wanted to cry... or run.

"I'll come over tonight, to help with the kids. We can pretend I'm their nanny again, to help you through. Just for a while. It's too soon right now, but later we can tell them."

"Tell them what?"

"That we're getting married. I'll be their mom now. I'm so excited. I bet Allie missed me. I sure missed her." She scurried around the apartment, making plans.

Shit, what have I gotten myself into now?

Whitney could not move in. Jack didn't want to marry her or anyone. He had to tell her though, and Jack didn't know where to start.

CHAPTER 9

Having to pretend that he gave a shit while waiting for Jenny's funeral to end had to be the best bit of acting Jack had ever done. Ray bawled as they lowered her casket, drawing all kinds of stares. He wouldn't have cared except that many of their clients and associates had attended and Ray made him look bad. Jack would have to deal with him somehow, but first he had Whitney and her ambitious pursuit of a fucking wedding to sort out. He'd managed to put her off for a while by making promises he didn't intend to keep.

She flipped out when he mentioned how bad it would look for her to move in. Then he gently explained how his kids might feel if their friends' parents talked about Whitney moving in so soon after Jenny's death. It might be devastating if they were teased about it. The lies just rolled off his tongue like butter. In the end, she agreed it might be better if they waited.

While Jack attempted to hang on to his single status, Ray called the nanny agency without consulting him and managed to find the oldest, most disagreeable woman on the planet to settle in his house. He did not want or need a live-in nanny. He got one anyway thanks to Ray.

Lillian was as wide as she was tall and as mean as she was

ugly. She'd arrived with only two bags but the house felt crowded with her presence. Rising at the crack of dawn, she made sure the rest of them woke shortly after, and then put the kids on a strict diet along with doling out earlier bedtimes. The kids were upset. Jack didn't blame them. But they learned after a week that to argue with Lillian got them nothing but extra chores, solitary confinement, and lectures Jack compared to psychological torture. Even he was a little afraid of her. Paul's last punishment for "sassing" won him the privilege of giving Lillian a pedicure. Jack shuddered at the thought. If only that were the worst of it.

What Lillian called "solitary" consisted of locking the kids in the spare room, which she stripped of everything but a bed. If they learned their lesson, they were out by bedtime; if not, they stayed. She brought in their meals and allowed them out only for bathroom breaks every few hours. Jasmine was the record holder for solitary with three days. Hell, Lillian had only been there two weeks, and Jasmine barely managed to stay out of the spare room for a day before she was back in. The last round, Lillian didn't even let her go to school. In Jasmine's mind it was cool at first, but that opinion changed when Lillian brought her homework in and stayed to watch her complete it.

Jack never stayed for coffee anymore. He got up and headed to Whitney's until he was ready to go to work.

"So, explain to me how it's better for your car to be seen here every morning, yet moving in together would cause scandal." Whitney asked.

"Fucking Ray and his fucking nanny. Jesus, Whit, I can't take a shit without her voicing her opinion about it. She's nuts."

Whitney laughed... and laughed.

When tears welled in her eyes, Jack lost his patience. "I don't see what's so funny," he grumbled, fingering his coffee cup and wishing he were still in bed instead of watching the sun rise through Whitney's kitchen window. "I'd fire her but I'm afraid of what my punishment would be."

"Maybe you could off her, like you did your wife," she

snorted.

His heart skipped a beat. "Excuse me?"

"Oh come on, like you didn't plant those bees somehow. I'm not an idiot, you know? I'm sure you were only trying to piss her off, but you got lucky."

"I did not kill Jenny. I can't believe you'd even think I could do something like that."

"Relax honey, I'm not telling anyone. I love you. Why would I care if you killed her or not? It was accidental anyway. It's not like you'd do life for it."

Whitney went to the coffee pot and poured him a cup before sitting across from him. She took his hands, a sparkle of amusement in her blue eyes.

Jack suddenly felt like smashing her know-it-all face off the table. How quickly could someone turn on you? Jack could tell you: in an instant if that someone was a guy who'd just killed his wife. "Whit, I don't want you thinking I set that up. I didn't. Had I wanted her killed, I'd have paid someone or cut her brake lines. I could hardly come up with something like that. Besides, she had her emergency kit ready. She'd been stung before."

"Whatever you say; I won't tell anyone what really happened. All you have to do is keep me happy and your secret is safe."

He stared at her for a long moment. Was she joking? If she thought he killed Jenny, did she seriously believe that he wouldn't get rid of her too? True, she was blonde, but until then, Jack had never considered her stupid. "I gotta go to work."

When Jack arrived at the office, he found Ray staring out the window. Paperwork overflowed from his desk to the floor. Such a mess usually drove Ray over the edge. Instead, he sat there staring vacantly at the street below. Jack closed his eyes, praying for patience. Obviously, Ray had already taken the leap into Crazy Valley.

"Good morning Ray." Jack shut the door quietly.

"Is it?"

"Is it what?"

"A good morning. I don't think so. Nothing's good anymore."

Did his lip tremble?

"It's like the lights went out when Jenny died and no one can turn them on. Can't turn the light back on…"

Can't turn the—what the fuck? Ray had finally crossed the sanity line and dived headfirst into lunacy. Jack didn't plan to reel him back in. Jenny was *his* fucking wife damn it. "Ray, this is getting ridiculous, and you're being an idiot. She was my wife, not yours. I don't care how many times she fucked you. You weren't married to her. I was."

Ray tapped his leg, blinking furiously.

Well shit, who'd have thought? Jenny traded down after all. "You were in love with her, weren't you?"

Ray stilled, but didn't meet Jack's gaze. For the love of Christ, he really did love her.

And I'm a fucking moron.

"You don't have to answer, Ray. It's obvious. You loved *my* wife. Don't blame yourself. When Jenny turned on the charm, she was quite impressive. I know how she works. She led you on, right? Told you what a prick I was. How I never paid any attention to her. She probably cried. Oh, Jenny's great with tears. Did she fuck you too, or just let you fumble around a little?"

Ray cringed.

"Look, I'm not mad at you. You're stupid, and you can't help that. But this grief is more than Jenny deserves. It's not like she even gave a shit about you. She only ever cared about herself."

Ray turned and stared. His lip trembled.

If he cried, Jack would push him out the fucking window. Prison or not, a man could only handle so much of this crap.

"Jenny was the most beautiful person I have ever known

and you were a fool not to see it." Wiping his nose on his sleeve Ray glared. "You have lost the best thing that ever happened to you and you can't even see it. She cared about me, and don't tell me she didn't. Don't you say she didn't. She cared."

"If we're going to continue being partners you need to lose this fixation with Jenny. Forget about the fact that it is just plain weird, you're only hurting yourself, man. Snap out of it! She's dead and she's not coming back."

Ray lowered his head and his shoulders shook but no sound came from him.

Fuck, here we go again.

He wiped his nose on the other sleeve and straightened some papers. "I know you don't understand it, Jack. You're not capable of feeling any real emotion. No feelings in you at all. That's fine. I'll be fine. I just miss her and I can't stop. Can't stop missing her."

What the hell? Didn't Jenny say she hadn't seen Ray in months? Of course, they'd both lied. It was plain as day now. How could he have missed it?

Because you got cocky.

Jack wished he could punch himself. Then he'd dig up his dead whore of a wife and cut her into tiny little pieces. Then he'd cook those pieces up and serve them to this pathetic motherfucker for dinner.

She's gone. What's done is done. Calm down.

"Maybe you should take a few more days then. Clear your head and then we can get back to work. If you want to take some stuff home so you're not buried in paperwork when you get back, then go ahead. Just get your shit together."

"Maybe I should, I don't want to leave you high and dry though. You need me to do the bids and the payroll and—"

"I did all of that before you were here. I can manage. Maybe you could take over at the house for a bit, get rid of Lillian."

"What's wrong with Lillian?"

"Everything. She has to go. The kids are miserable." Jack

took off his jacket and hung it in the closet next to the door.

"They need a mother figure. The kids need a woman in their life. Lillian is a good nanny and a good person. They just miss their mom. They just miss Jenny."

"I don't need her, though. She's a pain in the ass and she's taken over my house. I don't like it."

"You'll get used to her; she's good for you. Good to keep you in line. You tend to get a little irresponsible sometimes. She'll keep you in line."

"I could call Whitney, the kids love her. She can keep us in line just fine and I won't have to be afraid of going home anymore."

Ray flinched as though Jack had slapped him. "Whitney? You would dare bring her into Jenny's house? It's not enough anymore to fuck her all over town; you have to do it while your kids watch you stain their mother's memory? You've got to stain Jenny's memory?"

How did Ray know about Whitney? Of course, Jenny must have told him all about it to get him on her side. She might have been a lazy bitch, but he had to admire her cunning. And who the fuck was Ray to judge anyway? He didn't even try to deny that he'd fucked Jenny. "I don't think this is any of your business. You're crossing a line here buddy, and I won't take it. You were nailing my wife. Hardly makes her an angel, does it? Besides, Jenny is dead. If I want to bring in my own harem to fuck on the front lawn, I will. I've put up with enough of your bullshit, and I won't have you, my so-called best friend, telling me how to live my life."

"Maybe you should buy me out then. Buy me out right now. I can't continue this friendship anymore if you can't understand. You never did understand."

Buy him out? Not fucking likely. Jack would see him dead first. "Go home before we say things we'll regret. I'll talk to you in a few days." Jack pointed to the door.

"I won't change my opinion. You've gone too far and I won't change it. I won't stand for what you're doing to Jenny."

"She's dead, Ray. I can't do anything to her. Get out of

here."

Ray gathered his things in silence and left the office without sparing a backward glance.

He sat in the chair behind Ray's enormous pile of papers and thought the ridiculous episode over. Ray had to go; it was obvious he'd become a liability and a danger to Jack's freedom.

Buy him out? Right. Jack wouldn't give him one red cent. He was a pencil pusher, nothing more. But how to get rid of Ray without buying him out? He turned the possibilities over in his brain. There'd be no talking Ray around to his point of view. You can't rationalize with crazy. Jack's mind came to the same conclusion with each scenario he played. He would have to kill him.

Jack shrugged and leaned forward to sort out the mess Ray had left. "I've done it once, I can do it again."

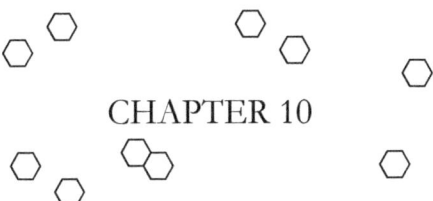

CHAPTER 10

Jack spent the rest of the day losing jobs to Thorne and Sons. No matter how unhappy it made him, he just couldn't work up a righteous anger. Thorne annoyed him, but now he presented less of a threat than Whitney or Ray. His mind refused to focus on clearing away the mountain of work. Two crews would start new jobs that week and he had two more jobs scheduled within the month. Jay-Ray—now just Jay—would not go under any time soon, so Michael Thorne might gain a reprieve. Let him think he'd won the race; it would make him careless later on.

After setting his pen down, Jack pushed away from the desk and leaned back in the chair; arms crossed behind his head. The bottom line was he had three issues to resolve as soon as possible: Lillian, Ray, and Whitney, and not necessarily in that order.

A migraine threatened to explode. Why could they not just let him live his life? Whitney knew too much, but he'd deny everything even while squeezing her pretty little neck. Ray was a different matter. Perhaps he deserved to get back what he put in when they partnered up, but not half of the business as it stood now. He'd never see that much money, not from

Jackson Murphy.

Lillian was just a pain in the ass; not enough that she had to die or anything drastic like that. He could get rid of her easily enough but for a devilish detail; it would give Whitney the excuse to move in. How to fire Lillian without letting Whitney in? Better to put up with Lillian's tyranny than to steer into the marriage trap. Jack rubbed his eyes. This was getting ridiculous. Panicking over nothing wouldn't help the situation. Lillian will go at any time and he could manipulate Whitney for a while. They weren't huge problems. Not yet.

But his partner posed an immediate threat with his lovesick ramblings and questions. How to deal with Ray? Jesus, Jack had pulled out all the stops to set up Jenny's death and he wasn't sure he had the genius for another. "Think, Jack, think," he grumbled. It shouldn't be too hard to set Ray up. The guy knew about numbers and little else.

Tapping the armrests of his chair Jack ticked off Ray's weaknesses. His only friends were Jack and the departed Jenny, he hated socializing, and most people found him too strange to tolerate. With all his weird habits, Ray wasn't easy to like. He lived alone. Until his mother died two years before, he'd lived in her basement. Though he owned the fucking house, Ray continued to live in the basement. Out of respect, he said.

What a moron.

Pity crept into Jack's heart uninvited. Closing his eyes, he thought of the times Ray had stood awkwardly by, when meeting a new client, and how he'd shook when he met Jenny that first night. At the time, Jack had wanted to help him, make him see that normal people needed friends. Instead of absorbing normalcy, Ray latched on to him and refused to branch out.

"No. He's a loser and a threat." Jack told himself. He'd outlived his usefulness. Hell, a guy could hire anyone off the street to do what Ray did for far less money. With Ray gone, he might end up ahead of the game.

A dull gloom hung over the room when Jack opened his eyes. He stretched his aching muscles and then glanced at his watch. Christ, it was after eight. He leaned over and shut the computer off before standing.

First, a good night sleep was in order and then he'd mull it over. His brain couldn't think anymore.

At a little past nine, Jack pulled into his driveway and his migraine returned. "Must be the air on this street," he muttered.

Well, at least the bitch turned the lights off.

He walked up the steps, thankful he'd made it home after the Dragon Lady had gone to bed. Fuck, he hated even looking at her. Jack winced as the hinges shrieked. He stepped inside, pushed the door closed, and reached toward the light switch. Something moved in the darkness. Jack flipped the switch, and nearly crapped his pants when he realized Lillian sat in the dark kitchen alone.

"What the hell are you doing?" Jack strode into the room. He was startled further by the sight of curlers and some goopy pinkish substance on her face.

"You are very late, Mr. Murphy. The children have been in bed for hours. I thought you might call or something."

"This is my house, Lillian, and I'll do as I please. It's only nine. What fucking time did you put them to bed?"

"There is no need to use such vulgar language. I don't approve."

"I don't care what you approve. You're confused about who the boss is here. I'll clarify for you: It is not the fucking nanny."

"Mr. Murphy, your children have just lost their mother. You remember their mother don't you?"

It took all the control in him to not kick her fat ugly face.

"They need structure and routine, and you must provide it. Beginning now, you will return home at dinner every evening. I don't care what you do when they are in bed, but between the hours of dinner and bedtime you will be home."

"You think so?" He stepped toward the table.

She leaned back.

That's right bitch, I'm the man of this house and you'll remember that.

"I don't think you understand the situation. This is my house and they're my children. If I want to stay out for a week, I will. It's your job to look after them. A job you're paid very well to do. If you don't like it you can leave."

"I will not leave those children. You will do as I say or I will call the authorities and you won't have them."

"You think I give a shit? I never wanted them, you stupid bitch. Call whoever you want. Maybe they can take them tonight and I'll be through with this bullshit."

She opened and closed her mouth a few times like a startled lamprey.

Grinning, Jack turned toward the stairs. Lillian had to go before the end of the week. The fat cow would not remain in his house a minute longer than necessary.

At his room, Jack jolted again after he opened the door. Jasmine lay sprawled across his bed, fully clothed and asleep. *What's going on in this house?*

"Jasmine?" Jack didn't know why people whispered when they wanted someone to wake up and after realizing he'd done it, he spoke louder, "Jasmine!"

Jasmine stretched, yawning and blinking a couple of times before frowning. When her dopey gaze fell on Jack, she sat up and looked around the room, rubbing the sleep from her eyes. "I was waiting for you to come home. I can't believe I fell asleep, but that bitch makes us get up before the sun so I guess it's no surprise."

He didn't bother to correct her language. "What are you doing here?"

"I want her gone, Dad. I can't take it anymore." Although her lip trembled, Jack commended her for keeping tears at bay. Poor kid probably wanted to cry like a baby.

Jack would send her away for showing weakness like that; he'd made that clear to all of them.

Still, she looked so vulnerable, like the spunky little toddler he remembered before Jenny ruined her. Jack might have let it slide just once. He shrugged, loosening the catch on his watch. "Without your mother I need someone here. Who would look after you?"

"Uncle Ray was doing fine, but you made him leave."

Fucking Ray, filling them up with bullshit.

Jack didn't need him or his stupid nanny. "I didn't send Uncle Ray away, honey. He was the one who brought Lillian. He set it all up. I don't like her much either you know."

"Can't you do something? I'm old enough to baby-sit Allie, aren't I?"

"No. Not for the hours I have to work. Besides, it's not fair to you. As long as you guys are here, I have to make sure you're taken care of. I can't work to provide a roof over your head and be here for you." As he handed her that line of crap, an idea tickled Jack's brain. Why hadn't he thought of it before? So fucking brilliant. "If you guys were away at school..."

"You mean like boarding school?"

"Never mind, you can't leave your friends. Everything you know is here. Forget I mentioned it." He removed his jacket and tossed it near the dresser, keeping an eye on her as she considered his idea.

"Wait," Jasmine's eyes brightened. She chewed her finger in thought, as her mother used to do.

Would he ever be free of that woman's memory?

"Where would we go?"

"Where do you want to go?"

"Some place foreign, you know, like Switzerland or Italy or something." She clapped her hands. "Oh my God, Missy is going to be so jealous."

It just got better and better. No matter what it cost him, they'd go.

"Sure, I could do that. Let me look into it tonight. I'll get some information and we'll have a family meeting tomorrow, without Lillian.'

Jasmine jumped from the bed and wrapped her skinny arms around him.

Jack stood frozen. He tried to recall her ever hugging him, and came up with nothing. Not since she was a baby at least. Not sure how to handle it, Jack patted her back awkwardly and then gently pushed her away. "Lillian has gone to bed. You can wake your brother and see what he thinks. I'll deal with Allie tomorrow."

"Okay." She turned to leave, stopping with her hand on the door. "Thanks Dad, you're really not the asshole Mom made you out to be." Then she was gone.

Nice Jenny, real nice.

Jack stared up at the ceiling. He'd known along she had fed them bullshit about him but hearing it from his daughter's mouth pissed Jack off all over again. He hoped she burned in hell.

Before turning in, Jack spent half the night on the Internet, looking up boarding schools in faraway countries. They really didn't cost a whole lot, after factoring in the cost of keeping them home. He wouldn't have to feed them, or pay for their sports, extras, or clothes. They wouldn't be running up the utilities or talking on his phone. He'd pay the tuition and aside from a small allowance that would be it. Perfect.

For the first time in nearly a year, he'd fallen into a dead sleep as soon as his head touched the pillow. A muffled thump woke him early the next morning. He glanced at the clock next to the bed.

Shit, five already.

He'd have to go to work to get some sleep. Yawning, he stretched, turned onto his side, and closed his eyes.

Then Lillian began her morning torture. She banged a pot, clanging mercilessly up and down the hall.

Moaning and grumbling followed from the kids. Paul and Allie got up. A rebellion erupted at the end of the hall, near Jasmine's room. Shit, he'd have to intervene just to get some peace. Jack couldn't wait until all of them were gone.

"I don't have to listen to you, so get out of my room you old bag," Jasmine screeched.

His head throbbed. Not a good sign.

Lillian's reply was muffled but it didn't sound good either. "Fuck off."

Jasmine's vocabulary had become interesting.

Feeling the quake of Lillian's three-hundred-pound frame lumbering down the hall, Jack rolled out of bed. Standing and stretching he reached for his pants, paused, and straightened again. This was his house and his room, if she barged in it was her problem.

The door burst open and Jack turned, a smile on his lips.

"Mr.—oh my," Lillian's hand fluttered to her mouth, the pot and spoon in her other hand she held in front of her like a shield. Dark eyes wide, she reddened and produced a strangled sound.

"What is it now?" Jack set hands on his hips as though oblivious to his nakedness. "Can't it wait until I get out of the shower?"

She stared at a point just beyond his shoulder, her face purple. "Yes, I suppose it can. Please, just hurry."

Jack slowly made his way to the bathroom after she waddled out. Hurry, his ass. He'd take all morning if he wanted. Let her deal with the kids. She was the one who wound them up with her boot camp bullshit. Jack couldn't wait to see her face when he pulled out the papers he'd printed the night before. He even made sure there were spots available at a few of the more promising schools for the kids, if he booked at once. Lillian had worked her last day at the Murphy house.

CHAPTER 11

Everyone, including Jasmine, sat at the kitchen table. Their hands placed before them, his children stared at an invisible point on the wall while Lillian lectured them on respect.

All eyes turned to the stairs when Jack cleared his throat. It was time to assert his authority. "It seems we have a problem and I've come up with a solution. Before anyone speaks," he glared at Lillian who pressed her lips into a thin line, "I want you to let me finish showing you what I've been exploring, and the benefits of it. Once you hear everything, I'm sure you'll see it's the best way to do things."

"Go ahead, Daddy." Jasmine smiled sweetly.

Jack couldn't believe the language that had come from that perfect little mouth only an hour before. "Thank you. Let's begin. I have here some enrollment forms for very exclusive schools. I was up well into the night studying this, so look them over carefully before voicing your thoughts."

He walked to the table and passed the papers to the kids.

Jasmine sorted through three pages before pulling one out. She looked at Jack, a grin on her face. "When do I leave?"

"Wait for the others, Jazz."

Reading slowly through the pages, Paul's expression

changed from afraid, to confused, to excited, as he reached the last. He looked up.

Jack stifled a chuckle at his goofy expression. "Well, Paul?"

"Can I really go here?" He waved a page.

"Sure."

"To Italy. I can go to Italy? On my own?"

"Yes Paul, but you're not alone. These are boarding schools. You will live there year-round, unless of course you prefer to come home on holidays and through the summer. The schools you are looking at have housing available all year. Most kids prefer to take advantage of the summer programs as well."

"I don't know if this is a good idea, Mr. Murphy. You can't treat them like baggage to be shipped off at your convenience."

"Of course he can." Jasmine jumped in before Jack could reply. "He's our dad, and if he says we can go then you can't stop him. Right, Dad?"

"That's right. You guys can be there before the end of the month if you want. Of course, if you want to wait out the school year, I'll understand. I just thought it might be nice to have the entire summer to make friends and get used to things."

"I don't want to wait," Paul said. "I'll go whenever they'll take me. This is awesome. Do you know the soccer stars that have come out of this school? It makes our soccer league look like peanuts. I can't wait to tell my friends. I get to live in Italy on my own."

"You will be in a dorm, with adult supervision."

"It's still cool."

Jack turned to Allie who remained silent, frowning at the pages. It dawned on him that she might not understand much of it. She was only seven after all; he'd have to convince her that she wanted to go. "Allie, do you have a favorite?"

"I don't want to leave. You'll be all alone." She looked up with watery blue eyes, the same color as his.

He sighed. Why did everyone feel the need to cry around him? "Don't worry about me, Allie-cat. I want you guys to be happy. Did you see the one with the riding program?" He leaned over and pulled out the form for a French school.

"Yeah, but you have to have your own horse. I don't have a horse."

"You could."

"Really?" She stood and then sat down again. "But this is in France, that's like another world and they talk funny."

"It's an English school, baby. The teachers will teach you French but everyone will also speak English. You have nothing to worry about."

"How would we get the horse there?"

"I'll call and find out if the school can arrange a horse for you. I'll pay for it."

"This is bribery and it is disgusting," Lillian interrupted. She took a couple of pages and waved them at the kids. "He's getting rid of you, don't you see? He doesn't want you here and he's trying to make himself look like father of the year while he banishes you guys. Your mother would never stand for this. You are being banished from his life, don't you see?"

"I'll take banishment then," Paul said, taking the pages back from her. "I don't care if he wants me, as long as I get to go to Italy, man."

Jack smiled at Lillian.

She glared.

"Lillian, it looks like you'll no longer be needed here. I'll pay you your two weeks but you can leave whenever you want. The sooner the better."

"You won't get away with this, Mr. Murphy. I'm calling Ray and he'll stop you."

"This isn't Ray's house and they aren't his kids. He may have hired you but he has no control. He's my business partner and nothing more. So you just pack your shit and get the fuck out. Call Ray. Call the police. I don't give a damn who you call, just get out of my house."

Lillian turned white then red before jerking around to head up the stairs to her room. A door slammed followed by scrapes and thumps. Jack figured she'd probably add a few of his things to her bag, but he didn't care. Why hadn't he thought of the schools before Ray found her? It would have spared him a ton of headaches.

Jack joined his kids at the table and listened to their chatter, mixed with Lillian's racket upstairs, content for the first time in a long while. The nanny was gone... or she'd be gone very soon, and the kids would follow. There was no need for Whitney to move in. He'd have to see about a smaller place though. A big empty house would be an invitation and Jack didn't want her thinking she had a future with him.

Jack hadn't seen Ray for three weeks. He'd expected him to run right over as soon as Lillian called, bitching about what Jenny would think of Jack's little plan. Instead, Ray didn't come into the office until the day after the last of the kids left for school. He stood against the door, shaking his head and making that clicking noise he made when he was upset. Even without the fucked-up clicking, Jack would have known by the look on his face that Ray had a lot to say.

"Hello Ray, how are you feeling?"

"I'm okay. How are you? Are you okay?" He sat in the chair opposite Jack, hands resting in his lap.

"I couldn't be better." Jack smiled.

Ray blushed.

The guy was too easy to read, and Jack knew exactly what Ray expected to hear. He wanted Jack to say he was a mess. That's how Ray worked. He'd lost his wife and then his kids. In Ray's mind, Jack should be seeing the error of his ways by now.

Not likely.

"What brings you here? Are you coming back to work?" Jack asked.

"Lillian called me a couple weeks ago. She called my house worried about you. Worried about you and the kids."

"And?"

"You can't just send them away. How could you ship them off like that? Jenny would be heartbroken if she knew her kids were separated. Just heartbroken."

"She didn't want them any more than I did. She bitched constantly about being stuck with them and forgot to pick Allie up nearly every week. They ate pizza or some kind of take-out five nights a week because she forgot about dinner. Jenny wasn't the saint that you insist on making her out to be."

"I won't let you spoil my memory of her. My memories are nice and honest. No, not letting you do that. I won't come back here again."

"You aren't coming back to work?"

"No, I'll draw up a release with the amount of the business you'll have to buy out." Ray stood.

Was he serious? "Save yourself the bother. I won't sign."

"You have to pay me. You know you have to pay me."

"I don't have to do anything, Ray. You're the one abandoning ship here. I don't have to give you any more than you put in."

Fuck him.

"I don't want this to get ugly just to get what's mine. Don't make me have to do bad things," Ray said, his eyes filling with tears.

Who was he kidding? Ray would love to take Jack to court where he could tell everyone what an asshole his ex-partner was and rat Jack out about the bids. But he couldn't do that without incriminating himself. Ray handled the accounts. So any wrongdoing was his too. There was no way he didn't know he'd go down with Jack. Unless Ray meant...no, he'd never go to anyone about the bids.

"We don't have to let this get ugly." Jack tried to sound reasonable. "But you aren't getting half of this business. You haven't earned half. I could hire anyone to do what you do. You helped me out and I'll give you what you put in, but I am not giving you any more than that."

"We'll see. We'll see." Ray spun on his heel and stomped to the door without another word.

Jack stared at it for a while after Ray closed the door quietly behind him. Pussy couldn't even leave a room properly. Jack snorted. He needed a foolproof plan that would get rid of Ray but keep his name out of it.

Tampering with his car wasn't an option because the shithead took the bus most of the time. The car had been his mother's and Ray didn't like using it. He did smoke occasionally. Not a heavy smoker mind you, he had one in the morning and one in the evening after work. Honestly, Jack didn't see the point in maintaining a habit like that. He wasn't even addicted; Jack would bet he'd only started it because Jenny smoked.

Fucking freak.

A tickling feeling spread through his brain—the same sensation he experienced as he thought of the bees—the one that heralded a brilliant idea.

Ray heated his house with gas; he'd had problems with the lines the year before. What if those lines weren't fixed properly? What if a valve was loose, or broken? They crack all the time. It might leak into the house for days without him noticing. Ray didn't even have a smoke detector, much less a carbon dioxide alarm. They irritated his migraines, and he swore they only malfunctioned when he had a headache. The gas companies usually added some shit to give the gas a rotten egg smell, but Ray had a problem with his sinuses; he couldn't smell right. Well, he claimed he couldn't smell... Jack was willing to put that claim to the test.

All he had to do was to get Ray out of his house for a few hours. That would require creativity. Jack had all day to think about it. It wasn't as if anyone was around to distract him.

If Ray was going to be gone for good, he should hire a bookkeeper. That was inconvenient. He'd have to call an agency and find out if they had anyone available, preferably someone who could do their job and leave him alone. People were way too involved. It drove Jack crazy how everyone had to know what everyone else was doing. Whitney tried to convince him to get involved in some shit she called "social networking." He got as far as Twitter and nearly lost his mind.

Twits definitely made an apt name for the freaks. As if anyone cared that they just wiped their ass or had blueberry Pop Tarts for breakfast. Whatever happened to minding one's own business? Everyone seemed to have an opinion on what Jack said and did. If he worried about what they thought, he'd consult them beforehand. Jackson Murphy did just fine on his own.

CHAPTER 12

Before he did anything with Ray, Jack forced himself to visit Whitney. She'd be pissed that he hadn't returned her calls the past couple of days, but once she knew what he'd been up to, she'd calm down. The only problem Jack struggled with was explaining why she couldn't move in. That could cause a tantrum.

His mind went to the last one Whitney pitched. It wasn't so much that she got angry, but what she did to punish him for pissing her off; the memory of hot wax ripping the hair from his balls made him shudder. He pulled his car in front of her building and rubbed his crotch at the memory. His hands shook. Whitney could be a tad on the nutty side... oh, who was he kidding? She was batshit crazy. He could never be sure how she'd act when she got angry, or even when she got bored. He feared some morning he'd wake up with his balls super-glued to his asshole or worse; which was why Jack seldom spent the night.

Walking to her apartment, he visualized the forthcoming discussion in his head. No matter which version he played, it didn't end very well. Maybe she'd forgotten about Jenny and her uncomfortably accurate guess about what happened. He'd hate having to get rid of Whitney. He'd grown fond of her and the sex was amazing. Jack slid the key in the lock and turned it. He opened the door, and entered the apartment. Empty.

It was early yet, and he seldom came to see her before dinner so she could hardly be expected to wait for him. In the living room, few things were out of place. Her bra lay over the pink lamp next to the couch and a pair of panties hung on the coffee maker. Her clothes were scattered about the apartment. Usually tidy, unless they were fucking, Whitney never threw her clothes about. She even folded them into the laundry hamper.

He cringed when he turned into the kitchen. Dirty glasses sat on the counter and the bong lay on the table. Did she have a party last night? Must have been pretty wild for her to leave such a mess. Jack picked up the bong and carried it to the sink to dump out the contents. Reaching over the fridge, he put it in the cabinet with the rest of her "supplies." Why would she leave that out? She was usually so careful.

He turned toward the bedroom. If she was going to be a while, he'd have a little nap. Jack could always go for a nap.

From the hallway, he glanced toward her bedroom. The door was closed. Odd. She never closed it. He crept to the door and turned the knob. Was that Whitney's voice? Jack pressed his ear to the door. Female, but it didn't sound like Whitney. Maybe she was going through her closet; she did that sometimes. She'd invite Rachel over and they would trade clothes or whatever it was girls did when they cleaned their closets. Jack didn't understand it and he wasn't about to try.

A buzzing sound preceded a definite moan and Jack froze. They were *not* cleaning the closet. After releasing the knob, Jack tiptoed into the bathroom that adjoined her bedroom. He might be able to peer through the gaps in the slatted door.

He inched across the floor, catching his foot on the corner of the vanity. It shuddered, sending a bottle of perfume tumbling. Jack caught it but bumped the wall in the process.

"What was that?" the unfamiliar voice asked.

"What was what? I didn't hear anything. Are you finished

already?" Whitney purred.

Ah, shit, he knew that voice. They were not cleaning.

"I thought I—Oh Jesus, Whit, you are good at this. Why do you waste your time with that asshole? You and I could be so good together."

"What are we doing right now? I like a cock most of the time but it doesn't mean I can't have you too. You can't bring everyone over to your team. Just enjoy what you've got."

Jack breathed again as they dissolved into moans and giggles. Although he wanted to feel offended that she was cheating, he just couldn't seem to muster enough indignation to do so. This was too intriguing... and damn hot. If it had been a guy in there, the shit would have surely hit the fan, but he didn't mind this development.

He peeked through a gap in the slats. Whitney straddled a dark-haired girl while she lubed up yet another vibrator. Christ, how many of those things did a woman really need?

Whitney moved down the girl's body, licking and sucking as she went until she reached her thighs. Then she lowered her head and—shit. Jack's mouth went dry. Sweat beaded on his forehead.

I'm too old for this.

He shifted his hard-on and focused on his breathing. Lightheaded, Jack worried he might pass out if his blood continued to rush south, and not where it needed to be to keep him conscious.

The other girl moaned and panted as Whitney went to work. God she was good; the girl was right about that. The way she worked her mouth along with that mechanical cock was fucking amazing. Riveted, he pressed his face to the door, unable to turn his gaze from the other girl's body as she climaxed. Then Whitney turned toward the door, stared right at him, and smiled.

Shit.

She couldn't know he was there. Could she? He hadn't told her he was coming over. Jack didn't even know it until the last minute.

"Now you do me."

The girl eagerly jumped up to kiss Whitney.

They exchanged a wet, sloppy, tongues-all-over-the-place kiss, before Whitney pushed the other girl's face down to her breasts. "Come on let's see if you're as good as old Jack. He's an expert at this, you know." She looked at the door again.

Jack stepped back. She did know.

The girl rubbed her breasts against Whitney's before following with her mouth. Then she moved down her body and Whitney's gaze locked on to Jack's. With a little grin, she pushed the girl down further. Always in control.

The girl did as instructed.

Before long, Jack's cock found his hand. Or perhaps it was the other way around. The coppery flavor of blood betrayed he'd bit through his lip to keep from crying out.

Whitney's climax would have drowned out any noise he made anyway. A small twinge of jealousy stirred in his belly.

"That was fucking amazing. You were almost as good as Jack," Whitney slurred. "But practice makes perfect."

"Maybe next time I won't get so stoned and you'll change your mind about how good I am." The girl slipped a hand between Whitney's legs. "Maybe we should try again now; I know I can do it better than any guy."

"Maybe another time, I'm actually expecting him soon. You better go." Whitney pushed her away and climbed off the bed.

"Whit, that's so rude." The girl pouted. "Why can't I meet this Jack? We could party together. It'd be fun."

"Jack is mine. I'm not into sharing." Whitney nodded toward the girl's clothes. "I'm just going to get in the shower, could you lock up when you leave?"

Whitney turned to the bathroom.

Jack jumped away from the door. What if the girl saw him? Was she crazy?

The girl mumbled to herself as she dressed.

Whitney opened the door a crack. She waited until the girl left the bedroom and then, grinning, walked into the bathroom. "Did you like that?" she whispered.

Jack wiped his hands on the pink towel hanging over the vanity, trying to regain some composure. Did he like that? What a stupid question. "How did you know I'd be here?"

"I didn't, but I heard you come in. You're the only one with a key, you know. It doesn't take a rocket scientist to figure it out." She grabbed his crotch and squeezed before pressing her mouth to his ear. "When Misty goes, we should have a shower."

"She's not gone?"

"I need to say goodbye first. She doesn't like to leave until I send her off properly."

"She's been here before?"

"We're like best friends, silly; of course she's been here. She sleeps over all the time."

Jack just stared. What could he say to that?

"Relax; it's just something girls do. Experimenting, you know? I'm not gay or anything." She slipped out of the bathroom.

He stood there like an idiot, his mouth open.

Just something girls do?

Why was it women always made their own rules about such things? If she had walked in on Jack and one of his golf buddies doing the nasty, Whitney would lose her mind. He'd be gay and that would be that. Women were a law unto themselves.

After turning on the shower and undressing, he wondered when the hell Whitney would get rid of the friend. Under the spray, he adjusted it as hot as he could stand it—the way Whitney liked it.

The curtain opened. "Hey baby." She'd pinned her hair on top of her head.

His heart picked up its already erratic pace. Good thing he took care of his health or a heart attack would have claimed him long ago.

Whitney sank to her knees and ran her teeth over his cock.

Fuck, he loved it when she did that.

She followed with her lips and he had to lean against the

shower wall as his knees buckled. If she knew that he imagined the other girl's mouth on him, she'd probably bite it off. Jack tangled his free hand in her hair as he came once more, her giggles deepening his pleasure.

"Okay, now let's watch a movie." She stood, wiping her chin.

Jack closed his eyes.

Please don't make me kill her.

They watched the video Whitney made of her encounter with Misty and they messed around most of the night with its help. Not that Jack needed help getting in the mood. It just helped sometimes to have a visual; made things more interesting.

Exhausted and sore, but with a wide grin plastered to his face, he chugged his coffee and got ready for work. Whitney hadn't mentioned Jenny all night. Jack's stupid mouth had to bring it up in the end and he nearly kicked himself as he opened the proverbial can of worms. "The kids aren't home anymore."

"Did you kill them too?" She leaned against the back of the ugly pink couch, as if amused with herself.

"Uh, no. I haven't killed anyone... yet. They wanted to go to boarding school, so I let them."

Her eyebrow shot up and she got that you-fucking-liar-look on her face.

Jack hated that look. The one where she smiled, but not really, and her chin jutted out a bit.

"They wanted to go? They just went willingly?"

"Of course, they appreciate what I've given them. It's a great opportunity. These are excellent schools."

"Please spare me the bullshit, Jack. You wouldn't care if they were no more than shacks in the woods, you'd have sent them away. Now you've gotten rid of Jenny and your kids, who's next?"

Alarm bells screamed in his head. "For the last time, I

didn't get rid of Jenny. The kids need structure that I can't give. I work long hours and I *must* keep you happy; where is the time for them?"

"I could have moved in to help. But no, you had to hire that whale, what was her name? Lucy, Linda?"

"Lillian. And she's gone, thank God. I told you why you couldn't move in. It's not because I don't want you. You know I need you more than anything." He pushed the tiny table away to make room and pulled her onto his lap.

Whitney shoved at him, stood, and moved to grab her purse from the counter. She fished out a joint and then a lighter, which she made a production out of flicking and sparking until she lit the thin smoke before squinting at Jack. "Why can't you say you love me? You've never said it, not once. Do you love me?"

"Of course I do, baby, how could you doubt that? Fuck, look at everything I've done for you. I pay your bills, I pay for your schooling, and when you want anything, I'm here. If I didn't care you'd have none of this."

"Say it then."

"What?"

"Tell me you love me."

"I do."

"Say the fucking words, Jack."

He jumped as she slammed her fist on the counter, scattering ashes everywhere.

"I love you?" The words sounded weak even to his ears. Of course he didn't love her; love was a waste of his time. But if that's what she wanted to hear, then he'd say the words a thousand times.

"Fuck off." She turned and butted the joint in the sink before storming to the bedroom.

What did he do now? He said what she asked him to say and now she was pissed. Jack was getting pretty tired of her crap. Everything had to be a fucking soap opera. "I'll just leave then, thanks for the hummer and all that," he yelled.

Something smashed.

Yep, she was really pissed. "You call me when you're off the rag and we'll talk like adults."

Another crash and a string of profanities.

Atta girl, let it all out. That damn pot always made her like that, paranoid and just fucking weird. Jack didn't stick around for the rest of the tantrum.

CHAPTER 13

Jack watched Ray's house for days before he finally figured out a pattern. A creature of habit, Ray did everything on a schedule and rarely strayed from his routine. If he still worked at Jay-Ray, it would be simple, but now Jack couldn't be sure when he'd be home.

Ray still got up at five and went for a jog every morning, which should have kept him in better shape. Jack wouldn't waste time sweating and bouncing his shit all over the place when a treadmill achieved the same results; with no gawkers to witness his attempts to fool Father Time. After the jog, Ray sat indoors doing whatever Ray did alone in his house. At noon, he went outside to do yard work. Even in the rain. After the yard work, he returned to the house until around three, when he fired up his mother's car, drove to the cemetery and sat first at Jenny's grave and then his mother's. That morbid ritual lasted one hour, no more and no less. Jack was a little creeped out by Ray's analness.

At four, he left the cemetery to do his banking, groceries, and whatever other errands he had on his list. He carried a list in his pocket all the time. Funny, Jack had never noticed a list before. Perhaps it was a new thing.

On two of the afternoons Jack followed him, Ray went to Thorne and Sons. What he did there Jack didn't know, but it made him more determined to be rid of the fucking traitor. He'd probably sold all of Jay-Ray's secrets to the competition. At the very least, he might have been working for Thorne and that was unacceptable. Ray knew how much he hated that guy.

Jack would have the most time to do the job in the afternoon, because Ray was away from the house for at least two hours. In the morning, however, there would be no one around to see him go in. It would entail less risk of anyone remembering.

Ray lived in an area full of old shits that had nothing better to do than peek through their curtains at one another. If one of those idiots saw him, Jack would have some explaining to do. They might not remember their own names most days, but they'd damn sure remember old Jack going into Ray's house.

Ray's jogs lasted no less than an hour. It definitely had to be in the morning. Unless Jack could do the job in less than thirty minutes, he would need to figure out something else. He toyed with the idea of strangling the little prick. God, it would be so satisfying... but it might leave evidence and Jack couldn't have that. It had to be as clean as Jenny's "accident."

He made his move on a Sunday morning. The sun hadn't yet risen, but the air was already warm. In a few hours, his car would be like an oven. If he truly had any luck, Ray would extend his jog to enjoy the beautiful weather, but he couldn't count on it, and Jackson Murphy wasn't a stupid man.

Ray jogged past the car, disappearing down the street. In the rearview, Ray's short body, clad in a white tank top and bright red, eighties Adidas shorts, bobbed away. Jack choked back the bile in his throat as his mind wandered to Ray *sans* underwear in those nasty little running shorts, his junk getting tossed to and fro.

Jack drove the car to the street behind his target and walked to Ray's house trying to look casual, strolling, as though enjoying the day that hadn't quite started yet. No one roamed the quiet street, and as far as he could see, no busybody peeked through the windows of the neighboring houses. He cut through the back yard and jogged to the back door that led into the kitchen. Ray never locked the back doors, always afraid of forgetting his keys and being locked out. Most men would break a window or call someone, but not Ray. He'd probably remain homeless until someone took pity and helped him.

Jack paused in the doorway to take a pair gloves from his pocket and slip them over his hands. The small kitchen was spotless, not a speck of dirt dared to fall on its immaculate surfaces. In the fridge, everything was organized in neat rows with labeled containers and the date he stored it. How OCD could one guy get?

"Psycho," Jack muttered. He closed the fridge and turned to the hallway next to the kitchen. Through a second door, he crept down to the basement. Damn if it wasn't cleaner than the upstairs. Ray's apartment took up half the open space, the other half made up the laundry and utility rooms. It took Jack a good fifteen minutes to locate the stopcock. Most houses nowadays had the gas shut-off located outside. This was as much for safety as convenience. But Ray's house was old, and the gas valve remained where they originally installed it, inside the basement. He probably worried about some "punk" tampering with it or something. Jack wondered how he managed to avoid the inspections when the city upgraded the gas lines a few years ago. Probably no one wanted to deal with the crazy fuck. Yeah, Ray was a genuine freak. Jack had been saying that for years.

After quickly nicking the line, just near the valve where it was hard to see unless you were looking for it Jack returned to the kitchen to cut the line that fed the stove. If Ray noticed one, he would fix it and assume the problem had been solved.

His heart skipped a beat at the sound of a key in the front door.

Jack bolted to the kitchen door, almost falling in his haste, jogged to his car and sped away. He didn't register his pounding heart and sweat-drenched hands until he reached the highway. Trying to slow his breathing, he pulled the car onto the shoulder and stopped. Keeping an eye in the rearview, for what or who he wasn't sure, Jack removed the gloves and placed them in a plastic bag he'd left on the seat. When he returned home, he would bury them in the trash.

Confident that no one followed him Jack started the car again and pulled back onto the road. He drove at a more sedate speed while stifling the urge to laugh hysterically.

On the approach to his street, Jack forced himself to breathe normally. He turned on the familiar tree-lined road, and nearing his house, he let his foot off the gas while his heart slowed to a pathetic crawl. Then his gaze fell on a rusted brown shitbox sitting in his driveway. Whose car was that? He didn't recall seeing it before.

Cops? Shit.

Getting out slowly Jack scolded himself for being paranoid. He grabbed the bag that contained the gloves and shut the door. The cops couldn't be there already. Ray hadn't been home more than ten minutes. But who the hell would stop by unannounced at six in the morning? No one he knew was dumb enough, aside from a few nosy bitches from Jenny's church. They had hounded him until he told them to fuck off and go find a widower who actually wanted to grieve over his loss. If they thought Jack had changed his mind, he'd tell them a thing or two. He'd shove their fucking casseroles right up their tight Jesus-loving asses.

Jack leaned over to look through the driver's window and scanned the interior.

James.

Purple dice dangled from the rearview mirror; seats draped in novelty seat covers printed with playing cards, blue lights around the back window, mats decorated in poker chips.... What the hell did he want? Didn't he pay off the greedy prick years ago?

What does the rotten, dirty son of a bitch want now?

Jack took a deep breath to steel his nerves before he ran up the front steps and pushed inside. He wouldn't even question how James got in; the bastard always found a way. Too bad the little prick had no one to blackmail now. Jenny was gone and James's little bit of information was useless.

Jack stalked purposefully down the hall and to the kitchen. His cousin James sat at the table with a large bottle of Jack Daniel's, his Jack Daniel's, surrounded by poker chips and Whitney.

Whitney? What the hell?

The bag suddenly felt hot in his fist. The two were playing poker, already drunk as skunks. How did he track her down? Did he have to? James could be a problem, blackmail or not.

"Jackie-O! I drove all night to get here and you're gone. Your beautiful friend was here when I arrived, looking for a way in, so I obliged the little lady. I hope you don't mind. I never could say no to a beautiful woman."

"What are you doing here? What the fuck is either of you doing here, drinking my booze, before the sun is even up?"

"The sun is up," Whitney giggled. "Where were you?"

"I was out. I do go out."

"I called last night and there wasn't any answer. I haven't seen or heard from you in so long, I thought maybe the bees got you."

Both dissolved into hysterics.

What did that stupid bitch tell him?

"I'm real sorry to hear about Jenny, she was a great girl." James belched after this solemn statement and took a swig from the bottle. "Really sad since you guys were working things out and all."

"How would you know anything about me and Jenny?"

"Whitney told me all about it. Shit man, what time did you leave? Cause we've been here for about an hour."

"I wasn't home. I had to go away on business."

James's eyes narrowed. "You always leave your coffee pot on when you go away? That's good coffee; it wasn't even burnt. Where do you get coffee that can sit on a burner for a couple of days without burning?"

"Your coffee maker is automatic," Whitney chimed in. "It shuts off after a certain time, doesn't it?"

"The timer's broken. It doesn't matter whether my coffee was on or off, you two broke into my house and stole my booze, and now you're trying to question me? I don't think so. Get out, both of you."

They laughed. Coming from James, it wasn't a surprise but Whitney not taking Jack seriously was a new thing.

"Sit down and relax," Whitney said, patting the seat next to her. "I missed you and James is here to support you in your time of need. Most people would welcome their family after their spouse died."

He glared at a woman he no longer knew. If she thought he'd put up with her shit, she had another thing coming. And James... Jack glared at his cousin. James and his fucking scheming would be an issue. That's all he did; lie, scheme, and use people. Jack's whole family was like that. He avoided the lot of them. James chose to ignore the fact. In Jack he'd found a human bank machine and he intended to use it.

"Listen, Jackie-O, I really did come by to see how you were doing. When I saw this hot little number peeking in the windows I had to find a way in. I thought I might get laid."

"Keep dreaming." Whitney rolled her eyes and pried the bottle out of his hands.

If Whitney had a type, Jack couldn't see James fitting it. Although he was similar in height to Jack, he was soft all over. That's what never doing an honest day's work in your life got you. Slightly younger than Jack, James couldn't be more than mid-thirties, yet most of his hair had taken off for parts unknown years ago. He wore a hat to cover its desertion. James preferred loud, tacky headgear, like purple cowboy hats, white top hats with brightly colored bands, even berets. Jack had seen so many eyesores topping his cousin's head that each time he doubted James could find uglier ones. Well, he did: a neon green beret with black smiley faces all over it, which he adjusted slightly as he squirmed under Jack's glare.

"If you just gave me a shot, I'd rock your world," he promised Whitney.

She laughed.

Fucking skank.

"Listen, I'm really tired and I have to go into work later, so can we continue this tonight or something?"

"Where am I going to stay, man? You're going to send family to a hotel? Whitney told me you're all alone here. Can I use Paul's room for a day or two?"

Jack stared. Letting James stay would be a mistake, but the bastard never appeared for no reason. This visit so close to Jenny's death couldn't be a coincidence. Better to find out what James was up to before he sent him away. "You have twenty four hours. I told you the last time you came here, I didn't want to see your ugly face again and I meant it. I don't want you here."

"Harsh, Jackie-O. You are so cold."

"He's not cold, he's private. I warned you he wouldn't be happy." Whitney smiled at Jack as though she'd done nothing wrong.

"And you, Miss Fuck Off, why would you break into my house because I don't call you after telling me off repeatedly? What the hell is wrong with your head?"

"I missed you. You know I get moody sometimes. I just really want us to be together now that we have the chance. I know you have a hard time with feelings, baby. I'm sorry I pushed you."

Was that a tear in her eye? It better not be a damn tear. Jack couldn't take another crying jag from anyone else. "If you cry, Whitney, we're definitely through."

Her chin trembled but she held on.

"James, you can sleep in the basement, but I want you gone by tomorrow morning. Whitney, unless you're going to make yourself useful I'll call you a cab and you can go the fuck home."

"Oh I'll be very useful." She was off the chair and over to

him in a heartbeat, pressing her lips to Jack's ear, her hand grabbing his crotch. "You won't ever want me to leave."

He'd want her to leave as soon as he got off, but he'd have to settle for when he left for work. "Go on upstairs. I'll be up in a minute." Jack watched her ass sway as she sauntered up the stairs obediently, and then he turned to James. "I better not see you when I wake up tomorrow."

"Just relax Jackie-O. Can't family lean on each other when they're in trouble?"

"I'm not in trouble."

"You could be."

"Out with it. What do you think you've got on me?"

James grabbed his chest in mock agony. "I'm shocked that you would think so little of me."

"You milked me for fifty grand last time I saw you. What else am I supposed to think?"

"I really did come to make sure you were okay. When I got here, Whitney told me the kids were gone and she described how Jenny died. It got me to thinking, Jackie, thinking a lot. Made me wonder how a girl who was always so careful and who'd had to inject herself many times with that kit, could ever panic and not inject herself properly. Makes me wonder if there was anything in that syringe, you know?"

"It's Whitney talking here, you idiot. Jenny didn't panic; she slipped. Even if she did panic, it's understandable. She had a lot on her mind and so did I." Jack would not give him a dime. The case was closed, anyway. They couldn't prove anything beyond a reasonable doubt. James had nothing to bargain with.

"You can't con a conman, cousin. I see what happened. You hire a gardener whose job it is to keep bees out of your yard. From what I heard, the gardener found a big old chunk of beehive in the bushes. Did it fall off the freaking roof and then jump under there? Doesn't sound right to me. How many beehives you see on a fucking roof, let alone a chunk of a hive randomly falling into a bush? I tell you, I never saw anything like that."

"So now you're an expert on bees? You know how they

build their fucking hives and how strong? Give me a break."

"Just let me lay low here for a few days and I'll be gone. Maybe we can make an arrangement and I can be outta here sooner."

"What kind of arrangement?"

Here it comes.

"Hundred grand and I'd forget I ever knew you. Two hundred and you'd be dead to me forever."

"Fuck off. That's what you said the last time, and here you are. I don't need to pay you anything because you've got nothing on me. I didn't kill her. Whitney is delusional and so are you."

James stood and walked around the kitchen, looking in drawers and running his fingers along surfaces. He shook his head and turned to look at Jack. "I could be a big pain in the ass though, getting the police all riled up about the possibility of this little plot. Come on man, how will your business do if you gotta go to court and prove your innocence? Will people want to have you in their homes knowing you might have offed your wife?"

"They'd never convict me because of a piece of a beehive. I'm going to bed." He turned away from James, through with his bullshit.

"But they'd try and that's the point here, Jackie-O. They'd try and that's all it would take to get people talking."

Jack paused at the stairs. Yes, he could get the police to dig a little bit. He knew about Whitney and he knew Jenny and Jack weren't as happy as they let on. A little suggestion here and there might not send him to prison, but it would sure as hell cause a lot of problems, especially with Ray's imminent demise. Two deaths surrounding one man would raise some eyebrows if James got to talking.

"Why do you need so much?" Jack asked.

"I've got bills to pay same as you. If you can't pay me that much, let me lay low here. Just for a while."

He'd been gambling with the high rollers again, stupid ass. He was desperate. Jack could use that. "I didn't kill her, James, period. You can stay for a while and I'll see what I can do to help you, but I'm not giving you a dime to shut you up."

"We'll talk about it. How's that sound? Thanks for letting me stay, man. I know you'll see it my way eventually. You're just hardheaded, that's all. I can wait."

You'll wait a long time asshole.

Jack climbed the stairs and wandered down the hall to his room.

What was he going to do about Cousin James? Too soon to plan someone else's death, even one that would be easy. The mob would be interested in James's whereabouts. He was a genuine asshole too. James had made enemies. Jack could get rid of him. One thing at a time. Slow and steady wins the race, right?

Whitney was on the bed, softly snoring. She lay on top of the blankets, naked. Well, at least that was one good turn of events. He'd get a hummer, a nap, and maybe he'd even get rid of Ray, all in one morning. After closing the door, Jack tossed the bag behind the dresser. The gloves might be useful again very soon. He climbed in beside her and slipped a hand between her legs.

She moaned.

"You didn't say you'd be sleeping," he murmured into her ear. "That would be a waste of my time."

"Just resting up for you, baby," she sighed.

Jack pinched one pink nipple.

She squealed, "Not so hard! I'm not in the mood to be rough."

"Well that's too bad Whit, cause I'm in the mood for a little bit of everything." Jack moved to straddle her face and waited.

"You're mad at me?"

"Just a little, you did break in to my house. Let's see if you can make it up to me." He nudged his cock.

Obediently, she parted her lips to take him in.

"And if you have anything to do with James again, I will be killing someone. You got me?"

She opened her eyes, ran her tongue over him, and leaned

back.

Jack grabbed her hair, yanking hard enough to force her to look at him. "You got me?"

She nodded.

He let go. "Good, let's do this so I can get some sleep." Sometimes a little fear produced great sex.

Whitney became all about keeping him happy and Jack was all about being happy.

As they drifted off to sleep an hour later, Jack made a decision. If James refused to see reason, he'd have to deal with him too. He was sure a few people would love to know where James had wandered off to, and Jack would be happy to help with directions.

CHAPTER 14

It took two full days for something to happen with Ray. Two days packed with tension and anticipation. Jack worked as usual, and ensured he did all he could to keep the appearance that they were still friends. He even left a message on Ray's phone, asking when he'd be back to work. Jack also hired a temp, and told her Ray was on stress leave. The only one not buying his act was James. As he said, you can't con a conman.

James stared Jack down as he tried to enjoy *his* coffee in the house *he* owned and was supposed to be enjoying, because *he* was supposed to have the fucking thing all to himself. Jack ignored him as much as he could. Still, his beady little eyes were tough to dismiss.

"What happened with you and Ray?" James asked finally. "I saw him at the bank and he says he doesn't work with you no more."

"He's a little stressed out lately, I told him to take some time off."

"Not what he says."

"I don't care what he says; he's off his fucking rocker. He lost it when Jenny died; they had a thing I know. I was willing to overlook it. Obviously I'm not perfect either, but he just can't let it go."

"Are you buying him out? Is that why you can't pay me?"

"I told you, I'm not paying you. There's no issue whether I can or not. Ray will be back, he just needs a break. He's not really that stable in the first place."

"Wonder when he'll wind up dead."

Jack pretended that he didn't hear. James was too good at the game to argue. This time, though, he'd underestimated Jack. James thought he had him but he wasn't looking at the big picture. He'd told him far too much about his current situation. Now Jack had the power to get rid of him without getting his hands dirty.

Whitney took off after the first day, making him promise he'd be over to her place before the end of the week. She was agreeable of course, and had to get back to classes anyway. Jack was a little concerned that she didn't call to nag him as she usually did, but then nut-bags tended to be moody. This time, she might be a little more than scared.

Finally.

She truly believed that he'd killed Jenny. He imagined his little threat rolled around her brain like a rock.

She should be worried. If he thought he'd get away with it, he'd off her in a second after her recent behavior. Whitney was fast becoming a nuisance. Ray, Thorne, and James created enough headaches without her adding to his stress.

Why couldn't everything just run smoothly? Why did everyone have to take a shot at bringing him down? Jack wasn't about to let them ruin what he'd busted his ass to achieve just because they were jealous of his success. Perhaps Ray would be the last problem he was forced to eliminate. Luck was a funny thing.

When he finally visited Whitney, it was mostly because he couldn't stand waiting for Ray to die with James breathing down his neck.

Jack ran both hands over his face. He peeked through his fingers and glared at the sunshine blasting through Whitney's damn window. Pink drapes did not block the morning. Of course, she didn't care. The girl could sleep through an earth-quake, followed by a hurricane, followed by the apocalypse. His cell phone blared and he nearly fell off the bed. Man, he needed a vacation. His house was calling his cell. "What?"

"Hey Jackie-O, I just got off the phone with the cops."

James had his attention. He sat up and glanced at Whitney. They had crashed hours before after making up in the best way.

She rolled over and blinked sleepy eyes at him. "What is it?"

Jack waved a hand.

She bit her lip.

"What were you doing talking to the cops?" Maybe he followed through on his threat. Damn. He couldn't do anything to James if he'd gone to the cops already. Fuck, they'd be all over that.

"They just called looking for you. Something about that guy you worked with."

"What are you talking about?" Jack's heart raced. Dizzy with relief, he laid down again.

Whitney touched his arm. It tickled, like a caterpillar crawling on his elbow. Jack resisted the urge to throw her hand off.

"They want you to call them; I'll give you the number."

Jack hung up as soon as James finished reciting the number. He had to get control of himself before calling the cops. The good thing was that Ray lived in a different area; a different department would deal with his death. He didn't have to worry about the same cop sniffing around the crime scene.

Relax Jack; it was the perfect crime.

"What's going on?" Whitney asked, her eyes still clouded with sleep. "Who was that?"

"Something happened to Ray. The cops called the house."

"Why would they call you?"

"I don't know, I guess he didn't have anyone else."

A couple of years ago, after his mother died, Ray was rushed to the hospital with a virus or something. He'd been really sick so he had them call Jack, told him he had no one else to list as a contact.

Jack punched the police number, recited his name to a girl, and then waited a full minute to be given another number. He cursed the inefficiency of Hanover Springs's public servants.

Another woman answered, "Detective Newman."

Little Jack stirred. Fuck, she sounded like one hell of a woman. "Hi, this is Jack Murphy. I just got a call about my partner, Raymond Campbell. Is he okay?"

Silence.

"Hello?"

"I'm at his house right now, Mr. Murphy. What's left of it anyway."

The weight that had followed him for weeks lightened. Had he done it?

"Mr. Campbell called 911 a few hours ago; he had taken some medication and got scared."

"What?" This wasn't right. He wasn't supposed to do it himself.

"Look, I'm sending a car to your house. You can discuss what happened with the detective. You might know something that can help us."

Shit. Not his house. Not with James there. "No need to trouble yourself, I'll come right over."

"Not to the scene, please sir. There's a coffee shop at the end of the street. Do you know the one I'm talking about?"

"Yes."

"A detective will meet you there."

She hung up. Jack's stomach churned. They hadn't asked him to go to the station, just the coffee shop. So that's good. God, he hoped that was good. Ray fucked it all up, of course. What the hell was he thinking?

The detective waited outside the coffee shop. He smiled and flashed his badge as Jack approached.

Jack shook the older man's hand. "I hope I can help you, but I—"

"Let's discuss this inside." The detective opened the door.

As he entered, the odor of stale coffee and baked goods assaulted Jack's nose. Funny, he imagined the guy would wear a suit; a brown one with a shitty tie. This guy, with a carefully styled crop of graying hair and dark, tailored suit, looked as if he might be taking off for a wedding, or a funeral, once he finished with Jack.

They sat in a booth at the back of the café. The dining room was empty. That sent fresh churning sensations to Jack's gut.

He smiled at the cop, who had yet to introduce himself. Weren't they supposed to do that?

Just take the heat of yourself, Jack.

"What happened? I mean, I just can't see Ray attempting suicide." If Jack had foreseen such a thing, he wouldn't have wasted his time trying to kill the little prick.

"My name is Thompson, by the way. Sam Thompson."

Jack nodded.

So? Get on with the fucking interrogation, Sam.

"The thing is he didn't overdose. When he called emergency services, he said he had done some terrible things and wanted it to be over. But he had second thoughts and called because he didn't want to die. I'm told the EMT's arrived in time; they called dispatch to let them know they were prepping him for transport. He was awake but disoriented. He asked the paramedics to get his wallet from the basement. I'm not sure what happened next, there's no one left to tell us."

So, Ray's suicide attempt turned him into a murderer, thanks to Jack.

Stupid fuck.

"How do you know all of this? I mean, no one's alive to tell you who did what."

Thompson cleared his throat. "Dispatch radioed to see if they could respond to another call. The EMT that stayed with your friend said they'd be a while and mentioned his partner was in the basement. We're still investigating, but shortly after they radioed to dispatch, there was an explosion. The house was destroyed and we had to evacuate a few of the neighbors because their homes caught as well. It's pretty bad there. Actually, I shouldn't even be telling you all of this. It's just such a... I just transferred to homicide. Thought it might be quieter than the drug unit. Hanover Springs's homicide rate is exceptionally low. Might've been a good feather in my hat before retirement, but my first week I get this shit." He shook his head. "I apologize. You don't want to hear my life story. It was unprofessional."

"Shit." Jack didn't need to act; he was genuinely shocked. "I don't know what to say. This is just unbelievable."

"I understand. I'm kind of lost for words too." Thompson laughed a little.

"Should I make a statement or anything?"

"We'd like you to help us locate some family. Obviously, his records are gone. The body isn't even identifiable."

Taking a breath, Jack sniffed.

Thompson must have mistaken the noise for grief, or shock, or whatever it was people who didn't want their friend to die felt when they did so in such a big way. "I'm so sorry Mr. Murphy, I shouldn't have said that. I know this is hard."

"It's okay; I just need a minute to think. Do I need to go to the station?"

"Detective Newman would like you to meet her as soon as possible. I understand you have a business to run, and now with this, you'll have arrangements to make."

Jack pictured Newman as a tall brunette with endless legs and a big rack. He'd love to meet her. "Actually, Ray kind of flipped out a while ago. My wife passed away, a freak accident. Ray doesn't deal with loss too well. He was a mess after his mother as well. I told him to take some time and he said some things...."

"You weren't working together?" Thompson took a small notebook from his jacket.

Fuck.

"I thought he'd get over it and come back after a while. He did that sometimes, broke down, then he'd be sorry and we'd move on. I never thought he was this bad. God, if I'd known I'd have been more understanding. Shit, I just told him to get lost, get his shit together."

"We don't expect anyone to do this Mr. Murphy; it's not your fault."

His compassion made Jack smile. "You're right, I know, but it's still so surreal. I just need to think."

"Come by the station tomorrow, around nine?"

"Okay, I'll be there."

"Are you alone Mr. Murphy?"

"Am I alone?"

"You should really call a friend or something. I don't think it's a good idea to be alone right now."

Aw, how sweet.

Thompson was concerned *he'd* do something stupid. "No, I can stay at a friend's house for now. I'll be okay."

"Good, I'll arrange a meeting with Detective Newman for you tomorrow. Nine o'clock okay?"

"Nine, right. Thanks Detective, I appreciate—" lowering his voice to a whisper, as though he might cry, caused Thompson to reach for his hand. Jack almost ruined it by laughing out loud. He was getting so good at pretending to give a shit it frightened him. "Take care." Jack stood and walked from the coffee shop.

He drove straight to Whitney's. The apartment was quiet when he entered. Her concern for his wellbeing was overwhelming.

He paused in the doorway to her bedroom. Still in bed, Whitney stared, pale and wide eyed. "Jack?"

Jack took a deep breath. "Ray killed himself," his voice sounded a bit shaky from his excitement.

"Oh no, that's awful."

"He took pills or something then called 911, I guess he had

second thoughts. The guys came and then something happened." Jack covered his face and walked to the bed. He sank down next to her. "There was an explosion and everyone is dead, the emergency guys... and Ray. God it's...."

"Why did they call you?"

"I'm all he has left, they had to call someone. I have to talk to the cops in the morning."

"You shouldn't go by yourself. I'll go with you."

Hell no you won't.

His wife died only weeks before and now his best friend. Jack could not show up with his college student girlfriend. "It's not necessary. I really should go by myself. I'll need the time alone to get my shit together. I don't want to look like a dick down there and cry or something. I've got an image to maintain."

"You can't be the tough guy all the time, Jack. People think you're a cold, calculating asshole because you never give them anything. A little crying is a good thing. It doesn't make you weak."

Fuck her and her psychobabble. Jack longed to tell her where she could shove all of it. At least she didn't think he planned this one. "Men don't cry, not if they've got any balls. I won't cry and I don't need anyone with me. Just drop it."

She looked like she wanted to argue but bent her head and lay back down on the bed. "Let's get some sleep and we'll decide in the morning, okay? You're exhausted."

"I won't change my mind."

"Okay. Just get some rest."

Jack remained wide-awake, his meeting with Detective Newman playing over in his head until he felt confident that he wouldn't mess it up. He'd be just a little vulnerable, shaken over the loss of his longtime friend so soon after his wife. It would be a terrible shock that he just couldn't comprehend. She'd be sympathetic and try to close the case quickly. If she looked as hot as she sounded, maybe Jack would play it up a little more. Maybe he'd get an invite to stop by again, have coffee... whatever. It was probably inappropriate for her to do something like that and she'd try to control herself, but he'd read the signals when he got there. Jack loved a woman in uniform.

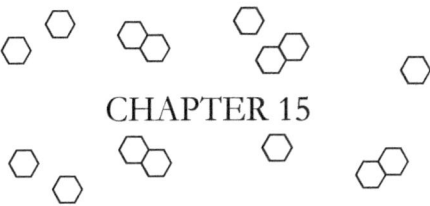

CHAPTER 15

Jack had some trouble convincing Whitney to stay home while he met with Detective Newman the following morning. It'd be awkward meeting a new woman while the old one hung off his arm. Maybe Newman would make a good side-fuck, just in case Whitney became too much of a nuisance.

After arguing about it most of the night, he finally made Whitney understand how awkward it would be to introduce his hot young girlfriend to a person who might question such a thing so soon after Jenny's death.

He left for the police station before Whitney woke, just in case she felt the need to offer moral support again.

Jack arrived a few minutes early and stood in the foyer of the police station, surprised at the order and calm within the stone walls. He'd imagined a noisy, criminal-filled lobby with cops everywhere. Instead, three officers wandered about with Styrofoam cups and a pretty receptionist sat to the side in a glass enclosure.

"Excuse me..." He leaned on a ledge that ran around the receptionist's desk and smiled.

The girl glanced up and sighed. Perhaps he'd interrupted her romance novel or something equally important. Beauty didn't make them any better. He learned early in life that women were bitches no matter what their package. But it was easier to tolerate them when the wrapping was nice to look at.

"Yes?"

"I'm here to see Detective Newman. My name is Jack Murphy."

She frowned, her eyes narrowing. He assumed she reacted to Newman's name. It's not like his should cause such a sour expression. She looked like the type who liked attention. Why put out the effort to look that hot if you didn't want a man to notice? But there was no need for such cattiness. Christ, she worked at a police station. Did she have to have all the men?

"One moment please." She stood, straightening a very tight black skirt over nice thighs and walked through a door at the back of the enclosure swinging her tight ass.

So many women....

Jack sighed and glanced around the room while he waited.

Two cops watched him. Why'd they always have to stare like that? Likely because they could. Who in his right mind would tell a cop to stop looking? They unnerved him so Jack turned back to where the receptionist had sat moments ago. She took her sweet time. Good thing he had nothing better to do.

"Mr. Murphy?" A gorgeous voice called.

His smile froze when he turned. The voice did not match the face. Jack struggled to recover but couldn't do anything but stare at her and gape.

"I'm Detective Newman, I've been expecting you."

"Okay..."

She smiled, making things worse. Wasn't there a weight restriction for a person to be in law enforcement? Maybe she'd gotten in under some kind of equal opportunity bullshit or something. The woman had to be at least six feet tall, and pushing two hundred fifty pounds, with a mole on her face bigger than her gigantic nose.

She'd restrained her frizzy black hair with a grey hair band that really didn't help anything. Thick glasses with red rims emphasized an angry scar on her chin.

The smile deepened and her face folded like a basset hound's to swallow the mole. "Let's go to my office. There isn't much I need, just a recount of the last time you saw Mr. Campbell. It might help us get an idea of the events leading up to the crime."

"The crime?" Had he been tricked?

"He did kill two people, and it may have been intentional."

"Oh." Glancing over at the two cops who had been watching him, Jack scowled.

They grinned so wide, their faces threatened to split in two.

The bastards knew exactly what he'd thought. How many suckers did they watch each day react like that?

Assholes.

She led him through a large set of steel doors and down two flights of stairs, to stop in a dim hallway with several doors.

"I just made detective, and there aren't any real offices available," Newman explained as she opened a door. "I get to use an interrogation room for a while. Just until someone retires."

If he were her, and he thanked God he wasn't, Jack would kill someone just to get out of such a hole. Obviously, her ambition only went so far, but when you looked like that, there wasn't much point in striving for anything. The room was brighter than the hallway with a small desk in a corner. Two steel chairs faced it and a filing cabinet sat propped against the opposite wall. A plant on top looked like it died years before. Someone, he assumed it was Newman, had taped concert posters to the cement walls. Sure, it might be hard to hang any real art on those walls, but Milli Vanilli's pouty lips super-sized made the already hideous décor worse in Jack's opinion.

"Are you okay?"

"Pardon?"

"You look, I don't know... scared." She smiled again.

He suppressed a shudder. Her jowls were like some kind of mouth chomping down on the mole, and then throwing it up when the smile went away. "No, I'm fine. I guess I'm still getting used to the idea that Ray is gone. I can't believe he'd set anyone up like that. He was so nice and kind, he cried more than I did when my wife passed."

"Yes, so I heard."

Jack glanced up.

She offered a knowing smile and touched his hand.

He resisted the urge to yank it away.

"Michael Thorne stopped by the scene early this morning. He was supposed to pick up some papers from your partner. Apparently, he didn't intend to return to your business. He was planning to partner with this Mr. Thorne. Allegedly, of course."

"Thorne..." Jack grimaced, as though she'd just struck him. "No, he wouldn't. He was just taking a leave of absence. He would have come back. Mr. Thorne is mistaken; Ray would never do that to me."

"Perhaps that's what pushed him over the edge," she suggested. When he didn't reply she continued, "I think he was depressed. His affair with your wife—you did know about that didn't you?"

He shook his head in a noncommittal gesture. "I had my suspicions, nothing solid mind you... no, I didn't know for sure."

She sighed.

Jesus, he wanted to forget the past few weeks. He wanted to pretend his wife didn't fuck someone like Ray. Maybe with both of them gone, denial could be a place he lived forever. It hit him in the gut like a brick.

"Mr. Thorne knew of it, he said everyone did—everyone but you, obviously. Anyway, I think he felt enormous loss when she died. Then, the guilt of betraying your friendship not once, but twice, was his breaking point. He was unbalanced according to his therapist and he just went over the edge."

"You've talked to his therapist already?"

What did he tell this old bag?

"When we pulled his medical records, we examined every

angle. It's common, especially in suicide cases, to pull up any psychiatric evaluations. She said he hadn't been there for three months and suddenly called on Thursday. His appointment was for Monday, but I guess he couldn't wait that long."

"Jesus, there's so much I didn't know. It's like I've been living under a rock. Ray and Jenny, it's just so unreal. I convinced myself that if anything had happened between them, which I had no proof of anyway, it was over. Jenny and I were trying to make things work before she died, Ray was all for it."

"There is no point in trying to understand it. You'll just drive yourself crazy."

He nodded. What the hell did she think he could add? She already had the whole story from everyone else.

"You said you spoke to Ray... let's see, a few weeks ago?"

"Yes, when he said he needed some time. He did try to quit and I told him to take some time to think about it. I just thought he needed a few weeks of rest."

"Did you try to contact him?"

"Several times. He wasn't taking my calls."

"And you never went to his house?"

Bravo, detective, you covered every base.

Jack wasn't going to trip up though. He'd figured one of those busy bodies must have seen him. "Well... yes, a few days ago, I can't remember which day, but I went to see if he'd talk to me. He usually goes out early for a jog so I tried to catch him before he left."

"You didn't?"

"No he already left, so I left a note. Just said I was worried about him and wanted him to give me a call. He didn't."

She nodded, as though his story fit with what she had in her little book.

Of course it did. Jack had gone into the house just like those nosy pricks told her and he'd admit to being there for a few minutes. Then it would make sense he'd simply write Ray a note and leave. With the place a pile of ash, she couldn't prove or disprove the note.

"I guess that's all Mr. Murphy. Thank you for your time."

She stood, offering her hand.

He took it, surprised that it felt dry and cool. Thank God for small mercies. He couldn't handle one more thing to gross him out.

"We've contacted his attorney who will be in touch soon. His estate and all of that has been left to you and your children. I guess he made up for his mistakes after all."

Ray left everything to him and the kids? Why? "Thanks, I appreciate that. I guess I get to plan another funeral." Jack laughed nervously. "Lucky guy."

She took out a card and handed it to him. "If you need anything, just call me. If you think of anything else that might help us figure out what happened I'd appreciate it."

"I will. Thanks."

Jack exited the station elated. He'd done it again. How charmed could a guy be? Two people he planned to get rid of and both got rid of themselves. Of course, he helped them along, but ultimately the cops had nothing against him. Jackson Murphy was fucking brilliant.

On to Cousin James.

CHAPTER 16

After the meeting with Detective Newman, Jack went straight to his office. Michelle, the temp, greeted him as she puttered happily away at Ray's desk. Fiftyish, with bleached out hair, short and spiky, and a rather attractive build, she might be something Jack could nail once or twice in a pinch. Her face wasn't too bad and she had amazing tits; obviously fake but hey, boobs are boobs.

"Good morning, Mr. Murphy. Mr. James called about twenty minutes ago, wanted to meet for lunch."

She had a voice like a five year-old girl, high-pitched and whiny. If he nailed her, she'd have to keep her mouth shut. Or full. "Thanks. Did he say where?"

"Frankie's. You know that Italian place on Clover? He said around one o'clock works for him."

She held out a stack of paper he assumed was his mail and then took out a new stack and laid it in the empty spot.

"How are you managing?" How much of a mess had Ray left behind? "I know it's a lot of work."

"Oh shit, this is nothing. I usually have to do the job of three or four people. This is a cakewalk. Your partner was a very meticulous guy. Everything is right where I need it.

Nothing is out of place."

"Ray was always tidy. So, are you looking for a permanent job?"

"Are you kidding me? Of course I am. Are you offering?"

"Maybe, let's give it a few weeks before either one of us commits. I may change my mind and so may you."

"Sure thing. Oh, and I was looking for a file and came across this." She handed him a brown envelope with his name across the front in Ray's neat scrawl.

"Great, let me know if you need anything."

Jack strode to his office and closed the door before sitting down to stare at the envelope. It wasn't very thick, so it probably wasn't work-related. Ray always handed him volumes of paperwork to read. He'd take them into his office and dutifully look at one or two pages before sending them back. Jack didn't have time to worry about the numbers. That had been Ray's job.

In the envelope, he found two handwritten pages. He read slowly, his stomach clenching tighter with every word.

Holy balls... I've been fucked.

Jack;

It pains me to do this, but I have to clear my conscience before I leave. I have accused you of many things in the past and most have been true. I cannot say though, that you have been a bad friend. That is my sin, against you. I have been the worst friend a guy could have and I'm writing this to confess all that I've done to you and apologize for it.

If you're reading this letter, I am either dead or we have parted ways. I hope that I am dead because I couldn't look at you knowing you've read it.

Last year I gave into temptation and I fell in love with Jenny. To be honest I have been in love with her for much longer, but as your friend, I did not act upon it. I spent a lot of time at your house and one night she called me crying, you were late again and she was worried.

I came over to comfort her. That really was all that I intended. When I arrived, she was standing at the door in nothing but her blue teddy. I was lost instantly.

She told me that you didn't touch her anymore and she was lonely. I told her it was a mistake, but in the end, I betrayed you. Then the lies began.

We planned to get rid of you on that cruise. I'm so sorry, Jack. Jenny was going to poison you and throw your body overboard. At the time, it sounded like a good plan, though I doubt she would have followed through. Deep down, Jenny was a good person. She would have had second thoughts. Plus, when I thought it over rationally, it wasn't a very realistic plan. Jenny wouldn't have been able to lift you over the side of a ship. They're rather high and people are always around. But does that really matter?

As you know, she died. I can't handle her loss and the guilt at one time. It is eating away at my heart. I wrongfully laid the blame at your feet because I couldn't admit that I was the one who'd done everyone wrong.

That alone is enough for me to deserve to die, but that is not all that I've done. You'll remember Michael Thorne, the new guy that keeps stealing our contracts. He didn't win those bids against us. I never put your bids in. I was trying to bury you, and ruin this business. I thought it would teach you a lesson but it was the wrong way to do it.

After our argument, I went to Mr. Thorne and offered him some information. I am so sorry that I've done this. It can't be undone now. He's seen the papers and knows things that he should not.

I told him about the bids, how you get the competition's bids from your source and cheat the system. I also showed him our books. I have doctored them just a little. Not enough to make you do time, but enough that you'll be in some trouble with Tony and his friends. I'm hoping to fix this before I die, but if I don't, I'm truly sorry.

I led Mr. Thorne to believe I cooked the books on your orders. He said he'd go to a friend with the information, but that I had to gather evidence to prove you'd forced me to do it. His friends might have considered me as guilty as you otherwise. I didn't let him keep them, although he wanted to. He offered me a job with him. I told him I'd think about it. I wouldn't have done it though Jack, I swear. He is going to tell these people about the bidding and you could be in danger. The guys you cheated weren't nice guys. I tried to tell you but you wouldn't listen. They are connected if you get my meaning and could retaliate.

I'm sorry for all I've done to you. I am ashamed that I let greed and envy get the better of me. I changed my will to include you and the kids as a sort of repayment for my betrayal. You will keep the business, all of it, although I'd like you to put some in trust for your children. You don't really have a choice. I made it a stipulation in the will. Ten percent must go to the kids.

That's all I have to say. I'm going to try to end my miserable life soon. I hope that I have the guts to do it.

Sorry. Ray

He knew it! She would have fucking killed him! He hadn't been paranoid. They had really been out to destroy him.

Blue teddy? Since when did Jenny wear lingerie?

Good thing he killed the bastard. Well, Jack hadn't actually killed him. Maybe in a roundabout way he did, but Ray wanted to die, anyway. Jack helped when Ray would have chickened out.

A knock at the door brought him out of his dark thoughts.

Michelle stood smiling, a paper in her hand.

Christ, he didn't even hear her open the door.

"Mr. Thorne is on the phone. Do you want to talk to him?"

"Sure. Is there anything else?"

"Can we talk about the books later? I think there are some issues; a lot of errors. I'm new here, I know, but I've been doing this for a long time. I know my numbers."

"I'll take this call and then we can take a look."

She disappeared around the door.

Jack stared at the ringing phone. He should make Thorne wait, but had to know what he knew and what he wanted.

"Jack Murphy."

"Hello Jack, this is Michael Thorne. Can I call you Jack?"

"I'd rather you didn't. What do you want?" Fuck him. Jack would not play his game. Why should he pretend to be friends?

"Okay, well let's get down to business then."

"Let's." Thorne didn't know who he was messing with.

Fucking jerk.

"You and I have some things to discuss, Mr. Murphy, and I

think we need to get together and do so."

"Why not right now?"

"This isn't something we should discuss over the phone. It's kind of sensitive information... I mean sensitive for you."

What a moron. Did he think he could intimidate Jackson Murphy? Thorne had more to lose than Jack did. He'd come too far, done too much, to have some faggot like Michael Thorne steal it from him. "Where and when?"

"I was thinking we could meet tonight. Over dinner?"

That prick was laughing; Jack could hear it in his asshole voice. Did he think Jack would run scared? Maybe he should play it like that, catch Thorne by surprise when he cut the cocky fuck's throat; metaphorically speaking, of course.

"I'd rather not meet anywhere I'll be recognized. I'm sure you understand," Jack said.

"Of course, let me think. Do you know Chez Martine? It's over on Tenth and Hickory."

"Yeah, I know it. That's fine. I can get there by eight tonight but no earlier. Is that okay?" Jack was a busy man after all. His business was already established and he had things to do; things that were more important than meeting with some pain in the ass that couldn't get ahead on his own merit. No, Thorne had to blackmail people to do it. Not this time. Jack wouldn't be ruined that easily.

"Eight is fine. I think we should be able to become friends, Mr. Murphy. It would be beneficial for us to watch each other's back."

"What are you talking about? I don't know you, and I don't give a shit about what you think would be beneficial. I've had enemies I'd trust more than friends like you."

"Let's not be hasty, I'm trying to help you out here. You'll understand tonight and then I'll be happy to accept your apology." He hung up.

The fucking prick actually hung up on him. Jack stared at the phone. Thorne would pay for even thinking he could put one over on him.

No one crosses Jack Murphy. No one.

When would people learn that simple fact?

Jack didn't leave the office until well after six. Michelle had no clue how to run a construction company. Where Ray could do material lists, estimates, and help with bids, Michelle could look after the books and only the books.

She did that well, though, and spotted where Ray had hastily doctored his figures. He forgot to finish what he'd started and she noticed it at once. Jack feigned shock and dismay and asked her to fix it. Obviously, Ray had been a little unstable before his death.

Michelle had reacted with a suitable level of horror after learning he killed himself. She promised to fix it so Jack wouldn't pay through the teeth come tax time. Jack had patted her shoulder and she beamed, loving every minute of his attention as she should. What woman wouldn't? When old Jack turned on the charm, he was irresistible.

Jack pulled into his driveway, tired and miserable at the thought of having to fire an entire crew of fuckups and then finding new men to take over their job.

People were useless; they wanted a butt load of money without doing any work. Before leaving work, his foreman had called and said they'd failed inspection. Not only would that set Jay-Ray back a couple of weeks, it cost Jack money and he didn't pay people to cost him money.

A million thoughts running through his head contributed to confuse his plans for the meeting with Asshole Thorne. Jack pushed the door open—jackass James never locked a damn thing—and tossed his keys at the hook next to the door. They clattered to the floor. "Fuck it."

He turned the corner and froze. James had made a friend, and was fucking her on the kitchen counter.

He just stood there, staring, rage bubbling to a boil in his gut. Who nailed some chick he barely knew on someone else's counter top? What the fuck? Nasty. That's what. Now Jack would have to rip the damn thing out and fumigate or something.

The woman looked as though she'd crawled out from under a bridge somewhere. Her hair had that skunky look: dark underneath with a blond-on-the-top layer. Why did women think that was even remotely attractive? It was just plain weird, that's what it was; weird and tacky with trailer-trash hair. She was on the fat side of chubby too; he could tell since her fat ass was plopped atop *his* counter. Dimply and scarred, it jiggled every time she moved. Make that every time James rammed her. Ugh. Jack tasted bile.

He'd seen enough, Jack strode to the counter. James had his back to him, oblivious to his audience. He picked up a pan from the stove, raised it over his shoulder, and cracked James in the back of the head.

The skunk screamed and tried to cover her sagging breasts while James swore, and grabbed his head as he jumped away from her. His erection couldn't withstand the blow.

"What are you doing, you fucking idiot?" Jack asked.

"Jesus Jack, why do you always have to go there? You can't just say excuse me? You gotta fucking hit me? With a frying pan? Shit, you are mental."

"I asked you a question. What is that skanky slut doing on my counter? Why are you in my kitchen nailing anything?"

"You're never home. I'm a guest. Gotta keep your guests happy, man."

"You are not a guest. You're a pain in the ass. You're supposed to be gone, and I'm tolerating you." Jack turned to the girl.

She was pulling her clothes back on as fast as her red claws would allow, with enough sense to look offended.

Jack pointed toward the door. "Get the fuck out and don't come back."

"You don't have to be so mean. God, James, I thought you

said he'd be cool."

"He is when he's not here. You better go. I'll call you later."

Jack stood by the counter getting more pissed by the second, and positively irate when the front door closed with a bang.

"Thanks a lot. Why can't you just relax?"

"I'll relax when you're out of my house and I don't have to look at you anymore."

"You know how to get rid of me. With your partner gone, you've got some extra cash kicking around. You don't have to share the take anymore. How convenient. Give me my money and I'll vanish."

"Only to reappear in a year or two? I don't think so, James. I didn't do anything wrong and I'm not giving you anything." He just wanted James to go, but couldn't afford to have him running around talking to people. What if he convinced someone to look further into Ray's death? Or Jenny's. It might amount to nothing, but he couldn't afford the damn shit storm it'd cause. If he paid James off, he'd bet that the little fucker returned in under a year. His only hope was to hold out long enough for James to find some other sucker, or for whoever wanted their money to come for him.

"Suit yourself." James shrugged.

"I will, thanks. No more women, especially in my kitchen. That's dirty and I don't like wondering what kind of nasty shit is on my food surfaces."

"Listen to you, Mr. Clean. Food surfaces? Give me a break, like you never did it."

"It's my house and if I want to put my germs on there, I can. God knows what assortment of diseases she had in that cunt."

"I'm offended. You think I can't pick up quality girls? She was really nice, and she's not a slut. She works at the club by your office."

"More like on the corner outside the club. What were you doing near my office?"

"Just checking things out, you weren't there yet. Michelle is very nice. Too old for my taste, but not bad."

"Stay away from my office too."

"Where can I go?"

"To Hell," Jack was tired of his face. What did he do about him though? He couldn't have another accidental death close to him. That might be too much; the cops weren't stupid. "I have a meeting so I'll be gone for a few hours tonight. You think you can clean up a bit?"

"Don't you have a maid?"

"I have a service that comes in once a week, but they aren't paid to clean up your mess. Pick it up." Jack walked away and headed up the stairs. What a loser. How did he come from such a shallow gene pool? He should have blown the whole lot of them up years ago.

Fucking useless.

CHAPTER 17

Chez Martine's was a fancy, pretentious French restaurant. Jack knew the owner, and he couldn't possibly have been more German.

Smart man.

Dress it like a bistro you'd find in Paris, on a larger scale of course, charge a fortune for crêpes, or fillet of whatever, and watch the rich assholes come running.

Guys born rolling in it made Jack want to puke. They had no clue about money, and spent it as though it grew on a tree in their backyard. If it cost too much they had to have it. *Bunch of fucking knobs.*

It figured Thorne would eat at Martine's; he had money to waste. Jack skipped these places unless a client insisted, and certainly never paid. It was robbery plain and simple; like handing them his wallet before bending over.

Thorne had arrived earlier at the restaurant, as Jack expected he would. The first rule he'd learned when he opened his own business was to be one step ahead of his opponent—or customer. Thorne thought he had the advantage, but he was wrong. Jack knew what he knew and Thorne didn't know that he knew, making him the one ahead. Jack suppressed a smile at the convoluted thought. He'd crush the arrogant prick before this was done. If he couldn't crush him financially, it would have to be literally.

The maître d led the way to Thorne's table. Pasting a nervous smile to his face Jack followed. Thorne sat at a table at the back of the restaurant so Jack had to walk past all of the snotty bluebloods on his way through. Heads turned to stare, and Jack stared right back.

Yes, his suit was off the rack. But when they all died, Jack would have more money than they would because he didn't pay through the nose for a tag on the back of his clothes; a tag no one ever saw until he undressed.

Stare, you stupid freaks, I can afford to eat here every day.

Jack hated these places. He hated the diners' ugly pinched faces even more.

By the time Jack stood at Thorne's table, his face hurt from forcing his cheeks to keep the smile in place.

"Jack, you're late." He didn't rise to shake Jack's hand.

All right then, he wanted no class? Jack could do that. "Sorry, I had to nail the girlfriend before I left. Gotta get my money's worth, you know? I put a lot of cash into that piece of ass so I tap it every chance I get."

"That's interesting. Weren't you married?"

"She died," Jack deadpanned.

Thorne's mouth opened, but no sound left his throat.

Jack laughed. "She was fucking Ray anyway. You remember Ray don't you? He was my business partner, and apparently, we partnered out of the office as well. Actually, he saved me a lot of hassle. With him banging her, she wasn't nagging me for it. Once they have kids, it's just plain unpleasant to look at. I tell you, Jenny was like the Grand Canyon after the last one. I could hear an echo sometimes, I swear."

"Okay, so you know about Ray and your wife. I figured you weren't so stupid you'd let that get by you." He smiled.

If Thorne loosened up and stopped being such an ass, he could be a nice looking guy. Blond hair and blue eyes, all-American for sure. Jack wondered why he hadn't married; rich jerks always had a trophy wife.

He's probably a fanny-bandit.

"Why are we here?" Jack asked. No point in drawing it out.

A waiter slipped a beer stealthily in front of him and vanished. He didn't order a drink, but at least it wasn't some gay man's cocktail. Jack took a swig and gagged. Piss warm. Mr. Thorne could pay for that. Jack did not pay for piss.

"Some facts have recently come to my attention, and they're... how do I put this? They're bits of information you'll find very interesting."

"Skip the fucking crap and just tell me what you want."

"You're a prick. Did you know that?" Thorne's voice cracked.

His cool guy image was obviously slipping.

Thorne continued, "I'm trying to be a nice guy and you are making it very hard."

"Why should you be nice to me? I don't want any favors. You're here because you want something so just spit it out."

"I know about the bidding. How's that?" He leaned back in his chair, as though he'd just revealed the Coke secret formula. "I also know about what you've been keeping from the IRS. I could crush you right now. You'd do the rest of your life for fraud, tax evasion, bribing officials, and probably a lot more once they begin to dig."

Jack gazed at him for a minute or two. Should he play the game and act shocked or scared?

"You don't know anything." Nervous was the way to go.

"You were very unkind to Ray and he didn't appreciate it. He might have had second thoughts later, but he came straight to me when you knifed him in the back."

"Ray was a fucking lunatic. I didn't do anything to him. He was screwing my wife as you well know. Was I supposed to be best buds with the prick that was nailing my wife? I don't think so. He didn't have the balls to do anything like what you're saying."

"Okay then, here are a few names: Jonny Tanor, Tom Kemp, Sammy D., and Lou Vito. All of these men cheated out of paying jobs because you stole their bids. You undercut them and I doubt they'll be pleased. Do you know what they do to cheats in their world?"

"Are you threatening me?"

"Of course not. I just want you to be aware of what I could do with my information. I could go to the IRS, or I could go to the Teamsters. I could go to these guys and whisper in their ears as well, but I haven't yet. I want to make a deal."

"A deal?" Here it was.

"I think it's a fair deal. You get to live, I get everything else."

"I don't get it."

Play dumb, that's the way to win this.

"If you want this to go away, you give me everything." He smiled, his perfectly straight, perfectly white, and perfectly expensive teeth sparkling in the candlelight. "Well, I wouldn't take it without compensation of course. You do have to live somehow. I want you to sell me your business. All of it: client lists, jobs, you know the deal. I will pay fair market value for it. I want you gone. You sell out, leave and never do business again."

"Do I look stupid?" He had to be a complete nutter if he thought Jack would go for that.

Thorne had nothing that would send Jack to jail. Michelle was fixing the books as they spoke. As for the mob guys, Tony, Jack's source, was in their organization. It wasn't like they weren't doing the same thing all over town.

"Of course you don't, which is why I came to you before doing anything rash. I thought you were a reasonable man who would see the wise thing to do here. I hope I wasn't wrong." He waved to the waiter for another drink.

Jack stared. What an annoying face he had. He longed to punch those perfect teeth out of his mouth. He wanted to smash his head off the wall until his hundred-dollar haircut was covered in blood and brain. Bastard thought he had Jack by the balls, but he didn't know anything. "I would need to see a contract and a few days to look it over."

Thorne reached under the table and brought up a briefcase. It looked as if he'd come prepared for Jack to give in.

Unbelievable.

"I took the liberty of having my lawyers draw something up. Of course, you have ten business days to look it over and get back to me. I welcome any changes. I'm not so hardheaded that I won't negotiate. The terms are firm, but the money I can move a little on. Just a little, mind you."

He handed Jack a stack of papers.

Jack didn't bother to glance down before folding them. "Don't think this means I'm going to agree." Jack stood. "I will consider what you've told me before I think it over. How am I supposed to know you can back up your story?"

"I knew you'd ask." Thorne produced a large brown envelope. "These are just copies. I have the originals."

"How did you get started in this business?" Jack asked, suddenly curious. "Did you have to work your way in?"

"Work my way in? No, I don't have the time for that nonsense. I bought it. I bought a little company that was going under and I bought my contracts until I was known."

Everything just handed to him. The thought made Jack ill.

"My parents wanted me to do something so I chose this. I can sit back, enjoy the money rolling in, and pay lesser people to do the work. My hands don't even get dirty."

"That's what I thought." Jack walked away with his stack of blackmail.

Two weeks to get rid of Michael Thorne.

CHAPTER 18

Jack stepped into the office and switched on the lights. He went to the Ray's-Michelle's desk to pick up his mail, and spotted a note on the computer. She had fixed the mess in the books and would see Jack on Monday. Michelle hoped he didn't mind but she needed Friday off. Family thing.

Well, he did owe her that much, but he'd have to make it clear that taking vacation whenever she felt like it wouldn't be happening at Jay-Ray... Jay. Just Jay.

Fuck.

What the hell was he going to call this thing now? It didn't matter. She'd find another job if she expected to take a day off whenever it suited her.

He opened the desk drawer to search for a post-it, and paused. A silver recorder nestled beside a box of pens. Jack pulled it out and pressed play. Ray's monotone voice rattled off a list of things to do, excluding of course his plans to kill his best friend. Jack smiled, pressed "erase", and slipped it into his pocket.

Once Jack settled behind his desk, he pulled out the envelope first. It contained a disc and a stack of papers, which he spread out across the desktop. The first papers were unmistakable: copies of pages in his ledgers.

"Fucking brilliant, Ray. You didn't leave the ledgers with him but gave him copies. Lovely." The next few pages stopped him cold. His mouth soured, bitterness bubbling from his guts up to his throat. The pages contained e-mails between Ray and Jenny, filthy little emails filled with hearts and fucking butterflies. They loved each other; *last night was amazing, we will be together very soon.* Well they could be together as much as their cold dead hearts wanted.

He read each one to make sure that whatever they wrote couldn't screw everything for him. In the middle of the stack was a short message from Jenny to Ray, dated three days before she died.

I just wanted to say hi. I'm so scared, Ray. I think he's going to have me killed. I don't know why, he's been so agreeable that I should be happy. If I make it until the cruise, I know I have to do what we talked about. If I don't, I don't think I'll make it home.

Please make sure if I die before that, you tell the police what you know. He can't be allowed to get away with murder. If I disappear or something like that, you know it wasn't an accident.

I love you,

Jenny.

Suddenly Jack was really glad he'd enlisted the bees. Shit, if he'd gone ahead and cut the brakes or something, he'd be in jail. So Thorne thought he'd use this? It was possible, Jack supposed. The police might look a little closer at Ray's death, and he couldn't have that happen.

He picked up the disc and flipped it over to the label: *Meetings: Ray Campbell.* Leaning back, Jack grabbed Ray's little CD player from behind the curtain, the one he didn't think Jack noticed. He listened to the recording for a few minutes before hitting eject. He already knew its contents. So Mr. Thorne had proof, flimsy and circumstantial, but proof nonetheless.

The love and crap spewed in the emails didn't bother him. Well... just a little, but only because it made him look like a dumbass.

Mr. Michael Thorne had just played a deadly card. Did he think Jack could allow him to live? He couldn't very well let him breathe while he had such information. Thorne had the originals though, and that was a problem. He couldn't get rid of him before obtaining everything; otherwise, he risked the information falling into someone else's hands.

"Fuck, fuck, fuck! Why can't I just live in peace? All I want to do is make money, get laid, and be left alone." Jack's fist on the desk sent the CD player crashing to the floor.

After a few deep breaths, he tried to think. He needed a plan and he couldn't find answers if he freaked out. That was not productive.

First things first, Jack.

How to get into Thorne's office? To do it he needed someone on the inside. Of course, Jack did not know anyone so that was a non-starter.

James.

A piece of shit never had so many possibilities. James was a conman who knew how to get things done. If Jack offered him enough money, he'd find a way. As long as James wasn't the one going in, everything would be fine. Of course, involving him would add to the material James could hold over his head but it might be worth it. James didn't have much longer on this earth anyway. It struck him as funny that his cousin was finally going to be useful. It wouldn't be a pleasant experience; asking James for anything was sure to be torture, but Jack's life lay on the line, and that justified any sacrifice.

When Jack pulled into his driveway one hour later, he cursed; every damn light was on, except the one in Paul's room where James slept. That ass probably went to bed and left everything on just to spite him. Glancing at his watch, Jack sighed. Just after midnight. James had probably been in bed since nine; knocked out by Captain Morgan.

Nice to see he had to worry about the bills. Slamming the car door made him feel marginally better, but it wasn't enough. He wanted to slam James and he couldn't. He needed him. He pushed the door but it didn't give. At least James remembered to lock up, so Jack's shit wouldn't be gone; but with the electricity bill, he wouldn't be able to afford to keep it. He fished the house key from the ring and stepped inside the house, rage bubbling in his gut.

"Fuck off." He didn't need to turn the light on to see that the kitchen was totaled. Dishes piled in the sink and unidentifiable bits scattered across the counter. One glance at the stove triggered a shudder. James would clean up or he would kill him. Forget about covering his ass.

"James," Jack called. No answer. Of course. Fuck it. He'd watch some TV and crash.

At the living room, Jack paused. James lay sprawled across the couch with a bag of chips on his chest, the remote in his hand, and dirty plates on the coffee table.

Something crunched beneath his feet but he refused to look down. "James!"

He jumped sending the bag tumbling to the floor.

More chips on the carpet.

Fucking lovely.

"God, don't do that. Why are you always yelling?"

Jack held his arms out and looked at the mess. "Why are you always trashing my house? You're cleaning this up, you know?"

"I know." James sat up and rubbed his eyes. "Maybe you could relax a bit. Shit Jack, you're going to give yourself a heart attack like this."

"If you weren't here, blackmailing me into letting you fuck up my house, I wouldn't be so pissed now, would I?"

"You know how to get rid of me." He shrugged and hiked the volume on the TV. Two women straddled one very lucky man tied to a bed. One woman turned—

Is that a mustache?

"Jesus, what the hell?" Jack snatched the remote and turned the set off. He was worse than a child. How did a man live thirty odd years and not grow up at all? "Listen, I am not paying you for doing nothing but making up shit about me. If I did that I'd be paying a lot of people."

James just stared.

Jack stuffed his hand into his pants pocket and pressed the button on the recorder. Then he mentally forced himself to count down. He had to stay calm. James could give him something he needed right now, and he had to be nice. Just for a while, he had to refrain from punching his face in. "If you want some cash, I could come up with a few jobs."

"What kind of jobs?" He looked interested, if a little wary.

Of course, he should be a little skeptical; Jack was more likely to send him out to shovel shit than give him a decent job. "There's one I need done right now. You wouldn't have to do anything... just make a couple calls for me. Five grand plus expenses."

"I'm listening."

"Promise first you won't use it against me later."

Fat chance.

"Fine, I promise whatever this job is I won't hold it over your head." He rolled his eyes.

Real convincing, asshole.

"Don't be so sincere. I might believe you'll actually keep your word."

"I will. Haven't I always kept my word?"

"Not exactly. Weren't you supposed to fuck off forever? I thought that's what I paid you to do the last time we spoke."

"I said I'd never bother you about your girlfriend. I can't help it if you keep giving me reasons to come back. If you'd just clean up your act, I'd have no reason to be here."

"Clean up my act? Are you kidding me? I should—never mind. Listen, this job is important. It can't be linked to me. My name is not to be used, ever. I'll meet with whomever you hire, but I don't want them to know my name. Clear?"

"Killing someone else? What's the matter, don't like getting your hands dirty?"

"I'm not killing anyone. I *haven't* killed anyone. I just need some documents. Whoever does it will have to break into an office. I'll give them the details, but I need you to find the right guy for the job."

"I know someone." James's eyes narrowed. "Ten for me and five for them."

"Fifteen grand!" Jack's heart fluttered. Maybe he was about to have a heart attack. "All right, that's fine. I guess it's worth it if the job is done right. You get nothing until the documents are in my hands. Call your guy and set up a meeting."

"It's not a guy. It's a girl. Actually you know her." James grinned. "I introduced you two already. Remember Skunky Slut?"

"She can't do this."

"Sure she can. You really have to stop judging people as soon as you meet them. It's limiting you know."

"Find someone else. This job is serious. I don't need someone to just walk in and ask for the documents. They'll have to break in, probably hack a sophisticated security system, and then find some papers, possibly break into a safe, and get back out. Fast and clean."

"I'm telling you she's the one."

"I can't be connected, dumbass. She knows who I am." Why was he constantly surrounded by idiots?

"So you wear a disguise when you meet. I won't tell her who it's for." He shrugged as if it was so simple.

What if she recognized his voice? What if James told her anyway? It's not like he was Mr. Trustworthy.

"I don't like it, James. I can't be connected to a break in. I'd rather have someone I don't know. Where did you find her anyway?"

"Friend of a friend, she actually got onto your buddy's crime scene to get me more information. She posed as a reporter and found out what they were doing and that the gas lines had been tampered with."

"I already knew that. Everyone knew that. The explosion kind of gave it away."

"She also got into the morgue after hours and copied the autopsy report." James added. "She broke into the morgue, Jack. That's not easy, you know."

Bingo. Just what he needed. "What did the autopsy report have that was so important?"

"Sadly nothing. I was hoping there'd be poison or something that made him go bonkers like that. But I guess I can't link you to that murder. Good work there."

"I didn't kill anyone." Jack felt like a broken record. Why was James so certain? When had Jack ever given anyone a reason to believe he would be able to kill somebody? Did he have a homicidal aura? Does anyone? And hey, he didn't actually kill anyone yet. Not directly.

"Whatever... Look, you want me to call her or not? My other connections are no good right now. I'm laying low, right? I can't do that if I'm calling guys to do jobs. Word gets around fast."

"Who are you hiding from?"

"No one in particular, I have debts that need to be paid. I told them I had to leave, go travel a bit to get it. I don't want you having any trouble so I didn't tell them where I was really heading."

"You think they wouldn't have you followed? Are you a complete fucking retard James? I don't need the mob coming to my house."

Not until I call them here anyway.

"I wasn't followed. I'm good at this game. Either take Candi, or do it yourself."

"Candi? Really? I'm supposed to have confidence in someone named Candi? Is that her real name?"

"Well yeah, I think it is. Why does it matter? She can do it. I promise."

Jack closed his eyes; a migraine threatened, his eyes burned and his head spun. He needed rest. This was ridiculous, running around at all hours just to keep his ass clean. His life was supposed to get easier with Jenny gone. Somehow, it had spiraled out of control. If he could find out where Candi lived, he would make sure her mouth stayed shut. Then it wouldn't matter that she knew him. But he still had to play this as James expected him to. "All right. Set it up for tomorrow night. In the morning I'll let you know where."

"You got it."

"Oh, and, James..." Jack gazed at his trashed living room and his headache intensified. "Clean this shit up before you go to bed, or you'll be the next person the morgue has to collect."

"Sure thing. I don't want you plotting against me. Although, that would be too many bodies lying around, don't you think?"

"At this point I don't care. Clean it up."

The stairs proved to be an effort. Once Thorne was gone, he'd get rid of the little prick. Then he could relax and enjoy his freedom. Shit, he thought getting rid of Jenny would solve everything. It was as if she sat down in Hell creating problems just to spite him.

CHAPTER 19

If the mob wanted James bad enough, they could have had him a dozen times in the last hour. Jack tailed his shitbox car through several red lights and down three streets. Christ, it was almost midnight, no other cars on the streets, but not once did James slow down, or speed up; nothing to indicate he noticed that Jack followed him.

"Fucking idiot," Jack slowed as James pulled onto a cracked sidewalk in front of a dilapidated house. James honked the horn and then opened his door.

Shifting into park in front of the house next door, Jack stared as Candi exited the house. Two miniature versions of Candi hovered in the open doorway. Jack grabbed his phone, held it up and shot a few pics of Candi and James, and one more of the kids. Leverage.

James still hadn't hauled his ass downstairs when Jack left the house on Friday morning. Jack didn't think he would have. He'd cleaned most of the mess he'd made over the weekend, in the kitchen anyway. He probably couldn't work a vacuum.

I can't ask for the world.

Hell, lately he couldn't even ask for his own piece of it.

Traffic proved challenging, and Jack practiced counting to ten backward, forward and sideways just to keep his temper in check. Mornings like this never presaged a good day. When the last light finally turned to green, the bitch driving a Jeep Cherokee in front of him proved colorblind. She sat leaning toward the radio while cars honked.

What the fuck?

She had the top open, so Jack leaned out his window. "Hey stupid!"

Sitting up—she knew her name—the bitch glared into her rearview.

"It ain't getting any greener, honey," he yelled.

Her gaze shifted from the mirror to the lights. She wrenched the wheel and turned right.

"Are you kidding me?" She could have turned the whole fucking time? Women.

He hit the gas, tires squealing in a fulfilling way as he almost clipped her ass end. He'd like to clip more than her ass. Jack nearly missed his turn and that pissed him off even more. He hated looking like a moron and slamming on his brakes when he was nearly past his turn made him look like a big one.

To further his frustration, the parking lot at the apartment building was packed.

What is this? Visitor's day?

Did the parking spots have numbers just to see if people could count? "Fuck."

Jack parked across the road. If he got a ticket, the superintendent would pay.

As he marched up the stairs, Jack ran straight into the old prick down the hall and sent his sputtering corpse careening into the wall to his left.

"Whoa son, slow it down," the man huffed.

"Fuck off."

Jack didn't wait for his answer, eager for the sanctuary of his office so that no one else could ruin his day any more. At the door, his day improved; Michelle was already at her desk. It was barely eight o'clock, and Jack thought he was early.

"Good morning, Mr. Murphy." She smiled. "I wanted to get a jump on things, since I took that day off. I think I've got everything caught up now. You need to get a bid ready for the Midtown mall job. There's an e-mail. They want it by Friday."

Shit, he'd forgotten about that job. It was huge. Fucking Thorne would have already dived in like the dirty prick he was. "I've got the material list done. I just need to add up the figures. If they call, put them through; I'll come up with something."

"Sure, I'll do that. There's just one thing.... I'm not an expert, but you don't have enough guys for such a job, do you? I mean you got rid of a crew the other day; you're kind of stretched for manpower."

Smart girl, he'd have to keep her around.

"I know. That's a bit of a problem, but I should have the guys when the work starts. They're still clearing the site and getting it ready. I'll manage. Just let me know when the jobs come up and I'll decide if we can take them."

"Sorry, I was just trying to help."

"I know, and don't be sorry. I like someone who asks questions, as long as they're intelligent ones."

She beamed.

Jack turned and headed toward his office. She'd be easy to keep happy; a little stroke now and then and she'd do fine. Most women were like that; give them a little cuddle and a fuck and they were smiling. Maybe if Whitney kept being a pain in the ass, he would give Michelle a turn. She might be old, but she was still doable. He'd certainly done worse.

Smiling at the thought of her tits, he booted his computer and started on the Midtown bid. By the time he hung up the phone, putting in a tender he felt sure they couldn't refuse, it was already noon.

Michelle peeked in, scaring the shit out of him by stuffing her head in the doorway, no knock or anything. "James is on the phone," she said, and disappeared.

Stupid ass.

Jack cleared his throat. "Are you just getting up?"

"Maybe."

"Do you know what time it is?"

"Look, Jack, I don't have a lot of time so I'm just going to give you the information. I gotta go. Candi will meet you behind Georgio's, that's a bar on Johnson Street, around ten tonight. Wait in the alley, and wear a blue jacket with a red tie so she'll know you're the guy."

The phone went dead.

Was he serious? Jack set the phone down. He was too dumfounded to be pissed about James hanging up on him.

Where did James come up with this shit? Why couldn't Jack just say "Hey Candi, I'm the guy." He was not wearing a red tie. James could kiss his ass. Besides, he didn't need a disguise. If they fucked him, they'd go down too.

Johnson Street and its surrounding area were full of delinquents and society's rejects. Apparently, they liked the bars. As Jack neared the end of Johnson, he spotted a flashing red sign that announced Georgio's. The second "g" was broken or someone had nicked it. At least it had been easy to find. He cursed his useless cousin again. James knew Jack had wanted to choose the meeting place. The only reason he let it go was because he was sick of arguing. Slowing the car, Jack pressed his lips tight. This was just ridiculous.

Across the road, whores flaunted their wares to passing cars; wares that hadn't been gently used. Horribly used would be a more apt description in Jack's opinion. He searched down the adjacent street, watched a drug deal go down, and gaped at a police car driving by without pausing. Nice neighborhood for a guy with a Rolex and a BMW to be wandering into.

Jack parked in front of Georgio's, between a rusted out Impala and a truck made of parts pilfered from other trucks, its back window smashed out and replaced with garbage bags and duct tape. Georgio's was just what he expected, rundown and very loud; the patrons spilled out onto the street, laughing, fighting, and making asses of themselves.

He climbed out of the car and walked quickly to the sidewalk, head down. His back to the wall of the building, Jack moved along the cool brick until he reached the edge, and slipped into the alley. He took a steadying breath.

Should've brought protection.

His gun sat in the drawer of his nightstand, doing him absolutely no good. He only carried a bunch of keys and his wits; dubious forms of defense in an area like this.

The backdoor to the club opened and Candi came out. She turned into the alley and paused. In her hand was a pocketknife, held up so he could see it. It crossed Jack's mind that maybe James had set him up, but he squashed the thought; you can't blackmail dead people.

"Candi." Jack stepped out from the shadows.

"Where's your tie?"

"I don't wear ties. That's just stupid."

She eyed him oddly and put the knife away. "You need to follow instructions if you want me to do this job for you." She moved closer. "So what do you want me to do exactly?"

"I need you to break into a business and get something for me."

She rolled her eyes. "I gathered that. What am I stealing?"

This was the slut who had her nasty ass on his counter not so long ago, Jack reminded himself. What made her think she could speak to him like he was an idiot? "It's not stealing; the stuff is mine. I want it back."

"Again, what is it?"

When he finished with her, he'd knock her skanky ass into oblivion.

Fucking bitch.

"Papers, copies of emails and ledgers, and some discs. I have a list here with how they might be labeled and where they may be kept."

She glanced at it briefly before shaking her head. "I need

ten grand to do this."

What? She and James were soul mates, bleeding him dry.

"First I don't like going into something blind. I can do it, but I don't like it. Second, you called me a skanky slut and you owe me for that."

"No, I believe it was *skunky* slut. Listen... just forget it. I told James you couldn't do this."

"I can do it."

"I won't pay more than five grand for it. Ask your boyfriend for a part of his cut."

Fucking ridiculous.

James was a moron. How did he ever think James would ever be good for anything?

"What's James getting? He told me he gets a cut of mine for getting the job. That bastard... I want what he's getting."

So James tried to screw her over too. Nice to see Jack wasn't the only one bending over for him, although he imagined she did it literally as well. "He's getting five, same as you." Like he'd tell her the truth. "Look, it's all I've got, take it or leave it. You weren't supposed to know me either and I'm letting that go."

"What if I told you James asked me to give him the papers first?"

"What?"

"What if James wanted to see what it was you wanted so badly? How much is it worth to you for me to give him something other than what I'm taking from this place?"

That little prick. The two-timing, backstabbing, piece of shit snake.

James would die a horrible death, Jack would see to it. "So you want ten grand? How do I know you won't give it to him anyway? How do I know you two didn't plan to squeeze more money out of me? I'm not an idiot, you know?"

"I don't think you're stupid, I know you're not. Rich guy like you, working your way up to what you got without a handout from anyone, you've got to have some smarts. You're right not to trust me. After all, I was fucking some guy in your kitchen for a mere hundred bucks."

"I knew he paid you. I knew it."

"The thing is I don't do anything for free. Not stealing, not killing, and definitely not screwing. I'm willing to help you, but I need to make it worth my while."

"All right." This was costing a lot more than Thorne was worth. Jack was tempted to say fuck it, and just get rid of Thorne himself. But he couldn't be sure those papers wouldn't see the light of day, and that was a risk he couldn't take. "If I give you ten, you don't show anyone those papers. You hand them directly to me. I'll give you something to give James."

"Make it twelve and you have a deal." She smiled sweetly.

Jack ground his teeth. These two should get married and have a couple of kids. Then they could clean the pockets of the world with their criminal genius. "Twelve and don't say a fucking word to James about this."

Her smile vanished as Jack advanced.

"So help me, if I find out you screwed me and went to him anyway, I'll hunt you down and wring your miserable neck."

"Hey, I told you I wouldn't, just relax." She backed away.

She looked sufficiently scared. He could be an intimidating guy when pushed. "I mean it, now here's a phone. It's a throwaway, so you can't link it back to me."

She took the phone and stuffed it into her pocket.

"I'll call you the day before the job so we can meet and go over the details."

"Okay, but I do have to work. I can't just come whenever you call."

"Where do you work?" Probably on the next corner.

"I'm a dancer." Her chin lifted slightly. "I need something regular to pay the bills, I got kids, you know?"

"I know." Poor little bastards.

She stiffened. "James told you?"

"Sure."

"Why do you think I let assholes like you and James treat me like this? I wouldn't if it weren't for my daughters."

"You think I won't kill you for fucking me just because you have kids? Think those kids are off limits? Think again. I won't hesitate to do what is necessary to cover my own ass. I mean it."

"Relax, you have a deal. I won't screw you. Unlike James, I never go back on my word."

Jack walked away before he changed his mind. Making a pact with the devil was risky business, but he had to get into Thorne's office, and Candi was the only available devil.

CHAPTER 20

The payphone looked dirty; the receiver caked in a white flakey substance that Jack could probably identify but it didn't make him feel better. People walked past. Now and then, a car backfired but he kept staring at the phone, ignoring the distractions. He did not want to pick it up. Jack pulled a sleeve over his hand to grab the receiver and punched in the number with his keys. He hadn't called the phone he'd given Candi all week. Hopefully she'd been smart enough not to use the damn thing and waste the battery.

The papers he'd made up for her to give James were in the car. She'd get them when the job was done. The little bastard would have no doubts that Jack was the one who caught him in the act.

Candi's phone went to voice mail. Jack had to try several times before she picked up. "Where the hell were you?" he barked.

"I didn't know the number."

"Of course you didn't know it, stupid. Have I called you before?"

"Well I know your home phone and this ain't it."

"Do you think I'm stupid enough to use my own phone?

Come on. Let's think about this for a minute."

"If you're done being an asshole, I'd like to get on with this. I have other things to do."

She had other things to do? Like bleeding him for twelve grand wasn't the most important thing on her agenda. "Right, you have better things to do. Okay, I'm going to drive by the bar we met at, and you'll wait outside. When I stop you get in, I'm not getting out, so be ready."

"Where are we going after that?"

"For a drive." Jack knew how guys got nailed by naming a spot. He wasn't about to give her a location so that she could set him up with the cops, or worse, have James lurking in the shadows with a camera and a recorder.

"I don't like this, it sounds fishy. James says I shouldn't trust you."

"James is the one you shouldn't trust, he's already lied to you once that we know of. I've been completely honest."

Well, sort of.

"What color is the car?"

No, she wouldn't catch him that way. "You'll know it's me. I guess we better get this shit over with. Are you free now?"

"As long as it won't take long. I need to be back by three, they're expecting me at work."

She's establishing that someone will miss her and come looking. How cute was that? "I suppose Saturday is a big tip night? Whatever. I'll only need an hour of your time."

"Okay, see you in a few."

Jack hung up before she could ask any more stupid questions. You never know what could be gathered from these cell phones. Jack wouldn't put it past government pricks to tape every conversation.

Driving to the bar in daylight was much different. Most of the delinquents would be in bed sleeping off their high, or in jail waiting for the judge to let them go. Georgio's sign wasn't lit up; the streets littered in bottles and... Were those used condoms?

Gross.

Candi stood outside, smoking a cigarette while examining her nails. She didn't look any better in daylight. She'd fixed her hair, sort of. Now it was dark brown with red chunks splashed through it.

Jack slowed the car, a rental this time, and opened the door.

"I thought you drove a Beamer," she said as she got in.

"I do."

"I see."

"I'm going to talk as we drive. That okay?" Jack hoped he didn't need to write everything down. That could get tedious.

"I'm listening."

He explained the setup, Thorne's office address, the type of security she could expect and what he wanted out of there.

She nodded and chewed on the skin next to her nails.

Jack resisted the urge to crack her in the face. He hated chewers.

"So how do you get the files from me?"

"I'll be watching you. When you come out, it will be the same setup as today. I'll be waiting. You get in the car and we drive away."

"What about James?"

What about him?

"I mean, he'll want to go so he can get the files and copy them before I give them to you. What do I do about him?"

"You tell him the setup; don't lie about any of it. Tell him I'll be waiting for you. Tell him you'll make copies while you're in there, so he will have what I have, except you won't really be doing that. You won't have enough time."

"I wish you'd trust me, I'm not going back on my word."

"I'm covering my ass, I don't trust anyone anymore. You shouldn't either, it gets you fucked and not in a good way."

"What did this Thorne guy do to you?"

"He's trying to blackmail me and I'm not letting him. He stole something of mine to put me under, only I'm not going quite so easily."

"Why don't you just, you know, get rid of him?"

Why didn't I? Stupid cow. Well it's just that easy isn't it? Why didn't I see that before?

"He has my stuff, do you get that? He dies, what happens to it? Who sees it and what will they do with it?"

"Oh. Gotcha." She put her hand on the door and turned.

In the dimness of the car, she was somewhat attractive. Thank God for tinted windows. He could see how in a dark club, vision blurred by booze, a guy might think she could be worth seeing naked.

"I'll do this for you, and I won't go to James. Maybe sometime you and I could—"

"I'm involved, but thanks."

Fuck that, you won't get me within a football field of anything that's been near James.

"I meant, oh never mind." She sighed and opened the door. "Tomorrow?"

"Yes, but I'll let you know what time. Keep the phone handy."

Jack waited while she strolled down the street. He couldn't believe he was letting a woman do a man's job. What choice did he have? At least if she proved to be a problem she'd be easy to get rid of. How many whores bit it while working the streets?

Making money was now priority. Jack drove back to work to make some calls. He'd get James's money back; James might not get the chance to spend it.

Michelle stayed at the office all of Saturday, kissing Jack's ass for her bullshit the week before. She knocked on his door before leaving, and handed him a note. "Some guy came by today and left this. I didn't open it. I assumed he wanted it to be kept private." She stood there while Jack looked at it.

"Thank you, anything else?"

"I know this is going to sound strange but—" She blushed and twisted her hands.

She was hot for old Jack, he could tell. Well maybe he'd give her a go soon, he hadn't had an old woman in a while. Variety was the spice of life they say.

"I know that your wife just died and you spend a lot of time at work. I was just thinking that maybe some night I could make you dinner, just so you don't have to eat alone."

Dinner. Right. "That's really sweet Michelle, and I may just take you up on that. It's been a long time since I've had a nice home-cooked meal. Jenny wasn't a cook, or a housekeeper, or anything else really. I miss her in other ways..." he let his words drift off.

Her face reddened to a tomato shade. She looked away.

"I'm sorry, I've embarrassed you. Of course, I don't expect you to give me more than dinner. That would be inappropriate anyway, I'm your boss, and you've probably got lots of guys lined up."

She laughed and shook her head. "No, Mr. Murphy, once a woman gets to be a certain age, it's not like they're waiting around the block for her. It's not inappropriate, really. Lots of coworkers sleep together and stay friends. I'm far too old for you though, at least ten years."

At least.

Well, maybe fifteen, but he wasn't going to ruin her fantasy of a younger man. "You can't be—" Jack said, shrugging and giving Michelle a taste of the old charm, "I don't care about age anyway; sometimes a person just needs a warm body. That didn't sound right, I'm sorry. Just forget it. I appreciate the offer of dinner."

"No, I want to. You are fading away as we speak. I know you aren't sleeping, and you look so stressed out all the time. Is Monday okay for you?"

Now she was determined. He'd let her seduce him just this once. Maybe he could teach the old dog some new tricks. "Sure, I'd love it." Jack smiled.

She blushed again.

"No strings?"

"No strings," she agreed. "Well, I better go. Are you coming in tomorrow? It's Sunday."

"Nah, I need some rest. You're right about that. I'll see you Monday bright and early. We need to line up a crew for the mall job."

"Okay, I'll see you then, Mr. Murphy."

"I think when it's just us, you can call me Jack." He'd throw her a bone. Why make it too difficult? Although he did like the idea of nailing her while she moaned, "oh my, Mr. Murphy! Yes sir, harder sir." A man can't always have what he wanted, Jack supposed.

"Thank you, Jack." She turned, but paused in the doorway. "I forgot to mention, you have a message from Whitney."

He did not have time to deal with her just now. "When did she call?"

"Once today. Twice yesterday. She asked if you'd call her when you had a free minute."

That would be never. "Okay, thanks."

"You're welcome." Michelle left, closing the door softly behind her.

Jack stared at the envelope on his desk for a long time before picking it up. Who, he wondered, would need to stop by on a Saturday and leave him a note? It couldn't be good.

Opening it, he let out a sigh of relief. The bids for the newest jobs. Funny, Tony never delivered them like this before. He usually just let FedEx handle them over. He pulled a sheet, paused and then ran through the figures. Thorne had bid low on all of them. He wasn't being realistic. How could he possibly be making any money? Maybe he used cheap labor but still, the materials alone would run him close to his bid. Unless he used shoddy goods, discount or recycled material. Within a few years, Thorne would be wallowing in lawsuits. Jack chuckled to himself. Inexperience, overworked men, crappy material, and a boss who was rarely on site—Thorne headed for a fall and it wouldn't be pretty.

Part of him wanted to let Thorne land flat on his face, let

him experience the humiliation. He could be satisfied with that, but he'd targeted Jack for annihilation, and that made it impossible for him to turn the other cheek.

Tomorrow he'd check out a few of the sites. The one that was easiest for him to get into without being seen would be the one he let Thorne have.

Setting the first page down, Jack scanned the second. Tony wasn't a letter writing kind of guy; he didn't like trails. But here was a little unsigned note from him. His guts somersaulted.

> *Just to let you know our correspondence must end. Company arrived today and they were very interested in what kind of friends I keep. Since we don't keep copies of our letters, I couldn't enlighten them. It's not likely you'll be able to do so either and that's just fine. They don't know my friends and I don't think you'll mix well anyway so I didn't introduce you.*
>
> *We have a large mouth to find and stuff so I won't be able to help you anymore. I must go away for a while so do not write. I won't get it. My big brother is watching the office and he doesn't like mail. I hope this is clear. If you have any of our correspondence, file it under G. Our friends can look for it there. Best of luck my quiet friend.*

Shit, there was a rat. Thorne? The guy might be a class-A twat, but he was far from stupid. But if it wasn't Thorne, then who? Jack knew this would happen eventually, but not when he had so much other shit to deal with.

Fuck my life.

Jack made a mental note of the sites, shredded the list, and checked his desk and computer for anything he might have missed.

Who was checking? Tony and Jack had been at this for years without being caught. Even with his other contacts, he'd never had an issue. Jack had a sinking feeling that Tony was in trouble right now because of him and he hoped, for his own sake, Tony's boss never figured that out.

CHAPTER 21

Candi answered the phone on Sunday afternoon. He tried to reach her earlier, hoping they could finish with Thorne in the morning, but she didn't pick up. Probably just hauling her ass out of bed. Her laziness didn't piss Jack off too much. It was safer to do the job at night. No one would be around and they wouldn't risk Thorne putting any overtime in, not that he was likely to be in the office on a Sunday morning, but one could never be sure.

James acted strange that morning. Jack supposed he was anxious to see the papers since Candi would have shared their plan. He tried to be nonchalant about it, but Jack guessed that the possibility of missing the papers was killing him.

"Where you headed off to on a Sunday night? I thought you were taking today off." He followed Jack around the house as he prepared to leave.

"None of your fucking business. If I want to go out, I'll go out."

"I was just wondering... shit you get angry at nothing anymore. You really need to take a holiday or something. All work and no play makes Jack a fucking asshole."

Jack turned and jabbed his finger in James's face. "I am angry because assholes like you try to blackmail me out of money I've worked hard for. I'm sick of lazy pricks doing nothing with their lives and living off my sweat. Maybe if you went home, I'd be in a better mood."

"No can do, cousin. I got bills to pay. If I don't pay them, I could wind up missing parts of my body. I'm actually fond of every bit I've got, so I'll be staying until you help me out."

Ignoring him, Jack grabbed his keys. James didn't need to know that he'd rented a car. And he'd find out later that he couldn't use the phone or the Internet. Jack couldn't have him contacting his little partner in crime.

Jack parked the rental at work and would switch there. He wanted to arrive at Thorne's before Candi so he could watch her walk in. When he couldn't reach her that morning, he'd checked the rear entrance to Thorne's office. His recent string of bad luck made him paranoid; what if she went in and copied everything during that time? What if she and James were cooking up a way to fuck him while he dialed her number over and over like a fucking retard?

He breathed a little easier when he found the back door to Thorne's building was barred up with one of those mall-type security gates. Instead of a lock, the latch was welded shut. Whatever it was, it worked for Jack. Candi had only one entrance and one exit.

When he finally got a hold of her, he laid down a timeline. He'd given her twenty minutes once she got in the door, hoping that wouldn't give her enough time to make copies of anything. She wouldn't get paid if she took longer, or if she didn't get everything he told her would be there. Of course, she wasn't happy about having a time limit, or the possibility of non-payment. She'd get over it. The longer she spent in there the greater the risk of being caught, and Jack couldn't see her taking the wrap for him.

He pulled up in front of Thorne's office. A few minutes later, Candi strode past, looking way to conspicuous in red leather gloves. What the fuck was wrong with her?

Jack watched as she pulled something from her pocket and

fiddled with the door. His heart jumped into his chest. If she got caught, he was gone. Seeing her disappear inside did nothing to calm his nerves.

He waited, playing with the radio, tapping the steering wheel, keeping his eye on the front door, watching for her bouncy form to emerge onto the empty sidewalk. The benefit of a Sunday night job was that in this neighborhood, with its hoity-toity offices and restaurants, no one roamed the streets. They were all sleeping off the hard day on the golf course, resting for Monday morning.

While he waited, Jack considered how he'd get rid of Thorne once he had the papers. Accidents seemed to be working out so far, and he didn't see any point in messing with a system that worked.

When the phone rang, Jack came perilously close to shitting his pants. Then he sighed. Whitney. She was probably getting lonely.

Doing chicks couldn't be very satisfying once a girl's been full of Jack. He let it go to voicemail. After a brief pause, it rang again. Sighing he picked it up.

"Where are you?"

"Well hi to you too, I've missed you," he said. "What happened to hello?

"I haven't heard from you in days; there's no reason for that now. I can't believe I let you treat me like this. Why can't you just call me?"

"I have nothing to say. What do you want me to do? You can't just call someone and say nothing." Women were ridiculous.

"Maybe you wanted to hear my voice, that's fine. Shit, it's like pulling teeth to get any scrap of affection from you. You can't use Jenny as an excuse anymore. Either you want me or you don't."

A shadow moved outside the car. Jack froze. Nothing moved in front of Thorne's building. He scanned the empty street in front of the car. Beneath the streetlight, a paper bag drifted and danced; caught in the breeze.

"Jack?" Whitney said, a sob in her voice.

"Oh I want you; that's never been an issue. Come on, give a guy a break. I'm a busy man. I can't just drop everything to call you, baby, even if I want to. I do miss you. How about I come over?"

"You want to get laid and I'm not that fucking easy. How about you come over and take me to dinner? You know, where everyone can see us."

Unbelievable.

"I'm going to take you to dinner at this time of night? Seriously, you're being unreasonable."

A faint whirring noise to his right set him on edge.

Candi emerged from Thorne's building.

His patience for Whitney's bullshit ended. "Listen, I need to go. I'll stop by when I'm done here."

"Where are you?"

"I'm busy. I'll see you in a bit." He closed the phone as Candi opened the door. Why did women have to be such pains in the ass? It was simple; they needed to spread their legs, cook his food, and otherwise shut the hell up.

"Are we going to just sit here and wait to get caught or are you going to drive?" Candi looked nervous.

That made Jack nervous too. She should look happy, proud of herself for a job well done. She shouldn't look ready to jump out of her skin. "Did you get the papers?" He put the car in gear and pulled out of the parking lot.

She nodded.

"Then what's the problem?"

"I tripped the alarm. I was almost out, and—shit, I don't know what happened. It went off as I was leaving. I was careful. Don't look at me like that. They had cameras, which I figured on, so I had my hat and glasses, and a jacket on the whole time. I shut the system off. You can't just cut the wires either; trips some of them. But it must have reset itself, because as soon as I opened that door it went off."

"The cops will likely take a while to respond. We're okay." He wasn't sure who he was trying to reassure. "The important thing is that you got everything."

She tossed a red shopping bag at him as he pulled over in front of an ATM machine.

"Not here, asshole, keep driving."

"They won't even notice us. Christ. Just relax. It's lit better here, and I want to see what you've got." The cops might see them, and the worst that would happen would be an arrest for solicitation. Why else would someone like him be alone with someone like her?

"Just go farther away. I don't think stopping on the same fucking street is the smartest idea."

"I need to switch cars, so we can go to my office. Will that make you happy? You can take this one home."

"Don't you have to return it?"

"Eventually, it's not in my name. James doesn't know it, but he's been doing a lot of driving lately," Jack said grinning, proud of his genius.

She looked horrified. "What? Are you retarded? You really are an asshole or just unbelievably stupid."

"You can get out right here, without your twelve grand. Who do you think you're talking to?"

"James has some really bad guys after him. They're connected. Now you've got him renting cars, putting his name all over shit, and they'll find him. They're going to kill him. Do you understand?"

What a moron. She thought he cared about James. One of them was a retard, and it wasn't him. "They won't find him."

Not until I'm safely out of the way.

"Jesus, you need to dump this car. Never mind, I'll take it far from here and throw them off his trail. You know if they find him, you're in trouble too."

He pulled into his space and looked at her. Of course he'd thought of that. Running a hand through his hair Jack sighed dramatically to spin another lie. "Look, I'm sorry. He didn't tell me anyone was after him. He said he owed some money. With James, it could mean a phone bill. If you could dump this, that would be great. I really appreciate it. Now let's see what you've got."

Uppermost in the bag were the e-mails. He flipped through a few. Satisfied that the incriminating ones were there, he set them aside and dug deeper. The copies of the ledgers were beneath the e-mails. He frowned when his fingers brushed a stack of disks.

"You said a disk. I didn't want to take the wrong one, so I grabbed everything."

Well she was thorough. Jack eyed one with Ray's name on it and pocketed the lot. He would inspect them later, just to satisfy his curiosity. The papers he'd compare to his own and make sure she hadn't overlooked anything. "Thanks Candi. Good job." He handed her a large envelope and a black duffel bag. "The bag is your money and the envelope is what I want you to give James. Now take off your shirt."

"You're kidding, right?" She tried the door and her eyes widened when it wouldn't open.

Thank you, childproof locks.

"I'm not taking off my clothes. I did your job and I'm not doing anymore. This is rape."

"I don't want to fuck you. Hell, I can do a thousand times better than you. I want to make sure you aren't hiding anything in your clothes. Take your shirt off."

"I will not."

"Either you take it off or I'll just check myself. You'll probably like that better, won't you?"

"Fuck you."

Jack waited.

Rolling her eyes, she lifted her shirt.

Jack looked down at her pants.

She cursed but managed to wiggle them down far enough to show she had nothing but herself in them. "Happy?"

"Yeah, real happy. Now I'm going to check for myself."

She glared "You said—"

"I know what I said, but I'm not stupid." He felt around her shirt. She had rolled some papers into a tube and tucked them up along with her shirt. Reaching under her ass, Jack came up with another disc with Ray's name on it. "Two discs? Clever girl, bring me all that crap and hope I am dumb enough to think you wouldn't fuck me over."

"I don't like lying to James. He's been real good to me. He's not a prick like you."

Jack searched the rest of her body, which wasn't as soft as it looked. Confident she hadn't stashed anything else he yanked the bag from her hands.

"What are you doing? I did the job—"

"You did, but you were going to fuck me over. So I'm taking the extra seven back. You get five, as agreed before you said you'd lie to him. He's getting ten, take it up with him."

"He's what?"

"He said fifteen grand, ten for him and five for whoever he finds to do it."

Get out of this one James.

"I could go to the cops."

"And say what?" She had to be joking. "You broke into a business and now you're angry because I took back some of the money I paid you? Are you going to go to jail to get even with me? Guess what, honey; you won't have any of the money then. You'll be in jail too."

"Fuck you and fuck your loser cousin." She grabbed the duffel bag.

Jack disarmed the locks so she could get out of the car. "I'm done with both of you. Don't ever ask for my help again because the first chance I get I'm nailing your ass to a wall."

She stormed off. Jack laughed.

Have a nice hike, bitch.

He put the cash in the shopping bag and set it on the floor of the car. It rattled. Jack grabbed it and reached inside. His hands closed over a prescription bottle. Interesting. Thorne's name was on the label. It was heart medication. Thorne had a crappy ticker? What an interesting development.

Why would she take these? Jack paused, his mind racing. Why should he care? It gave him an opportunity. A man's heart stops because he's lost his medicine. No one can be blamed for that. He couldn't control a heart could he?

But wait... Jack stared at the bottle.

Evidence of my involvement.

Thought she'd fuck him, did she?

Thorne's heart medication on the passenger seat set Jack on edge. He stared at the bottle, expecting it to explode or for someone to pull him over and arrest him. For what, he wasn't sure; but he couldn't keep them. Sure, he could throw them away, but where was the fun in that? Instead, he'd wiped off his prints, wrapped the bottle in tissue and shoved it in his pocket.

Jack approached the cul-de-sac he'd followed James to the previous week. Herchimer Lane, according to the bent, rusted sign. He slowed, and parked the car at the end of the street. Whistling as he walked, Jack nodded to a young girl pushing a stroller while dragging a toddler behind her. Yep, Hanover Springs's finest right there. Poor kids were probably hopped up on drugs just like their crack-whore mothers. Glancing at the house numbers as he walked, Jack looked around when he came to the cruddy piece of shit shack that was Candi's place. The house was dark: a good thing. Her kids must have been at a sitter's house.

Jack walked up the front steps as though he belonged. People noticed when you crept. Isn't that how they always found burglars? Eyewitnesses described suspicious characters as "lurking" so he wouldn't lurk at all. He tried the knob and it turned. Stupid move. People should always lock their doors. He pushed, but the door wouldn't budge. Stepping back, he cursed. Fucking deadbolts.

Jack glanced once more to the street and then stepped off the porch and walked around the house. Candi's back yard consisted of a crumbling cement pad, and a few white plastic chairs stacked against the house. The patio doors that led out to the pad looked crooked, with a wide gap between the top of the frame and the wall. Jack checked the neighboring yards for potential witnesses, and then moved toward the doors.

He prayed to whatever power had helped him so far as he reached for the handle, and paused before closing his hand around it. Jack pulled a pair of gloves from his coat pocket and slipped them on. He pushed the door and let out a sigh of relief as it jostled along the track. It stuck after about a foot, forcing him to wriggle through the narrow gap to get into the house, ripping the back of his jacket in the process.

"Fucking welfare slums," he muttered. Inside the tiny house, Jack cringed at the stench of pot and piss. A cat darted by his feet, sending his heart into his throat. Then, the useless ball of fur sat next to a crooked staircase and licked his balls before raising dopey eyes.

"Hello, Piss-Smell."

The cat blinked.

He turned to search through the coats and scarves hanging on the wall behind the door. He touched something smooth and slightly sticky. "Bingo."

Jack yanked the coats aside, and opened a bright red imitation leather bag and dropped the pill bottle inside. He arranged the coats over it and headed back to the patio doors, glancing back at the cat. "And it's as simple as that, Piss-Smell."

Candi wouldn't find them until she switched purses. If the slut was like Jenny or Whitney, she did so regularly. Why a purse had to match any of their clothing was beyond Jack.

Whistling, he closed the door and walked back to his car.

CHAPTER 22

In the papers that Candi stole, Jack found everything Thorne had shown him and then some. There were photos of him at Ray's house saved to one of the discs, as well as photos of him and Whitney... in her apartment. Damn telescopic lenses. Jack recognized the pink haze that distorted the pictures. Stupid pink curtains. He'd told her she needed blinds. It was a damn good thing Jack hadn't just eliminated the crafty prick or he'd have been thoroughly fucked.

James had stormed into the office earlier that morning. Candi had called him and she'd been more than a little upset.

Whiny cunt.

James figured he should have given her what they'd agreed on. Jack informed him that she was lucky to get anything but a bullet in her ugly face. Of course, that didn't win him over.

"You are the biggest asshole I've ever met in my entire life. Now she'll never speak to me again. We had something, you know?"

"What, you were going to run away and get married? Fuck off." Jack hated whiners, he hated liars, and James did a good job of both. "You're just angry that she was the only one willing to let you stick your skinny cock in her for a few bucks, and now you're back to jerking off in the shower."

"If that guy winds up dead, she'll go to the cops. How about that? You won't get away with this one. She seen all the stuff you told her to take, she knows all about what you did."

"She doesn't know a damn thing. She seen some emails, maybe a picture or two. That's not enough to say that I'd try to kill anyone; which by the way, I didn't."

Jack thought about the pills and wondered if she really had intended to set him up. If she did, she hadn't thought it over very well. It's not as though a guy with a heart condition wouldn't notice his pills gone. Thorne probably carried another bottle around with him. If Jack were cursed with a crappy heart, he'd make sure he took care of those things.

"If she does try to nail me, you won't have anyone to blackmail; just remember that."

"I didn't say I wanted her to; she's pissed at me too. Why did you go and tell her about the money? Now she wants half of mine."

"That's your problem. You set the price."

Jack didn't waste any more of his time arguing with James. He'd grabbed his keys, mumbled something about a job, and ushered James out of the office.

Driving through Hanover Springs's Main Street, he searched the buildings as he thought about James. He'd have to put that idiot from his mind. Nothing would ruin his good mood tonight. He had a dinner date with Michelle and actually looked forward to it.

Whitney excited him when he'd been a married man, but lately she'd grown stale. The same old fish every night didn't satisfy Jackson Murphy. A man needed variety now and then, a little adventure. The whole marriage kick she was on scared the shit out of him too. Jesus, if she believed he got rid of wife number one, why in God's name would she want to be number two?

At Michelle's building, he checked his watch. Thirty minutes late, as planned. Couldn't let Michelle think he was eager to see her. He got out of the car and headed to the door at the front of the building, impressed to see a uniformed old porter.

What it would be like to bang an old lady? Jack pondered. Probably wouldn't be as bad as being with poorly preserved old ladies. Michelle took care of herself and looked to be about thirty-six or seven— maybe forty without makeup—but he didn't intend to be around when that was gone. He wondered if old crotch was different than young crotch. Jenny's used to be nice before the kids, but afterward... Jack shuddered.

The old porter barely looked up and certainly didn't rise from his chair. Jack pushed through the door, walked to the elevator at the base of a winding staircase, pushed the button, and waited.

"Elevator's out," the porter growled.

A sign might be a good idea. He started up the stairs, his good mood cracking.

Rounding the tenth set of stairs in Michelle's dilapidated building, Jack nearly gave up. Why everyone though the top floor was the "best" escaped his understanding. Last one to get out in a fire didn't sound appealing. Christ. Next time they'd just rent a motel. If he felt she was good enough for a next time that is.

"Mr. Murphy, I thought you forgot."

Jack almost jumped out of his skin. He hadn't noticed the door open... one of only three in the hallway. Michelle laughed nervously as he walked toward her.

Shit, she must have been peering through her windows and then raced to time it just right. If that's how she acted when a guy was late, she must be really lonely. Whitney would have flayed his balls. "I thought we agreed you'd call me Jack." He smiled. Mr. Charming would be present this evening. Tomorrow morning when he wanted her to fuck off, he could go back to boss man.

"Oh, I guess I'm just used to calling you the other. Jack it is. Come in, it's not much but it's home."

Jack walked past her into a studio apartment decorated in black and white. Not what he expected. He'd pictured soft pastels and creepy dolls lining old curio cabinets passed down from her grandmother.

"This is nice. The rent must be phenomenal." He noted the bedroom in the far corner divided by Chinese screens, with splashes of red that offset the monotony of the décor.

"I bought it with the insurance money after my husband died," she said.

How long ago was that? She didn't seem very upset. Of course, he wasn't one to judge such things given the party mood Jenny's death brought on for him. Perhaps her old man had been an asshole.

Another nervous laugh bubbled from her mouth. "I don't have to pay rent which is nice, given the nature of my work. I bought a few other things, but maybe I'll show you those later."

Jack's gaze dropped to her chest. Purchase one and two, he'd bet. "How did he die?" Maybe they had more in common than he thought; or maybe he should run while he had the chance.

"Poison." She went to the tiny kitchen and pulled things out of the oven and the cupboards.

Poisoned by whom?

She glanced at Jack and laughed. "I didn't do it, silly. He ate some bad fish, got sick, and died. He wasn't very healthy to begin with, and he refused to go to the hospital. I stupidly let him have his way and now he's dead."

"Was it very long ago?"

"Five years or so. I guess I didn't really care for him. He was overbearing, mean; just an all-around asshole. I was planning to leave him but then he died. I guess it's a good thing I hung around when he got sick."

"I guess." Man, she was cold. Jack shuddered at the level of iciness that ran through her veins. Old or not, she was a fine woman. He sat at a little table next to the large window in the living area. Michelle brought the food over and prepared his plate. At least asshole husband had trained her well. Jenny wouldn't even cook the damn meal let alone set it out for him.

"Ironically, we're having fish. It's okay though, I bought it fresh today. I won't get anything if *you* die right?" She laughed.

Maybe he wouldn't stay for dessert.

"Loosen up, Jack. I'm sorry. I should have saved that story for later. He ate the fish at some roadside diner on the way home from a business trip. Nothing I cooked would ever kill anyone."

"I know. I'm just kind of tired. It's been a while since I've been out with someone. I guess we're not really out, but you know what I mean. It's strange too because you work for me."

"Let's pretend we just met then and you've paid me to show you a good time." She wiggled her eyebrows. "So tell me sailor, do you want to finish dinner or go straight to dessert?"

"I'd rather dessert; the menu is kind of killing my appetite."

She laughed again.

Jack speculated as to where the nervous, uncertain Michelle of a few days ago, might be hiding. This new version unsettled him. For once in his life, he wasn't sure how to act.

Without another word, Michelle stood and walked toward the bed. Jack followed, after pausing long enough to gather his thoughts. Of course she was going to fuck him. He was the best option she'd probably ever had. As Jack walked around the screen, his phone rang. He wanted to chuck it through the wall but took it out of his pocket and looked at the number.

Whitney, shit.

"I need to take this."

She nodded, reaching behind and unzipping the back of her dress. "I'll wait here," she promised and let the silky material drop to the floor.

Jack's mouth watered. She didn't look old at all. Fucking Whitney. "Jack Murphy," he snapped into the phone.

"How dare you use that tone," Her words slurred together and her voice sounded high and whiny. Drunk. "You fucker, you don't show up for like a week and you have the nerve to be testy with me."

"Sorry, I wasn't thinking. I'm working on a big job. Can I call you later?"

Michelle stood in front of him unbuckling his belt. After

lowering his pants, she rubbed his cock against her cheek.

Interesting.

"Jack! Are you listening to me?"

Jack groaned, and closed his eyes. "I'm sorry, but you've caught me with my pants down here. I'm trying to finish up as fast as I can."

"No you can't call me later, asshole. I want you to come here now. I want you to make up for treating me like garbage."

Michelle ran her tongue over him.

He drew a shaky breath.

"What are you doing? You sound funny."

"That's what hard work sounds like. Listen I'm sorry about not calling you back, but I've got so much building up... now that Ray's gone. I—oh fuck!"

Michelle's mouth had more suction than an industrial vacuum. Jack's last words came out like a boy hitting puberty. Whitney knew that voice well.

"Are you with someone? Jack so help me, if you are fucking some other—"

"I'm just helping my secretary to finish a job so we can both get off at a decent time." His voice still shook but he'd recovered the tone nicely.

"You don't sound like you're working."

"I bumped into the desk. Look, if I don't get off the phone and finish up, my head is going to explode from the stress. I'll talk to you soon."

"I'm sorry—"

He didn't care anymore. Let her get pissed and wax his balls, or whatever took her fancy.

He closed the phone, tossing it next to his pants as Michelle sucked his balls into her wonderful and airtight mouth. Jack nearly passed out. But then she let go of him and stood. Jack stared. Apparently, she wasn't finishing that way.

She made up for his disappointment soon after, kissing him hard, her teeth grinding against his lips.

Jack could have done without that and quickly broke away. He grabbed her arm and dragger her over to the bed where he tried to press her down on it, but she proved strong for such a small woman.

"You lay down," she purred and forced him onto his back.

If Jack wasn't all about making it fun, she'd have been on her back, but he didn't mind letting her do all the work.

"Can I tie you up?"

Bad idea.

"I'm not really into that," he said.

She dangled a set of cuffs.

"Especially not with those."

"Come on, I promise it will be fun."

"Maybe next time, we hardly know each other."

Fuck did she think he'd just let her lock him to her bed? He wouldn't be able to leave until she wanted him to. Who knew if that story about her husband was true or if she poisoned him herself?

"Fine, I understand. You're used to being the boss. Can't let go of control." She tossed the cuffs. As they clattered to the floor near the screens, she climbed on top of him.

Her muscular body lit by the light of a tiny lamp next to the bed held Jack's eye. Her tan looked fake and her muscles a bit manly. Jack wasn't sure if he liked that, but then she lowered herself onto him and it no longer mattered.

"Just another thing I bought with my husband's money," she whispered.

"What your—?" Jack looked down in horror. No, he would know a fake cunt. He would. *The tightness...oh, fuck.* Laughter brought his gaze back to her face.

"Not that. I've always had that. I had them fix it up a bit, to make it match the rest of me. Tight and firm. Get it?"

"They did a fantastic job," he groaned. The relief in knowing he hadn't mistaken a guy for a girl intensified the pleasure of her moving up and down him. "If I'd know they could do that, I'd have sent the wife in."

"It's hard to find a doctor willing to do it. With the right incentive though, they can be convinced."

He didn't ask what incentive she gave and he didn't care,

distracted by her unnaturally large and high boobs as they moved with her. Strangely, they didn't bounce as much as they swayed. He liked them to bounce a little.

Just as he got into it, Michelle shuddered and collapsed on top of him.

What about old Jack?

"Is something wrong?" he asked.

"Nothing at all, why?" she mumbled into his chest.

Is she serious?

"Is that it?"

"Oh, you weren't done? I'm sorry. I usually don't come until after but you have got the biggest dick I have ever seen."

Jack knew that, but shit, at least suck him off or something. "Why don't you finish me then?"

"But you've been inside of me—"

"So?"

"Wash it and I will."

He blew off Whitney, a sure bet, for this bullshit? This bitch was fired as of tomorrow morning. "Either you suck it or I'm out of here."

How do you like them apples honey?

"Come on Jack, it's not the end of the world. Women usually never get off. Just once you have to deal with it and you're losing your mind? Real mature."

"I don't know what goes on in your world, but in mine a woman does her job and I get off. That's it, end of story. If you aren't going to suck it, then we have nothing more to say to each other. I'm out of here."

She stood, grabbed a black robe from the bedpost and stepped out to the kitchen.

Jack's throat burned, and he stared around him in shock.

She walked away from me.

Maybe she should see how a man treats a tease. Jack grabbed his pants from the floor and pulled them on. After returning the cell phone back in his pocket, he followed her, his temper rising with each step.

When he entered the kitchen area, Michelle set a teapot on

the stove and glanced up. She was not budging. He could see it in her eyes. Well she could find some other moron to take this shit.

"Thanks for nothing." He said. She better not bother coming in to work. Maybe he'd change the locks.

"Are we—are you firing me? Jack, I—Can't we talk about this? You can't afford to fire me, and I can't afford to be out of work. It would be silly to let something as silly as sex come between a good working relationship."

He paused. Her voice sounded strange. Too calm.

Son of a bitch....

She'd set the whole thing up. She wanted him to get angry, and she wanted him to fire her. He almost played right into her hands. She'd been into Jay-Ray's books, seen stuff from Tony. Michelle knew enough to cause a cluster-fuck of enormous proportions.

Jack couldn't afford to piss her off. For now, he'd have to play things her way. Later, Michelle would be one more body to add to his never-ending list. Jack counted to ten silently and then smiled.

Michelle looked uncertain, her gaze darting around the room, unable to meet his.

"You're right. That would be a horrible thing for me to do. I'm frustrated and I took it out on you. This sex thing isn't going to fly, but that doesn't mean we can't work together. I'll see you tomorrow morning."

Jack grabbed his keys off the counter and walked to the door. He paused, one hand on the knob and turned. "Thanks for... whatever that was."

He closed the door softly behind him. Try to fuck him over and see what happened. She'd have to get up pretty early to pull one like that on Jackson Murphy.

In the car, Jack drove through town and past his street. He'd go see Whitney. At the stoplight, Jack reached into the glove compartment for the cologne Whitney had bought him for Christmas and sprayed it liberally. He leaned to put it back, but thought better of it and sprayed a couple of shots in his pants, hoping to get rid of Michelle's stench. He'd use the bathroom when he got to Whitney's and remove everything else if he could. It wasn't likely she'd be in that kind of mood anyway.

As he turned onto Whitney's street, his phone rang again. He pulled it from his pocket and slowed the car. What did he want now? "James, you are getting on my last nerve."

"Where are you? Still on your hot date?"

"Just starting number two, why?"

"Maybe you should turn on the news. There's a little story running that you might find interesting," he sounded odd, giddy almost.

Jack didn't like it. "Just tell me what it is, James. I don't have time for your bullshit."

"Okay, but I have to say first that you are lucky I saw you yesterday and then you called from work. I swear I'd have thought you were a genius if I didn't know you had no part of this one."

"Spit it out asshole, I'm busy."

"Really man, you need to relax or you'll have no friends."

"I don't need any friends."

"Sure, if you say so. Anyway, the story; I turned on the news after you left, I don't usually waste my time but the game was starting and—"

Jack sighed.

James stopped talking.

What a dipshit.

"Oh sorry, you're busy. Okay that guy, Thorne, that you got Candi to—"

"Think about what you're saying for a minute, fucknut, and how you're saying it." For a conman, he was pretty loose with his mouth; on a cell phone, no less.

"What?"

"I didn't get anyone named Candi to do anything. I don't even know who you're talking about. Isn't that the bitch that dumped you a few days ago?"

"What the hell are you talking about?"

Jack pressed his lips together and breathed through his nose. Finally, it must have sunk into his cousin's thick skull.

"I forgot you never met Candi. I was thinking of my other cousin. You do know Thorne, right?"

"Of course I do, stupid. We're in the same business."

"Just checking. Anyway he's dead."

"He's what?" If James was fucking with his head, Jack would strangle him with his bare hands. Or maybe he'd cut the little prick's tongue out first so he could gag him with it.

"They found him this morning, I'm not lying. His secretary said he was tearing his office apart yesterday. They had a break in, you know?"

A pause.

Did James think he would admit to knowing that?

"He was looking for missing papers, all freaked out and shit. She left. He said he had some business to deal with so he was staying. Do you know he lived alone? I thought with a name like Thorne and Sons, he'd have, well, sons."

"Do you have to take the detour just because it's there, you fucking moron? Can't you just tell the story and leave out the bullshit?"

"I should let you find the rest out yourself. You're really beginning to bother me. You're a mean old prick."

"That makes two of us." Jack maneuvered into Whitney's parking lot and waited for James to finish. He had no patience left.

"Anyway, he had a heart condition. They said he was born with it. He took some kind of drug so his heart didn't like spaz on him and quit. It got bad when he was really excited, would suck for sex I guess, but that's probably why there's no Mrs. Thorne. Boring sex isn't going to win over the ladies."

"James—"

"Oh yeah. Sorry. The doctors figure he was agitated and had an episode, that's what they called it. He usually had his pills in his desk. He kept some in the car too, but he was in the office so they were no good."

Jack counted to ten.

James continued. "So the thing is, his pills weren't in the drawer, they were gone. He must have forgotten to get more or something. He croaked. They found him in the hallway. They figure he was going to get the ones in his car. Talk about a bad day, huh?"

"Did you tell your girlfriend about this yet?" She *did* set him up. Sadly for her, it backfired.

"She's barely speaking to me, but she's probably seen it. She watches the news too you know. She's a smart girl."

"If you say so. When you do talk to her, tell her that I said she did a fine job."

"You've lost it man. She's not going to understand any of that. I don't understand any of that."

"She will. Just tell her." Jack closed the phone, cutting off James's stuttering questions. He couldn't believe how brilliant he was. He'd only wanted to send the stupid bitch a message.

Thorne was gone, and technically Jack had nothing to do with it. He didn't take the pills. Candi caused his death. True, she was working for him at the time, but he didn't ask her to take them. He wouldn't have, even if he'd known about the prescription. Fate obviously agreed that Jack should live without assholes in his life. Why else would three assholes take care of themselves? Now, finally, he'd work on James.

CHAPTER 23

Whitney didn't meet him at the door as she usually did. Jack didn't believe he'd get a replay of the show he'd been given the last time she didn't meet him. He whistled a little tune as he entered and stood on the mat, waiting for Whitney to look at him. She didn't. Instead, she sat on the couch and glared at a spot on the wall.

"Are you going to sit there all night, or are you going to be mature about it and talk to me?"

She didn't move, but her eyes narrowed just a bit.

Whitney figured she was a grown woman in every way and hated any reference to her immaturity. Well, the truth hurt. "Come on, I have a life you know. Lots of things have been happening lately. I can't just drop everything for you. I'd like to, but I can't."

"I should be part of your life, Jack, not a convenient little piece of it when you feel like bothering. I won't wait around much longer. You either start getting serious or we're through."

Fuck, she was pissed. He needed to keep her hanging on for a while but didn't want her think he would marry her. Jackson Murphy wouldn't be snared into that trap again.

"Okay I'm sorry. I've been a jerk and you have every right to be mad. I just got caught up in trying to get my shit together. You know why James is here, don't you? He's trying to take me for a ride, and I just want to get rid of the bastard without paying him off. Then there's been all the stuff with Jenny and Ray's deaths. I've had a lot to deal with."

"Maybe you should get rid of him too. I mean, you did it once and he's not going to be missed. I wouldn't tell anyone."

"Fuck, I haven't gotten rid of anyone. When will you get that straight?"

"Whatever. Are you going to start taking this seriously? I mean it. I won't be just your whore."

What else did she think she could be? Like he'd marry someone who fucked random chicks and married men. "I said I'm sorry. I'll try to treat you better."

She smiled.

He relaxed a notch; the worst was over. "Look I really gotta piss. I drove here as soon as I cleared my desk. I'll use the bathroom and then maybe we can find something fun to do."

After the fiasco with Michelle, if he didn't get release soon he'd explode.

"Okay. Can we watch a movie? I rented a couple of new ones. I thought I'd be alone again, so they're not really your type."

Chick flicks. Great.

"That's all right. I'll watch whatever."

Jack hurried to the bathroom and washed up. He grabbed some kind of lotion from the cabinet. It smelled like bananas. Jack squeezed the yellow goop on his hand and rubbed it everywhere Michelle might have been.

Better to smell like a fruit than Michelle's snatch.

When he emerged from the bathroom, Whitney had curled up on the couch remote in hand. Jack settled down and pulled her close. The movie looked awful and Jack prepared to sleep with his eyes open. He couldn't stand bad acting. The hacks in Whitney's movie were beyond terrible.

She giggled a few times, but Jack didn't see what she found

so funny. He watched halfheartedly before a thought crossed his mind. Something didn't seem right. "Aren't there any women in this movie?"

Whitney didn't answer.

It should have been a clue that something wasn't right.

The scene switched to a shower where two football stars—best friends if he understood what was going on—lathered each other up. From that point, it turned into a car wreck that Jack couldn't look away from. Damn, he really wanted to. The blond guy moved his hand down to rub the dark guy's ass and his chest and then they kissed. "What the fuck?"

"Shhh Jack, it's just getting good."

Getting good?

He'd have to gouge his eyes out and scrub his brain to erase the memory.

The dark guy turned around and braced himself against the wall while the blond hunk grabbed his hips. Jack closed his eyes. The sounds were as bad as the visuals.

"I'm done." He jumped up and shook himself. "Whitney, you honestly thought I'd watch this shit? Fuck, I know you're pissed at me but come on."

"We watch girl on girl all the time and I don't complain. Why can't we watch this? It's very erotic."

"You *like* doing girls. You fool around with them all the time. I don't go around nailing my friends like you do. This is totally different." What was wrong with her? He didn't do gay porn. No guy who was into chicks would do gay anything.

"Okay, fine. I'll shut it off. You owe me, though." She switched off the movie and turned, a smile on her lips. "We do whatever I want tonight."

"What do you want?"

"Come with me and I'll show you."

Jack followed her to the bedroom.

She produced a pair of cuffs. "I'm going to punish you."

He stared. He had a fifty-fifty chance of torture or ecstasy. Jack didn't like gambling on those odds.

"But you'll love every minute. I promise." She winked.

"Sure baby, whatever you want."

Driving home a few hours later, Jack regretted that promise. He'd have been better off as some guy's bitch in a maximum-security prison. He didn't even know how she managed what she did; just that he'd been too shocked to react.

He hobbled into the house, tripping up the stairs as fast as he could. Jack cursed Whitney, her mother, her father, and anyone else responsible for her existence as he leaned over the tub to crank the hot water. As he removed his clothes, he considered burning everything to get rid of the memory of what she'd done... and where.

After a scalding bath, he wrapped himself in a towel. He worried he may never walk properly again. Before he was through, Jack would stuff not only his cock, but whatever else he could find into every fucking hole in that woman's body. She'd be whimpering and begging for mercy just as he'd been. Would he show it? Not a chance. What happened at Whitney's proved that his fear of cuffs was founded.

Never again.

James moved around downstairs. Jack weighed his options. He could go downstairs and talk or he could just go to bed. Behind closed eyes, the maddening low hum of a vibrator would pounce on his mind. He'd talk to James.

At the bottom of the stairs, he thought maybe James had retired for what was left of the night. He went to the coffee maker and frowned at a thump in the living room. Nope. James was still there.

"You're drinking coffee? It's four in the morning."

"I have to work in a couple of hours. I need caffeine." Jack ran water in the pot. Why did James think he had to explain his life? He was always asking questions; so many questions.

"I got Candi to talk to me tonight. What did you do?"

"Nothing." If she didn't tell him, Jack wasn't going to.

"She freaked out and told me not to call her anymore. She

said if she ever laid eyes on you again, she'd cut your nuts off."

"Well we'll see if she has the parts to do it." Jack wasn't worried about Candi. She was nothing, and she would never do anything to hurt him. Jack held all the cards in Candi's game and she knew it. If she fucked with him, or tried to extort money like his douchebag cousin, Jack would make sure she found herself in a jail cell. She must have found those pills in her ugly purse. Why else would she be so pissed at good old Jack?

"So you must be leaving soon." Jack said. "There's nothing else for you here."

"When I get my money I'll go, and not a second before." James sat across from him at the table.

Jack glared. He'd have to work on getting rid of James now. One more and he would be home free. James was the only one left who could lay anything on him. "I'm not paying you any more than what you earned, so forget it."

"You will. Did I mention that Detective Newman called after I hung up with you? Oh, I didn't because we haven't talked. She'd like to see you again."

What did she want? He thought they'd taken care of everything. "Did she say what she wanted?"

"No, just that she had a few questions she needed answered. I'm sure it's nothing since you claim you haven't killed anyone. Maybe she wants to get laid."

The thought of Newman bouncing on his cock made Jack shudder. He didn't care what was at stake; he'd never fuck that buffalo. "I'll call her from the office. I'm sure it's nothing."

"I had a nice chat with her, you know? I could have talked all night, but then I knew we were working on a deal here and I didn't want to jump the gun."

"What are you talking about? You don't have anything on me." He was bluffing and he knew Jack knew it. James wouldn't send him up the river without his money. He'd do it after Jack paid him, and that was exactly why he wouldn't.

"I know you broke into Thorne's office. True, you didn't kill him, but burglary is a crime. Then there are the bees, and

Jenny's strange death, and the fact that Ray was trying to fuck you over and slept with your wife. His death looks very suspicious when you take all of that into consideration." James grinned.

Jack's temper rose. If James wasn't careful he'd do him right then, consequences be dammed. "Fuck off James. I'm not paying you another cent. Do what you want."

Jack gave up on the coffee and picked up his keys. He didn't need to hang around and listen to this bullshit. He'd go to work and set the wheels in motion that would see James gone once and for all.

At the office, Jack headed toward the spare room, hoping he could sleep without images of Whitney's vibrator haunting him. Michelle wouldn't be in for a couple of hours, if she showed at all. He left the lights off. Lying in the bed staring up at the ceiling, he revisited the events since Jenny's death. No matter what James said, they couldn't pin anything on him.

Ray, wanted to do himself in anyway, Jack just made up for his lack of balls. If anyone, other than Thorne, had any pictures, he could explain them away. Ray had been acting pretty odd for a few weeks. Jack didn't need to come up with anything fancy. He rubbed his eyes and squeezed the bridge of his nose as another headache threatened. He'd worry about Ray's death if it came up. Hadn't he mastered thinking on his feet?

Thorne might prove to be an issue. Jack hadn't established an alibi for the night of the break-in. If Thorne had kept anything else, like notes or more pictures, Jack would have much explaining to do. But, would he? Would Thorne have been so frantic if he had anything else stashed away? Of course, with an alibi his ass would be clean. Maybe Whitney.... Jack shuddered. He didn't want to go back there any time soon. What choice did he have though? She was the only one he could use.

A siren wailed somewhere below and Jack closed his eyes, holding his breath as it faded away. He'd talk to Whitney before he called Detective Newman. It wouldn't hurt to let her in on a few things. He couldn't trust Whitney, but if he could get her to lie to the police and provide him an alibi, he'd have something to keep her toeing the line.

Thoughts swirled around his brain. Questions, problems, and fears, mixed with possible solutions and the wish that he'd never thought of those damn bees.

Michelle's voice startled him.

Jack glanced at the little clock on the stand next to the bed. Eight already? He must have dozed at some point.

Michelle's voice didn't sound happy. She must be on the phone, given the pauses in conversation.

"I tried. You know I take this seriously. The problem is this guy is really an asshole. He doesn't care about anyone but himself."

A pause. Whoever she was talking to was long winded. The silence dragged on. Thinking she'd hung up, Jack sat up and rubbed his eyes. Perhaps it was time to make his presence known. He stood and crept to the door.

"Look I'll try but I don't think we're getting anything out of him. Really, he's a fucking snake. I even tried the poison story and he still agreed to mess around with me. He didn't even blink when I said I'd sue him."

Who was she talking to? James? The cops? Fuck, would they pay her to set him up?

"Okay, I know. I'll stay, but only for another week and I'm out of here. He gives me the creeps. Did you know his wife and his partner are dead? That's a huge coincidence don't you think? Yes, you're right. I'll see you Saturday. I'm going to need something to warm me up after being so close to Mr. Frosty. You can help me with that. Yeah, I know. But you can find someone to... okay. Bye." She hung up.

Jack stayed at the door for a few minutes. How should he play this? It couldn't be the cops. She wouldn't have asked about Ray and Jenny if it'd been Newman on the phone. That left James or maybe the mob. James would've told her about Jenny and Ray right away, so she'd know he knew about them.

So that leaves him off the list.

Was Tony gunning for him? Maybe they thought he'd helped James. Wait, Tony's note. He said something about a rat. Fuck. She said she wanted something to warm her up. Booze? No. She could get that herself. But Tony had a hand in many pots, not just construction bids. He could hook her up with all kinds of drugs. Maybe she was a plant. Tony was making sure Jack wasn't their rat. It had to be the mob.

He ran back to the bed, fiddled with the alarm clock until it went off, and let it scream for a full minute before hitting the snooze button. After making a bunch of racket, he went to the door.

"Hey," Jack tried to sound groggy. "When did you get in?"

"I've been here a while. Why were you sleeping in there? Don't you have a house?"

"Yeah, I came back here to get some work done last night. Didn't you watch the news? Michael Thorne kicked the bucket yesterday. I figured his contracts would come up for the rest of us to finish. I've been trying to figure out how to take a few."

"You don't have enough crews. We talked about this yesterday."

She was all business now, which Jack found amusing. Her eyes said she wanted to put a bullet in his head.

"I know, but if there's no one to take over his business, there will be a lot of guys unemployed. I could place an ad out and see if any of them want work. It would be perfect. They already know the jobs, right?"

"You think fast, Mr. Murphy. I wouldn't have considered that within a few hours of such shocking news."

"I told you before... You can call me Jack. Nothing has changed." He'd play her little game.

"I'd rather not. It's uncomfortable after last night. I would rather forget the whole thing happened."

"Whatever works for you. Listen, I've some calls to make and possibly an appointment in a couple hours. You can set up the ad. Ray had some files in the cabinet of where he would post them. Use those. I'll check in with you once I'm finished in my office."

She didn't reply.

Jack didn't care. He went to his office with a smile on his face, but it quickly vanished when he sat and stared at the phone. Now to find out what Detective Newman wanted. The actor in him had better be ready to perform.

CHAPTER 24

After punching Whitney's number, Jack picked up Newman's business card, which had sat next to his computer since returning from their previous meeting. Whitney had to back him up or he was in serious trouble. But what would she want in return? The phone went to voicemail so he tried her cell. Voicemail again.

Shit.

He tried again. This time she picked up.

"Jack, I'm in class," she whispered. "Can this wait?"

"Actually, can you get out of there for a minute? This is important."

She sighed. There was shuffling and then the click of a closing door. "Okay, I'm in the hall. This better be good, we were discussing possible test subjects for experiments in deviant sexual behaviors."

He had to admit it was kind of sexy when she talked like that; like she was intelligent. "I'm sure it won't be hard to find volunteers."

"You would be the perfect guinea pig. I can attest to that," she snorted.

He knew she was on his side then. What he'd endured the

other night should make up for ignoring her for the next five years. "Are you alone?"

"I'm in the hallway, but there's no one here. What have you done now?"

"I haven't done anything and that's just the problem. This guy, Michael Thorne died yesterday, and I guess it's suspicious because they're calling me in for questioning."

She giggled. "Why? Did he sleep with your wife too?"

He took a breath. Jack didn't want to piss her off but it was killing him not to tell her what he thought of her sense of humor. "Not that I know of. I barely knew the guy. Now I need an alibi because they want to pin it on someone. He was competing for new business in town, and he was loaded. He won a few of my jobs. They may think that's a motive, I guess."

"What do you want me to do? I can't call off the cops, honey. Even I'm not that good."

"I just need you to say that I spent Sunday evening with you. That's all."

"Where were you?"

Fuck, couldn't she just do it without the bullshit? How hard was it to just do as you're told? "I was at home. That useless tit James is refusing to tell them I was there unless I pay him. I'm not giving him a damn cent either. Honest baby, you won't get into trouble because that's where I was."

"Why don't you just pay that asshole and get rid of him? He strikes me as the type who will eventually disappear."

"He'll fucking disappear all right. I won't be paying him though. Not a fucking cent."

Silence.

Maybe he should open his big mouth and just stick a foot right in. If James disappeared, she'd have to go shortly after. "Will you do it or not?"

"You once promised me something pretty to show off to my friends. You know, like something sparkly and expensive?"

No, he certainly did not promise her anything of the sort. "Did I? Well then, I guess I'm going shopping while you speak to the cops."

"Will I have to swear to it in court? I have a future, you know. If they can prove I lied in court, my credibility is ruined."

Not just your credibility sweetheart, you'd be an accomplice.

"You just need to tell anyone who calls that I was with you. That's it because it won't go to court after that. They're just checking any lead they have. The guy had a heart attack, simple. I don't know what this is all about. I just want to make sure you'll stand behind me if I need you."

"Of course I will, Jack. Unlike you, I make sacrifices for the people I love. Maybe after this you'll get it. Will I see you tonight?"

"No more of that bullshit you pulled the last time."

"That was fun, wasn't it? I had fun."

"Fuck off."

"Jack," there was laughter in her voice. "You should be nicer to me."

"I know, but that was nasty and I'll end this now if you ever pull a stunt like that again."

"It's okay, I taped it. So I don't need you to do it again, I can watch you beg for mercy anytime I want."

She taped it? How could he be such a fucking moron? He should have guessed she was up to something. The stupid bitch taped everything. She had enough material to take the porn world by storm. "Get rid of it."

"Maybe. Bye Jack. I love you." She hung up.

Jack slammed the phone down. Now he'd have to find the fucking tapes and get rid of them. He couldn't have that shit floating around. Maybe some of them would be okay, but not the latest. He'd die before he let anyone see that... or she would.

Jack sighed, picked up the phone again and keyed in Detective Newman's number. He couldn't imagine what she could want. Thorne's death was an act of God. He had nothing to do with it. Well, maybe the pills could get him into a little bit of trouble. But really, if Thorne hadn't tried to blackmail him, he wouldn't have gotten so riled up and given himself a heart attack.

"Detective Newman," her voice was still sexy as hell.

It felt so wrong that he was turned on by it. It was cruelly unfair of fate to give a woman such a voice and then pair it with a disgusting body; just plain mean.

"It's Jack Murphy calling," he kept his voice friendly, as though he had no idea why she'd be calling him again. "I was told to call you. Is there more information on Ray's death? I thought we were done with that."

"Well, there is some new information on that, but it's not why I'm calling. Your partner's death was an unfortunate accident. Sure, lots of strange coincidences that piled up to end in tragedy, but still an accident. I'm calling because I need you to come down and answer a few questions I have about Michael Thorne. You knew him, didn't you?"

"Yes, he owned another company, but I didn't know him too well. He's only been around for a little while. We met once or twice and I thought he was okay."

"Well we can go over that in your statement. Can you come down this morning sometime?"

In his statement? What the fuck? "Am I in some sort of trouble Detective Newman? I'm a little confused." *Try a lot confused.*

"You're not in any trouble at the moment, but if you'd come down we can clear up a few things that have come to my attention. Just some troubling pieces of information that I've come across. I'm sure it's nothing."

"Of course it is. I'm just a bit concerned that I'm being questioned about some guy I barely knew. It was a heart attack, wasn't it? That's what the news said."

Play dumb Jack. You don't know anything about anything.

"Relax. I'm sure these are just some misunderstandings." Her voice sounded soothing and had probably calmed many psychopaths.

Good thing Jack wasn't a psychopath or he'd confess everything to that voice. "I can come down now, I guess. I'd rather get this over with as soon as possible." He tried to sound offended and upset.

"Thank you Mr. Murphy, I'll see you in a little while." She hung up before he could reply.

Jack wanted to play up the innocent man thing a little before going down there, but he could do it just as well in front of her.

Jack set the phone down, stood, and stretched. Fuck, he was tired. By noon, he'd be lucky if he could even see straight. He locked the door to his office behind him. "Hey, I'm going out. Meeting."

Michelle barely looked up from her paperwork. She'd be disappointed to find that his office was now locked.

"There might be a guy coming over sometime this morning; my lawyer. I expected to be here but this meeting just came up. Tell him I'll join him for dinner at the usual place and we can talk about things then." It was a total lie but he loved the way her eyes widened at the word "lawyer."

Just try to pull one over on Jack, you old bitch. I'd bury you before I let your douche bag ass take me for a ride.

"I'll do that," she murmured. "Will he need anything from your office?"

"No, he's just coming for a brief. There are some legal issues I'd like to deal with. These things snowball if you don't attend to them right away. I'm sure you understand why I won't discuss them; there could be a conflict later on."

She stared for a moment, her cheeks just a little flushed. Then she looked down. "Of course, your business is your business, Mr. Murphy. I don't need to know everything about this place. I'm only a temp after all."

"It's not business." He smiled as he left.

Chew on that you fucking whore.

Jack got to the police station before traffic piled up too badly. The ride home, if the meeting took too long, would be a nightmare. Traffic at midday in Hanover Springs could be described as simply mental. With any luck, he could charm his way out of whatever it was Newman thought he'd done, which meant he had to rely on the obvious fact that the bitch received little positive male attention, if any. The only way she'd ignore Jack's charm, which worked nearly every time, was if she was into chicks.

Lesbians did not like Jack, and he wasn't fond of them either. Sure, they were fun to watch, but any woman who claimed she didn't enjoy a real cock now and then had something wrong with her. How could you prefer a rubber substitute to the real thing? Jack didn't think they should be allowed to use dildos. Someone should make a law or something. Hell, they had laws about who you could marry. Why not a law about how you pleasure yourself? If they don't like guys, why should they get to use anything closely resembling a man's important bits? They made their choice and that choice was cockless.

After slamming the car door, he stepped out of his car and jogged up the steps to the station doors. Why the hell did all legal buildings have to put a hundred steps out front? Was that mandatory? Christ, by the time anyone got in, they forgot why they'd come. He pushed the big steel door and walked into the foyer. A different girl sat behind the desk. Gone was the cute little thing. In her place sat a woman of about seventy with thinning hair.

"Excuse me."

She looked up from her crossword puzzle.

"I'm here to see Detective Newman."

She didn't leave the desk to get Newman as the other girl had done. Instead, she picked up the phone.

Perhaps the other girl had left to compose herself. She probably had been in on the little joke that was Detective Newman.

The old woman's false teeth moved as she spoke into the phone.

Jack's lips curled.

She hung up and pointed the way down to Newman's office. He wouldn't merit a personal escort this time. Newman was either really busy or she thought he was a petty criminal who didn't deserve common courtesy. Downstairs, Jack knocked on her door and entered without waiting for a reply.

Newman sat at her desk in her dungeon cell, head bent to a pile of papers in front of her. She didn't look up.

"Good morning." He smiled.

She glanced up to return a very unconvincing smile.

"I hope we can clear all of this up today; I'm really busy."

"Shouldn't be a problem. Just some simple questions that require simple answers." She made notes in a little book as she spoke.

He had to force himself not to lean over to read them.

"Okay, so here's the problem I have. Well, the first problem anyway. I need to know where you were on the fifteenth, all day and all night."

Shit, he thought they'd only ask about the time of the break in. "Was that last Saturday?"

"Sunday."

"Oh, that's easy. I was at home most of the day with my cousin. He's staying with me for a while until he gets back on his feet. He's had some financial trouble lately." Jack leaned forward and lowered his voice. "He has a gambling problem. We've tried to help him but he just continues to go into debt with some very scary people. His presence at my house is kind of a secret."

"So he was the man I spoke to on the phone earlier? Okay, he also said you were there for the day, so that clears that up. The evening?"

"I was with my girlfriend. She's a student, kind of young for me, but you only live once, right?"

Whitney would raise eyebrows, especially if her earlier connection to Jack's family had to be revealed. That would just make him look like an asshole though, not a murderer. He didn't care if it came out.

"Can you give me her name and number?"

"I can call her right now if you want." Jack took out his

phone.

She shook her head. "That won't be necessary, I'll call her later. So you can verify your whereabouts for all of Sunday, that's good."

Did he imagine a faint smile? The mole moved just a little. Maybe she'd started to warm up a bit.

"There is another issue that I think needs clearing up, even if your alibi is solid."

If that fucking Candi told them anything, he'd strangle her. "Okay, ask away."

"We found a contract in Mr. Thorne's office that makes me a bit concerned. It appears to be a deal, unsigned mind you, for the sale of your business. It also states that you promised never to enter into any business in any way related to building, construction, or renovations."

Jack couldn't move, couldn't speak. Shock swept over him. He didn't need to act at all. Why hadn't he thought of the contract? If they could pin a motive on him for hiring someone to break in...

"That's interesting." He shook his head hoping he looked bewildered. "I did have dinner with him, at his request. He asked if I'd consider selling out. He and I were competitors and he was trying to move to the top of the ladder. My first reaction was to tell him to fuck off, but then I thought better of it. I want to retire in a few years, so what could it hurt? I told him to make an offer and I would think it over. No way would it have been enough, but I was curious to see what kind of figure he tossed out."

"So you agree that he did approach you with such a proposal."

"Yeah, but it wasn't even an option. I don't know why he'd bother drawing up a contract."

"Your cousin seems to think Mr. Thorne was blackmailing you."

James. *Fucking asshole-motherfucking-jackass-cocksucker.*

"Is there any reason why he'd think that?" she asked.

Maybe because everyone was trying to take a piece of him.

James was in serious trouble. "I mentioned the dinner, but I never said I was being blackmailed. But, you know, James is one of those guys that thinks everything is a conspiracy. He thinks that the mob is out to get me for having him at my house. He's convinced that they're going to kill everyone close to him. Seriously, Detective, I don't understand him at all and I don't think you should read too much into what he says."

"I did feel he wasn't telling me everything. Is he involved in organized crime beyond the gambling?" She raised her eyebrows. Her frown made her face uglier, if that were possible.

He hesitated. Should he put the bug in her ear to set himself up for James's eventual disappearance? Should he leave it alone and use it later? "I don't know, really, he only shows up when he's in trouble. Turns out, he's gambled away most of what he had. Now, he says the mob is after him. I really don't think so. I think he owes money to a couple of casinos, but they're probably not too concerned. They get guys like him every day, don't they?"

"I'm sure they do, but some prominent casinos have ties to the mafia. You should be careful with this, Mr. Murphy. Let your cousin know that I can put him in contact with some agencies who can help him. If he has committed any crime, I'm sure that they can work out a deal in exchange for information. Loyalty to people who are out to kill you is senseless."

Ah, what a sweet gesture. She wanted to protect his darling cousin who just tried to send Jack up the river. No one could protect that bastard. "Thanks, I'll tell him. I do think though, that it's all in his head. I doubt he has any connections to anyone like that. He's not the brightest bulb, if you know what I mean. They'd have gotten rid of him by now just on sheer stupidity," Jack laughed.

She smiled.

He liked it better when she smiled and the hairy mole disappeared into the folds of her face. It gave him a slight reprieve from looking at the disgusting thing.

"I think that just about does it." She handed him the notebook she had been writing in. "If you could just sign that what

I've written there is true, we're finished."

Jack read through. He was home on Sunday with James, at Whitney's in the evening, and no, he did not agree to sell his business to Thorne but held no animosity toward him. It sounded good; Jack signed it and passed it back to her.

"If you think of anything else I would appreciate a call."

They couldn't pin Thorne's death on anyone. They weren't even looking for the culprit in the break-in. They would have had video, at least until Candi shut it down. It'd be a woman they wanted. Candi didn't even wear a disguise. He knew Newman didn't want his alibi. This was a poor attempt to mask the importance of that damn contract. That's what she really wanted to know about. Maybe she thought the contract would lead to a motive to kill Ray. She'd never pin any of that shit on him. But Jack couldn't resist playing with her a little.

"Of course, I'll call." He said. "Are you thinking he didn't die of a heart attack? I'm just curious."

"No, he died of natural causes. We're investigating an incident that he reported before he died. His secretary thinks some very sensitive information was stolen, we have to check it all out." She stood.

Jack took the gesture as his dismissal.

After shaking her hand, he left as fast as he could. Whitney had better keep her word and back him up on the alibi. If he went to prison, he'd make sure they had a better reason than hiring a thief to steal a bullshit contract.

CHAPTER 25

Whitney kept her word, and swore to Detective Newman that Jack had been with her all evening. She even offered to let Newman know what they did, but the detective declined. Whitney thought it was funny to hear the disgust in her voice.

Jack held the phone from his ear as her shrill laughter echoed through his head.

"She sounds hot, Jack. Are you sure you aren't just giving her reasons to haul you in?"

Picturing Whitney and Detective Newman together, caused an awful ache in his brain. "Oh she's a knock out. She's at least two hundred pounds and most of that belongs to a hairy mole on her cheek. You'd like her. Should I fix you two up?"

"I think you're lying," she laughed. "Are you coming over tonight?"

"I don't know yet. It's early." He didn't want to go over there, not with the night from hell still fresh in his mind... and his ass. "I'm trying to set up a meeting with this guy. Can I call you?"

"Sure, if you aren't coming until late then Misty and I might catch a movie."

With any luck, she would stick with Misty and he wouldn't

have to get rid of her. Wouldn't that be perfect?

"She was hoping maybe you'd come over and play."

Sweat formed on his forehead as he considered the idea. He'd give anything to be involved in something like that—before all of the other crap happened. Now, he didn't know if he trusted Whitney enough to get into her games anymore. What could two of them do to him? He shuddered. "She's not really my type but whatever you want is fine. I owe you one."

"You owe me a ring, asshole."

"A what?"

Oh hell no.

"Forget it. I don't want you to do things because you owe me. It's supposed to be about love."

Fucking love again. She'll never learn.

"I'll call you and we'll decide."

Jack didn't acknowledge the mention of love, and he wouldn't. She could love him as much as she wanted; he wasn't about to marry her. He liked variety, and although she was experimental and welcomed other women, Whitney always had to be involved. Where was the variety in that?

Jack hung up and called Tony's service. Tony's letter said he couldn't write, but he said nothing about communicating by phone. He left a short message stating that Jay called and needed to contact him urgently. He didn't leave a number. Just a brief mention of the "regular number" and that they could meet at Tony's place or the booth. His "place" was their code for an apartment Tony used for business transactions—most of which Jack was happy not to know about. "The booth" was a phone booth he used to make his calls from, Tony never used his own phone for business.

James had sealed his fate when he blabbed to the police. How could he do something like that to his own cousin? How could he do that to his meal ticket? Jack eagerly awaited Tony's call. He couldn't wait to let James know that he knew what the little prick had been up to.

Jack sensed something strange as he entered his house. First, there was darkness. James never turned the lights off. Jack paused to listen. Was that music? Movement to his left brought Jack's gaze to the doorway of his living room. The glow of a candle chased the shadows around. Jack hoped it was a candle and not an all-out fire. His mind raced with possibilities. What could that fuckup cousin of his have been up to?

At the living room, Jack stopped just inside the doorframe, his hand moving to his mouth as it became clear in the flickering light came from a candle. It also became clear that James had problems; Jack hadn't even touched the surface of how messed up the guy really was. Jack's ears burned, embarrassed to witness the debauchery. His chest ached with fury as he cursed the weirdo for soiling his living room. "Do you have to ruin every room in my fucking house?" Jack roared.

James looked up, eyes glazed. He sat in Jack's lazy boy, a rope around his neck—which he'd anchored to the doorknob. Naked. The freak was naked. Jack's gaze moved down to James's hands and he quickly averted them. "Jesus, Mary, and Joseph."

Risking a look at the chair again, he couldn't look away this time. No matter how much he wanted to.

James finished masturbating, his face turning an unhealthy grey shade as his body seized.

"James!" Jack yelled.

He looked like he passed out, or better yet, like he'd died. "Why are you yelling at me?" James's body shuddered one last time, eyes closed, his voice a hoarse whisper. "Most people would just turn around and leave. They don't interrupt a guy in a private moment."

"It's my house, in case you forgot. Most private moments don't happen in the living room, and they do not involve strangling yourself to get off. For most people dying is a turn off." Jack switched off the radio and closed his eyes. Another headache loomed.

"I read about it on the Internet," James said as he untied the rope.

Jack resisted the urge to run over and pull it tighter.

"It does work, you know. When the brain lacks oxygen, something fucking amazing happens. It's like you feel everything a hundred times more intensely."

In Jack's opinion, his brain hadn't had much oxygen for a very long time.

James wiped at his crotch.

Jack fumed. "Is that my dish towel?" How many of those had touched James's cock?

"I'll wash it, relax."

"If you tell me to relax one more fucking time I'm going to finish what you started there and wring your fucking neck. You want to do shit like that, find a damn room. Do not do it in my house."

"This from the king of sex-capades," James muttered. "You do far stranger stuff than I do."

What was he talking about? The hairs on the back of his neck rose one by one. Jack tried deep breaths to keep himself from blowing. "What are you talking about? You don't know what I do. You see, I like privacy. I don't use someone's living room or in their kitchen to get off."

"Maybe you should forgo the camera too then. It's hard to keep it private when you tape it for the fucking world." He glared.

Jack opened his mouth, but no words would come.

James's glare faded, a grin taking its place. "You didn't know? Come with me cousin, I've got something you'll want to see."

Jack didn't want to. He suspected what James had to show him. But a perverse sense of masochism deep inside him had to see, had to know for sure. He followed him to the study and realized James must have picked the lock to get in. Good thing he didn't keep much in there that was secret. "Just so you know, you're not allowed in here, asshole."

"Then how do I use the computer? You shouldn't keep it in here if you don't want me to come in." He pointed to a chair behind the desk.

"How the fuck did you get into it anyway? You need a password just to get past the main screen." Jack sat.

"Not a password that can block me, Jackie-O. I know how to fix spliced cables too. By the way, I want my cell phone back or you owe me a new one." James turned on the computer. When it booted, he punched in an address—a porn site—and scrolled through a list. "Now, your face is blacked out but I know my family when I see it. Even if I didn't, Whitney didn't bother to mask herself, she's quite popular."

He clicked onto a picture that Jack recognized as Whitney's room, blurry but definitely her room. It was tagged "Whitney's Wonderland; Diving to the Depths of Depravity."

"What the fuck..." Jack muttered.

The video showed Jack cuffed to the bed on his stomach. He didn't need sound to know what was said, but James had it turned up anyway. When she brought out the first of many tools she used that night, he shut off the screen. "That's enough. I'm going to fucking kill her."

"Jack, come on. What guy wouldn't love to have his exploits caught on tape. Some of them are pretty good, I'm jealous."

"There's more?"

"Shit yeah." James switched the screen back on and typed something in the search bar.

Titles filled the screen to prove that Whitney was a busy girl. He wasn't the only guy she had on tape. Jack counted the videos. Three poor bastards and several women graced her collection.

"I can't believe you didn't know about any of this; you're usually so... smart."

"I knew about the girls, and I knew she taped sometimes. I thought it was for herself not this. I'm seriously going to kill her. Fucking bitch."

She'd fucked random guys as well as her friends. Added to

that crime, she put his ass on the Internet. He would kill her very slowly.

"There's a lot of money in this shit. You can't really blame her. She's one of the most popular contributors here. She makes money every time someone watches one of these. I'm thinking of doing it too. Why not?"

"No one wants to see your nasty ass on video." Jack shook. His rage triggered a red haze that marred his vision. Even James's grinning face faded to a toothy red blob. He would slowly squeeze the life from her body. He wanted to hear her beg him to stop and then he'd punch her perfect face into a bloody mess. There would be no accident for Whitney. It would be murder, plain and simple. Jail would be a worthwhile consequence in this instance.

"You need to calm down." James sat on the edge of the desk, a serious expression in his face. "You can't afford to do something stupid. The cops are already looking at you for one death. You can't be making yourself look unbalanced."

"This from the guy who ratted me out in the first place?"

James paled.

"Yes, I know all about your little chat with the cops and you're lucky I don't shoot you right now. Maybe I'll call up your friends and invite them for dinner. How would you like that, cousin?"

"I panicked. They were asking about me, and why I was here, and it just came out. I couldn't let them ask too many questions; these guys are in with the cops. You aren't in trouble. I knew you'd cover your ass. There was never any doubt in my mind."

"I'm glad you were so sure. I should have known you'd turn me in as soon as the opportunity came up. You're a fucking liar and a cheat, not to mention a coward." Jack stood, unable to bear being in the same room as James any longer. "Your days are numbered. Get out while you can."

CHAPTER 26

Jack drove to Whitney's as soon as he watched every video she had posted. Nearly everything they had ever done was right there; online for everyone to see. With every minute that passed, Jack's blood boiled hotter. How did he miss it? How could he have been so fucking blind? He knew what women were like, and he knew Whitney was a freak.

He'd trusted a whore, and she proved what Jack had known all along: women were good for fucking and cooking. When they weren't good at either one of those jobs anymore, a smart man tossed them. Whitney never was one for cooking and she'd just lost her appeal for fucking.

He arrived at her apartment ready to squeeze the life out of her and stormed in, only to come to a full stop, almost tripping over his own feet. "You're kidding me."

Whitney sat on the couch next to someone Jack never expected to see there. The breath blew out of him and he just stood unable to move, staring at the two women. Had he been so wrapped up in his shit that he didn't see the obvious?

"Jack, how nice of you to join us," Whitney smiled. "I guess there's no need for introductions. I believe you know Michelle."

Michelle blushed.

The bitch knew there would be trouble.

She smiled and waved.

Jack didn't smile back. Would it be possible to strangle both of them? Maybe he should just knock the scheming sluts out and tie bricks to their ankles to find out how fast shit would sink.

"The question is how do you two know each other?" He tried to be calm; a monumental effort. "I came here to talk to you about something, Whit, but now it seems less important than why you have this fucking nasty bitch sitting in the living room of the apartment I'm paying for."

"That's no way to speak to someone's mother." Whitney waited for his reaction.

Jack didn't give her anything but a stunned blink as the pieces of the past few days fell into place.

"How would you like it if your future son-in-law spoke to you like that?" Whitney asked.

"You think I'm marrying you? Honestly, Whit, you're out to fucking lunch if you think I'm going to get caught in that trap. I was just surfing the Internet before I came over. Any sites you think I should check out next time? I know I came across some really interesting ones, but maybe you can direct me to more."

Michelle glanced at her daughter.

He had to give Whitney credit. She didn't hesitate. "You found my site? I planned to show you but I wanted to make sure it was going to be successful first." She stood and went to the kitchen.

She didn't fool Jack for a minute. That she went to her little cupboard and pulled down a bag of pot and her papers told him he'd scared her. She smoked to calm her nerves.

"Are you angry?" she asked. "You look a little angry. I don't know why, most men would love to show what their women are willing to do for them."

"You can't do shit like that without consent, you know? It's illegal and if you don't take everything with me in it off, I'm going to the cops."

Michelle rose too, a contemptuous smile on her face.

She couldn't be Whitney's mother; it didn't make sense. Why did he never push the issue when Whitney refused to talk about her family?

Because you were too busy getting fucked, stupid.

"You won't go to the cops. I know you have a few things that you don't want them knowing about as well. Whitney is only trying to earn some extra cash. She has a wedding to pay for in a few months."

"I'm not marrying her." How many times did he have to say it? "Did you plan this when you invited me over to get laid? Did you know about her, Whitney? Is there video of that too?"

"Wouldn't you like to know?" Michelle moved to the kitchen to roll a joint for herself. "Here's the thing, I don't like you at all, but my daughter seems to love you very much. She's never been real smart about men, but you are able to take care of her and me so I'll allow it. You will marry her, and you will look after me. If you don't, we will go to the cops with what we know."

"You don't know shit," he laughed. This had to be some kind of sick joke. It had to be or Jack now had three problems on his hands. "Whitney backed me up for the other night, by lying to the cops. They'll nail her for that, even if she didn't know I wasn't guilty of anything. So, what do you think you're going to tell them?"

"First there's the sexual harassment suit that your poor little secretary will be forced to file against you. It's a shame you can't control yourself Mr. Murphy. Second, there's the information I've gathered, and that the IRS would definitely be interested in seeing. Third, I believe there is the issue of your wife conveniently dying when you were about to split up."

The floor moved beneath him. He'd set himself up so perfectly that he was nauseous with disgust at his own stupidity. Jack couldn't believe he'd let these two plot and scheme behind his back without a thought to the possibility that they could turn on him. Hell, he didn't even make the connection between them. He'd made the biggest mistake imaginable. But they had nothing. Sure, she could go to the IRS with the books, but he could figure a way out of that. The rest? Jenny's case was closed, with no real evidence to cause them to reopen it. And a fifty-something woman, with a surgically enhanced pussy claiming she was sexually harassed by a younger man already fucking a woman, who happened to be her daughter, less than half her age? He almost busted his gut trying not to laugh.

"First, let me just say, bravo to both of you. Excellent con job. Brilliant. Well... brilliant if you hadn't fucked up some really important parts of your plan."

"We've got you, and you know it." Michelle said.

Oh no you don't, bitch.

"Do you? Let's look at the giant holes in your little scheme, shall we? I've been banging your daughter since she turned eighteen. Are you telling me that you didn't know about your daughter's affair with a married man who has kept her for more than five years?"

"I—"

"Don't deny it. You knew. How could you not? Then you applied for a job with Jay-Ray without telling me you were Whitney's mother and you ask me over for dinner and seduce me. A judge would find that kind of strange, don't you think? Bye-bye sexual harassment case."

Whitney pressed her lips to a thin line. Jack might have left it at that, but Michelle's mysterious telephone call crept into his brain. It was Whitney on the other end. How could he be so fucking stupid?

"A judge might see that as odd, but you can't guarantee I can't talk my way around that one." Michelle smiled, crossing her arms over her chest. "No one has proof I've even been in touch with Whitney. Maybe we were estranged. It's possible that a set of coincidences, such as me applying for a job with the man she's in love with, brought us back together."

She might be able to talk the right judge into believing her; except for that phone call. "Really? You think so? Well if that happens, I'll have to produce the tape I have of a little chat you and your *estranged* daughter had the other day, when you thought you were alone. Remember that call, Michelle? I already figure out who you were. I was just waiting to see what you two were up to."

He didn't have a fucking tape, but these two didn't know that. Jack grinned.

"Jack, I'm sorry it's come to this," Whitney said softly.

I bet you're sorry, you fucking liar.

"I know you want to do the right thing, I know you love me. When you said you weren't going to marry me, I called my mom because I was so upset. You should be happy I'm not the type that cares about infidelity."

"Infidelity? You are talking to me about infidelity?" Could she really be saying these things? Jack shook his head and went to the door. He'd had enough and needed to think. He couldn't do it with them standing there. "You've very nicely put your little escapades on video for the world to see, I'm not the one who was unfaithful. You guys set me up and I don't like it at all."

"Don't leave angry." Whitney rushed around the table to grab him. "Let's talk about this. My mom has worked hard her whole life and I want her to be looked after too. Is that so much to ask? You've got enough money to make sure she's okay. Once we're married, I'll give up this place, and instead of paying my rent, you'll just give the money to her. It won't cost you anymore money really."

Her hand rested on his arm and Jack removed it. He couldn't stand the idea of her touching him anymore. His mind went back to the degradation of the last time they were together and shuddered at the memory. This was the last time she'd fuck Jackson Murphy in any way, but he'd fuck her at least one more time. He was through with Whitney. She no longer had any value to him at all.

"Michelle, don't bother coming in to work tomorrow. You're fired." Jack looked down at Whitney.

She looked away.

That's right you fucking slut, I'm not going to play your games any-

more.

"Whitney, you will remove all of those videos of me and you will do it tonight. I can't be with someone who would betray me like that. When I've had time to think this over, I'll be in touch. You two pull any shit before I come back, that taped call will go straight to the police. I'm sure the cops won't have too much trouble identifying Whitney's voice on the other end of the line."

He left without waiting for their reply. Jack didn't care what they had to say. Michelle was Whitney's mother. What the fuck? His world closed in and Jack didn't know which end was up anymore. When would he be free to enjoy the life he'd earned? Why was he surrounded by assholes?

As Jack reached his car, his cell phone buzzed. He got in his car and glanced at the display.

Tony.

Jack wondered how much time he really had to deal with James. Well, he couldn't afford to put it off now. He'd called Tony about it. One monkey off his back, anyway.

"Hey what's up?" Tony said as Jack started the car.

"I think I have some information your bosses might find interesting. Can we meet?"

"Sure," he sounded nervous. Tony didn't get nervous. "Can we meet at work? There's a little problem with the usual."

"JR's?" Jack asked. That was their code for Jack's office. They didn't have one for Tony's since he didn't really have a job description let alone an office to work from.

"An hour." Tony hung up.

Jack glanced at his watch. It was almost midnight. He'd been up for hours and now he had to meet the mob about a hit.

He needed more rest. Jack figured if he could get his shit together, he wouldn't be tangled in the web he was so thoroughly trapped in. He couldn't think clearly because he was tired. He couldn't sleep because his problems kept multiplying. Now Michelle had to go too. He wondered if he should do the mother and daughter together; if one went the other was sure to raise the alarm.

One thing at a time, Jack.

James first and then the sluts. If he'd known that Jenny's death would snowball into this, he'd have eaten a fucking bullet and been done with it.

Tony sat at Ray's desk when Jack entered his office. He didn't ask how he got in. Tony could master any lock. Sometimes he unnerved Jack with his creepiness. He'd never considered paying Tony for anything but bids; until now. What was he getting into?

"Mr. Murphy," Tony drawled. "This must be important. You wouldn't have contacted me after I made it clear I didn't want you to."

Jack's mouth went dry and his hands grew moist. "Sorry Tony, but this is really important. You're the only one that can help me. I have a problem, which might also be a bit of a problem for your boss. I hope I wasn't presumptuous in thinking I could eliminate my problem by sharing with him."

"What kind of problem?"

"A pain in the ass."

Tony stared until Jack's ears burned under his scrutiny. Tony was a cool guy. He could be your best friend, but cross Tony, and it didn't matter if you were his mother; he'd slit your throat.

"This pain in the ass has a name?"

"James Murphy, my cousin."

Tony mulled this over.

He probably wondered why Jack would turn in family. Tony would understand when Jack explained that James was the worst kind of asshole, the kind that got people killed or worse—imprisoned. "You think my boss is interested in your cousin? Why?" Tony rested his chin on one hand while he tapped away at the computer in front of him. He was no longer staring.

Jack relaxed a notch. "He owes your boss a lot of money. I know this because he's trying to blackmail me into giving it to him. He's a rat, and he's dangerous. I know he's hiding out, he doesn't want anyone to know he's at my house."

"Sounds like you know a lot about his business. He can't be very smart."

"I don't know all of it, only what he's told me and what I've figured out from past experience. He's a fucking leech, and if he doesn't get his way, he turns on you. He's already talking about going to the cops to get protection. I told him that was crazy."

"What will he go to the cops with? What does he have on Milo?"

"I'm not sure. He won't say what he's going to give them. I know he's been gambling again. He left Vegas to come here. He's already knifed me in the back and I was helping him out."

"So really you're asking me to solve your problem. I don't know how Milo will feel about solving someone else's problem, Jack." Tony leaned back in the chair and smiled. "Myself, I like you and I'd do this for you. Milo, he doesn't like us to contract out because it brings heat. You understand? We've got a lot of heat right now, as you know. I don't know if one little pest is worth risking more heat."

This was not going as planned. Jack's desperation circled his gut like a bad case of chili shits. "Fuck Tony, if I didn't believe he was bad news to you I wouldn't have called. I covered him this long so I could see if he really would turn on you guys. He will. He's a liar and a cheat. He's only looking out for his own ass." Tony had to see James as a threat and Jack wasn't averse to lying like a snake to see that he did whatever it took to get that hit called.

"It's late, and I'm tired." Tony stood and walked around the desk. "I'll go to Milo and tell him what you've told me. I don't make any promises, though; Milo does what he wants. That's what bosses do, right? Tomorrow I'll come by here again. Stick around. Wait for me."

"Thanks Tony, I wouldn't waste your time. I really think

he's a loose cannon. He's been looking up FBI informant stuff and talking about disappearing for a while. You guys have been good to me and I would hate to see a little prick like him cause any problems."

"Like I said, I'll get back to you. Tomorrow." Tony nodded and left.

Tony wouldn't do shit if James didn't pose a threat to his boss. Jack knew better than to plead his case further.

The whole exchange didn't go as Jack hoped it would. They should be jumping at the chance to get rid of a snitch, but he hadn't prepared his case very well. Did James know anything to snitch about? Jack didn't have an answer, and he should have had, even if he'd made something up. The mob would be of no use to him. And if he couldn't get rid of James, he had a problem. It was only a matter of time before that fucknut opened his big trap to someone. What would he do if they found something, or just made shit up to nail Jack? Simple. He'd run. But to where? To Mexico? He had a fake passport, cash waiting, and no Whitney, Michelle, James or Detective Orca. Perfect.

Weary and fed up, Jack dragged his tired body to the spare bedroom and collapsed on the bed.

He slept fitfully.

The sound of Michelle's key in the door brought him wide awake the following morning. The bitch apparently needed to have an order drilled into her tiny head. Didn't he fire her?

Jack lunged from the bed and stalked to the front room straightening his rumpled shirt. He approached as she closed the door. She turned and jumped so high, Jack would have sworn she shit her pants in fright.

"Jack, I thought you'd still be at home. It's only seven."

"I am aware of the time. What are you doing here? I fired you didn't I?"

"You were upset, I'm sure you'll see sense once you've

rested. Go home and get some sleep."

"I wasn't upset. I was lied to. You two plotted against me and set me up. Upset doesn't even come close to how I feel. I am pissed. There's a difference, and unless you want me to show you just how angry I am, I suggest you get the fuck out of my office."

This wasn't about her fucking job. She never started at seven o'clock. He chewed his lip. Michelle's eyes darted to the desk and back to him. She stepped forward. Damn it, she'd come hoping to get in and out before Jack even got there. "Get away from the desk, Michelle."

Now he'd have to change the locks and go through the entire place. Everything in his desk and Ray's would have to be locked up. Not at the office, though, perhaps at a safe deposit box.

"You're still not seeing the bigger picture here. You can't fire me."

She was committed to her lie, he'd give her that. But Jack was no fool. Michelle didn't give a shit whether she worked for him or not. She wanted fuel for her little blackmail scheme.

Jack advanced until his face was inches from hers. She paled but stood her ground.

He would bury this bitch if it was the last thing he did. "Dead people can't tell anything to anyone, can they, Michelle? Do you honestly think I'll let you live long enough to go to anyone with your bullshit? I've worked too hard to get this far, you and your little slut won't ruin it for me now. Don't forget the little conversation you and Whitney had the other day. I play that tape for the cops and who do you think they'll believe?"

"You can't threaten me. The cops are already on your ass." She moved around him and to the desk.

Was she retarded? Why did she insist on bothering him? "Get away from the fucking desk. Now."

"I think you need to cool down and think about things for a while. Whitney and I care about you, and we don't want to give the cops anything. But if you keep acting like a lunatic, we won't have any choice."

Jack pointed calmly to the door. "Get out before this lunatic does something you'll regret. I'm dead serious. I want you out of my sight."

She paused at the desk and looked at him for a moment. With a sigh, she picked up her purse and made her way back to the door. "I expect to be paid for the day. You are the one who sent me home when I tried to do my job."

She'd get everything she had earned and then some.

He waited for the door to slam shut behind her and then slipped behind Ray's desk. Nothing but a couple of photocopies of job bids lay on top.

Into the shredder with those.

He pulled open the top drawer and scanned the ordered pens, paperclips, and various other items that Ray stashed inside. There was nothing damning. So far so good.

The bottom drawer didn't budge. She locked his fucking desk? Of course she did. So she could come back later and remove whatever she'd hid.

From the top drawer Jack grabbed the pearl-handled letter opener that once belonged to Ray's mother. He stabbed it into the flimsy lock until it clicked.

"Fuck me." A pile of discs rested on top of the neatly stacked paper inside. Each disc was labeled with a year and Jack's name. This is what she'd wanted. Jack picked up the phone as he began snapping each disc into pieces.

"Harvey here."

"Hey, Harv. You busy?"

"Jack? No, I'm never busy. Need something?"

"Yeah. You remember those guys your firm had switch out your computers and shit last year?"

"Sure, it was my wife's brother-in-law. He's cheap and keeps his mouth shut."

Perfect. "I want to update the computers here to start fresh. Jay-Ray is no more, so I want to start with all new files, close the old shop up. Know what I mean?"

Harvey was silent for a minute. "So you want the hard

drives wiped?"

"I need everything on them to vanish. Is that possible?"

"Sure it is. You can have the lot of them destroyed for the right price."

"Price doesn't matter. Can you have him come in tomorrow and get rid of these computers, after making a backup of accounts and contact databases, of course, and then install entirely new systems? I want my computers at home done too."

"I'll see what he's got going on. Hey, thanks for thinking of him. Guy's got a new baby and—"

"You tell him if he can do everything by end of business tomorrow, I'll give him twice his regular rate."

"Done."

"Thanks."

Suck on that, Michelle.

CHAPTER 27

Tony arrived that evening when Jack had nearly lost his mind waiting. To keep his sanity, Jack busied himself by calling his supervisors to check on jobs nearing completion. He had a company that did payroll and invoicing, so if he wanted to step back from the business he could. Jack's main job was to get the contracts, and he paid a quantity surveyor on the side to handle the tedious details, but he just didn't like not knowing what was going on. Everything seemed on schedule. At least, he didn't need to worry about that. Shit, who was he kidding? Jobs would be pretty fucking scarce if his luck stayed in the shitter.

Jack also checked that his money had moved around. He'd started this when things went downhill with Jenny. Little amounts that wouldn't be noticed and under names and business numbers that wouldn't be checked right away. If something happened, he had a cushion. A guy going to prison could lose everything. It would be a damn shame to lose what he'd worked so hard to keep.

Out of sheer boredom, he called the kids. Allie was anxious to come home, but loved her new friends, and hated the idea of leaving her new horse. "I miss you, Daddy."

Jack's heart did a strange thing at the sound of her little voice.

Just like the fucking Grinch.

The stress must be making him crazy. He didn't care about his kids, not enough to miss them. "I miss you too, Allie-Cat." Did his voice just catch in his throat? Well, Allie was the best of the bunch; his mini-me. So, of course he'd miss her just a little.

"Will you come get me at summer?" she asked.

"Sure, if you want to come home for part of the summer, I'll send the plane ticket. Okay?"

"Cool. But not until July. Okay Daddy? The Show is in June, after classes are out. They said I could help and if I learn how to stay in the saddle, I get to go in the parade at the end."

Jack smiled as she listed off the friends who invited her to summer homes and on vacations. "Hey, if you want to do that stuff, go ahead. Don't worry about me. What's important is that you have fun. I'm a dad, I already had my fun."

"You're silly, Daddy."

"I know. Just let me know what you're doing when the time comes. Okay? No decisions until then. I have to call your sister now, so I'll talk to you soon."

"Kay. Love you."

"Yeah. Me too." Jack hung up, hating the lump that rose to his throat. His life just did not allow kids. Fuck, if they'd been around through this mess he'd really have a shit-show happening.

After keying the number for Jasmine's dorm, Jack gave her room number to a crackly voice that answered. He waited, and waited. Then there was yelling and a short discussion. He heard Jasmine saying to take a message. Then a sigh. "May I ask who's speaking?"

"It's her fucking father, and you can tell Jazz if she doesn't come to the phone I'm revoking her tuition and she can come back to public school."

There was more talking and yelling, then silence.

Jack tapped the desk, ran a finger over the dust on the

computer, and leaned back in his chair.

"What?"

"Hey Jazz, I miss you too." Jack was a little irked that she didn't jump at the chance to speak to him.

"Sorry, I was busy. Homework, you know?"

"Sure. Homework. So you like it there?"

"I love it. Actually, I was going to call you next week sometime. See, Julia, she's my roommate and her family is ridiculously rich, you can't even imagine, anyway: she asked if I could spend the summer with her. On her yacht! Please, can I go?"

"Of course you can, honey. That sounds like fun. Will her parents be there?"

"Well duh, yeah."

"Okay. Just checking. I'll let you get back to your... homework."

"You're the best. Love you. Bye."

Jack set the phone down. Jasmine would never come home. As long as Jack sent the money, she'd be content to stay away forever.

He searched the rolodex for the number to Paul's school. The man who answered forwarded him to Paul's room. Interesting. Paul had a "room," not a dorm line. Jasmine would be so jealous.

"Hey Dad. What's up?"

"You have your own room?"

"Yeah, most of us do. Just the scholarship kids have to share, really. We get houses. It's pretty cool."

"So you like it? You want to stay?"

"Fuck, yeah. I mean of course. You won't believe the soccer teams around here. Amazing!" Paul droned on and on about his soccer team and some girl he met.

Jack drifted away a few times. Paul could talk to a fucking rock and be happy. His grades probably weren't the best, but as long as Jack paid, he would stay in that school. Or rather, as long as Ray paid since Jack now used their trust money.

After a glance at the clock, Jack decided to order pizza

while he waited for Tony, afraid to leave in case he showed. One thing Jack knew for sure: if the mob told you to stay put, you didn't go making them try to find you.

Paul ran out of boring shit to talk about and they said their goodbyes.

By the time the door opened, the pizza had come and gone.

Tony walked in, a smile on his face.

Jack took that as a good thing.

"Jack, we have a problem." He still smiled which seemed strange considering his words.

A problem? Fuck, James was like a fucking stray cat that just kept coming back again and again. If the mob couldn't get rid of him, how could he? "What's the problem?"

"It seems you've attracted a lot of attention in the past months, my friend. The kind of attention we don't like. Milo is concerned that taking care of your cousin might draw some of that attention our way."

"James drew that attention to me and the little prick will do the same to you. Why can't you see that?" Maybe the mob was a bunch of retards too. It didn't surprise Jack that he found more idiots as he went along.

"Yes, I see your point. What you need to understand though is that he has nothing on us, but a lot on you. He's really no threat to us right now. You get me?"

"Yeah, I get you. Christ, what am I going to do then?" Jack paced the floor and his insides tightened at the thought of that bastard breathing another day. "He's lying to the cops, they're asking questions about shit I had nothing to do with. He's blackmailing me and he's going to get away with it. I need him gone, completely."

"I have a suggestion, if you're interested. It's not something most guys would consider but I think you are a special kind of guy. I think you could handle this."

"What?" So wrapped up in his own misery Jack didn't really think about what Tony said. When Tony touched his shoulder and Jack looked at his face, he knew this wouldn't go his way.

"Sit, listen. You have some decisions to make."

Jack sat.

Tony smiled.

He was not an attractive guy. Short and compact, his hair receded rapidly and his nose had lumps from too many fists slamming into it. But when Tony smiled, you forgot all of that. That was his secret: a smile that could win anyone over.

"The way we see it, James is mostly your problem. He could potentially cause us some discomfort but not enough to risk the cops looking too closely at our organization. Milo has had some bad press lately and he's trying to keep his nose clean, so to speak."

"James is already talking to people. Isn't that going to make eyes turn to you guys?"

"Possibly, but he has nothing. Do you honestly think he'd be around if he could hurt Milo? He'd be in the dirt by now entertaining the worms and the bugs. No, we're bothered, but not worried. You, one the other hand, have a major problem. He could really ruin everything you have here. Now, I've come up with a plan that should satisfy all of us."

Jack wasn't interested in this plan. It meant bad things for him. More work and more problems. Fuck, why couldn't he just live in peace? Hadn't he earned that?

"We are willing to give you the contract on your cousin."

What?

"You get rid of him and we are in your debt, if you need something we will get it. Well... as long as it's reasonable, we will. Milo doesn't want to be linked in any way to it, but he would appreciate the favor."

"So you guys want him gone but you don't want to do it. Fucking lovely, I told you the cops are looking at me already. How am I supposed to do this?"

Tony grinned again. "I have some ideas. Are you up for them?"

Well why not? What did he have to lose except everything?

"Fire away. I don't have a lot of choices here."

"Everyone has choices, Jack. Most of us are afraid to make the right ones. You, my friend, you know what needs to be done. I have great respect for you. I know you don't let problems fester and grow until they blow up in your face. Nice job with Ray-man by the way."

Jack's eyes narrowed as his testicles climbed inside his body. Shit. How did he know?

"When you're in the business of getting rid of problems you recognize a solution when you see one. It was a great one, but your next job was sloppy. I hope there are no more witnesses for that, or the cops will be at you."

"Only James and his ex-girlfriend. She won't talk though. I've got enough to sink her. She's too smart to risk it."

"She could be an issue, but you'll deal with her later. Here's what you need to do, okay? First, get James out of your house. Don't do the job there. Too many possible issues and having someone die in your house always raises the wrong eyebrows."

Tell me about it.

"He needs to disappear, without leaving behind an easy-to-find body. There are many ways to do this. I'm sure you'll figure that out. Make sure he is gone, like a ghost. Not a trace left of him. This will work, because your cousin drifts. He never stays in one spot for long."

"He's too busy finding a new target to con. I thought I had gotten rid of him years ago, yet here he is like a bad rash."

"You should have taken him out then. You'd have less to worry about now. You need an alibi too. If they notice him missing—or if you fuck up and someone finds his body—the cops will ask questions."

"I won't fuck up. If I'm going to do this, I'll do it right."

"Good, I know you'll be fine. We've got a picture of James. I had my guy snap a few today while your cousin was walking to his car. We're going to get him a passport. Not real of course, but I guarantee it'll get him on a plane. Don't tell him where you got it, of course. And I need an alias for him. You guys book your flights on different planes, a day apart, and stay in different motels. Not just different rooms, you hear me?" Jack nodded. "When you propose your plan to him, tell him something like you don't want us to link his escape to you.

Trust me, he'll be so worried about saving his ass, he won't question it. Now, let's go over a few ideas I have and then I'll leave it to you. I don't need to warn you about keeping your mouth shut do I? If you get caught, you'll still go to jail even if you do rat us out, and Milo's reach is very long."

"I'm offended that you'd even think I'd turn on you, Tony. I'm not like that."

"That's what I like to hear. Maybe when the heat's off, we can help you with that piece of ass you've been hanging onto for a while. Hey man, I've got Internet too. She's pretty hot, but I gotta tell you, no matter how fine the ass, it's not worth the hassle."

"You have no idea. That one I can manage on my own. Thanks anyway. Her fucking mother is another story. I'd like to see a bullet in her head today."

"Just saying, I'm around."

By the time Tony left, Jack's plans were made. James would go on a permanent vacation.

As he was about to call it a night, Jack fielded another call from Detective Newman.

"Sorry, Mr. Murphy. I know it's late."

"Yeah, so?"

"Can you come down and see me again?" she sounded nice. *Too nice.*

"Shit, I just don't have time to go anywhere right away. Can I come in closer to Friday? I've got all these damn jobs to run. I can't keep up here on my own. Is it urgent?"

"No, Friday is fine. See you at nine thirty?"

"Perfect. Thanks."

She hung up.

Jack stared at the phone. His curiosity would have to wait until Friday. He had a business trip after all, one that couldn't wait.

CHAPTER 28

James was not happy about going anywhere. He wasn't a total dickhead and knew it wasn't wise to trust anyone—especially the cousin he kept trying to ruin—but Jack eventually convinced him that it was in his interest to go along.

"Listen, I've heard rumors and I think your best course is to just lay low. What better place to go than out of the country?"

"What have you heard?"

You've got him now, Jack.

"Just things here and there. My friend Tony was asking about you; he knows some people and was wondering who you were and where you came from. You know I don't like you, but I can't afford another body turning up. If you don't come you're causing me a lot of problems."

James looked doubtful.

Jack kept pushing. "As I've already explained, I got a lead on a huge job in Canada, not too far away. We can fly out, I can meet with the guys I've called and then maybe just travel a bit. Canada is a nice country to disappear into. No one asks a lot of questions either. I hear they just nod and smile. They're kind of slow; probably from the cold. Anyway, I got you a fake

ID, so no one will know where you went. You book a flight and a room somewhere with that ID so anyone looking will just find me traveling alone. You won't be on the flight. We won't be seen at the same hotel."

James seemed to be considering it as he chewed his thumb-nail.

Fucking chewers.

The beauty of Jack's plan was that he had made some contacts and *did* have a meeting, which provided the alibi he needed. He'd never take a job in Canada. It was too cold and full of illiterate morons. Also, he could barely understand their messed up English. *Here, monsieur, eat some poutine and wear the toque when yer ootside, eh? No, don't be a hoser, just put the dang thing on. Good stuff. Now, have ye ever swam in the lake in January? Oooh, yer in fer a treat, eh?*

"Are you coming or not?" Jack asked.

"How long are we staying?"

"Depends on how long it takes me to negotiate a deal with this company. I'll probably stay a few days at most I think. You? I don't know. I need someone to keep an eye on things if I get the contract. With your new identity, you can stay as long as it takes for Tony and his pals to forget about you and you could earn that money you need so badly, and hide out from whoever you pissed off."

Forever asshole.

Jack figured he should have a bag packed just in case things went to shit. Some cash to get him through until it was safe to begin using his secret accounts, some clothes, a fake passport and he'd be good to go. Maybe he'd stash James's car some-where too; somewhere easy to get to, but not too obvious. Whitney's? Perhaps. If he couldn't get to it, then Plan B might be his only option.

James shrugged. "Okay, I guess I don't have much choice. Who's Tony?"

"Tony is the guy that gives me the bids, you know? He sets me up to get the jobs. I pay him a little cash and he looks after my interests. He works for a family though, and I don't think you want him sniffing too close."

Sweat formed on his brow and his eyes widened. "You should have said something before."

Yeah, you worthless little prick; you are in deep shit.

"I didn't think about it. Before the cops started looking at me, thanks to you, I didn't care if you went swimming with cement shoes. Now, it kind of looks bad on me if you do. It's not because I give a shit whether you live or die, I want you gone as much as they do. I just can't afford for you to disappear right now."

"Give me my money and a passport, and I'm gone." He shrugged as though it were that simple.

"I can't afford that either, stupid. If I pay you off, there's a trail. If there's a trail, then they're on me for helping you get away. No, it's best for us to just lay low. Maybe you could stay up there with the fucking Eskimos for a long while. I'd pay for that."

"When do we leave?"

"As soon as you can pack. Your flight leaves tomorrow night. I'll follow on another flight. I've got your motel booked and I'll call you as soon as I get to mine. There's too much bullshit around here. A few days working up in the arctic wastelands will cool things off, I think."

On the way to the airport, Jack called Detective Newman to confirm he would be in at the end of the week. She nearly lost her usual calm when she heard "Canada" in his plans, but regained her control quickly, and demanded the names of people he had to see, and dates and times. He was happy to oblige.

Try to break this alibi, you bovine bitch.

As far as the world and the police were concerned, Jackson Murphy traveled to Canada alone. The passport James used was probably for a dead guy the cops hadn't found yet. Tony, or someone working for Tony, had slipped the documentation under his door just that morning. Jack didn't tell James who made the fake passport, and James didn't ask.

Newman mentioned James, asked how things were going with his little "issue." Jack replied he'd fucked off the day before.

She sounded surprised.

He explained that his poor misguided cousin never stayed anywhere long.

He hung up as James exited the bank wearing Jack's sunglasses and his jacket.

James opened the passenger door and tossed the bundled cash he'd been given at Jack. "I'm surprised you didn't take this and run."

"Still have plenty of opportunity, don't I? I just want to get the fuck out of here before those guys show up. You remember you promised me half to stay up there. Otherwise how am I gonna live?"

"I said I would, and I don't break my word."

The money wouldn't go to James at all. It'd be safely tucked away into a Canadian bank account so he could transfer it later to one no one would find.

"Now are we going?" James asked.

"Just one more stop. I need you to do the same thing at another bank. It's kind of nice how your forgery skills are working for me now, rather than against me."

"Yeah, fucking great," James grumbled.

"Look, if I take it out myself, they know I paid you. If you do it, and I can prove to Tony that it wasn't me, then they have no idea I sent you anywhere. Works for both of us."

James didn't reply.

They made it to the airport in plenty of time to catch James's flight. Thanks to Tony's advice that he should buy a second round-trip ticket for the day after his flight so the cops wouldn't be lurking around on the actual day of departure. Tony said that cops liked to nail people at the airport, and Jack didn't need Newman seeing him with James. That would blow his story out of the water and render it impossible to get rid of the little prick. Jack bought his real ticket after seeing James off. Paid through the fucking nose for it, but any amount was worth ticking another problem off his list.

They made it to Toronto without incident. Maybe Fate had once again found Jack's side.

The first day, he called James and told him they'd meet up the following afternoon, leaving James to do whatever it was James did in a motel room.

Canadians were a polite bunch, courteous and intent on keeping Jack happy. Usually he had to impress the man with the money, but in Canada, the man with the money tried to impress Jack. Maybe business in the cold North wasn't such a bad idea. Jack could hire some of their guys and take the job after all. A major retail chain wanted to build stores all over the country. They needed a construction company that could do the jobs right, but cheap. Jack was up for it.

He scheduled a dinner meeting with them for the following day. He could get rid of James, and then make some money. Everything would be so tight that they would have a hard time putting Jack at the scene of the crime should his body be found. First, he must decide where the crime scene would be.

Tony gave him a few ideas and he checked them out, covering it up as a "tour" of the great Canadian landmarks. James enjoyed himself, he loved Canadian women; whom Jack had to admit were pretty fucking hot, and a lot more accommodating than most of the women he knew, even if they did talk like rednecks.

That first night Jack managed to snag a red-haired beauty, who worked with the men he'd met with about the contract. The couple of hours spent with her were more to cover his tracks than anything, but he definitely wanted to keep in touch, eh?

It wasn't until they came through a tiny town north of Toronto that Jack found the spot. They'd gotten turned around on a dirt road and ended at an abandoned quarry: a huge hole filled with murky water and crumbling rock. The old buildings that once housed the guard station and what looked like a maintenance shed, were overgrown with brush and covered with dust and grime.

"What a wasted opportunity to make money," Jack said.

James joined him next to the edge of the immense hole. Jack estimated it to be a twenty-foot drop into the water below. The water itself must have been at least that deep again. "Fuck, these people just leave a goldmine to rot. What a bunch of morons." Jack shook his head.

"It's a hole in the ground."

"It's a quarry, numb nuts, they blast the rock off and grind it up to be sold to construction companies, shingle manufacturers, and things like that. There's still a lot left to be used."

"Maybe you should move here and start a new company. I think the Canadians might just be good for your attitude."

"I don't think so. I have enough going right now."

James leaned over to peer down at the water. The temptation to push him off was almost unbearable. Jack knew though that while it was almost certain the fall would kill him, there was a small possibility he could survive. James would do that just to spite him.

"I'll get the camera out of the car; a guy I know may just be interested in this."

James shrugged, unconcerned.

Jack hid the grin he couldn't keep from his face. The hassle of the trip would be so worth everything he'd endured because of James.

That fucker won't know what hit him.

He lifted the trunk and took out the gun Tony had arranged for him to collect in Canada. Once he was rid of James, the gun became the issue. Getting it had nearly caused him to have a heart attack. He took a letter Tony had given him to an address where the biggest, ugliest motherfucker he'd ever seen answered the door of a quaint little house on a dead-end street. Jack stammered and produced the note. The man smiled, exposing a mouth full of rotted and broken teeth, slapped Jack on the shoulder almost knocking him over, and invited him inside. He'd given him the gun, ammunition, and a warning about what would happen should it ever be traced back to him. He showed him how to take the gun apart and suggested that the pieces not be found together. Jack had gone on his merry way hoping never to see the man again.

As he walked back to the quarry, Jack began to shake. He wasn't scared, but excited and a little worried the whole thing had gone too smoothly. Nothing went smoothly for Jack anymore. Something had to go wrong.

"Have you given any thought to staying here?" Jack asked as he approached James.

"Why would I stay in this shithole? No, I'll go back to my own country thanks." James glanced at him briefly then turned toward the car.

"I think you're staying." Jack raised the gun and pointed at the back of his head.

James stopped as though sensing the danger.

"You have fucked me over long enough, James. It ends today."

"You won't do it." He didn't turn but clenched his fists. "You can't get away with something like this. The cops know you're here. Once they find my body, they'll put two and two together. You'll be fucked."

"Who says they'll find a body?"

The shot echoed across the quarry, deafening Jack who watched as though in a dream.

As the bullet hit him, James spun. His eyes widened with shock before falling to the ground to look at the sky.

Jack walked over, the gun aimed at his face.

James blinked and shook his head. "You're fucked, Jack," a whisper.

He fired again.

James's face exploded in a shower of bone and flesh. Some of it covered Jack's shoes and the bottom of his pants. That might be a problem.

"No, James. You are fucked."

He paused long enough to savor the moment. Jack wanted to remember this feeling later. Taking care of things himself was very gratifying. So much better than the *accidents* he had set up before.

Jack shook his head and forced his thoughts back to reality, then set about finishing the job. He dragged James over to the edge of the quarry; a heavy piece of shit too. He searched the body until he found James's wallet. After pocketing it, Jack selected a large enough boulder along the edge of the clearing, close to the tree line, gathered a roll of electrical cable from the car and fastened it to James's waist. He made sure to tie enough knots so that the damn thing would not come loose. Couldn't have him popping up too soon.

Pushing him over proved to be a problem. Jack shoved the body over the edge, but the boulder held fast.

Fucking great.

James hung, dangling over the edge, blood dripping everywhere. Of course, he couldn't make this easy for Jack. The bastard would be a pain in the ass right to the bitter end.

He tried to push the boulder over but it was stuck; it wouldn't budge. To use the car was out of the question; if he scratched the paint or dented it, to explain the damage would be a problem.

Fuck!

Panic threatened at the back of his mind. "Think, Jack, think." He glanced around until his gaze fell on a shed under the trees. Jack ran over to it and kicked a rusted padlock, but it held. Frantic, he ran back to the car and searched the trunk until he found a tire iron.

At the shed, he pried the hasp off the rotted wood. "Thank you, Fate. I love you."

When his eyes adjusted to the darkness inside the shed, Jack spotted a shovel and other tools leaning against the far wall. Running back to the boulder, Jack dug at the edge of the quarry and under James's cable. Slowly, the dirt and gravel gave way and the boulder moved. He gave it a push and it went over the rest of the way. Jack's heart raced as the boulder plummeted with James trailing behind it.

It landed with a huge splash, then bubbles rose, and then nothing but murky water rippling as James sank into the depths. Fucking brilliant, if he hadn't taken the wrong turn he would have never found this place. Tony was right, when you keep your eyes open, good things happen.

But now he had to clean up the blood and there was a lot of it. Jack shoveled the mess from James's face and brains to the edge of the quarry and then over. Then he scraped the spatters around the area. The blood down the edge of the rock face was impossible, but then, if no one leaned over and looked closely, it would blend with the soil.

His clothes were an issue. He'd have to get new ones before returning to the motel, but to do so he'd have to go into a store.

His careful planning hadn't been careful enough. He ran back to the shed. Inside he found barbed wire, which he used to shred his pants and add a few cuts to his shoulder and hands.

Working out his story as he got into the car Jack grew confident that he just might pull this off. Barbed wire stung like a bitch. He got lost, had to take a piss and tried to climb a fence. As the stupid city folk that Jack was, he got tangled in barbed wire.

Perfect.

Back to the main road, it didn't take too long to find a gas station and get directions back to town. The guy even gave him clean clothes and helped him clean up and bandage his hands. In the tiny, disgusting bathroom of the gas station, he dissembled the gun and then wiped and wrapped each part in paper towel. He put part of it in the sanitary napkin box that hung precariously on the chipped brick wall and the remaining pieces in the garbage can out front. The attendant, seeing him struggle to fit his garbage inside the almost-full bag, came over and removed it, carrying the garbage to the dumpster out back. These Canadians were so hospitable; a guy could get away with anything. A guy just did, actually.

The next morning, Jack met with the retail chain's head honcho. He gave them his bid, which was a little too high for their liking, and said his goodbyes. Jack promised to keep in touch and look over the figures again.

All in all Jack was proud of himself. He'd committed the perfect crime, and could arrive home a day earlier than planned. Just two more to go and he would be home free.

CHAPTER 29

Detective Newman didn't wait for Friday to arrive, but Jack figured she wouldn't after learning he'd taken an earlier flight. As soon as he stepped off the plane and powered his cell phone, it rang. Jack peered at the number and knew he couldn't put it off. He had to go see her. Maybe she didn't think he could be guilty. Maybe she wanted to nail good old Jack and was calling him in just to look at his handsome face. Women like her were either stalkers or lesbians, so it was a possibility.

"Jack Murphy," he answered.

"Mr. Murphy, nice to have you back. All went well in Canada, I hope."

If he put a bag over her head, wore gloves, and made her talk dirty the whole time, she might be doable, as long as he didn't have to touch her with any part of his body. "Not really. It was a lot of running around for nothing. My bid was too high for their liking. I'm not giving up though. So far I'm the only bid they have."

"Good, I hope that works out for you." She paused.

Jack waited. No, he couldn't fuck her, not if it meant his life. He just couldn't imagine trying to straddle that beast.

"I'm actually near the airport right now, could we talk somewhere? It's rather urgent that I speak to you."

"Is this about Thorne again? I told you, I barely knew the guy."

"No, it's not about Mr. Thorne. Some things have come to my attention; disturbing things that make me question a few of your statements. I just need to clear up some confusion I have, nothing else."

"Sure, where are you now?"

"I'm at the airport."

Fuck, she was determined. She was probably waiting all night for him to fly in. "Okay, I'll just get my bag, put it in the car and meet you in the bar. How's that?"

"Sounds fine." She hung up.

Jack went through the baggage recovery routine, running over possible problems in his mind. He carted the bag to his car, and then headed to the bar. Ray? There could be problems there. What if someone decided the lines had been tampered with? He'd placed himself at Ray's already. What if she figured that he had no reason for being at Ray's house? What if a neighbor saw more than he thought? Jack wouldn't put it past those fuckers to be peering in the windows.

Detective Newman sat alone at the bar. A few guys gathered at the far end, giving her lots of space. She was probably used to sitting alone, drowning her sorrows in a Bloody Mary. He waved.

She smiled.

The guys looked at him with pity. They probably figured he had to be gay... or slow, to be hanging out with such a walrus.

"Mr. Murphy, I'm glad you could spare a few moments. Should we take a table? It's a little more private."

"Sounds good." Though he could kill for a JD and Coke, Jack ordered a beer and joined her at a table in a dark corner.

She produced her notepad. "I'll get right to it if you don't mind."

Jack took a deep breath. She was all business.

"Cut yourself?"

"What?"

She pointed to his hands. "Your hands are cut. How did that happen?"

Right, his barbed wire story for the Canadians. "Oh, I was looking over a job site and we had to climb through some brush. I wasn't prepared for such a rural environment so I didn't have any gloves."

"I see. You should have them looked at before they get infected."

"I intended to make a doctor's appointment when I got home, but you called me first."

She smiled. "Let's get down to business then. I was speaking to your girlfriend and she backed your alibi, but something strange happened later. We have reason to believe that Whitney was with her mother on the day and night in question. When I called Whitney, she gave me her lawyer's number. Any thoughts?"

"How about you tell me who is claiming that I'm a liar?"

"It was an anonymous email."

What kind of shit was this? What did she think she knew? "I'm not sure I believe you."

"Doesn't matter what you believe. We had a tip through our website, which provided me with some emails and directed me to a site run by yourself and your girlfriend. This site has been running for some time, since before your wife's accident."

"I had no clue about that site until last week. No one can say that I did. I'm fucking pissed about it to be quite honest." Fuck! He knew that would bite him in the ass more than once.

"That's interesting because the money generated from those videos is placed in an account linked to your business. Can you explain that to me?"

She probably masturbated until her fingers cramped to those videos. That was likely the best sex she's ever experienced and now she's going to use it to nail him. Jack would bet she went straight home and watched them all again. "I set up an account for Whitney a long time ago. I wanted to make sure she stayed in school." Lie like a rug, that's what he'd do. "I didn't know that account was used for anything else. Perhaps you can check if besides transferring her monthly allowance I've ever handled it. I don't even know the balance. Had I known Whitney had another source of income I would have stopped pouring money into that account. Sure, I'm an idiot. But there are millions of guys like me out there. It doesn't make me a murderer."

"No, but it does put things in a different light. Why didn't you mention that you were seeing this woman when you were questioned after your wife's death?"

"I was freaked out, and in shock for crying out loud. It's not the kind of personal thing most people would volunteer unless asked directly. Jenny's death was an accident. That much is clear. I loved her, and I love Whitney. I wouldn't hurt either of them."

"Hmmm... you understand my reluctance to believe you?" She stared.

Hatred bubbled in his chest. He had to control it. This was one woman he couldn't afford to piss off. There was too much at stake and he hadn't solved the Whitney-Michelle problem. He had to make her believe him again. "Look, I know I'm an asshole. I can't help it, I need more than one woman can give me. I've even cheated on Whitney since Jenny died. I just can't seem to stop myself. I did love my wife. When she died, we were planning a second honeymoon. I wanted to end things with Whitney and make my marriage work. I can't prove it because Jenny is gone and can't tell you what we discussed." Jack tried to work up some tears, but he was only so good and settled for lowering his head in shame.

"But what about her affair with Ray?"

Fuck, that annoying piece of information would haunt him forever. He'd forgotten she knew about that.

"Ray and Jenny? That wouldn't have lasted. She just wanted to make me jealous. Tit for tat, and all that stuff."

"From the evidence I've looked at, they had more than a meaningless fling. I think your wife was planning to leave you, and I think you knew that."

Act surprised, act pissed. Give her the performance of your fucking life.

Jack worked up his indignation. "Are you kidding me? We were working things out. Ray was my best friend. They were.... Oh my God! If they were alive, and Jenny was in love with him—which I don't believe for a second—Ray's guilt over betraying me would have overwhelmed him and it would have ended." Jack stared into her eyes, hoping he looked like he believed the bullshit he just handed her.

She looked down at her notepad, obviously uncomfortable.

Good job, Jack. Give her some more.

"Why would my wife suggest the cruise then? If she was so fucking in love with Ray, why would she be so insistent on working things out with me?"

"Mr. Murphy, I'm not sure what's going on here, but I think maybe I should have investigated more before giving you this information." she blushed. "I'm not sure what correspondence you've read between your wife and Ray, but in those emails that were given to me, your wife and your partner were planning to kill you. I can't tell you the contents exactly as it is still a murder investigation, but it makes you look suspicious."

"I guess if I'd known they were doing that I might, but there's nothing like that on the computers at my office. I read all of Ray's email. Not one thing about killing me. How can something I knew nothing about be used as motive for murder? How would I have known?" His hands trembled. Good effect. Wait a minute. How the hell did she get her hands on new emails, unless she'd gone into his office before he shredded the stuff from Thorne, and had Harvey's brother-in-law wipe the computers? "How did you come by these new emails? I mean, who gave them to you? If someone went into Ray's or Jenny's computer and copied them, then—isn't it a crime to read someone else's personal email?"

"Okay, that's all I need for now. I think you need some time to clear your head." She stood and gathered her things. "This isn't over though, I'm sure you can understand that. I don't know if you are lying or being truthful, but what we found is an excellent motive for murder. Given that the two people who betrayed you died from freak accidents, I'm going to keep digging until I am certain of what happened."

"They were accidents."

"In my experience, the more unusual the "accident" the more likely it wasn't one. I'm just doing my job. If you are innocent, I'll prove it. If you're not, I'll see you pay for your crimes."

He stared after her. What a fucking messed up situation. Candi wouldn't be so fucking stupid, but Michelle was the only other person who could access those emails. She would be that stupid. If he went to prison, that miserable slut would suffer. Jack wouldn't go to prison though.

CHAPTER 30

The days after his meeting with Detective Newman went by in a haze. Jack thought he caught people staring everywhere he went, and realized he was becoming paranoid when he imagined cars watching his house.

Think logically, Jack.

Really, who would be watching his house? There was no reason for the police to waste valuable manpower to watch him when he'd done nothing wrong. Nothing they knew about anyway.

He finally spoke to Whitney after she failed to return the dozen messages he left her. She agreed to meet outside the University.

When she saw him, she smiled, but slowed her pace, as though uncertain of the wisdom of the meeting.

That's right, you little bitch. You should be scared.

"Jack, I'd have called, but I thought we broke up." She said.

"I thought we broke up," Jack mimicked her honeyed voice. "I told you I'd be in touch and you're fucking ignoring me. Sounds like you really give a shit about me. What happened to marriage and all that fucking crap? I know I said we were done, but look at this from my point of view for a hot second. How would you feel if you walked into the shit I did? Imagine someone you trusted conspiring to fuck you over. Maybe you didn't intend to do anything shady, but don't try to tell me your mom's on the same page."

"You don't want to marry me." She pushed past him and toward her car. "I don't want to force you into anything. I value my life more than that."

Grabbing her arm, Jack dragged her to his car.

She opened her mouth to scream.

He kissed her hard and then drew her closer to whisper in her ear, "Keep your fucking mouth shut if you want to make it home. I'm serious Whit. I've reached my limit. Get in that car; we are going to your place. If your mother is there, we can go to my house. We have a lot to talk about and you aren't getting off that lightly. Clear?"

She nodded.

Jack opened the door. When she hesitated, he pushed her in and quickly jumped in beside her.

"You've lost your fucking mind. This is kidnapping. You'll go to jail for it." She crossed her arms and stared out the window.

He was dealing with a child; he had to remember that. She was no more mature than Jasmine and didn't see the danger of her situation. "Is your mother at your place?"

"No, she fucked off with some guy a few days ago. She'll be back once she's taken him for all she can."

"Why do you want to ruin me, Whit? What have I done to deserve this?" He wanted her to feel bad, to want him again.

She surprised him by laughing. "I don't want to ruin you. I want what you have. I want what I've earned the past few years. You fucked me and went back to your wife, thinking a little cash would be enough. You get rid of that wife and then try to get rid of me; what do you expect me to do?"

"I've never tried to get rid of you. I don't want to get rid of you." Lying seemed to work every other time. "Shit Whitney, we had something amazing and now I can't trust you."

Jack pulled into the lot in front of her building.

She shot out of the car.

He had to hurry to catch up with her. She wasn't going to get off that easily.

"Just go away," she said at the door. "Either give me what I want, or go away."

"Fine."

"What?"

"Fine. You want to get married? You got it. Set the date."

She stared, her mouth wide open.

Jack almost laughed but knew she would blow if he did. "But the site goes and your mother goes."

"I'll close the site, but you can't ask me to never see my mom again." She recovered from her shock and opened the door.

Jack pushed her in ahead of him; no point in giving her a good target. He knew the value of never turning your back on the enemy. Hadn't he taught James that recently? "The cops just told me that Ray and Jenny were sleeping together, and planning to kill me. Wonder how they know this? I'll tell you. They know this because of the emails your mother stole from my computers."

Whitney looked suitably surprised.

"She's a fucking menace, and she can't be a part of our life. I won't tolerate her bullshit."

"Just pay her bills, and we'll move away where she won't be able to come see us often. She's my mom, come on."

"You're lucky after all the shit you've done to me that I'm even considering marrying you. You're not in the position to be making demands."

She spun around. "And you think you are?"

By the way her eyes darted around, and the tremble in her body, she was close to losing her shit. Good. He could deal better with anger. Whitney didn't think clearly when she was pissed.

"Where's James?" she asked. "Can you tell me that? You disappear to Canada for a week and James is suddenly gone. That smells a little fishy to me."

"I paid him off and he left. End of story."

She raised an eyebrow.

Fuck her, he didn't answer to her. Jack couldn't wait to put a bullet right between her fucking eyes. "You honestly think with all the heat your mother has brought on me I'd risk getting rid of him any other way? Shit, you are stupid. I haven't killed anyone. Get that through your tiny little head."

"Don't call me stupid." She moved into the living room and sat on the couch. "You know I hate that. What do you expect me to think? You're not the guy I fell in love with. You're different. Ever since your wife had her *accident* you've changed."

"Give me a break. Are you kidding me? Wouldn't you be different? My wife dies. A few weeks later my best friend dies. I have cops breathing down my neck about that, and about some asshole I didn't even know who clearly had a heart attack."

She didn't look at him.

Jack knew she mulled over the possibility that he might be innocent. He made a great actor, and she was not a great judge of character. "I'm not a murderer. I just want to be left alone to enjoy the life I've earned without the bullshit."

"I'm sorry." She met his gaze and surprised him by smiling. "I don't believe a word you say. I know you set Jenny up, even if your hand didn't kill her. Ray... I'm not sure but *I know* you had something to do with it. James is gone and that reeks of you as well."

"Why the hell do you want to marry me then?" Women were fucking mental. Plain crazy and he was done trying to figure this one out.

"I love you," she said. "And I know you can love me with the right incentive. We can be good together, Jack. You'll see."

She stood and stepped into the bedroom, glancing back to give him her special smile.

Well hell, why not? If there was one thing she was good at it was fucking. He might as well get it while she breathed. "Does this mean it's a yes?" He trailed behind her.

"Yes, we're going to get married...."

As much as he despised her, his cock didn't share his feelings; it grew hard as soon as she started to unbutton her shirt.

"....tomorrow." She removed her clothes.

CHAPTER 31

Tomorrow?

Fuck, his life got worse every minute. He'd hoped to get a few days to plan how to get rid of her before the wedding. Now he had fewer than twenty-four hours. How was he going to get rid of her in less than a day? Perhaps it would have to wait for the honeymoon.

Maybe he'd tie her up like she did to him, and let her see how getting more than just his cock shoved up her ass felt. She'd probably like it. That was the sad part. Whitney was a strange animal, and Jack a fool not to have seen how dangerous that could be.

After a disappointing round of boring, married people sex, she jumped up and grabbed the phone.

"What are you doing?"

"I'm calling my friends. They'll want to be there."

No fucking way, this would be a secret wedding. Then, when she disappeared, it wouldn't be so interesting to Detective Newman. "Can we just keep this between us for now?" He removed the handset from her hands.

She turned, hands on her hips.

Shit, now she was mad again. "Just think about it for a

251

minute. It will look really odd for me to remarry already, to the woman I've been fucking since before my wife died. They're already questioning me about it. They'll think you and I planned it."

Good lie, Jack. Thank you Jack, I do try to please.

"What? Why would they think I'd kill her?" She looked panicked.

Perfect.

"I told them it was bullshit but they don't buy it. If we announce it to everyone, you're going to look like a pretty believable murder suspect along with me. Do you want that?"

"Shit, you should have waited for that cruise and dumped the stupid bitch into the ocean," Whitney said. "That's what I would have done. Then, she'd just be missing. They wouldn't have anything on you."

If Jack had to have a partner in crime, Whitney would have been cold blooded enough to do it. Too bad she turned out to be about as trustworthy as a rabid wolf. "I didn't kill her. I won't say it again."

His cell phone warbled. He reached to the floor next to the bed where he'd discarded his pants.

Detective Newman.

Jack pulled his pants on as he answered.

She didn't give him time to say hello. "Where are you Mr. Murphy?"

"I'm at a friend's house. Is there something wrong?"

"I've just received a call saying that your girlfriend was abducted from the University parking lot by a man who fits your description."

"You're joking, right?" Who would call and say he kidnapped her? Did the Fates switch teams again?

"No, I'm not. Are you at her house now?"

The fucking cow should be the next one to go. Too bad he couldn't afford to snuff a cop. It would be a pleasure to get rid of her. "Yes, would you like to speak to her?"

"I would."

Jack handed the phone to Whitney. "It's the cops. They

think I kidnapped you and probably think I'm torturing you right now. She wants to talk to you."

Whitney took the phone. "Yes, this is Whitney. No, officer, I'm fine... I don't know where you heard that, we're fine... No, he didn't... Okay, if you think you should... Yes, I'll open the door... Thank you, bye." She closed the phone and burst into laughter. "Oh Jack, your little cop girlfriend is coming to check out the situation. Should I be timid and scared? Should I cower at your manly presence? Is that what she wants?"

"Don't you dare. Just act like yourself."

Fucking cops. Goddamn rhinoceros-looking, fucking whale, stupid bitch, cops.

Why wouldn't she leave him alone?

She must have been outside because the buzzer sounded within minutes.

Whitney answered.

Detective Newman strode into the apartment, one hand reaching around to her side, eyes alive, scanning the room.

Did she think he had an army in there? Jack glanced at Whitney and suppressed a laugh at her expression. That must have been what he looked like when he first saw Miss Newman.

Whitney quickly recovered and returned Jack's glance in amusement.

"I'm sorry, but I have to check out these calls," Detective Newman said. "I saw video of you forcing her into the car." She peered at Whitney. "Are you sure everything is okay?"

Whitney chuckled. "I'm so sorry, I should explain." She looked at Jack. "Is it okay if I explain, baby?"

"Sure." A void opened on the pit of his stomach. Whitney had the look about her that said that she was up to no good.

"Well, Jack and I like to play games. I don't know if you've seen our website, but it's something we do quite a bit. I told him some day I'd like to role-play an abduction. I wanted him to snatch me from somewhere public and then "rape" me all afternoon. It was just a game. I didn't think about what people around us would think. I feel so silly now."

What a piece of work. She was ruining his credibility. Jesus, she was killing him.

Detective Newman blushed. "Oh, I guess that makes more sense."

She'd wonder about the sex, and definitely look for the video on the site tonight; Jack just knew it. *Too bad bitch, you won't be dildoing yourself to my tight ass tonight.* There was no rape scene to tape. "So, you aren't going to cuff me and take me downtown?"

Newman looked like she'd punch him.

Try it you stupid cow.

"I told you I'm innocent, I don't know why you think I would be capable of any of this."

"I'm just doing my job, Mr. Murphy. It's nothing personal." She turned to the door and paused. "I'd like it if you stayed close though, just in case I need to speak to you."

"What do you mean?"

"I mean don't be traveling anywhere; you are a murder suspect."

"Is that official?" Fuck her. If she didn't have a reason to arrest him, he'd go where he wanted.

"No. I can't stop you from doing what you want. I'm just asking you to stay around here. It's wise to do as I ask. Traveling out of the country again makes you look suspicious."

"I'm already guilty in your eyes."

She turned to glare.

He gave her the old Jack grin, designed to melt the panties off normal women. Newman wasn't normal. "I may as well do as I please until you arrest me for this bullshit. When I prove that I'm innocent, you'll look like an idiot."

She didn't reply. The gloves were off. Jack realized she'd do whatever she could to lay Jenny's death at his feet. He wouldn't be surprised if she tried to bundle James's disappearance and Ray's botched suicide there too. He'd die before going to prison. No joke.

"What a train wreck," Whitney giggled. "That beast is just gross. You weren't kidding. She has a hate on for you too. What did you do? Is she mad because she's the only female on the planet you didn't try to nail?"

"I don't know why she hates me, could be the fact that you and your mother keep giving her reasons to think I'm a fucking creep and a liar. I told her that site wasn't mine and you say it is. Shit, I can't believe you."

"It's not a big deal. I'm taking it down today anyway. Married women don't do that sort of thing. Besides, I won't need the money. I'll have my husband to take care of me." She wrapped her arms around his neck.

Jack let her kiss him.

Your husband will definitely take care of you. He'll take care of you real *well.*

"I guess we better get packed then."

"Where are we going?" She pulled away slightly. She still didn't trust him.

"We are going to Vegas, baby. We've got a wedding to attend."

She squealed and ran to her room to pack.

It was a shame she wouldn't be around to enjoy the honeymoon.

CHAPTER 32

Whitney talked all the way to Vegas. By the time the sign welcomed them to the city, Jack wanted to cut her tongue out. She was too excited to speak after that; just stared at the casinos and the lights glittering in the night sky. No need for real stars in Vegas.

"This is amazing. I can't believe I've never been to Vegas. We should move here."

"I like where I am just fine. We're here to get married and then we're going home." Like he'd live in this place; bunch of fucking con artists and sluts. No thanks. He had enough of those at home.

"I wish we could have invited someone. My mom would love this place."

"Kind of hard to invite her when you don't know where she is."

He didn't believe for a second that Michelle was gone. Whitney knew where she was and she'd probably told her what they were up to. Jack tried to keep an eye on her, but women were sneaky. She probably hid a phone in the bathroom. That long shower was likely to cover her excited call to dear old Mom.

"Little Slut to Big Slut, we've got him now. He's such a sucker. Don't worry; I'll have his account cleaned out by Christmas. Then we can move on to a new schmuck."

Wouldn't they be surprised when he turned the tables on them? "I thought we'd go sightseeing first, and then we'll go to the chapel."

"It's dark. How are we going to see anything?" She looked at Jack like he'd gone nuts.

Maybe he had. After all that he'd been through, who wouldn't be a little crazy? "The guy at the chapel said he couldn't fit us in until midnight. We've got like two hours to kill. I asked him what we should do in the meantime and he said if we drive out into the desert, there's an amazing view at night. I've got the directions right here." What a brilliant liar he was becoming. Jack did have two hours to kill—her.

He pulled out his phony directions.

She looked at them briefly. Whitney was about as useful as a blind monkey at reading directions. She could get lost going to the store. "Sounds boring, let's go to a casino."

"Then we might miss our appointment. Those places have no clocks and believe me, you'll lose track of time. Once that ring's on your finger, we'll go blow a few grand, maybe win a few more."

She bought this lie as well.

Away from the city the darkness was absolute, but for their headlights flooding the road. It was perfect.

Whitney crossed her arms over her chest. "How the hell are we supposed to see anything? It's pitch black out there, I think you've been fooled. That guy wasn't serious. I bet he's laughing at us right now."

"Okay, I lied."

She turned.

Jack caught a spark of fear in her eyes. It made him want to laugh maniacally. He didn't. That would ruin his plan. "I wanted to have my way with you out here. Imagine it, no one for miles, just you and I, fucking like animals in the dirt."

Her eyes lit at the thought of something new and deviant.

Jack had counted on her need for nasty, weird sex, when he planned his little jaunt.

"How far are we going?" she asked, breathless.

"I think we'll turn off the road soon. It looks like you could drive anywhere here; it's all a dirt road really."

"Let's try to find one of those cliffs," she said.

Jack was a little put off by this suggestion. It was what he planned to do but her wanting to do it made him a bit nervous.

"I want you to fuck me right on the edge."

"That's a little dangerous Whit. What if the ground gave way under us?"

"You're no fun. The whole point of it is the danger."

"How about I take you from behind facing the cliff? Then you can look down at it, almost like you're hanging over it."

He turned off the road and the car bumped through the barren desert. He'd never get a good trade on this thing now. Beamers were not meant for off-roading. He should have got a rental.

"I guess that will have to do," she sighed and looked out the window. "Leave the headlights on and talk to me like you're a rapist and you're going to kill me."

She was seriously fucked up. Why hadn't her odd behavior triggered alarm bells in his brain earlier? "Why would you want that?"

"It's been in my head since I made up that shit for that cow cop. I think it will be fun."

"Whatever my girl wants, my girl gets," Jack said.

She reached over to run her hand over his cock.

Of course it was hard. He could barely wait to find a spot and wondered what it said about his mind that killing Whitney while he fucked her turned his crank. Probably nothing good.

They approached a spot where the ground rose, before dropping sharply into a canyon that looked to be a good depth. That should keep her happy. Jack slowed and turned off the engine leaving the lights on as she asked. "Here we are. Where are you going?"

Whitney had hopped out of the car and scurried to the

edge. "I don't want to do this. Please just let me go and I won't tell anyone," she begged.

What the—right, kidnapping. The game was on. "Get on your knees bitch," Jack would give her what she wanted. It would be pretty convincing too. "Do what I say and you might live through this."

"Oh please, I just want to go home," she cried.

He wanted to laugh at the look on her face. Although her voice trembled, her eyes shone in anticipation. Jack checked his pocket for the cord and moved toward her.

She backed away, stopping at the edge of the small cliff.

"I said on your knees."

She dropped to her knees and lowered her head.

Fuck, this was going to be so easy. "Bend over like the bitch you are." He pushed her.

She fell on all fours and whimpered, but looked back grinning.

"Turn around. I don't want to look at your slutty face."

Her smile faltered but she turned.

Jack lifted her skirt to rip a tiny lace thong from her body.

Her breath came in short pants.

Jack roughly shoved his fingers inside her; she was flooded. Yeah, she would love *almost* every minute of this. "You like that? I knew you were nothing but a fucking whore."

"Please no, I just want to make you happy. Then you can let me go."

He jerked his hand.

She gasped.

He knew what she liked. For Whitney, the rougher the better.

"Oh my, I don't know what to say."

"Tell me you want me to fuck you like a dog," he said into her ear. "You want it hard and fast don't you?"

"Yes, I want it hard. Like a dog. Like a bitch." She pushed her ass against his hand. "Just don't go too fast."

"I'm not going slow, bitch. I'm going to pound until you beg me to stop. Then I'm going to keep going until you bleed."

As he rammed his fingers, she gasped for breath. Jack knew she wanted to turn the tables, but she was too into it to object. He removed a condom from his pocket. No evidence. Slipping it on, Jack whispered into her ear. "Are you ready for me bitch?"

"Yes, please don't hurt me," she sounded like she meant it, which made Jack want it more.

It was a shame he had to get rid of her. He'd have a hard time finding someone else like her.

He pulled the cord from his back pocket, and positioned himself before grabbing a handful of her hair.

She didn't protest, but went very still.

This was fucking brilliant, he couldn't wait until he had Michelle on her knees and then, finally, his problems would be solved.

Jack entered her fast.

She cried out.

He didn't slow down, but kept pumping her until he climaxed.

She struggled to be free of him.

He yanked her hair to keep her in place.

"Jack, you're hurting me. This isn't funny."

"No. Is it? Now you know how I've felt since you fucked me over."

She tensed.

Jack let go over her hair and slipped the cord around her neck.

"What are you doing?"

"Game's over Whit, it's time to say goodnight." Jack twisted the cord tight and pulled.

She scratched and wriggled beneath him as the breath left her body. The cord broke the tender skin of her neck, causing her blood to drip onto the dirt.

"Your mother will get the same," he whispered into her ear.

She stopped struggling, her eyes bulging rather unattractively from her face.

"No one fucks me. I told you that before. I earned what I

have and no one is getting any of it."

"My mom, she knows I'm here," her voice came out in a hoarse sigh. "She'll take you for everything."

"I've moved all of it, you stupid bitch. As far as anyone else is concerned, Jack Murphy is broke. She won't get a fucking dime and she wouldn't live long enough to spend it if she did." He pulled the cord tighter, watching her face as the last breath rasped through her lips. Blood trickled down her chin, the cord rubbing against the delicate bones of her throat.

As she went limp, Jack realized he was still inside her. He pulled back. He didn't fuck dead chicks.

Jack waited awhile to be sure she was dead, even kicked her a few times.

She stared, unblinking at the night sky above.

Five down, one to go. Now to get rid of the body.

CHAPTER 33

Jack buried Whitney in a spot farther down the desert road, deep within a crevasse, certain she wouldn't be found for a very long time. Well, as long as she didn't get dug up by the coyotes, everything would be just fine. Did they have coyotes in the desert? Jack didn't know, but she was so nicely packed into the dry ground it wouldn't matter.

Her purse and her bag Jack threw in a dumpster at some shitty little town on the way home and he drove through a car wash to remove the sand before heading home. He had his story. Whitney took all the cash he had and vanished. So sad he'd been such a fool. Now he'd lost everything because his cock overruled his brain.

Take that Detective Newman.

The pleasure he derived from taking someone's life disturbed him a little. But Jack consoled himself by choosing to believe the satisfaction meant the deaths were justified. These people tried to fuck him. He just got there first. Really, who wouldn't love to destroy someone who was trying to screw them? Jack knew that any guy, given the opportunities fate had gifted him, would have done the same without hesitation.

Now his problem was Michelle. How to find her? And

when he did, what to do with her? Where was easy: she'd come to him when Whitney didn't report in, or rather when she ran out of money. He'd have to be ready. Jack was fairly certain she'd go to Detective Walrus. He had to prepare. His story was solid, but that didn't mean that Newman would buy it.

Jack drove like a madman to arrive at Whitney's just before five that morning. A total of nine hours away from home; time enough to have been asleep all night oblivious that his new fiancée had left in the night with everything he had. Jack would be frantic, of course, and a little pissed.

Scanning the parking lot for unusual cars or people, and tallying the same vehicles that were parked in the numbered spaces every day, Jack went up to her door and went inside.

Everything was as they had left it. Even the note he'd slipped on the counter remained sealed on the same spot. No one had been in. Perfect again. Maybe he should have been more open to a career with Milo and Tony. Nah, he couldn't handle the stress, one lie leads to another as his mama always said. Things got complicated when you had too many of them to remember.

Jack opened the note; it would be the first thing he noticed when he woke to find Whitney gone. Oh, what a terrible thing it was to read. The writing was Whitney's. She left it for her Mom at Jack's gentle urging. There were no names but the note itself, when read as though directed to Jack, took on a different meeting. He mimicked her writing the best he could and scrawled "Jack" across the top in her girly, bubbly, hand. It looked the same as the rest of the note.

He scanned it one more time, marveling at his genius.

Jack,

You're probably wondering where I am. I know I said the wedding would be tomorrow but I couldn't wait. I'm writing because I know you'll worry and you're probably pissed. Things just haven't gone as we planned, and I'm sorry for that. But you took off and I can't wait for you anymore. I have to watch out for myself in the end. You've taught me well.

You'll find the accounts empty. I know that wasn't part of our deal, but you can take care of yourself. It's only money, right?

Till we meet again I want you to take care, and please don't be angry with me. Love you, Whit.

Whitney hadn't cleaned any accounts out before leaving, but Jack had told her to add that because it wasn't right for Michelle to have access to Whitney's hard-earned money. She believed his line of shit, and even suggested they close the account. If the old bitch believed Whitney had nothing, she'd run back to her daughter's, raising hell. Just as he hoped she would. He had finished cleaning his accounts before leaving for Vegas, so that the letter would verify his later claims. He'd put some of the money in Whitney's personal account, to make things look good, the rest he'd moved around to places he hoped the cops wouldn't look. With the mess at the office, the video surveillance of James posing as him at various banks, Jack could lay the blame for his missing money at James and Whitney's feet. Neither of them would be able to say otherwise.

He made a cup of coffee and sat on the balcony.

Almost time to call the cops.

He wouldn't ask for Detective Newman; that would be too obvious. He'd do what any other person would: ask for their fraud department. After all, he'd been robbed.

Sipping his coffee Jack stared out at the quiet street. A few people emerged from their apartments for work or their morning run. One old man walked a pathetic-looking dog further up the street. The thing was the size of a rat and wore a purple sweater, because everyone knew that summer weather was so fucking frigid. Any man who would take that thing out in public deserved to have his balls cut off.

Probably named it something stupid like Killer.

He glanced at his watch and set his coffee down. Cell phone in hand, Jack ran the story over in his head. This time he could play the victim. Once he was through, Jack couldn't wait to see Michelle try to play the damsel in distress. Her daughter just stole from him, and fucked off. Worse, she did it on the eve of their wedding. What kind of mother raised a daughter like that?

Jack keyed his bank's number first. "Hello, this is Jackson Murphy. I'm afraid there might be something wrong with my accounts." The voice on the other end sounded alarmed and promptly put him through to the manager. "Yes, thank you for speaking to me. I seem to have no money left in my accounts. I was wondering if perhaps I was mistaken."

A couple of moments of silence as the manager searched the computers to verify this information. "There have been several withdrawals. Are you saying this wasn't taken by you, Mr. Murphy?" he asked.

"No, it wasn't. So it is gone?"

"Seems so. Two transfers went to outside accounts that I'd have to track. I'm not sure if I can reverse them. Then there were several large cash withdrawals a couple of days ago. I'm afraid we have signatures for those that match what I have here on file as your signature, so there's nothing that can be done on our end until we can check the videos. This is probably a legal matter, I'm afraid."

Of course it's a legal matter. The bank had the right signature. James signed for them and he could forge anything. However, a good look at the videos would prove it wasn't Jack. Naturally, the police would believe James had taken off, and therefore could not be a murder victim. Not by Jack's hands anyway. "Should I call the police?"

"Yes, as soon as possible. If they find who did this, we might be able to return some of the money to your account. If they can't...."

"Understood. I'll be in touch."

Jack smiled as he hung up and then keyed 911. Someone planning such a thing might dial directly, but not a guy who happened to be an innocent victim of a dishonest whore.

A pleasant female voice responded, "Emergency services, how may I direct your call?"

"I've just been robbed. I think the bitch took everything."

"Who took everything sir?" she sounded a little irritated.

Good.

"My girlfriend. We were supposed to go to Vegas today to get married. She's gone. My bank account is empty.... God, I'm so stupid."

"Are you okay sir? Is anyone hurt?" she sounded condescending now.

After all, Jack was just a stupid ass who got himself taken for a ride. Why would she treat him with respect? "If I find the little bitch, someone's going to be hurt."

"Okay, calm down and don't leave your location. May I have your name and address please?"

"Jack Murphy, I'm at her place. I woke up and she was gone. Fuck, we were supposed to get married today. What am I going to do now? I've got nothing. Does insurance cover something like this?"

"I don't know sir, you would have to call your insurance broker and check that out. I'm sending a car to your address, Mr. Murphy. Just stay there. The officers will take your statement when they arrive."

"If I wait here she's going to get farther away isn't she? Shouldn't you be sending someone to check the airports? What if she leaves the country with my money?"

"The officers are outside right now, they can direct you from here." The line went dead.

He smiled. Nice fucking service. Who cares about some poor sap who got duped by his girlfriend?

Rapping at the door brought Jack to his feet. He suppressed a snort when he greeted the cops standing outside, and coughed to cover it up. One tall and skinny and the other quite round made a perfect "ten." Before they could speak, Jack yelled and ragged about what a miserable slut Whitney was.

"I cheated on my wife for her. Do you know how much money I spent on her already? I'll tell you. Lots. Too much. Fucking paid her way through school and this is the thanks I get."

The officers blinked, neither offering their condolences nor bothering to calm him down.

Jack switched tactics. "God I loved her. How stupid am I? We were getting married today. Going to Vegas and—shit. I've been a complete ass."

"Sir, can I ask why you believe she took your money?" Fat cop asked.

Jack tossed the letter at him. "That's why. I called my bank, but we still have to check it all to be sure. I think she got everything in my business accounts. Her mother has all of the access codes, pin numbers; she looked after my books so she had access to my personal information. I thought it was strange that I couldn't find a couple of important files on my computers the other day. Is it possible for someone to just wipe the hard drives? Fuck, I'm finished."

They read the letter and tall cop took out a little notepad. He made some notes and then the questions began. Jack found them very helpful after that. By ten thirty, he was on his way to work and they had launched the search for Whitney.

While Jack waited for Whitney to be found he planned his revenge on Michelle. He could taste the sweet victory already. He was almost free from every pain in his ass.

CHAPTER 34

Jack rummaged through files, checked his numbered accounts, and tried to figure out how to disappear. After four hours of plotting and scheming, he'd almost figured it all out. The phone rang and he grabbed it off the desk, not bothering to check the number. "Jay-Ray Construction."

"Mr. Murphy, I hear you've run into some trouble," Detective Newman didn't sound pleased.

"Yes, I have. Word gets around fast."

Let's see you turn this one on me you filthy pig.

"Well, you are a subject of interest here. When your friends go missing, it tends to be a permanent move. Is there anything you want to tell me?"

"You're joking right?" What did she expect him to do? Did she think he'd just confess? Some genius he'd be if he gave it all away. Jack moved closer to freedom with every minute that passed; she just didn't realize it yet. "That cunt steals my money and you're asking me if I want to tell you anything? Yeah, I want you to catch the bitch before I do, or *I will be* guilty of murder."

"Have you heard from Mrs. Wilson?" she asked.

"Michelle? No, she's probably with her thieving bitch of a

daughter right now. I won't hear from either of them Detective." Jack wouldn't tell her if he did anyway.

"Hmm... are you quite certain you haven't seen Mrs. Wilson?"

What was this now? "No, I have not. I fired her only a couple of weeks ago. She's not likely to give me a call just to say hi."

"Are you at work?"

As if she didn't know exactly where he was. "Yes I am."

"Stay there. I'm sending an officer over to escort you home." She hung up.

Why would she be escorting him home? Fuck her. Jack had money safely stashed at Whitney's; they'd never find him. Forget planning the getaway, he'd just go. Jack barely managed to pick up his keys when the door opened.

Two large men in uniform stood there, hands on their guns. "Mr. Murphy, please come with us."

"What's going on? I don't understand... have I done something wrong?"

"Just relax sir, you aren't under arrest. There's been an incident at your house and we'd like you to come with us for your own safety."

An incident? Jack's phone warbled and his heart missed a beat. Christ, if he didn't die from the stress of the past month alone, he'd have to commit himself to a mental institution. Almost afraid to look at the number, Jack took it out of his pocket.

The payphone.

Shit, Jack couldn't answer his call with these two in front of him. Fuck, he'd have to. The last thing he needed was Tony breathing down his neck. "I should take this, it might be my girlfriend—ex-girlfriend. Lost girlfriend. The one that took all my shit."

They nodded.

"Jack Murphy."

"Are you alone?"

"No."

"Call you back in an hour." The line went dead.

What the fuck? An hour from now the cops might have his phone and Jack could be rotting in a cell. "Wrong number I guess." He shrugged and walked past the officers. "Can I take my own car?"

"No sir, we'll take you home. We can send someone by to get your car if you'd like."

I don't think so asshole.

"That's all right. I can take a cab in the morning. It's not like I don't have to come back here every day anyway."

They insisted that Jack walked between them. He mulled over the day's events as they walked down the hall. They couldn't have found Whitney; Newman would have said something. If they had, he'd be in handcuffs, not walking casually between these two Neanderthals. While this was all fine and well, it didn't mean Newman wouldn't find a reason to arrest him. Tony's call didn't bode well either. Maybe someone had found James. It was highly unlikely, but still not impossible.

Jack got to sit in the back of a cruiser parked right in front of the building.

Just fucking great.

He frowned and lowered his head. Now everyone could see the cops taking him away. That would do wonders for his already shitty reputation. He could see his crews freaking out. *The boss is in jail, we don't have anyone to pay us. Oh no, what are we going to do?* Jack figured he might as well kiss his business goodbye.

Things didn't look much better when they arrived at his house. Police cars crowded the sidewalk, two right on the damn lawn. Yellow tape stretched around the property. Neighbors came out to see what was going on, maybe to find out who else died in the Murphy's house. Jack didn't look at any of the assholes.

Let them wonder.

Inside, Detective Newman spoke to a man in a white suit. She glanced up and said something quietly to the man. Smiling, she walked over. "I'm sorry we keep meeting under these circumstances. It seems every time we speak, someone is dead."

"Strange."

Snotty fucking wildebeest.

"I'm afraid we have a problem here. There appears to have been a break-in, and a murder."

"What?" Jack didn't have to pretend to be shocked. He was. Who would break into his house? Who did they murder? "This is unbelievable. Please tell me this isn't happening."

"It is happening and I do have one piece of good news for you."

"What's that?"

"Apparently you have an alibi for the time of the murder. Isn't that convenient?"

"Slow down here a minute. Can we take this from the top? Who broke into my house?"

"Michelle Wilson."

"Michelle?" So this is where she went. Whitney must have hoped she could get his banking information and whatever else they were going to take. "And who is dead?"

"Michelle Wilson."

"So you're saying that Michelle broke in and then killed herself? That makes no sense."

"I'm saying that the neighbors watched her break into your house. A few hours later, one of them called to report screaming and we sent a car around. We found Michelle dead."

"Why didn't they call when she broke in?"

Rotten bastards. Nice neighborhood my ass.

"That's unclear. It didn't seem important at the time. I can ask, but I'm getting the impression that you weren't well liked by your neighbors."

"They can kiss my ass, the pricks. This is supposed to be a community that uses a neighborhood watch system. Nice to see my co-op fees at work. They'll watch all right, while I get cleaned out."

"The issue here is what happened after Mrs. Wilson broke in," she reminded him.

Not in his books it wasn't. She got what she deserved.

"Someone came in around eight this morning, almost exactly at the time you were on the phone with 911, and they shot her in the head, execution style."

"Are you saying what I think you're saying?"

"Mr. Murphy, I need to know if you have any connections with organized crime."

"No. Why?"

What have you done Tony? I said I'd do this myself didn't I?

"You said your cousin had ties to organized crime. I'm thinking that either the bullet in Michelle's head was meant for your cousin, and this was a matter of someone being at the wrong place at the wrong time, or this was a hit."

"A hit? Why would you think that?"

Play dumb, Jack. She's a woman after all, without a man's natural instinct.

If she were a man, she'd have caught on to his act long ago.

"She was on her knees, her hands bound behind her, and shot in the back of the head. The assailant was standing. That's a hit."

"Umm... anyone could have done that intentionally. I mean, we've all watched the Sopranos. How do you know someone didn't make it look like a hit?" Stupid, Jack berated himself. It was like putting a big neon hand over his head.

Her eyes narrowed. "How well did you know your girlfriend's mother?"

Shit, he should learn to keep his big mouth shut. "Well enough I guess."

"She told us earlier that the two of you had issues. That you forced her into a sexual relationship she terminated because of her daughter. She said you began to threaten her after she ended it, and later you fired her."

Fucking cunt. Just had to hammer a few nails into his coffin before she died. "That's bullshit. I didn't even know she was Whitney's mom until last week. They set me up and I'm ashamed to admit I fell for it. Our sexual relationship lasted one night, and she didn't even have the courtesy to finish the job. Then she tried to blackmail me. She threatened me, not the other way around. She was a con, and so is Whitney."

"Do you want to know what I find strange, Mr. Murphy?"

"What's that?"

"Your girlfriend's mother is dead; a woman you despised and who you claim was blackmailing you. On the same day, her daughter suddenly vanishes with your money. Seems rather odd to me. Do you have any idea why these coincidences keep occurring around you?"

"You're the detective aren't you? Tell me why a man would arrange a murder in his own house? I'd need to be psychic to guess when she'd be breaking into my house so I could do the job, wouldn't I?"

"Still, Michelle and her daughter crossed you, and now she's dead."

"I'm just a regular guy who's had a lot of bad luck. I've all but lost my business. I have no money, and there are assholes coming out of the woodwork to take a piece of me wherever they can get it. Whitney took my money and fucked off. She probably shot her mother. She's not one for sharing. She did it here so that I would look guilty. But as you said, I have an alibi. I'm not able to be two places at once. So it doesn't really matter what I think, does it?"

Newman glared.

Jack wouldn't have thought she could be uglier but now he knew better.

Fuck you. I know my rights.

"I think we need to look at this from my point of view, Mr. Murphy. Then maybe you'll see why I find myself wondering about you."

"Please, go on."

"First your wife dies, stung by bees that you pay a gardener to ensure are not on your property. She carries a bee kit, but the coroner finds nothing in her system, which leads us to believe the syringe was empty. Strange, but not sinister by itself. It may have been a simple mistake."

Jack nodded. No one could pin that on him.

"Second, your business partner who just so happens to be sleeping with your wife blows up his house. This is after trying to commit suicide and calling the paramedics for assistance. An otherwise sweet man, liked by everyone, intentionally kills two strangers and himself. Stranger than your wife's death, yes, but still not evidence to take you to court. It's still under investigation, just so you know."

Jack's heart beat faster. No, he'd been so careful. They couldn't prove anything, could they?

"Third, a man who has been giving you some competition, and who wants your business, suddenly dies of a heart attack. An attack possibly brought on by his distress over a robbery at his office. The medication that is usually in his desk mysteriously disappears, as well as some important documents. Of course, you had an alibi for the robbery. The problem there is that your alibi is suspect. One person corroborated it, but she has reason to lie for you."

"It wasn't a lie. I was with Whitney."

"So you say." She moved to the kitchen and took her notebook out of her pocket. "Fourth, your cousin vanishes just before you schedule a work trip to Canada. He has yet to return. Why would a man, who is wanted by the mob according to you, and was blackmailing you to get out of this trouble, just vanish without his money?"

"My bank manager said they didn't know who cleaned out my accounts. Maybe it was James."

"Didn't Whitney's letter indicate she took your money?"

"Maybe they worked together."

"Does that sound like something James would do?" She asked.

"I gave up trying to figure him out long ago."

Fuck you. I'm not going to break.

"Fifth," she continued, "your girlfriend takes off in the night with your money. A man, who has proven himself intelligent enough to climb his way to the top from nothing, is taken by a young girl. A girl who only a few days ago, claimed you were getting married. Why would she do that if she were going to have access to the money anyway? Why now?"

"She's a whore. She didn't want to be tied down. Maybe she didn't like that she'd still have to ask for money. It's not like she could legally get into my accounts, even if we were married. Maybe she figured out that she'd only get *half* of what I earned after the marriage." Jack smiled. "I don't know why she did it. If I did, I'd have been able to stop her. I trusted her."

"Sure you did. Last, your fiancée's mother is shot, execution style, in your living room. Coincidentally, this occurs while you are at her daughter's apartment on the phone or with the police because your future wife has taken you for a fool. You can't explain of course, why the mother broke in or who would shoot her in your house. Do you see the common threads here?"

"I'm sure you'll tell me, but I feel I should remind you that Whitney confessed to stealing my shit. Her mother was probably planning to clear out the safe at my house. Maybe Whitney had the same idea, but didn't know her mother was already there. Ever consider that Whitney shot her to set me up so she had more time to run?" Jack opened the fridge and took out a beer. Her disapproving frown pissed him off. Jack drank half of the bottle before letting out a loud belch. It was his fucking house.

"Six people dead within a few months. Every one of them linked to you in some way. Every one of them had crossed you, or had been costing you money. Each person is dead under questionable circumstance, and you don't have what I feel is a believable alibi for any of them except the last."

"Doesn't matter what you believe. What matters are the facts. That's all the courts care about, Detective. And you're mistaken. Four people died. Not six." She couldn't spring that trap on him. James and Whitney took off, like he said. He'd never admit to anything else. "Two of that four had a very small connection to me. One of the other two was depressed and suicidal. The other one, my wife, had been planning a second honeymoon with me. I wanted to work things out with Jenny and I believed she did too. In the end, she was the one who planned to kill me. I'm the victim here, detective, not them."

"I'm sorry, you're right. Four dead, two missing."

"Two took off. They can't be considered missing when they left willingly."

"I want you to stick around for a while. No traveling or anything like that. If you leave, we might have enough to arrest you. Do I make myself clear?"

"You can't arrest me. I've done nothing wrong."

"There is a dead body in your home, Mr. Murphy. The woman is someone you strongly disliked, and that raises some red flags for me considering these other events. You had the motivation and the means to kill her even if it wasn't by your own hand. Although you have an alibi, it's not impossible that you hired a hit. While it makes little sense for you to have it carried out in your home, there is the possibility that something went wrong. You can leave any time and go anywhere you like, but consider how that might look to law enforcement. You are a suspect, and suspects don't leave town if they're innocent."

"They do if there's a cop trying to railroad them. What do you have against me?" She had nothing or he would have been in cuffs.

"I have nothing against you, if you are innocent; I'm having a hard time accepting that six people are dead, or missing, and you had nothing to do with their deaths or... disappearances. I'm just doing my job. If you are innocent, I will give you a full apology. If you are guilty, and I will prove it if you are, I'll see you rot in prison for the rest of your life."

"When I prove that I'm innocent, I'll have your fucking badge."

Take that Detective Orca.

"As long as we're both clear on where we stand." She smiled and the hairy mole, which he'd nicknamed Steve, disappeared into her cheek folds.

She was gross... and desperate. Her boss was probably breathing down her neck to get this shit wrapped up. She'd take any patsy she could find. Jackson Murphy would not play the patsy.

CHAPTER 35

The house was a crime scene and Jack couldn't stay. He packed some clothes, watched closely by two cops, and went back to the office. He couldn't go back to Whitney's because the cops were all over that shit.

Fuck. Way to screw it all up, Newman.

He called Harvey.

The lawyer freaked out. "Shit Jack, what have you been doing? Four people dead? Two missing? Fuck, I'm a corporate lawyer not a defense attorney."

"I know you can do this." Why was everyone abandoning him? "They haven't pressed charges because I'm innocent. I just need someone to look out for me. They're trying to pin it on someone, and that someone, unfortunately, is me."

"There's a guy in the firm that deals with criminal law. I'll call him and see what he thinks. You said you've got alibis for these murders?"

"Harv, two were accidents, one was a heart attack, two took off, and only the last was a murder. I only need an alibi for that one and I have it. The fucking bitch who has the case hates me. She's just trying to trip me up." He figured the guys listening to his calls knew the bitch that was Detective Newman.

"Fuck man, I need a drink. This is major. Like cluster-fuck major. You said Whitney took everything? That could be a problem."

What? Was he kidding? After all the business Jack had given him, he would haggle over money? "Listen, she didn't get everything. I have a few clients who owe me money. I can probably round it up, just not right away."

"Stop, I don't want to hear anymore. The partners won't represent you without a retainer. I'm sorry but I can't take on a case without their approval."

"I just checked with my bank, and someone impersonating me made large withdrawals. They have the bastard on tape and it isn't me, but I can't touch those accounts because the police are still investigating."

Harvey sighed. "Can you get five grand?"

"No, I can't."

Unbelievable. Snakes, the whole fucking lot of them.

"Call me when you have some money. I'll still talk to my partner and we'll have everything in order when you can pay the retainer."

Furious with the world at large, Jack ended the call. How was this happening? He'd been so careful. Now, it unraveled at the speed of a runaway freight train. If that old bitch hadn't broken into his house, he'd be on his way to freedom. Instead, he wasted time trying to stay out of prison with no fucking attorney. If he wasn't in so much hot water, Jack would blow up the entire firm of Waters, Whalen, and Scott.

Assholes.

Then he remembered Tony. What happened to an hour? Should he call him? He suspected the lines were tapped, so he wouldn't call Tony from a landline. Jack still had the cell, which was in Paul's name.

Tony picked up on the first ring.

"T?"

"Yes, I drove by your house and thought it wouldn't be wise to call you for a bit. I knew you'd call me eventually."

"What happened?"

"Are you at JR's?"

"Yeah, I don't have anywhere else to go."

"You need to go to the booth. There will be a note. Follow the instructions. We'll talk when I see you again." He hung up.

It was then that things began to clear for Jack, and he cursed himself for being so stupid. Tony said he'd scratch Jack's back if Jack scratched his. He'd taken care of James and Tony knew about Michelle. Jack wouldn't have been surprised if she was connected to Milo in some way, and wondered if she had tried to take one of theirs for a ride.

Grabbing his keys off the desk, Jack left the office. He didn't take his car. If he had a tail, he could lose them in the streets easier than on the road. He took two taxis and four buses, getting off at random stops and getting back on immediately. When he was sure he didn't recognize any passengers at three stops Jack boarded a bus to the booth.

He checked the streets, but no one seemed to be paying any particular attention to his movements. When Jack reached the booth, he took out a quarter and picked up the receiver.

Nasty dirty things.

Grimacing, Jack drew the receiver to his ear and pretended to argue with someone on the other end of the line, while slipping two fingers into the coin return to retrieve Tony's note. He tucked it into his fist, cursed at the imaginary person on the phone, and slammed it down. Before leaving the booth, feigning indecision, he glanced around. When he failed to spot anything amiss, he walked away and turned down an alley to read the note.

Frankie's. ASAP. T.

Frankie's? He wasn't dressed for that overpriced shithole.

His T-shirt and jeans curled the maître d's nose as he entered Frankie's.

"Monsieur, we have a dress code at Frankie's."

Jack scowled.

The bastard pronounced Frankie's like "Fronkee's," his fake French accent mangling the word.

"I'm meeting someone. Tony?"

"Oh. Right. One moment, *monsieur.*"

Jack sighed as he waited for the skinny little jerk to check his story.

He came back moments later carrying an ugly-brown sports coat and tie. "I must request that you put these on."

Jack shrugged into the jacket, which was a size too small, the sleeves hitting just above his wrists. The tie clipped on and he hated clip-ons. He looked down at his shirt. "Uh, this won't work."

The jerk sighed and snatched the tie from his hand. "Follow me, *monsieur.*"

Jack trailed him to the far corner of the restaurant; it was the VIP area, apparently.

"Good to see you." Tony smiled from his little table in the shadows.

He took the chair across from him.

The maître d' hovered, wringing the tie nervously in his hands.

"A scotch for my friend." Tony beamed.

The idiot trotted away.

Tony's smile vanished. "You okay?"

"No, I'm not okay. My house is a crime scene, the cops are on my ass like a fucking stubborn will-not and I'm looking at jail time for something I had nothing to do with."

"Nothing?" Tony shrugged. "Seems to me you had a favor coming; I gave different instructions but my guy got excited."

"Why my house?"

"Long story. He's been taken care of. Milo was very unhappy. He hopes you understand that we were trying to return the favor. Brilliant work in Canada, by the way. One of my guys tailed you, checked your work, and said we should take you on."

Jack didn't want to say much about James, in case someone was listening. "Look, I didn't ask for what happened at my house."

"I know you didn't say it specifically, but I promised to help you out. She was out to ruin you. When my guy picked her up, she fucked him, drugged him, and stole his wallet. She was asking for it. He didn't even check in, he just followed her and did her when he caught her alone."

"Stupid bitch."

"She was pretty smart, just chose the wrong guy. Mikey was a bit unbalanced, you know? Better to be rid of him anyway, he'd fuck up and end up nailing Milo eventually."

"Good for you. What do I do now?"

"Deny, deny, deny. That's all you do. They got nothing on you, Jack."

"They're asking about mob ties. Your guy made it look like a fucking execution. In my house. In my fucking house."

Somewhere behind them, plates crashed. Jack nearly fell out of his seat. Once he stilled his heart, he smoothed the ugly jacket.

Tony laughed. Leaning forward, he leveled a menacing glare, not a trace of laughter in his dark eyes. Hell, even his cheesy mustache looked threatening.

"Your lips are sealed. I don't care if you're going up the river; you don't open your fucking mouth." Tony's face reddened just a little.

Hairs rose on Jack's neck. He didn't know which would be worse, the cops or the mob. Both would hand him a fate worse than death. "I won't rat, that's not me and you know it."

"I hear word that they got us for anything, I mean just a hint, you'll hear from me. We won't be pals anymore, you got me?"

"Why are you doing this? I'd never do that." Jack didn't like this new Tony.

"Just so you know, that's all. You need money?"

"No thanks."

"You need to disappear?"

"Not yet, but I'll let you know." Like he'd let them know where he was going if he did take off. "I need a lawyer because mine won't represent me without a fucking retainer."

"I'll talk to Milo, he knows some people. We won't let them screw you over."

"Thanks Tony." Jack wouldn't offend Tony, but he had no plans to use a mob lawyer. He had to think and plan how to get out of this.

"You go get some rest. I'll talk to Milo." Tony threw a fifty on the table and stood. "From now on, don't call me for any reason. I'll contact you if I need to. I think the less we have to do with each other the better."

Fucking right.

"Okay, I got it. You have nothing to worry about. I'll just fuck off eventually. Once I clear my name, I don't want to be around any of this anymore."

"Where will you go?"

Wouldn't you like to know?

"I don't know yet. I've got some family back East. I could stay with them until it's safe to get to my money. I can't disappear. My kids are at school. They'll need me."

"We can look after your kids. If you need to disappear, so can they."

Shit, now he wanted to help with the kids. Those little bastards couldn't keep their mouths shut anyway. That would definitely raise Newman's hairy eyebrows. "Don't worry, thanks to Ray they're taken care of for a while. I just don't want to abandon them."

Tony patted Jack's back and nodded sympathetically.

Jack only needed him to believe he wouldn't fuck off and leave him holding the bag. "I'll wait to hear from you. With any luck, that bitch cop will give up on this. She's got nothing on me but tiny little crumbs, and she can't do much with that."

"I've seen them use less." Tony patted his shoulder again and left.

Fuck, the shit had piled so deep it pressed in on his neck. He wouldn't go down like that. No prison... and no mob execution either.

CHAPTER 36

Detective Newman called Jack twice more that week for questioning.

The bitch had nothing new to say to him though. Why did the cops insist on asking the same shit over and over again? When would they look at those fucking bank videos and see that James took his damn money so he could access it?

Harvey hadn't done much either. Jack couldn't put together money without leaving a trail and blowing apart his story about Whitney. It took a lot of planning to move cash around, and yet he needed money for lawyers.

How fucked up was it to be rich and broke at the same time? Unless Jack sold the house, he had nothing he could put his hands on and he couldn't sell the house because the cops were still investigating their stupid crime scene.

She was shot in the head, assholes. How much more do you need to know?

Jack sat at a smelly, crappy café, a cup of stale coffee in front of him and an old lady picking her nose in the booth ahead of him. He called Harvey to see if he'd at least help him get the house back.

Harvey didn't seem optimistic.

"Come on, Harv. I'll pay you double your usual retainer if you can get me the house. I just have nothing I can touch right now unless I can sell that damn house."

"I don't know. They need time to finish up. I can't see it taking too much longer."

"The police know I have no money. They must know that if I get the house back I can get an attorney by selling it. They don't want me to have any means to defend myself. They want to pin this on someone and I'm their guy."

"It sounds like a conspiracy," Harvey chuckled.

Laugh it up jerk off. You'll be the next fucking crime scene.

"Really, you're getting paranoid. I'll talk to them, see if I can't get them to allow you to at least list it and clear out your shit. How's that?"

"I don't think you heard me. I said I'll pay you double if you can get that house back into my hands."

"No worries, it will be the standard rate. But we will require that retainer. Maybe you should have sold the business buddy, considering the recent turn of events. Rumor is you're sunk."

Fuck off, you stupid lush.

"Yeah, so I hear. If I can get the house, I can get a loan against it and pay you while getting everything straightened out at Jay-Ray's."

"You'd be further ahead to just disappear."

"I can't disappear without money."

"You aren't stupid. We both know that. You said you had money coming. Get it. I don't think you're an idiot, so I'm sure you've got other resources hidden away. If you could vanish too, like your girlfriend, you'd have it made. The cops would've arrested you if they had anything. They haven't done that yet. Legally, you can go anywhere you want. Can't harass a guy when you can't find him."

"They told me I can't leave."

"Like I said, they haven't arrested you yet. Technically, you can do what you want. I wouldn't tell anyone where you're going, though. They could arrest you just to keep you here. There is an awful lot of circumstantial evidence from what you've told me. That's all they really need to hold you for a few days, or weeks, until they can get an arraignment."

"I don't know Harv... they can't send me to prison on that bullshit."

"I've seen guys go for less. You're lucky, though... usually. I think you'll be fine. Just keep telling the truth buddy, get the money and my partner says he'll help you."

"Thanks." *For nothing asshole.* "I'll be in touch."

Jack hung up the phone and laid his head on the table. He thumped it a few times, the pain a welcome diversion to the constant whirring of his panicked thoughts. What the hell could he do now? He sighed, and picked up the phone again. He couldn't wait for the lawyer to call Newman. Jack punched her private line, now memorized, into the phone and waited.

"Hello."

Her voice ceased to turn him on. He wanted to strangle her every time he heard her mocking tone. "It's Jack Murphy, I was hoping you could tell me when I could expect my house back."

"I'm not sure. Do you need something out of it? I could send an officer in with you."

"No, I need my house. I have no money. In case you forgot, someone took off with all my cash. I need to sell the house. Maybe you could start looking for the real felon here instead of holding my fucking house and my bank accounts hostage."

"We're not holding anything hostage. The house is a crime scene and they have to process everything. That takes a while. You have a large house. The bank accounts are also a crime scene of sorts. Once we've established that you haven't taken the money yourself, you'll have access to them again. Why are you selling the house anyway? You could go to the bank and get a loan against it. Wouldn't that would be simpler?"

"I want my house, not a loan. Anyway, if I did go to the

bank I can't get a fucking loan when I'm a murder suspect and my business is going under. Banks don't trust suspects in homicide cases. You've made it very clear that's what I am."

"Mr. Murphy, I'm sorry you're having such a hard time. If you'd be honest with me, this would go easily. Without your input, we are working blind and that takes time. If you have any information about the murder of Michelle Wilson, like who did it, we could work something out."

"Like a deal? Are you joking?"

She has to be joking.

"If the mob did this, and if I had that information, I wouldn't make a deal. Do I look stupid enough to go against the mob? I'm not, and I'm not going to make shit up either just to satisfy you."

"Then we'll have to turn up the heat. You know, get this investigation moving along. Watch your television Mr. Murphy. You'll see what happens when you lie to me."

"I'm not lying to you," he growled. "I am not guilty, and I didn't do anything wrong."

"Why would someone you don't know, except maybe through a brief encounter, be executed in your home? That doesn't make sense, and when something doesn't make sense to me it means someone is lying."

"Fuck off." Jack hung up.

The old lady stared at him, her thin lips forming a small "o."

Jack sneered.

She looked away, picking at a mutilated piece of pie in front of her.

Newman had cooked up something really fucked. Jack touched the phone. He should call Tony and warn him. No, he couldn't call him. Tony specifically said not to call him. How did he warn them she was on to them?

After tossing a dollar on the table, Jack stood and walked to the door of the café.

The waitress smiled.

He waved. If only his life wasn't so messed up, Jack could

have taken the time to get her number. She was cute. No. He couldn't do any of that.

Fucking bullshit pain in the ass jerks, messing up his carefully laid plans.

All he wanted was what he'd earned. His money, his business, his freedom; all of it was gone.

Trudging toward his office, Jack pushed through the doors and grumbled under his breath. As he got in the elevator, a man and a woman exited. They eyed him warily, allowing an extra few inches of space as they walked out.

What? Never seen an angry guy before?

Nosy assholes.

Jack stepped off the elevator and headed down the hall, getting maybe ten feet from the door to his office, when he paused. So this was why they stared at him. Tape covered the door; yellow police tape.

What the hell? Jack reached for his phone.

Detective Newman picked up on the first ring. "Hello Jackson, what seems to be the problem?"

"You know what my problem is, you stinking cow. How dare you do this? It goes against my rights."

"What are you talking about?"

"My office." She'd be floating belly up in the fucking river before he was through with her. "Why have you taken my office?"

"Oh that... well, it is a crime scene, you know. Michelle worked there and it was one of the last places she was seen alive. There might be valuable information in those computers. We had to cover all avenues."

"Do you have a court order? You can't stop me from going in."

"Look down the hall."

Jack did.

The guy he first dismissed as another tenant when he came in watched him closely. His hand rested on a gun holstered on his belt.

Fuck.

Jack looked the other way.

There was another cop. The strange expression on his face made Jack believe he hoped for something to justify an arrest.

"You nasty bitch." Jack said.

"If you'd like to see the court order, you can ask the officers. Have a nice day, sir." She hung up.

Jack stood immobile and furious. No way could he get into his office. Staring at the door, the image of the computers filled his mind. The new computers. She'd get nothing there. But did he get everything else? The discs. The letters. The pictures. Jesus Christ, Jack couldn't be sure now that he hadn't missed something.

Jack turned. No. He would not panic.

You were careful, and you covered your ass. Computers are gone. The car is spotless.

Newman thought he had no resources. She was wrong. He had cash at the house if the fuckers would let him near it, one of James's credit cards, and his car. Gamble or die, it was as simple as that; anything but going to prison. After everything he'd done just to be free from bullshit, no way would Jack go under because of the one fucking body that had nothing to do with him.

Stomping down the hall, and past the cop with itchy fingers, Jack took to the stairs. Waiting for the elevator with these pricks watching didn't appeal to him. Rounding the last flight, rage covered everything in a red haze. Had he killed Michelle, she'd never have been found.

Hadn't Jack proven there was such a thing as the perfect crime? Why would he order a hit in his own house? Jack was smarter than that. Smart enough not to get involved with the mob, stupid assholes that couldn't even follow simple instructions. Tony heard him say that Michelle and Whitney could wait. Hadn't he promised to take care of them himself? Their favor just ruined everything. If they weren't so dangerous, Jack would have put a bullet in each of those assholes.

When he breezed past a black sedan, the driver straightened in his seat. Undercover?

Real great job you're doing there, dipshit.

Jack waved and fished the car keys from his pocket.

Where now?

In the car, he paused and tapped the steering wheel. The plan had been to run, but now he had almost nothing to work with. How did one get around the cops and the mob and get to Mexico without any cash? Jack could access his safe deposit boxes, rent a car they wouldn't recognize, and then make a run for it. But would he make it? The only other option left to him was death. If he couldn't run, he'd simply eat a bullet or something equally quick and painless. No way in hell would they put him in jail. Jesus Christ, things were getting desperate. He needed somewhere to think this through.

The motel looked cheap. The sign outside only had one working bulb, the door taped to cover a large hole in the glass. It looked perfect. Newman would look for him at a fancy, high priced joint, never at some seedy, cockroach-infested shithole.

He parked around the back, under a "Staff Parking" sign, and went in to pay for his room. Thank God for James's credit card. Too bad his cousin was such a loser that his credit limit wasn't high enough to pay off Harvey. *Screw that drunken ass.* That dick wouldn't get any of his money now.

"Room 105, sir," the pimply clerk said, and offered a key on a rusty chain.

Fuck, they couldn't even afford a decent key ring? What would his room look like?

Room 105 was at the far end, next to an ice machine. He let himself in and went straight to the bed ignoring the light; he didn't want to know what the room looked like.

Two hours later, squeaking springs brought him awake. Jack rolled over, reaching to the nightstand for the lamp. Something tickled his hand. He jumped back, shaking off whatever it was.

"Jesus," he muttered, reaching again to hit the switch as fast as he could. A smallish cockroach scampered across the floor and disappeared under the dresser.

A pale yellow glow illuminated a tiny space, the television on the far wall only about a foot from the end of the bed. Jack cringed at the stains and burn holes on the bedspread's ghastly floral pattern. He slid to the end of the bed and hit the power button on the television. The local news flashed its logo and the room filled with the nasal delivery of the anchor. "Special Report," she exclaimed.

Jack knew he was deep in shit when Detective Newman's ugly face filled the screen. If he ever hoped to get away, he'd have to move to plan B.

CHAPTER 37

Detective Newman fucked Jack like no one had fucked him before with her TV performance

"We have had a break," she opened her tirade, "in the recent burglary-turned-homicide and I'd like to share what we have, so that anyone who may have seen anything can call our hotline."

She smiled, shuffled some papers and looked up.

Jack's gut clenched. That bitch looked right at him. The newsflash was making him physically ill.

"A suspect in the case has provided details that lead us to believe this homicide was a contract killing.

"Because of this, we've added Anthony Frenetti to our list of suspects. If anyone knows the whereabouts of this individual, please call the police. Do not attempt to approach Mr. Frenetti; his links to organized crime make him a very dangerous individual.

"We are also searching for Milo Farese as an accomplice to this crime. You may recognize the name. Mr. Farese is the alleged head of the most powerful crime family in the country. Please use caution when dealing with these individuals. Do not approach them or try to apprehend them. Call the number at the bottom of the screen and allow law enforcement officials to handle the situation.

"The suspect has also volunteered information that builds a strong case against Farese in other investigations. His bravery in coming forward is commendable."

Fucking bitch, rotten lying bitch!

Detective Walrus thought she could play Goliath and fuck him like this? If not for the mob breathing down his neck, he'd see her giant ass in a body bag. Jack's phone buzzed. He stared at the TV screen, terrified to answer. So close to freedom, to getting away with everything, and now.... That fat piece of shit just ruined any hope Jack may have had of working with Tony to get out of this. Within the hour, they'd be after him.

He glanced at his ringing phone to realize that "within the hour" had been wildly optimistic. An avid news watcher, Tony wouldn't miss the local news.

"Tony, I don't know where she got her information, it wasn't me. She's out to get me, I told you."

"We have ourselves a problem, friend, and I don't know that I can fix it."

"Fuck Tony, you know I'd never turn on you. Shit, I'm not a complete retard, you know."

"I know that and you know that, but Milo; he's not so un-derstanding. He's ordered you gone. Where are you now?"

Fuck that.

"I don't think I should tell you."

"Smart, but we'll find you. It's nothing personal on my end. I have to do as the boss says. I wish it hadn't come down to this. We did you a favor, and now it bites us in the ass."

"They've got nothing. I won't testify." Sweat trickled down his neck. First, they had to catch him.

"You see... we've heard that before, Jack, from very good men. When it's your ass on the line, things change. It doesn't change the fact that it appears you've already turned. Milo has big plans once he has you. If you come to me now, I'll talk him into a quick death. What are friends for?"

"No, I won't do it, Tony. I'll kill myself first. I didn't turn on you. Why won't you listen to me?" Fuck, he had to get out of there. He'd used his credit card to get the room. How long before they traced it back to him? Jack looked around. He'd brought nothing. He had nothing. He'd never make it out of this alive.

Fuck it. Plan B.

As he dashed out of the room and turned the corner into the parking lot, Jack skid to a halt. His bowels threatened to release. Stepping back, he peered into the tiny parking lot. Two cops searched his car. Shit. Would a car wash remove everything? I If not, they'd find sand, and maybe even a little of Whitney's blood. He'd cleaned the interior, but that shit stayed for a long time. Fucking Newman, he'd make that bitch pay. She would not take him in. No way.

The motel was surrounded by buildings, no shrubbery, or any other vehicles to hide behind. Perhaps he could go back inside, and stay out of sight until they left. Jack risked a peek. Too late. They headed to the door. Jack's head swam. He swayed and the growing bubble of fear lodged in his belly burst, shooting up like hot lava to his throat. He could barely breathe.

The cops went inside.

One, two—Fuck it. Go Jack!

As Jack reached his car, shouts exploded behind him.

Shit, get in the car.

He fumbled with the door and cracked his head off the roof as he dove in.

The cops barreled toward their car.

He should have slashed their tires first. *I can lose them.*

Still got a lead.

Jack shifted into drive and stomped on the gas. The car lurched and spun out of the lot.

Jack drove blindly, turning down side streets and weaving in and out of traffic until he felt relatively confident he'd lost the cops. What now?

Ditch the car.

His license plate alone was like a neon sign. JKSBBY, a gift from Jenny when he'd bought his first Beamer. Jack hated personalized plates.

On the highway, he drove a few miles before the road forked. Stay on the highway or take the dirt road? Jack turned right. Dirt road. Definitely.

He drove without seeing; ignoring signs, houses and the farms he passed. The car was a liability, but he couldn't walk. On foot, they'd have him for sure. A large metal sign caught his eye. Bullet-ridden letters rusted with age, the post dented from too many drunks on a road tour, answered Jack's prayers. Bob's Salvage.

Perfect.

The gate hung by one hinge.

Nice security.

Jack slowed only as he approached a smattering of small buildings. In the center stood a barn-like structure.

A short, chubby man eyed Jack's car doubtfully.

Jack hoped he didn't ask too many questions. He was desperate enough to commit one more murder if he did. "Hey." He got out and waved at the scowling man. "I was wondering if you do trades."

"Trades? I'm not a dealership son; I'm a wrecker. That doesn't look like a wreck."

"I know. I'm kind of in a little trouble here. I need to unload this for a while. Do you have a car?"

"Yep, but it ain't no fucking Bentley."

Stupid redneck, it's not a Bentley.

"Neither is this, but it's just as valuable. Can we make a deal?" Jack rounded the back of the car and knelt to remove the plate.

"Depends on the deal. I got no money for a car like that."

"I don't want money."

His eyes narrowed.

Okay, thought Jack. He isn't totally stupid. "I want to trade my car for yours. If I come back for it, I'll pay you for your trouble. If I'm not, you can grind off the serial number or something and get a lot of cash for it."

"Seems kind of dangerous for me. Why would you want to dump this? What did you do to get into trouble?"

He was already in this deep, might as well go for it. "You know Milo Farese?"

"Not personally, no. I think it would be wise to stay away from the likes of him."

"Yes, well I seem to have learned that lesson the hard way. I need to hide. There's been a misunderstanding and now I'm in a lot of trouble. If you get rid of the number and maybe give it a paint job, no one will know this was my car. In return, I just need something to get me the fuck out of here."

"How did you get mixed up with the mob, son?"

If he called him son one more time, Jack would lose it. "It was a total misunderstanding. Look I don't have a lot of time, can we trade or not?"

"Sure, I suppose. But I wouldn't feel right with an even trade. I'll give you some cash for it." He disappeared inside the barn.

Jack silently urged him to hurry. He didn't know how long the cops would take before they figured out that Jack would ditch the vehicle. He wasn't far from the city, so they'd be able to track him fairly fast.

"How's five hundred and my old Taurus over there?"

Five hundred. Great. It would buy him time. "Perfect, thanks so much. Hey, can I leave your plates on?"

The man pointed to a pile of old parts. "There's some old plates in that pile of crap there. The plates on the car are registered to me, and I don't want none of what you got linking me to you."

Jack walked over to pick up a plate. "Make sure you get rid of the number, I'd hate to see them find my car here."

"I can handle myself."

Jack took off. If he drove all night, he could be miles away from Newman and Tony by morning.

His pocket buzzed.

Jack swerved, almost driving straight into a ditch. Righting the car, Jack pulled his phone out and checked the screen.

Newman.

Right. Like he'd answer and have them trace the call. Maybe he should just shut it off. Couldn't they trace a call whether the phone was answered or not? Jack hit the power button and tossed it on the back seat. He'd keep it for later. It might come handy to throw them off.

Panic wreaks havoc on a man's brain. Wasn't that car behind him an hour earlier, when he pulled off the highway? The highway. That would be the best way to lose anyone.

His head throbbed as Jack came to the end of the dirt road and turned back onto the highway. First, he'd find another room. Now that he had cash, he'd be able to sleep knowing they couldn't trace him. He wouldn't give Milo the privilege of killing him. Not Milo's way. Death would be a mercy compared to what those fuckers would do to him. Death didn't scare him but he preferred to go on his own terms. Plan B. If it proved to be the only way out, he'd do it. Those bastards wouldn't get their man.

The lights of a motel blazed in the distance. Enough was enough. He pulled into the empty lot and after finding the darkest, most difficult spot to see from the road, he got out and made his way inside.

The clerk looked better than the previous, his face at least was clear. Jack registered as John Smith. It wasn't very creative, but he could have used Donald Trump's and they'd never ask. It would be *"Okay Mr. Trump, ice machine is at the end of the hall. Maid service is every morning after ten. If you're here at eleven, that's one more night."*

His legs threatened to buckle. Jack trudged the few steps to his room. Once inside he locked the door, turned on the news, and lay back on the bed.

Jack's face filled the screen. Not his best photo. His hair looked brown—really, it was dark blond—and his eyes looked dull on screen. Hadn't Whitney called them electric blue? The anchorman droned on "this man is armed and dangerous."

Jack chuckled. He wished.

CHAPTER 38

The sound of sirens jolted Jack awake. He blinked at the brightness of the sun shining through the patio doors on the left side of his room.

Should've closed the blinds.

Were the sirens for him? Maybe they screamed for someone else. Taking his phone from the nightstand, Jack turned it on. It rang at once.

Tony.

It wasn't like Tony could trace the call and Jack planned to leave right away. He'd talk while he drove. "Yeah."

"Jack, what are you running for?" Tony sounded irritated.

Of course he was. Milo would be up his ass over this. "Wouldn't you run?" Looking over the parking lot, and finding nothing in sight, Jack risked a dash to the car.

Tony breathed heavily. "Must be running right now. You don't sound so good... Yep, you are running."

Jack wrenched the door of the old Taurus open and jumped inside.

Fuck the seatbelt.

The tires squealed as he tore out of the lot and onto the highway.

Tony laughed, but it sounded raspy, tired.

"That car your grandpa's? The cops are tailing you too. Makes my job a little difficult since, thanks to you, they're after me. Have you ever tried to follow someone the cops are after without letting the cops know you're doing it?"

"So leave me alone. Fuck Tony, you guys did her without even asking me. If you let me take care of her myself, you wouldn't be in this situation. I didn't ask you to kill her."

"You didn't ask me not to. I said I'd do it and you didn't tell me not to," his voice rose with every word.

"You won't find me alive."

"You don't have the balls, Jack. Don't give me that bull-shit."

"I have been running for months now. I'm tired of every-one fucking me over. If you don't catch me, I face prison. I won't go to prison. I'll die in there." Jack knew he was beat. The rearview confirmed his thoughts. The car behind him gained ground with every second that passed. Jack accelerated. "Is that you behind me?"

"No, that's the cops. I'm in the car behind them. Wave, that's me in the black sedan."

Looking in the rearview again, Jack spotted a black car.

"Game over, Jack." Tony said.

"You can't do me in front of the cops. What if I just pull over and turn myself in?"

The road narrowed to one lane as they drove along the mountains. One side of Jack was solid rock face, the other a guardrail. Just a few pieces of wood and wire kept his car from the rock and the water below.

"I'll do the cops. Milo will take care of me. He wants you gone. You fucked him."

"They haven't arrested him yet." Milo couldn't be in jail or the cops would have left Jack alone. Bigger fish. They wanted Milo more than Jack.

"They can't find him. That's the genius of Milo. He can disappear like a ghost. So will I... once I'm done with you."

"I'll drive into the city, go to the cops directly. You going to take out the entire station?"

Fuck you Tony, I'm not that stupid.

"Like you said, you won't go to prison. Even if you think maybe you'd survive, you ran, so the cops know you're guilty. This is going to end with a bullet in your head. Makes no difference to me whose bullet it is." He had a point. Jack had no choice but to run. That was likely his plan all along.

A beeping sound. Jack's heart skipped. The fuel gauge hovered on empty. Fuck, it was now or never. Looking over the edge of the cliffs Jack watched the tide coming in. Yes, now was the time. "Bye Tony."

"You won't do it Jack."

Jack threw the phone out the window. It clattered to the rocks below. He could do it. One turn of the wheel and Jackson Murphy would be no more.

Do it Jack.

"Mr. Murphy, this is the police." A voice boomed over a loudspeaker.

I know that you fucking knobs. Who else would be speeding after me along the edge of a fucking cliff?

"Pull over now. You are under arrest."

Do it Jack.

"I repeat, Mr. Jackson Murphy, you are under arrest."

I heard you the first time, shithead. I'm not pulling over unless it's over the edge.

The incessant beeping of the fuel gage intensified Jack's headache. In the rearview, the cop's car closed in. Tony's wasn't far behind.

Jack glanced back at the sea and the waves below.

Do it Jack.

Fuck, did he really want to do this?

Do it Jack.

He couldn't. Everything he'd done, for nothing? He'd die instantly down there. It was guaranteed. Unless the tide had come in.... Swerving he cursed as his body instinctively pulled the car back.

Do it Jack.

"I know, I know. I have to!" Jack yelled. The road ahead would widen and go back to the highway soon. He'd lose his chance in seconds.

Do it Jack.

Ding, ding, ding, ding.

Fuck off you piece of fucking shit.

Why did this pile of crap even have a fuel alarm? No one driving it would be able to afford fuel anyway.

"Jackson Murphy, pull over and we can discuss your options. This is not the end."

No, this was pretty much the end.

Do it Jack, do it now.

Ding, ding, ding, ding.

"Fuck! Fuck! Fuck!" Jack's vision blurred as sweat rolled down his forehead and into his eyes.

Do it Jack.

The cops closed in, and bumped his fender. The car swerved. What were they doing?

Do it you fucking pussy.

Ding, ding, ding.

Jack turned.

Tony overtook the cops. His face looked odd. Why was he pointing?

The guardrail disappeared beneath the front of the car. Then there was nothing, but blood pounding in his ears. Jack smiled. Thank God that fucking beeping stopped. His stomach dropped as the waves moved closer.

CHAPTER 39

Sirens blared and cars lined the highway as close to the yellow tape as they could. The legend of Jackson Murphy was already building. Only hours after Jack's car dove over the cliff, Detective Newman spoke to other officers as they inspected the scene.

"Why did you do it?" her colleague asked. He was a veteran officer whose position she would have taken when he retired, had Jack Murphy not ruined it all for her.

"We had him, Harry, I know we did." She watched as forensics pored over the wreckage of the car and then looked away toward the water. "I didn't know the mob was chasing him too. He didn't do this on purpose. That asshole loved himself way too much. He screwed up, not me. The investigators said as much. We did get Tony Frenetti though. That's big."

"Not big enough honey. We've got nothing on Milo and your suspect is dead."

She hated when they called her "honey." Jesus, she had more balls than any of them. Jack would have gotten away with everything if left up to those spineless fuckers.

"The brass doesn't care that you got Frenetti. He's too

smart to talk, and you caused a man who was innocent until proven guilty to drive over a fucking cliff."

"He was guilty. We found the girlfriend's body last night. His cousin I'm sure is dead too. I didn't force him; he could have given himself up if he was innocent."

"You held that press conference and gave false information, Newman, you're lucky to have your badge."

"So I'm told." She turned as the medical examiner approached.

"The windows are shattered." The man, more a kid in Newman's opinion, barely out of training, reported. "The dive team said all the doors are closed, but they suspect he was ejected when the car hit the water. His body should turn up along the shoreline soon enough though."

"There was no body in the car?" Newman's nerves quivered. Impossible wasn't it?

He rubbed his eyes. They'd worked most of the night to locate the car, and she suspected he'd been here waiting to examine it. "No, but it landed in the water which leaves any number of possibilities as far as where his body might end up. They're trying to drag the car in to shore, but the tide pulled it quite a ways out. The water would've washed any DNA away."

"I need a body." It would be just like Murphy to swim away from this unscathed.

"Look, Detective, he went over at high tide; it's gone out since. His body could have been swept out to deeper waters. Once the car's in, we'll go over it with a fine-tooth comb, but as for his body, I can't promise much. The divers are going to continue looking in the morning, but we may never find it."

"What if he got out?"

Harry sighed and patted her shoulder. "Newman, give it up. He's gone."

"That man is too lucky to die. I don't buy it."

"Let it go. The man is dead. Case closed." He touched her shoulder again, turning her away from the scene. "Jackson Murphy didn't get away. You need to accept it. Do your desk time and get back on the horse. I see a bright future for you.

You just need to learn how to follow procedure."

"I know. I'm just pissed." She looked out at the water and cursed her luck. "That bastard killed six people and really, he did get away with it all."

CHAPTER 40

Waves crashed on the beach, seagulls squawked overhead searching for dinner, and an island beat floated softly on the air. For months, the stranger went out each morning to stare at the water. He laughed each time and sat there for hours. Several times, in the evening, he bought pretty ladies drinks, and then took them back to his fancy villa just over the cliffs.

Henry watched the man seated alone at the bar. He had money. That much was obvious. He was powerful; everyone gave him space, not wanting to get too close to his dangerously handsome face. Blue eyes, colder than a north wind, stared into your soul. He wore an amused look no matter what he discussed. The long scar that ran down his left cheek only added to his charisma. He never spoke of it and no one dared to ask. When he arrived, the man bought the villa and the sugar plantation that adjoined it. It stood empty for so long, Henry had nearly forgotten about it. Slowly, the man had built it into a thriving business.

Why would a wealthy American come to this shitty island just to bust his ass building a dead plantation back up again? Where did he come from? He appeared to have no friends, just his employees, of which there were only a few.

One man, Paulo, lived at the villa with him. Paulo, the arrogant ass, wouldn't even speak to the rest of them now. He stayed in that fancy house and rarely came down. The man whispered in his ear and Paulo went running. Lucky bastard. Henry would give anything to see inside that house.

The man signaled for another drink.

A gorgeous blonde had found a seat next to him.

As he approached, Henry perked his hears, hoping to gain a little piece of the American's puzzle.

"At the risk of sounding corny, can I just say that you are beautiful?" The man said to the blonde.

She smiled and leaned closer. "Not corny at all. I haven't seen anything other than the natives since I arrived here. You're a breath of fresh air. I've just arrived with my husband. We're on our honeymoon."

"What a shame. A woman as stunning as you, I wouldn't allow you out on your own. I'd be fucking you silly, especially on our honeymoon."

Henry thought for sure she'd slap him and walk away. To his astonishment, she laughed and touched his thigh. "My husband is very old. He's resting now. I've got at least three hours before he comes looking."

"Really? We could learn a lot about each other in three hours."

"We could. And your wife?"

"She's not around anymore."

"You're divorced? I'd never leave a man as handsome as you."

Fascinated, Henry stared openly as the man glanced at him and grinned. He didn't seem to mind that Henry listened.

"She had an unfortunate accident. I've just focused on getting away from it all since then. That's my villa up on the cliff there. Just over the beach."

"Oh so you're the wealthy stranger the locals talk about."

"I am indeed.... And you are?"

"My name is Jennifer."

The man stiffened for a moment. Something flashed in his

eyes, but he recovered.

"Interesting, I knew a Jenny once. Perhaps we should go to my villa and find out if the name makes the woman."

"I can't possibly leave with a stranger. If you'd tell me your name, then we could explore other, more interesting subjects."

"I'm David," he smiled, his perfect teeth sparkling in the sunlight.

They couldn't be real. Henry knew real teeth were not so white.

"Well, Jennifer, let's get to know each other better before your husband wakes from his nap. We don't want to give the poor man a heart attack by having to search for you. Not on his honeymoon."

"No, that would be terrible."

"Tell me, are you allergic to bees? I have some on the plantation. Just a hobby."

"No allergies to anything. Maybe we could find a use for all that honey."

"Maybe we could."

THE END

COMING SOON

OTHER THRILLING NOVELS BY

RENÉE MILLER

RENÉE MILLER

Till Doubt Do us Part

Do you ever truly know someone?

Charlotte sat at the kitchen table, cell phone in her hands. Bright morning sunlight shone through the window over the sink, burning her sleep-deprived eyes. She called Ben's cell twice before going to bed the night before, but he didn't answer. Why did he always get his panties bunched over Justin? Even if she and Ben split up, she'd never turn to Justin; she loved him like a brother but he was no more than a big child. No matter how vehemently she denied the attraction Ben imagined was there, he refused to believe her.

The sound of tires crunching gravel brought her out of her dismal thoughts. Charlotte set the phone down and waited. While she felt bad for ambushing him after he'd worked all night, he couldn't ignore her now. She hated when he shut her out like this. It'd be better if he yelled, threw things, or even hit her. At least then the torment would be short-lived.

The front door opened. Closed. A jingle of keys announced Ben's walk down the hall before he rounded the doorway to the kitchen.

"Hi," she said.

"Hey." He tossed his keys on the counter and leaned against the doorframe.

"Forgot how to use your phone?"

"I'm sorry. I just needed to cool off."

"I hate it when you do that to me," she said, but smiled.

"I know. It's just how I deal with shit. You'd think after ten years one of us would change pattern."

She laughed. "I love you, Ben. Only you."

He pushed away from the counter and walked toward the table.

Charlotte stood and waited for his arms to close around her.

"I love you too, baby. I guess all this shit that's going on; Kat going missing, neighbors being raped. It's got me on edge. God, I can't imagine what I'd do if it was you."

"Can you put yourself in Justin's shoes? He's probably barely holding it together. Kat is my best friend, and his fiancée. He needs support right now."

"That's just it, Charlotte. He's not freaking out at all. You saw him on the news. He seemed so cool. So normal."

She wouldn't tell him that she called Justin. No point in stirring the pot. But Ben was wrong. Justin wasn't cool. He was worried. Unlike Ben, Justin didn't know how to show his feelings. He hid everything deep inside.

Ben released her and pulled out a chair. God he looked so tired.

"Want some breakfast?" she asked.

"No thanks. I'm beat."

"Okay. Well I have a couple of assignments due by noon, and then I'll be out of the house for a few hours so you can sleep."

"No. Don't leave." Ben turned, his stern blue eyes meeting hers. "Actually, call your mom. I want you to take off for a while. Get away from Maple Valley."

"That's silly. I'm not going to run away."

"It's called being smart."

"Smells a lot like running away."

Ben smiled. "Listen, I have to stay on nights for a while. They offered me shift supervisor. It pays almost twice what I make, but I'll have to do a couple of doubles every week. That'll be like sixteen hours with you here alone. I can't handle the thought. Not with a murderer roaming around out there."

"Murderer? There hasn't been a murder." Not yet.

"Char, you've gotta look at the facts. So far, the women he's attacked, they've returned within hours. After the attack, he drops them somewhere alive, but each rape gets more violent, more vicious. Now Kat's gone for more than twenty-four ours. She won't be coming back."

A shiver crept through Charlotte. He was so certain. How could he just write Katrina off like that? "We don't know that the guy that took her is the same one raping women. I don't know that I believe anyone took her at all. Maybe she took off. She and Justin are a bad influence on each other. And she's run off before. I mean, after college, I didn't see her for a year. No one did."

Ben stared.

Charlotte wouldn't allow herself to believe Katrina was gone. Not until she had proof.

He nodded. "Maybe I'm just thinking the worst. Even though Kat was a bitch, she didn't deserve to die. I really hope you're right and she's just pitching a Kat-sized tantrum. But you have to promise me you're going to be safe. Don't let any man but me in here. I mean it. No one. Even guys we know. They think it's some stranger but we can't know that. It might be someone who's been watching us all along. Someone we care about."

"That's really creepy."

"Yeah, but you can't truly know anyone."

Natalie doesn't believe in vampires,
until she meets sweet and handsome Gabriel.

RENÉE MILLER

Ancient
Blood

Sometimes love is worth every bite

The girl crashed through the dense vegetation, desperate to escape. With no moon to light her way, she ran away from the road and deeper into the woods.

Risking a look back, she lost her footing. Not far behind, two green lights trailed. No man's eyes could light up like that. It couldn't be a man. As she stumbled through the trees and thick underbrush, she cursed. How could she have been so stupid? She should have bolted from the bar when he called her by name. *He knew my name.* Instead, she allowed herself to be carried away by his charm and good looks. Later, Shelley ignored the warning bells ringing in her head and left the bar with him.

They went back to his house, if this was his home. Shelly didn't know where she was or how long they had driven to get there.

Inside Shelly's small car, she lost track of everything except him. He wore no cologne, but his scent was overwhelming. She inhaled his sweet musk, her head reeling. Soon they pulled into a winding driveway where he helped her out of the car. She followed him inside.

It was unlike her to lose herself like this. Now she ran for her life.

"Shelly," he called.

Even now, terrified as she was, Shelly fought an insane urge to surrender. She didn't know why she should want to and shook the feeling off.

"Don't be silly, Shelly," he sounded closer with every word. "You cannot escape me out here. There is no reason to run. I won't hurt you."

Liar! Not after what had happened at that mausoleum he called a house. *Silly Shelly my foot!*

He had pulled her close and nuzzled her ear—whispering to her in a language she didn't understand as he trailed his tongue down her neck tasting her skin. Then, when she expected a kiss, the bastard bit her. Her neck still throbbed where he had sunk his teeth. He pulled away, blood on his lips, but worse than that, his eyes shone with a pale green light. Shelly ran as fast as she could out the nearest door only to find herself surrounded by strange woods.

"I didn't want it to be this way, Shelly. If you stop, it will go much easier for you. I'm afraid there are worse things than me out here."

At his words, Shelly missed a step again. What could possibly be worse? She doubted anything could be worse than returning to him.

"I can smell your blood and so will they," he warned right behind her.

She spun and stumbled backward, her heart skipping a beat. A few feet ahead, he floated in midair, his arms held out.

Her mind reeled. He wasn't human, he couldn't be. *Then what?* If he was a man, the creep must have slipped something into her drink. Either way he was bad news. People didn't hover. "Who are *they*?" Shelly stalled as she backed away.

"The others. You didn't think I lived in that big old house alone did you?"

Her heart raced and a sob escaped her lips as she tried to move away from him. His blond hair was no longer tied back, it floated in a white-gold halo around his body.

"Please let me go," she begged. "I won't tell anyone what happened. I don't even know where I am. Please, I promise."

He shook his head, disappointment in his eyes. "Why does it always comes to this?" he murmured. "You humans are all the same. Such cowards. You *do* know my name, Shelly." He reached out to brush a strand of red hair from her face.

Shelly shook her head and retreated until the rough bark of a tree dug in her back. She tried to step around it to put something between them, spinning around in fright as he moved with her, his feet light on the ground like a dancer's.

"Oh God," she cried.

Behind her stood another man, shorter than and not nearly as attractive as her pursuer. With a swift movement, he grabbed her arms and held her close. He grinned at her upturned face to display long canine-like teeth, his eyes blazing with orange light rather than green.

Her legs trembled. Lightheaded, Shelly thought she may faint. *Maybe it will be better to be unconscious for your own murder.* No, they would likely wait for her to wake up before beginning her torture. She turned back to the blond man; her best bet would be to appeal to him. "I don't remember your name," she lied. "I was so drunk, really. Please I swear. I won't say a word to anyone."

"She smells heavenly," the man holding her growled with a thick accent she couldn't place. "You are sharing aren't you Boss?"

"I wasn't going to," he said, and stepped forward to toy with a red curl. "But I seem to have lost my appetite having chased her so far. Actually, I don't desire her at all now."

Shelly looked between the two men. She wasn't sure which one frightened her more, the one who held her close and licked the wound on her neck at even briefer intervals, or the cold and imposing blond who stared down at them. "I just want to go home," she sobbed, her knees buckling. "Please let me go home."

The blond man moved so that his body touched hers. Her skin tingled. Nice. She looked up and wondered why she suddenly wasn't frightened. His eyes were beautiful; she couldn't look away from their glow. Staring into them she felt light, as though she would simply float away or dive into their green waters.

"Your hair is like fire," he whispered. "I so wanted to make you one of us, Shelly. I wanted to bring you into our family. This would have been your home forever. You would have wanted for nothing." He touched her cheek.

She turned her face into his hand. Maybe he wouldn't hurt her after all. Maybe she could get out of this alive if she played along. He wasn't ugly, far from it. A little strange, perhaps, but if she humored him until morning, she might stand a chance to run away. She looked up and gave him a shaky smile.

"It's too bad," he sighed. "You were nearly perfect, but I'm afraid nearly isn't enough for me."

He walked away and the blackness rustled around her. Orange lights glowed from the gloom. "Please Aedon," she called. "Please, don't leave me here."

He turned at the sound of her voice and smiled. His strange teeth shone in the darkness. "I see you've remembered my name," he said, and disappeared.

"Aedon," she screamed as more shapes materialized from the night to surround her.

"She's bloomin pretty," one growled in a thick brogue. "Let's take 'er back and play a bit."

"No. We can't do that," the man who held her said. "The boss wants us to do her out here and leave her for the wolves."

"Bloody hell. We canna have any fun anymore. Since he made that blasted bleedin' heart one of us it's been nothing but caution an' cowardice."

Shelly listened to them argue and searched for a nonexistent chance to escape. There were at least six of them. She was doomed and her spirits plummeted in despair.

"Would you fools stop your bitching and get on with it?" a woman's voice cut in.

Shelly turned to a tiny, dark-haired woman standing to her right. She was beautiful, her skin like ivory. Her luminous eyes didn't glow and hope stirred once more in Shelley's chest. "Please help me," she whispered. "Please don't let them hurt me."

The woman leaned closer and brushed Shelly's cheek with one long fingernail. Shelly searched her face for a sign of mercy but her hopes plunged when the woman smiled and bared the same long teeth as the others. Shelly recoiled against the brute pinning her but the woman entwined her fingers in her hair and forced her to be still by yanking it roughly.

"Oh, they won't hurt you a bit, love." The woman moved closer to brush her lips across Shelly's. She should have been disgusted; women were not her thing. Instead, her belly fluttered in unmistakable arousal.

"I think we should let it be ladies first tonight, lads," a voice from the darkness drew a flurry of laughter.

"You'd have been better off with us lass," the man who

held her whispered into her ear. "Olivia isn't known for her tenderness." He let her go and moved away.

Shelly stood rooted to the spot, uncertain. Shouldn't she try to run? She couldn't just let them kill her.

"Running would be very stupid," Olivia warned, as if reading her thoughts. "I hoped you would be a companion, as he had promised. It's a shame our Aedon is so fussy. I would have enjoyed playing with you. You *are* very lovely."

Olivia pulled Shelly against her and tugged on her hair forcing her head to the side. "I see he's already started for me," she whispered and kissed the wound on Shelly's neck. "Do you know how close you came to heaven?"

"I'm sorry," Shelly sobbed, but didn't try to move away. "Tell him I'll do whatever he wants. I just want to go home."

Olivia's nails dug into tender flesh, returning Shelly to reality. She tried to turn away but the tiny woman jerked her back with a rough tug on her hair.

"Oh no, sweet Shelly," she whispered as her eyes lit with the orange light. "You will never go home again."

*Dirty Truth. A grain of truth so dirtied by lies
that it becomes fiction.*

RENÉE MILLER

Dirty
Truths

*Fate gives Kristina Riley what she wants most,
but keeping it may be a dirty job.*

Joe McNeil sank onto the stool, his face shadowed, haunted.

"Rough night?" Wade set a Coors in front of his friend. "Just let me lock up and I'll join you."

"Thanks. Shit, I forgot you closed early on Wednesdays. I'll finish this and get out of your hair. I just needed somewhere to calm down."

Wade slid the bolt across the door and strode back to the bar. Joe's leg vibrated against the stool as he took a long swig of his beer.

Kristina. It had to be. Nothing else could get Joe worked up like this. She could get Wade pretty worked up too, but for different reasons.

He lifted a glass from the rack and scooped some ice into it. Grabbing the bottle of Jack Daniels off the shelf he walked around the bar to join Joe. "Kristina?"

Joe nodded and finished his beer. Wade filled his glass and slid the remaining whiskey to his friend. "Probably not the best idea. I could kill that little fucker."

"Who?"

"Who do you think?"

Wade didn't speak. Daniel Riley. Useless piece of shit. He waited. Joe would share what he wanted to share and no more. It was his way and Wade wouldn't push.

"When we got there, Kristina said she was carrying the baby and fell on the stairs." Joe's voice broke. He cleared his throat and rolled his shoulders. "I told her she better stop lying to me. No one breaks their ribs and gets a shiner from falling on the stairs."

"He hit her?" Rage burned in the bottom of Wade's gut.

"Christ, when isn't he hitting her? This time, he punched her, kicked her, bit her…fuck. Then he hit the baby. Might have been his worst mistake."

"The baby?" A red haze distorted Wade's vision.

"She had a small bruise on her cheek, but she's okay. You should see Kristina. Wait." Joe dug into his jacket and pulled out his cell. He pressed a couple of buttons and passed it to Wade. "There. See for yourself."

Hands trembling, Wade looked at the images. The eyes, once a bright blue so full of life it made a man ache just to look into them, held a hopelessness that broke his heart. He skipped through the pictures, unable to look at them for longer than a moment, stopping at an image of Kristina's abdomen. The right side covered by an angry purple bruise, swollen and scraped in spots. "Did you call the cops?"

"She did. After we made her."

"You know, I could take care of this. Call it a favor. Just between me and you. No one would hear from him again." He would pay Joe for the privilege of killing Riley with his bare hands.

"No."

"How many times are you going to just let this shit go? He's going to kill her and your granddaughter."

"You know what Kristina's like. Just let her do this on her own. I think she's finally had enough. If we get involved, she'll know and she'd never forgive me."

"Joe—"

"No, Wade. I mean it. Leave it be. Please." Joe glanced up, his eyes pleading.

Christ. "Fine. But if you ever change your mind, you know where to find me."

"I do."

"He hurts her again, I don't make any promises."

"Me either."

COMING SOON

For the Love of Gods

A DIVINE SERIES BY

RENÉE MILLER

For the Love of Gods

The gods have fascinated mankind since… well, forever. These all-powerful beings seem to have it all; knowledge, strength, beauty, immortality. But what is all of that without love? Whether they bask in the white glory of Mount Olympus or lurk in the shadows of the underworld, most gods can barely understand love, much less feel it.

And this is why the gods can't resist humans, no matter how insignificant they feel we are. *"For the Love of Gods"* shares the stories of how a handful of unfeeling, untouchable, and oh so sexy gods find themselves at the mercy of the human heart.

Thanatos, God of Death, Morpheus, God of Sleep, Tisiphone, Avenger of Murder and the most fearsome of the Furies; just to name a few of the mighty who will fall… in love.

Thanatos, god of death, has a flawless record...
until the birth of Caerus Thornton.

RENÉE MILLER

For the Love of Gods®

Lucky

Is he falling for the woman he's spent
more than two decades trying to kill?

"It's okay, baby. I've got you. Watch the steps. Okay, just breathe. Good girl." The tall, thin man in the too-short khakis and frayed jacket practically carried his pregnant wife to the car. An impressive feat to an onlooker, considering the woman must outweigh him by at least fifty pounds.

Thanatos never enjoyed bringing death in these situations. Expectant parents were always the most emotional. As if they thought their happy little bubble made them impervious to Fate.

The man closed the passenger door of the rusted red Chevy and ran around to the driver's side. Dusk had just settled over the rundown neighborhood. The porch light over the small gravel driveway was too small to illuminate more than the rocks directly beneath it. The bare bulb only served to highlight the shabbiness of their rented two-bedroom home.

On the upside, the cramped rooms would feel just a bit bigger when this night was over, although Thanatos knew they wouldn't see that as a positive thing.

Flashing into the backseat, he observed their nervous excitement. The man could barely fit the key into the ignition. He laughed when it finally went in and she touched his arm, a tender smile on her face.

Thanatos cringed at their eager anticipation of the child that would never be. He could do it now, or wait until they arrived at the hospital. It didn't matter to him much either way, but sometimes his job went more smoothly if he arrived before the doctors could muddle things up.

The woman cried out as the baby fought to break free from her tiny prison. If he did it now, he'd save the woman a little physical pain, as well. The process of bringing a human life into the world seemed positively barbaric. With all of the technology humans had at their fingertips, it baffled him why they still allowed the arrival of new life to rip the mother apart, as though they believed pain made it more important, more meaningful. If only they knew the reality.

Squealing the tires as he left the driveway, the almost father took off at full speed, which wasn't all that fast for the old car.

Thanatos smiled as the man fought to keep his eyes on the road and not on his panting wife. So much emotion over something natural and commonplace. Each one thought their little bundle of joy was special and unique, even though they knew thousands more just like them entered into life every day.

They breezed through a red light, honking horns in hot pursuit, and Thanatos leaned forward, his hand poised over the woman's distended belly. The car lurched and her husband's arm shot out, blocking Thanatos's path. Their fingers touched and the man shivered.

Damn.

The man's face paled to a sickly grey. He clutched at his chest, panic filling his bloodshot blue eyes. This had never happened before.

"Charlie?" The woman's voice was breathless from the contractions.

"I don't—can't..." Charlie gasped.

And then he collapsed. Unplanned perhaps, but a casualty or two was not unusual. Occasionally the Fates felt the need to add to his workload without telling him. Thanatos sat back as the car left the road. The woman screamed, her dead husband oblivious to her distress, as they careened into the ditch. A sickening crunch preceded their stop, and she lay still for a moment.

Thanatos exited the car through the roof and observed the carnage before him. Once upon a time such things affected him, but not for very long. Erebos made it clear that gods had no use for emotion.

The humans couldn't see him, not until their time came, so he was free to roam the scene and make sure the heart he came for had stopped beating. He tried to make it as gentle as possible, but sometimes his sisters required more force and less finesse. No one questioned the Fates, not even Death.

The woman's door opened.

Not done yet.

A car sped through his body, screeching to a halt before the twisted red metal. A man leapt from the driver's side, cell phone to his ear.

Dusk rapidly turned into night, and he stared for a moment before running to the woman, who struggled to exit her vehicle.

"You okay?" He helped her to her feet.

"My husband," she glanced at the wreckage of their car, wincing as a contraction ripped through her abdomen. The child was a fighter apparently, like her mother.

"Help is on its way, ma'am. Let's get you out of here."

Thanatos folded his arms over his chest. The Good Samaritan coaxed her from the car and her dead husband, toward his own vehicle. Sirens screamed in the distance. Thanatos walked toward them, intent on finishing his job. As he approached, the Good Samaritan tripped, falling almost into his arms. Instinctively, Thanatos put out a hand, touching the man's head. A heartbeat later the man stumbled forward as he fell through Thanatos's intangible form.

For the love of...

Stumbling to the road, unable to gain his footing, the man did a nosedive onto the pavement. The sirens grew deafening as the emergency vehicles shrieked to the scene, the lead one screaming over the Good Samaritan's head. This had to be the worst day Thanatos had ever experienced.

"No!" The woman screamed again. Holding her belly, she hit her knees in the ditch. At least it was dark enough now that most of the gore was hidden from her view. The paramedics, quite agitated over what just happened, jumped from the ambulance. One ran to the squalling woman and the other shining a flashlight on the dead man under the tires.

Thanatos glared at the scene. His sisters would have a fit.

*The god of dreams has deserted his post, and a good
night's sleep becomes a thing of the past.*

*To save humanity, Morpheus must sacrifice something
he did not believe existed: his heart.*

Hypnos paced the hallway, running a finger along the cool marble wall to soothe is burning rage.

"We cannot do as you ask, brother. I am sorry." Thanatos stood in front of the door to his sisters' chamber. He'd spent only moments inside, supposedly pleading Hypnos's case to the Fates. Of course, they proved as contrary as always.

He faced Thanatos. "I don't believe they gave me more than a passing thought. Wretched witches. Tell me, what could possibly be more important than Morpheus returning to his post?"

"It is not the girl's time to die. Fate has given the girl a long life thread, longer than any human I've ever encountered."

Impossible.

Hypnos ran a trembling hand through his hair. This could not be happening. Phantasos stood at Morpheus's post, protecting the land of sleep, and the dreams within it, but he was no Morpheus. He could not give prophecy. He could not guide the humans to the paths they must take. Hypnos doubted he even cared to do so. Although he reached for his brother's power, hinted that it would change much, Phantasos paled greatly in comparison to his older brother. This would not do.

Thanatos cleared his throat, bringing Hypnos from his musing.

"There is another option." Thanatos said.

"Please share then, brother. I'm all ears."

"The Fates say this girl is special, not quite what she seems. They say that someone must have learned her secret; a secret they believe even the girl is unaware of. Atropos hinted at a plot to use the girl to usurp Morpheus from his position. A gamble to win his power."

"What secret?"

Thanatos glanced back at the door and crossed the hall to put his lips to Hypnos's ear. "She comes from Eros."

Hypnos shoved Thanatos away. "That's...Aphrodite would never allow such a thing. They lie!"

"My sisters do not tell tales." An edge sharpened Thanatos's calm tone. He returned to the door, crossing his arms over his chest.

While they were brothers, Hypnos feared Thanatos's wrath more than he feared the fury of the Fates. He forced his frayed nerves to calm and took a gentler tone. Pissing off the god of death wouldn't serve his purpose. It would only see his problems multiply.

"Forgive me," Hypnos took a breath and measured his words. "I don't see how it is possible for the girl to have sprung from Eros's loins. Aphrodite would not let her pet from her side long enough to do such a thing."

"It only takes a moment, and he leaves her side more often than you think. What do you say of this plot? You appear more concerned that Eros has done as we all know he always does than you do about someone conspiring against Morpheus."

Hypnos thought the matter over. Eros was taken with the humans. He'd dallied now and then, much to Aphrodite's dismay, but a child? Even Eros wouldn't dare. But plotting and scheming could be Eros's second name. He might concoct such a secret to cause trouble for another god. But to steal Morpheus's power? Never.

"I cannot imagine who would dare plot against Morpheus." Hypnos said. "Eros seems the only likely culprit, but it is more likely a plot to amuse him than one to steal power. Does Aphrodite know of this rumor?"

"It is fact. The Fates do not engage in gossip. But in answer to the question, I do not know if even Eros knows of her existence, so use caution when you approach him. My sisters were rather vague. They know it to be true, and her parentage means that Zeus will not allow a mortal death to end her life thread. But, brother, don't you see? It is not necessary to kill the girl. You need only find the puppet master working her strings."

"And you believe it to be Eros?"

Thanatos shrugged. "I only know that one god likes to engage in trickery when it comes to matters of the heart. However, again I urge caution. It might be someone closer to home. Someone closer to Morpheus."

Hypnos nodded, but in his heart he knew none close to him was capable of such deceit. "I must visit Eros then, and force him to release Morpheus from this madness."

"If it is truly madness, then yes, that is what you must do. But keep in mind that Morpheus may have real feelings for the girl."

"The Oneiroi cannot love."

Thanatos smiled. "So said the God of Death, once upon a time."

Eris, Goddess of Discord, has kept Gavin Maenad's parentage a secret from the gods so she might nudge him to do her will.

RENÉE MILLER

For the Love of Gods®

NEFARIOUS

But the Furies get wind of Gavin's misdeeds.

Gavin strode the boardwalk, his gaze on the woman only a few feet ahead. There was a darkness about the small blonde; one that made his blood cold. She strode with purpose, her leather-clad legs not faltering as she all but glided across the ground. Those around her seemed to simply melt from her path.

Curious.

The sunlight sparked off her golden hair as she approached a food truck. She glanced over her shoulder as though feeling his stare on her back. Gavin slowed, but she turned back just as quickly, focusing her attention on the mob of black suits before the truck.

It was not quite noon. The lawyers and executives that spent their waking hours in the building only steps from the water's edge rushed out for their five minutes of sunshine at exactly the same time each day. Creatures of habit, zombies in his opinion, they appeared to order the same lunch from the same truck day in and day out. He would rather die than live with such conformity.

The woman stood watching the crowd, arms crossed over her chest. She was pretty, almost eerily so. As he approached, Gavin caught a glimpse of her blue eyes, coolly assessing a small group of men at the front of the truck. They waited to place their orders, no one speaking. She didn't appear to be looking at anyone in particular, and it baffled Gavin that not a single man looked her way. The black leather pants and bra thing she wore kind of stood out. While the professionals wore suits, others on the boardwalk dressed in shorts, dresses, and tank tops. No one else looked like Satan's stripper.

"Excuse me," a woman's voice.

Gavin turned. A tall redhead tried to wedge herself between his back and a tree. She tossed ginger curls over a bare shoulder and smiled. Gavin stepped back, offering a smile in return. Pretty faces always distracted him, and knowing he could flirt his way into their bed made it doubly hard to ignore their fluttering lashes. "Sorry, am I in your way?"

"Yes. And I'm already late." The woman moved past him,

her hand grasping his briefly.

As she sauntered toward the food truck, slender hips clearly outlined beneath the fabric of her white cotton dress, Gavin clutched the paper in his palm. Too easy.

A black shadow crossed his vision. He snapped to attention as the leather-clad blonde approached his redhead. She didn't speak, but removed the black leather gloves Gavin only then noticed she wore, and then touched the redhead's shoulder, eliciting a shiver before continuing on her way.

"Curiouser." Gavin said.

The redhead turned from the food truck, not bothering to place an order. She rubbed her arms, as though chilled. As she stepped onto the boardwalk, a roaring sound filled Gavin's ears. Something dark and cold lingered around them. He looked to the blonde, who calmly slipped her hands back into her gloves. It had to be her.

Gavin had sensed many bad and evil deeds done by others. This talent for reading a person's heart was how he chose his victims, but never had he sensed something like this. The woman didn't feel evil as much as she felt...dangerous. All of his senses told him to run far from her presence.

She stood with the black suits, watching the redhead intently. Gavin followed her gaze.

"No." He heard himself say as a bicycle screamed toward the redhead.

Gavin bolted, although he knew it was too late to stop the disaster.

The bicycle and its rider struck the redhead, sending her careening to the ground. Her head struck a large stone that lined the walkway, nestled among happy little flowers. Rivulets of blood stained the rock and her eyes stared vacantly to the heavens.

Something brushed past him and Gavin turned, meeting the blue gaze of the blonde. He grabbed her arm. "Who the fuck are you?"

Her eyes widened. "You can see me?"

"Of course I can." Gavin said.

"Well, that *is* a problem." The blonde said, shrugging free of his grasp. She removed her leather gloves once more. "I'm sorry, buddy."

She touched his arm, and Gavin jumped at the spark that ignited his body. "Jesus, how'd you do that?"

The woman looked concerned. Shouts echoed from behind them, sirens screamed in the distance. "You are unaffected." She said.

"By what?"

"Death."

"Come again?"

She searched his face, although the answer to her unasked question might be waiting there. She put a small hand out. "I am Caerus, the instrument of Thanatos, god of death, and you are?"

"Gavin." He took her hand in his, feeling the spark again, but fainter this time.

"Gavin who?" she asked.

"Maenad."

"You're joking."

He shook his head.

"Fucksakes, we'll never be free of that bastard."

"I'm sorry. I didn't know my name was a bad thing."

Caerus said nothing. She touched his arm, closing her eyes. When she opened them, she sighed. "Well, Gavin Maenad, I'm afraid you'll have to come with me."

"Where?"

She smiled. "To Tartarus. Hades will be delighted to meet you."

"He will?" Tartarus? Hades? The woman was insane.

"No, I was being sarcastic. But your father has some explaining to do."

"I don't know my father."

She smiled again. "You're blessed then. I know Dionysus only too well. Pray your ignorance works in your favor."

"Why?"

"If it doesn't, you will die."

ABOUT THE AUTHOR

Renee Miller is a freelance writer living in Tweed, Ontario. Small town life is busy, but she's managed to sandwich a book or two between the demands of housewifery and hiding from the neighbors. Her first novel, IN THE BONES, is available at online retailers. THE LEGEND OF JACKSON MURPHY, is her second published novel.

Reneemiller@bell.net
www.twitter.com/ReneeMJ
www.facebook.com/pages/Renee-Miller/548882035137022

Website: www.OnFictionWriting.com
Blog: www.authorreneemiller.com